Touched

Lilly Wilde

Touched

www.lillywilde.com
Cover Design by Lilly Wilde
Photo Credit: 123rf.com/profile_kiuikson

This book is a work of fiction. Names, characters, places and incidents either are the product of the author's imagination or are used fictitiously. Any resemblance to actual events, locales, or persons, living or dead, is coincidental.

Copyright 2015 Touched by Lilly Wilde

Except for the original material written by the author, all songs, song titles, and lyrics mentioned in the novel *Touched* are the property of the respective songwriters and copyright holders.

ISBN-13: 978-1507896969 — Print
ISBN-10: 1507896964 — Print

Acknowledgments

Thanks to the many readers who have joined *Team Untouched*. This has been an amazing experience. Your enthusiasm and enjoyment of Aria and Aiden's story has truly touched me.

I'm thankful for the opportunity to share this amazing journey with my Street Team, The Wilde Lillies! Your support has been invaluable!

And a huge thanks to my husband — your unending patience has been remarkable. Thanks for enduring my bouts of excitement with this series.

Contents

❧Chapter One❧

The day had been another horrendous test of my patience and emotions. I'd formally accepted the position of CEO of Raine Publishing House yesterday, and while that within itself would be cause to celebrate for anyone with aspirations such as mine, it somehow felt like a collar — I felt trapped. Aiden Raine, the newly appointed head of Raine Industries, had presented me with the offer, and from my perspective, I'd been coerced into acceptance. I couldn't resign without risking my chances of securing a comparable position at any other reputable publishing company. Aiden had made it very clear that he would block every job opportunity that presented itself, and given his immeasurable resources, I knew he could and *would* halt all my efforts to leave RPH.

I didn't understand him at all. Why was he doing this? Did he think it was the only way to keep me close? If that was his logic, he would soon discover it was pointless, because proximity didn't matter — I could've been stuck to him like lint on a cheap suit and it wouldn't change how I felt. I was done. At least that's what I kept telling myself every hour — and so far, my reminders had proved effective. But I'd be lying if I said I knew how I would feel once I saw him again.

My new responsibilities at RPH required dedication and

focus, yet each time I saw the RPH building, or even the logo, I felt a pang of betrayal. The first few days after Aiden's departure were hard. I'd struggled to shake off the remnants of his effects, at least as far as work was concerned. But in regard to my personal life, I'd taken it one hour at a time.

"I'll see you in the morning, Raina," I said, walking past my assistant's office door. She looked up from the file on her desk with perceptible concern in her beryl blue eyes.

"How are you? I mean—how's everything with Mr. Raine?" she asked.

"Everything's fine…or as fine as can be expected," I replied bleakly.

Raina was my executive assistant, and I didn't typically concern her with matters that weren't related to RPH. However, she was now privy to some personal aspects of my life due to my involvement with her boss…actually *my* boss, too—Aiden Raine.

"I can see the toll this is taking on you. I'm willing to listen if you need someone," she offered.

"I've had to digest more than my fair share of changes as of late, Raina, but I'll be fine," I replied, though I was unsure as to the truth of that statement. "Speaking of which, we need to rearrange some things on my calendar to prepare for our move to the top floor."

"Yes, ma'am. I actually started revising your schedule this

afternoon," she said.

I extended a smile, hoping it appeared genuine. Although I was very fond of Raina, I had no desire to discuss Aiden with her, or with anyone for that matter. I wasn't in the mood for much more than complete isolation from everyone and everything.

"Thank you, Raina. Don't stay too late," I said, turning to leave.

I'd admitted, at least to myself, that my heart was breaking…a little more with each passing day. Aiden had filled a part of me I hadn't known was empty. And for that I'd be forever grateful.

Beneath the pain was the reality of the end of whatever it was we'd shared. I missed Aiden, and his absence was profound. He was no longer the focal point of our business meetings, and the tempting interruptions to my work day were gone also. The texts that once made me smile, and often squirm in my seat, were over. The heat of his touch, the deep resonance of his voice, and the way his hypnotic eyes bored into mine — these were all etched into my brain. Memories were all I had left, and I couldn't escape them. He was everywhere, yet he was nowhere at all.

Every morning, Aiden was my first thought, and I spent the beginning of each day reprogramming my brain, reminding myself that it was over, that he was gone, that it had all been a lie. This morning had been no different.

Every day I expected to hear from him, but there had been nothing. The first few nights after he left, I cried myself to sleep. Had the tears been just for him? I hadn't figured that part out. Part of me wanted to think my despondence was less about him and more about what he represented. He'd given me something I'd never wanted, that I'd never dared think of—he'd given me hope.

And now, in the absence of that hope, I needed something to pour myself into. In the past—before Aiden—that *something* would have been work. I could have easily and quite happily worked for hours on end. My best friend April was convinced that I used work as a distraction from life's pains—I didn't see the point in denying it, because I did. Thanks to my recent choices though, I no longer had that crutch, because work was now tainted with thoughts of Aiden.

I let out a long disheartened sigh as I entered the Boston traffic, and headed toward the condo. Home didn't feel the same either. It was no longer a refuge, because it, too, held memories of him. There was nowhere to run and nothing to run to. I'd broken pretty much every Fuck Rule in the book for that man, and now I was paying the price for it.

Things weren't good, but they were bearable. I knew if I never saw Aiden again, I'd be okay. I could ride the wave until it all evened out. But I *would* be seeing him again, and I knew it would be soon, and I was dreading it.

Aiden would be out of the country on business for the remainder of the week—not that he'd communicated with me, but a memo had gone out to that effect. He was visiting many of the overseas subsidiaries of Raine Industries, employing calculated strategies to strengthen an already mega-successful company—hence my recent promotion to CEO. We were initially informed he had plans to work at RPH the remainder of the week. Although I shouldn't have, I couldn't help but wonder what had transpired to alter his schedule.

Entering my condo, my eyes rested upon the largest physical reminder of Aiden—the piano. Aiden was just as impressive on paper as he was off, and one of his many talents was his ability as a pianist. I was completely blown away upon hearing him play. When I'd mentioned I wanted to learn, he offered to teach me. And typical of him, he'd gone one step further when I'd asked for his help in selecting a piano, by surprising me with a baby grand, complete with an inscription on the back panel that made me weak in the knees.

I was in love with music, and as a child I'd longed to play the piano, and if the desire to learn wasn't so strong, I would have refused the lessons he'd arranged. As per his usual intrusive self, he had Raina fit in an appointment on my schedule with a local pianist who'd started weekly lessons with me. Each time I practiced, I was flooded with memories of Aiden and, needless to say, the lessons weren't going as well as they could have.

The ping of an incoming text pulled me from my thoughts. Smiling upon seeing the name of the sender, I quickly tapped a reply. I then dressed for my workout, grabbed my phone and headed downstairs to the gym. Stopping near the entrance, I tapped the control panel in search of a workout playlist. Once the sound of Disclosure's *Latch* filled the room, I began stretching as my mind did the thing that had become the norm for me as of late. I wanted to stop thinking about it, but the memories popped in as often as they wanted. After a while, I convinced myself the mental replays were a good thing — I could retrace my steps and figure out where I'd gone wrong and what I *should* have done. But even after my mental critiques, the result was the same.

The last few months had split my world wide open. Blake Meade, RPH's CEO at the time, had voiced his suspicions that RPH would be under a magnifying glass, but neither of us suspected the lens would be an intern named Aiden Wyatt.

We ultimately learned that Aiden was the son of Connor Raine, the CEO and President of Raine Industries. While I'd been extremely impressed with Aiden's abilities during his tenure as an *intern*, after only one meeting with him in his capacity as CEO, I'd discovered he was much more of a powerhouse than I'd ever imagined.

In one swift move, Aiden had relieved Blake of his duties as

CEO and presented the position to me. I'd wanted to prepare Blake for his termination, but Aiden had forbidden it. I reached out to Blake after the dust had settled though—Aiden couldn't stop that.

A week after the transition, Blake and I enjoyed a great discussion over lunch. He was disappointed, of course, but he was extremely happy for me. He went as far as to say, if he had to be replaced, he couldn't have chosen a better successor. He was currently interviewing for an executive position with Little Brown that looked promising, and I offered to serve as a reference in any capacity. Although I could see he had questions, we didn't discuss Aiden or Raine Industries.

Stepping onto the treadmill, I pressed the button for one of the pre-set workouts. My phone pinged a second time—it was Kellan again. My heartbeat quickened as I read the message. He was coming to Boston, and he wanted to see me.

Kellan and I started communicating soon after the Aiden debacle, mostly by text, and it was easy—no pressure. I could handle that. But an actual visit—I wasn't sure I should go there while still wrapped up in my feelings about Aiden.

Ugh. I was so tired of processing. Although I wasn't sure it was the best move, I replied telling Kellan it would be great to see him.

Returning focus to my workout, I started with a brisk walk

which quickly transitioned into a full run. How amazing would it be if I could actually run from the aftermath of Aiden Raine? The fallout at RPH had been mild all things considered, but the internal explosion I was experiencing was shattering. And what made matters worse, I had no reference point. I didn't know how to recover from a broken heart. Aiden had been my one and only relationship. I never engaged with men to the degree I had with Aiden...a fact that continued to confound me. He possessed a magnetism that I'd never encountered with any other man. It was undeniable and utterly indescribable. I totally lost all reason when it came to him. All my defenses abandoned me. It had felt as though I was doing things against my will, but at the same time I greedily savored every second of it. I was so sure I'd never suffer a broken heart, so I never gave much thought to it; yet here I was...the blubbering mess I'd despised.

I didn't expect men to do anything more than lie and leave—two things my father had taught me. My abhorrence for love and relationships had festered for over a decade, so even the slightest of lies tapped into the pain and heartache of my past, and that was exactly what Aiden had done. He'd taken me back to the time when my father left. He'd reminded me that I shouldn't trust men. That conviction and the fear of heartbreak had driven me for years. But even after this painful reminder from Aiden, I couldn't stop wanting him, and that was the part that was tearing me up inside.

You'd think my past would be the stronghold I needed to make sure I never suffered this fate. Well, that and the other safeguards I had in place: I never mixed business with pleasure, I never had boyfriends and I never allowed anyone to get any closer than sex...but for the first time, all my precautions proved useless—Aiden had pushed them all to the side.

Everything about him had encapsulated me; I'd been held prisoner to his whims, his voice, and his touch. Even now with the absence of contact, I was somehow still his captive.

He'd changed me. He'd loved me. He'd damaged me. To be fair, I'd already been damaged though, long before he'd touched me. But how can someone so damaged suffer more damage without being irrevocably altered?

The intercom buzzed, and when I grabbed my purse to pay for the takeout I'd ordered, I thought of my first dinner with Aiden. He'd appeared at my door with food and I'd referred to him as a delivery guy.

Having poured a glass of wine, I sat at the table and then sighed as I realized I was thinking of him again. Was I in his thoughts as much as he was in mine? Was he thinking of me even a little?

When he'd made his abrupt exit in July, I'd heard nothing from him the entire time he was gone; however, when he resurfaced he'd said he'd missed me every day. He'd also told me that he loved me…yet he was gone. I didn't fully know what it was like to feel love from a man, but I knew enough to realize this couldn't be right.

Had he expected me to say it in return? That I loved him? Did I have the slightest idea of what love was? I did once…back then, when I was in Dayton living under the ruse of a happy family. I also knew how it felt to love my job or love my best friend, and even to love my mom again. But loving a man? This man? I didn't know. I had told myself it was love. That he'd touched a part of me no one had ever come close to — a part I didn't know existed. But was that love? Mom told me that I loved Aiden. If anyone knew love, it was her. The depth of her love for my father was so intense it nearly killed her.

And for that reason, for years, I only wanted men for sex, and I wanted it on my terms. Never had I desired anything remotely close to what I'd begun to share with Aiden. I hadn't thought it possible for me to feel this way for a man, yet here I was, in a haze of want and confusion…and hurt. Actually, *hurt* was much too mild a description. I was burning. I was left with a gaping hole that threatened to exacerbate my already broken state. Sure, I'd been broken before Aiden, but I was nicely bandaged — and all the pieces were secure. I'd gotten by with that, and I had no desire for anything different. Unlike most, I was keenly aware of my dysfunction, and I was fine with it, until now...until him.

Every interaction with Aiden had entailed an undecipherable and potent mist that flowed freely from him to me, piercing me, changing me. I wanted to revert to my pre-Aiden state: happy, in love with my career and in control of my emotions. Yes, I'd been alone, but there was a reason I was alone; I was comfortable that way. Most of that comfort had rested in knowing that the distressed pieces of Aria Cason were safely locked away, lying there untouched. Now they were scattered about, taking life and penetrating the very essence of who I was...or who I'd *thought* I was. Aiden had somehow found the key to open that forbidden box and now I was frantically scrambling to close it again.

After tossing and turning for hours, I finally fell asleep and into a dream that seemed so real that I'd bolted awake. In the dream, Aiden and I were hiking in the woods, and I'd somehow managed to fall behind. When he realized I was no longer trailing after him, he turned back and retraced his steps. Once I was in his line of vision, he began walking faster, and relieved to see him, I hurriedly advanced in his direction. With each step though, Aiden's appearance altered. I slowed as I tried to make sense of what was happening. But when Aiden finally reached me, he was no longer himself — he was the spitting image of my dad. And when he reached out to me, I screamed—waking up, drenched and trembling.

Crawling out of bed minutes later, I stripped out of the wet clothes, tossed on a dry T-shirt, and headed to the kitchen for a bottle of water. The dream wasn't hard to interpret. I'd placed so much distance between myself and the memories of my father, and I was attempting to do the same thing with Aiden, but my tactics proved futile; I couldn't escape him…even as I slept. I hated him, and I hated what he made me feel. But would I take him back if his reason for leaving was one I could accept? I knew the answer was yes.

I thought back to the last few moments I'd spent alone with Aiden. When he'd left my office that afternoon, I'd stood there rubbing the lips he'd so savagely attacked with his kiss. Watching him walk away, it felt like my heart had stopped beating. Tears filled my eyes as my body slowly eased down the wall and onto the floor. It was as though I was inside a nightmare. Falling, falling, falling…wanting desperately to wake up before I hit the ground. But it wasn't a dream and I wasn't going to wake up.

I must have sat there for nearly an hour, wiping the seemingly endless flow of tears, each deep breath somehow failing to fill my lungs. Eventually I got up and fled from my office, not caring who saw me or what they thought.

Once in my car, I sped from the garage and darted toward the interstate. I'd wanted to drive fast enough and far enough until I disappeared. When I was away from the confines of the city, I still felt trapped, so I pulled over to the shoulder, lowered the top and then rejoined the flow of traffic. Turning up the volume as loud as it could go, I drove deep into the night as my hair blew crazily in the wind, drying the tears as quickly as they eased down my cheeks.

And now here I was…in my bed weeks later, curled up in my blanket, clutching my chest as I sobbed in the darkness of my bedroom. I was a mess, but I didn't blame Aiden for my misery; I blamed myself. I allowed this to happen; I went along with all of it. And for the life of me, I didn't know where to go from here.

❧Chapter Two❧

It had been a month since I'd last heard Aiden's voice, with the exception of the voicemail messages he'd left. I'd finally forced myself to listen to them. The first was sinfully seductive, as was anything that escaped his lips. The second message was a bit more forceful but alluring all the same. The last message revealed his frustration, or maybe anger was a better word. I considered reaching out to him, but ultimately decided against it because I simply wasn't prepared to reopen that door.

I'd pushed him aside just as I felt he'd done me, and his absence allowed for some of the pieces of my life to reassemble. The single good thing that had come of opening up to Aiden was that I was now rebuilding my relationship with my family, which added a different but happier layer to my life. I deeply regretted the amount of time and distance I'd placed between us over the years, but I was trying to make up for that now. We all were.

My sisters Lia and Bianca had blossomed into beautiful, mature young ladies, and I totally adored them. Mom was more and more like her old self—the animated, attentive mother I had wanted and missed for so many years. She'd sensed something was bothering me. I denied it, but she wouldn't let it go. I was wary at first—thinking my story would remind her too much of her own—but despite my reservations, I finally broke down and told her.

"Mom, I don't understand these feelings."

"This is a new world for you, and I'm sure you're fighting it at every turn, but I think you know exactly what you're feeling for Aiden. You don't want to admit it because it goes against who you've forced yourself to be for so many years."

I took in what she said—knowing she was right on both counts.

"This can't be what love feels like. Why does it hurt so much?" I asked.

"Because it's real, Aria."

"If this is love, I don't want it. I don't know how I can ever be the same after this."

"Aria, I know you don't want to hear this, but the truth is, you won't be the same. The kind of love you feel for Aiden alters you."

"It's certainly done that. My life hasn't been the same since the day I met him. It was as if I was someone else. I don't like this. I hate feeling this way and I just don't want it anymore," I said.

"If you're committed to letting him go, it's going to take a while, and you'll have some scars, but in time they'll heal."

I knew I'd have scars that would always be a reminder. But what I felt was far more than that; there was a gaping wound that

I feared would never close. I was silent, attempting to hide the fact that I was crying.

"Sweetheart, I think you should try to contact him. You two need to talk. Based on everything you've told me, I think you've jumped to some conclusions. This pain might all be unnecessary."

"I don't know how I could ever trust him. He lied. Every day I was with him was a lie. Not only did he lie over and over, he forced me into this freaking job and he's been so cold-hearted about it all."

"Aria, if you didn't want that job, you didn't have to accept it."

That was true—I didn't. But my career was important to me. It was all I had.

"It's best to let this run its course so I can get back to being me. With him, I'd become someone I didn't recognize, someone I don't want to be," I replied.

"I don't want to pressure you, but please consider my advice. It wouldn't hurt this badly if you didn't care so deeply for him, sweetheart."

"I don't know how I feel. I just want my life back the way it used to be. I feel powerless in this situation…that's not a feeling I'm comfortable with."

"Aria, you're such a strong woman. I saw that strength and resilience in you as a child. You know who you are, and you know who you want to be. Never let anyone take that from you. You *will* bounce back from this because that's who you are. Don't ever forget that."

"I won't Mom, and I'm sorry for worrying you."

"Please don't apologize. I'm your mother, and you can come to me anytime with anything. I can't begin to tell you how it feels that you're sharing this with me. I didn't think I would ever have the chance to be a mother to you in this way again." Her voice broke.

We were both silent for several minutes. I didn't know how to respond to her. This felt strange, but at the same time it felt good. I didn't want her to worry about me, but I was relieved I wouldn't have to go through this alone.

"Thanks for listening, and thanks for your advice. It means a lot," I said.

"I hate that you're hurting, and I'm here any time, day or night. I love you, sweetheart."

I paused and let her words register. I also allowed myself a moment before replying, "I love you too, Mom. I'll talk to you soon. Tell the girls I said hello and that I love them. I can't wait to see you all in a few weeks."

"I'm anxious, too. It'll be our first holiday as a family in so many years," she said.

"I know. I'm so excited," I said.

"I'll talk to you soon."

"Okay. Goodbye, Mom."

I pressed end on the phone and tossed myself across the bed and cried. It felt like someone had repeatedly kicked me in the stomach. I hadn't told my mother the depth of the pain I was feeling, because I couldn't. It would burden her too much — remind her too much of Dad.

Sitting up in bed minutes later, I wiped my tears. I was so grateful to have Mom to talk to about Aiden. I would expect anyone else to think I was foolish to still feel the way I did for him, but not Mom. If anyone could identify with my pain, it was her. Funny how I thought it would be weird talking to her about a failed relationship, but it was as though she'd been in my life in that capacity all along.

Her reassurance of my strength meant so much; I needed to hear it. And she was right. I was Aria Gabrielle Cason, and I'd be damned if I empowered Aiden, or any man, to take that from me. I didn't want to suffocate in the memories anymore. I didn't want to miss him anymore. I didn't want to cry anymore. I wanted my life back. The life I had before Aiden Raine.

Readjusting my thoughts over the next several days was a painful and lonely process. I couldn't tell anyone the gravity of it all, not even my best friend, April. The talks with Mom helped, but it still felt impossible to reclaim my former self until the day I sat at my bureau and looked at my reflection and saw Melena Costanzo staring back at me — a woman with deep sodden eyes, malnourished, often catatonic, and just a mess. After the shock of seeing my mother in the mirror, a switch flipped — no way in hell would I become the person I'd fought over half my life to avoid.

My appetite for food and work — which had become nonexistent — finally came roaring back. I'd lost a little weight, which angered me. I couldn't believe I'd allowed myself to travel down that dark path.

Aiden had permanently altered me. I accepted that. There was nothing I could do about what had happened, but I could learn from it. No one would be able to break my heart like this again. And I knew I needed to make some changes. I needed to live and I needed to love. I would no longer run from it; I would embrace it — but somewhat more cautiously than I had with Aiden.

Bright and early Monday morning, I walked into RPH in the same fashion as I had *before* Aiden — with my head held high and with the confidence that made everyone stop and take notice. I was eager to tackle the new challenges that accompanied my recent promotion. It was an invigorating feeling, one that readied me to take on any complication that RPH could present, even if that complication was Aiden Raine.

"Good morning, Ms. Cason," Raina said, as I approached her

desk. She took in my appearance and smiled. She knew I was back, too.

I returned her friendly exchange. "Good morning, Raina," I replied, sauntering past her desk. "Can I see you in my office, please?"

"Yes, ma'am," she replied, standing to follow me.

My new office was even more impressive than the previous one. It wasn't overly extravagant—that wasn't my taste. It was elegant in its simplicity, with lots of squares and clean lines. A handcrafted marble wall fountain imprinted with the RPH logo was on the side wall, and the back wall was all glass. A meeting table sat to the left of my desk, and there was a fairly large sized seating area on the right of the room, complete with a stocked bar.

After placing my purse on the rack, I walked toward my desk. I'd been unable to part with the one from the twenty-fifth floor—it was too much a part of me, so the interior decorator had brought in some additional furnishings to compliment it. She'd done such an amazing job, that I'd hired her to redecorate my condo. In deciding what I wanted to change, I opted to keep the piano, but I wanted a look that better accentuated Little V. I'd given her that name because each time I touched the keys, it reminded Virginia of Kingston. Shaking my head, I couldn't help but smile as I thought about the secret names I'd coined our most intimate body parts.

"Can you get Chase on the phone? I need to get him on board with the book tour," I said.

"Yes, Ms. Cason. You also have a conference call at nine and a staff meeting at ten."

"I should only need a few minutes to speak with Chase. We will not dance around his whims," I said. "We have dozens of authors dying for this opportunity; it seems he's forgotten that. He needs to shit or get off the pot."

Raina attempted to hide her smile at my last comment. I could see the relief in her eyes. She'd been worried about me. *Well, that makes two of us, Raina.*

"And we need to get an appointment scheduled with Stephanie for the marketing campaign. We're falling behind schedule."

"Yes, ma'am."

"Also, get in touch with Raquel; she needs to schedule a press release for the new paranormal series."

"Mr. Raine's assistant notified me that he would be joining us for today's staff meeting," Raina said, carefully assessing my reaction.

"No problem, Raina. Thank you for the heads up," I replied, as I continued looking through the many memos on my desk.

I wasn't at all surprised by this news. Sure, I was affected, but I'd expected he'd pop in from time to time—to torture me if nothing else. He had the upper hand for now, but I was quickly moving toward a remedy for that. Although I would have preferred to maintain my position at RPH, I'd decided it was best if I moved on. Aiden would make it impossible for me to obtain a similar position in this industry, therefore I had Plan B. I'd been quietly seeking other opportunities, and if those failed, I'd been in contact with my investment banker and instructed him to take a few risks which were paying off handsomely. At this rate, I could retire very comfortably — not that I wanted to do that, but it was reassuring to know I didn't need RPH.

"Can you get the latest sales figures from accounting for me also? Adam was supposed to have gotten those to me yesterday."

"Yes, ma'am."

"That will be all for now, Raina," I said, looking up from my desk.

"I'll get started as soon as I return with your tea," she said.

"Thanks, Raina."

A few minutes later, she entered with my favorite morning beverage. "I'll get Chase on the phone for you now, Ms. Cason," Raina stated as she placed the cup on my desk and exited my office.

Raina connected me with Chase — it was a very brief conversation. He was one of our most successful authors, and for some unknown reason, the publicity department had been unable to secure a date to launch his book tour. After a quick reminder of his contract and a subtle threat to pull his next book, Chase eagerly agreed to the date that was initially suggested.

After receiving confirmation on the release of the paranormal series from Raquel, I opened an email from Adam to review our latest numbers. Not that I'd expected a decline due to the change in our hierarchy, but I wanted to be aware of any area of possible concern. After jotting down a few questionable figures that required Adam's elaboration, I grabbed my tablet and headed across the hall to the conference room.

I wasn't expecting Aiden to have already arrived, so I was taken aback to see him standing near the front of the room in conversation with a sharply dressed dark-haired woman. I stopped dead in my tracks. Knowing I would see him and *actually* seeing him were two entirely different things. I could feel the quickening thump in my chest and the butterflies… fuck, they were fluttering so fast that I unconsciously placed my palm on my stomach in a feeble attempt to banish them. I appraised his magnificent frame from head to toe—he was as provocative and breathtaking as I remembered. He looked up and stopped mid-conversation when his eyes found mine.

I swallowed the lump of trepidation and took a few involuntary steps forward, stopping short when he began walking towards me. He moved with a leopard-like grace, polished and emblazoned with the Raine name, radiating dominance and privilege with each step. The power and control he exuded were practically immobilizing.

"Good morning, Ms. Cason," he said, as he stopped in front of me.

His nearness elicited feelings for which I was utterly unprepared. The sense of betrayal, confusion, and hurt all slipped to the background, allowing only the desire I'd always felt to spring forward.

"Good morning, Aiden." I was sure it was more appropriate to refer to him as Mr. Raine, but no way in hell was I doing that.

I wanted to step away, but I couldn't. His eyes wouldn't let me—I was at a momentary loss as I stared into them; they brimmed with vigor, sparkling like two green jewels atop a bed of snow. In that instant, I realized my recollections of him were flawed; they hadn't captured the gloriousness of this man. His beautiful face, his full pink lips, his prominent cheekbones — they appeared chiseled by a master craftsman, sculpted and pared to perfection. My heart hurt just looking at him. The memory of our closeness, of his voice, of his touch, of the precious gifts that were his kisses, of his hard, deep plunges inside me… it was all suffocating.

Obviously sensing my temporary loss of speech, he said, "I'm sure Raina alerted you to my arrival."

"Yes, of course," I replied.

I tried not to gape at him, but fuck, it was like asking me not to breathe. His demeanor was just as appealing as it had always been, but I couldn't allow that to draw me in any further. I needed to keep my glances brief. I didn't want to remember any more, and I didn't want to get pulled back into the maelstrom of emotions and yearning that came with appreciating him the way I desperately wanted to.

"It's so good to see you," he said.

He was too close. I needed to move. "If you'll excuse me, I'm sure I'm about to be amazed by your brilliance, and I want to get a good seat."

My sarcasm made him smile, but I didn't return the exchange. Stepping past him, I walked toward the table and took a seat near the front of the room, leaving the chair at the head of the table for him.

He followed me, assuming the chair to my right.

"How are you?" he asked. "Are you settling in?"

"I'm well, and yes, I'm quite settled. How are you?" I asked, diverting my attention to my tablet, swiping the screen. His inebriating scent started its attack—slowly filling the space between us, and grasping ahold of my insides. I adjusted my positon and moved slightly to the left, but that didn't help at all— I found myself fighting the urge to lean closer to him. I never understood how he smelled that way. It was as if he showered in pheromones and then dashed on *I Want to Fuck You* aftershave.

"Just like you, I'm well."

He looked at me as if expecting more. There was more, much more, but I knew this wasn't the time or the place. Actually, there would never be a time or place...not if I could help it.

Adam entered the room and walked directly over to greet the new Raine Industries CEO, who stood and faced away from me. I strained to hear Adam's discussion of Aiden's itinerary for the remainder of his visit, but I couldn't quite make it out.

The other staff members were steadily filtering in, their expressions as somber as mine. I guessed that they, too, were concerned about the impending changes.

The dark-haired woman walked over to Aiden and whispered something to him. She then took a seat beside him and he started the meeting. Even in this context, his voice was like silk...smooth and sensual. I stole a quick glance at him. He was the page of a glossy magazine, and he was sporting that sexy stubble that made me want to touch it. He was gorgeous, controlled and powerful, and I felt as though I were seeing him through new eyes. I'd always considered him inexplicably refined and I mistakenly assumed it was something he'd picked up and cultivated, but now I knew better. It came from simply being a Raine.

Aiden Wyatt Raine was the president and CEO of Raine Industries, a vast multi-national conglomerate, and until very recently, he'd been my lover. He was impossibly gorgeous and unbelievably seductive, even without an attempt on his part.

I looked down at the agenda and closed my eyes, allowing his velvet voice to flow over me, easily recalling those intimate moments we'd shared when that voice was directed solely towards me...saying things that made me blush. Saying things that made Virginia respond uncontrollably—just as she was doing now. I bit my lip when the slight pulses of my sex caught me off guard. *What the hell?* It was all I could do to just relax in my chair and let them roll through me. *Holy fuck! Did that really just happen?* Aiden's voice had always been a turn on for me. And to be honest, it was enough to deliver several tiny orgasms, instead of the single one I'd just experienced.

As Aiden continued talking, I glanced awkwardly around the table, hoping I didn't look as insane as I felt. My response to his presence was not something I'd expected. Why did my senses take leave when it came to that man? Wasn't the first burn enough? The pain of his deceit was fresh and the wound he'd caused was uncovered. Yet like someone under the influence of mind control, I was involuntarily drawn to him. Obviously one burn wasn't enough, because I wanted him. I still wanted him. The part of me that knew the risk was there lurking. But the part of me that he satisfied was the only part I was listening to.

After the first hour, we stopped for a short break. Some of the staff refreshed their beverages, others went to the restroom, me among them. I wanted to regroup, not to mention wipe up.

Returning to the conference room, I took a deep breath and headed to my seat. The meeting shouldn't last much longer, I mean, how many more ways could Aiden say he was revamping key divisions. Although the information he'd detailed was critical to our operations, I didn't want to hear any more of it. I was anxious to get away from him, but I had the sense he wasn't thinking alone the same lines.

Adam had taken the chair opposite mine and was in conversation with Aiden as I approached, but Aiden concluded their side-bar upon my reappearance.

"There's a great deal of information you'll need as quickly as possible if we are to transition efficiently, so I would like to send Chicago Bryant here for a few weeks to help out," he said.

Chicago had served on the Raine Industries board for years, and he was very involved with the workings of the company.

"Help me out? Do you feel as though I need help, Aiden?" I asked, glancing briefly at him. I made no attempt to hide how offended I was by his suggestion.

"If you were really listening instead of taking insult to my offer, you'd know I wasn't saying that. Promoting you was the best move for RPH. That said, I know how important it is for you to be on top of everything, and I need that as well. I want you positioned for success, and I'll provide you with every advantage possible, starting with Chicago. He'll be an excellent resource for you."

"I have Raina. There's no need to send one of your lapdogs to watch over me," I said, my voice loaded with impudence.

He lifted his brows in amusement.

I didn't find it funny in the least. Why would he place me in a position in which he felt I needed help?

"Once you meet Chicago, you'll see that *lapdog* isn't a description that would ever fit someone of his caliber. And although you do have Raina, Chicago is well versed on aspects of Raine Industries that your assistant isn't privy to."

"Aspects such as?"

He didn't answer. Instead he looked down at his phone. There was a message notification he obviously appreciated, given the quick smile that appeared on his perfect lips.

"I've been in contact with Chicago, and he should arrive Monday morning," he stated, looking up from his phone.

"Wait? You arranged this without speaking with me? Why the fuck didn't you just give me a direct order instead of presenting it as an offer?"

The brio I'd seen in his eyes earlier disappeared as he cast a warning glance at me. "Aria, calm down," he said, frowning his disapproval.

The others had returned and were taking their seats. I glared at Aiden as he resumed the meeting by introducing the dark-haired lady as Brooklyn Pierce, his personal assistant.

I was fuming and Aiden knew it. I wanted to tell him to stick his offer up his privileged ass. But that wouldn't be professional, now would it? Deciding to address this later, I pushed down the emotions, molded my expression into one more work-appropriate, and sat quietly as he proceeded.

After the meeting, I jotted some last-minute notes on my tablet and quickly rose from my seat. "I need to speak with you before you leave, *Mr. Raine*," I said.

Aiden glanced up from Brooklyn, nodded his acknowledgment, and then immediately returned to his conversation with her.

Less composed than I was at the start of my morning, I walked back to my office to see Raina exiting.

"I made another cup of tea for you. I thought you might need something calming after your meeting with Mr. Raine."

"Why would you ever think that, Raina?" I asked dryly.

"He seems to always press your buttons, and I didn't think today would be any different," she replied, looking at me sympathetically, her lips pursed.

"It seems you're correct, Raina," Aiden said, as he entered my office. "I think I may have done just that."

I looked at Raina, and she was obviously embarrassed. "I'm sorry, Mr. Raine," she said as she scurried for the door.

"Nothing to apologize for, Raina, you're simply stating the truth. I do somehow manage to upset Ms. Cason, but I'm hoping she'll allow me the opportunity to remedy that."

As soon as the door closed behind Raina, I turned my attention to Aiden. "I will not have you arranging things without my signing off on them first. If this is your plan for me as CEO, why not release my shackles and allow me to work someplace else?"

"Someplace such as Little Brown and Company?" he asked.

I'd interviewed there just yesterday. How could he know that?

"I'm very much aware of your meeting with them," he said, observing my reaction. "I have a very long reach, Aria, and I'm aware of more than you could ever realize."

"So…what does that mean? Are you spying on me? We both know it won't be the first time," I said, bitterly.

"There's no need for me to spy when I have such loyal business associates."

"That's illegal. You of all people should know that," I said.

"Brooklyn will work with Raina to coordinate Chicago's

accommodations and your schedules while he's here," he said, ignoring my previous comment.

"You're unbelievable. You're once again forcing something on me that I do not want or need."

"And you're once again fighting me on something we both know is good for you. Frankly, I'm disappointed that an intelligent, forward-thinking woman such as yourself can't see the value in this."

"Well, you know me...I love a good fight," I said.

"Even one you know you can't win?" he asked.

I knew there was more to his statement than his imposing Chicago on me. He was referring to us. And he was wrong—this was a fight I intended to win.

"Who says I won't?" I asked.

"Must you be so obstinate?"

"Must you be so intrusive?" I shot back.

He didn't reply.

"I'm sure our exchange of insults will be the highlight of my day but I have a very busy schedule, so I would very much appreciate if we could forego this nonessential prattle. Is there anything else you wish to force down my throat?"

"Well, if you're offering..."

Fuck, wrong choice of words. "I'm not in the mood for your word games, Aiden," I replied angrily.

"It was not my intention to insult you, Aria, just as I'm sure it wasn't your intent to display such flagrant insubordination in the meeting. I understand you're frustrated with me, but we *will* convey an amicable working relationship when we're in public. I need to make sure you understand that."

"So not only do you think I need your help to fulfill the role as CEO, but you also think I'm an idiot?"

"You know I'm not saying that. But the tension you displayed earlier is not acceptable."

"Excuse me for not being as nonchalant as you, Mr. Raine. In the future, I'll do my absolute best to convey the aloofness you've obviously mastered. Is that all?"

He sighed as he stood and walked toward me. "What am I going to do with you?"

"Nothing," I replied.

Cornering the desk, he grabbed my chair, sliding it back towards him. His eyes momentarily locked with mine, and then suddenly his hands were on my arms, lifting me from my seat. Before I could register my thoughts, he'd gripped my braid in one hand and grasped my chin with the other, forcing my mouth to his. And then abruptly, he sealed his lips over mine. The kiss was harsh and demanding, like the forceful grasp on my hair. I felt the subtle tug as he pulled the braid, allowing him more access, as the pressure of his thumb and forefinger on my jaw opened me to him — enabling his tongue to dart inside my mouth. Mustering all the strength I could, I pushed him away and slapped his face, my palm landing flush against his cheek.

"What the hell was that?" I asked, rubbing my lips.

"Do I really need to explain it? Besides, I didn't do anything we haven't done before."

"That was then. We no longer have that type of relationship, and you damn well know it," I said.

"Do I?" he asked, stepping away from me.

"And if you ever do something like that again, I'll—"

"I was caught up in the moment," he said, his eyes focused on my mouth.

"There was no fucking moment," I replied, glaring at him as he coolly raked his hand over his assaulted jaw.

He donned that lop-sided half smile that once made me want to rip his clothes off. Not today. Today I was livid — how dare he be that presumptuous with me. I wanted to wipe that cocky-ass smile from his face with another smack.

"What? Are you going to slap me again?" he asked, as if reading my mind.

"If I thought it would make a difference," I replied, glancing at the red mark on his cheek.

"Are you assessing the damage?" he asked.

"No, and don't expect an apology, because you don't deserve

one. You can't just do whatever you want with me anymore."

"When did I ever do what I wanted with you without you negotiating the hell out of it?"

"Regardless, if you do it again, you're going to find yourself on the receiving end of much more than a slap."

"Calm down, Aria — it was an impulse," he said.

"It was what it has always been — you taking what you want, when you want it."

"Is that what you really think of me?"

"Quite frankly, I don't give you much thought at all," I lied.

"Oh, but I think you do. You wouldn't be this worked up otherwise."

"Still arrogant."

"And you're still uptight. If your offer to shove something down your throat still stands, just say the word," he replied, leaning in closer.

"This is a place of business, not your bedroom," I said, backing away and taking a seat at my desk.

"So, kisses are reserved specifically for the bedroom?" he asked. "I clearly recall a different scenario in an office. One that went much further than a kiss."

He'd obviously taken the slap as a joke. Did he see this as a game? I'd been in his presence for approximately two hours, and he'd already launched a new campaign. And it was already affecting me. Would he always get under my skin? Had he any idea how badly he'd hurt me? Would he care if he did? For him to come at me like this, he obviously didn't.

"You know, I was thinking it wouldn't necessarily be a bad thing if you did get on the inside of Little Brown," he said, changing the subject. "We've been looking at that company for a while now, hoping to absorb it as an entity of RPH."

"What? Are you kidding me?" I asked.

"What do you mean?"

"You'd actually consider planting me inside LB and C? Is that how you do business?" I asked.

"Aria, don't be naive. Raine Industries is successful for a reason. We didn't get where we are today without stepping on a few toes," he threw out casually.

"I had no idea you were so unscrupulous. I can see why your own deceit was practically effortless."

He cocked his head, looking at me as if he couldn't figure out why I was outraged. "I'm a businessman, Aria—I do whatever it takes to get the job done."

"Obviously." *Lucky me. I get to see yet another side of Aiden Raine.*

"Just how ambitious are you?"

"What?" I asked, confused as to where this was going.

"If they were to offer you a position and you accepted, you

could give us the edge we need to make a swift and quiet takeover."

"You can't be serious," I said.

"Very. You'd be perfectly positioned for us to move on this. But I take your response to mean you're not interested," he said.

"And you would be absolutely correct. Besides, Blake is there now."

"That could also work to our advantage."

"I said no. I'm not going to be the person to Blake that you were to me."

His face briefly betrayed him.

What was that? Was he actually remorseful?

"Aria, you know I hate how—"

"Aiden, are there any additional business matters we need to discuss? If not, I'm late for a lunch meeting."

"Actually, there are several things we need to reexamine, which were left pending with Blake's departure, but first I really think we should talk about us. I know I'm going about it all wrong and I—"

"Aiden…please," I said. My tone was laced with the pleading and agony I felt, and it must have been reflected in my eyes, as I watched the vibrancy in his dissipate. I couldn't do this with him.

"No. I think we're done," he said, backing down.

I could see he wanted to say more, but I was relieved he

didn't. "Good," I replied, reaching for my cell phone to check the text I'd just received. It was Kellan. We'd agreed to a lunch date while he was in town. I sent a quick reply asking that he meet me downstairs, not wanting to chance any additional unpleasantness with Aiden.

Looking up, I saw Aiden still standing in front of me, watching intently. What was his fucking deal?

I slid my chair away from the desk and walked toward the door to grab my purse. He could stand there for an eternity if he so chose, but I was leaving. Opening the door, I was surprised to see Kellan seated outside my office.

"Sorry, I just got your text. Are you ready?" he asked, standing and walking towards me.

"Yes. Definitely."

Kellan glanced over my shoulder and saw Aiden in my office.

Grabbing Kellan's arm, I urged him in the opposite direction. We headed towards the exit, not bothering to say goodbye to Raina. I just wanted out before anything happened with Aiden.

"Is everything okay?" Kellan asked once we were in the elevator.

"Yes. I guess," I replied, sighing.

"Let's talk about it over lunch," he said. "We can't have the most beautiful girl in the world stressing, now can we?"

I looked up and smiled at him. I was so glad we'd kept in

touch since we'd met in St. Barts. He really was a great guy, and at that moment, he was exactly what I needed.

We'd decided on lunch at the Grotto, my favorite lunch escape. Seated at a booth near the window, I casually perused the menu as Kellan offered highlights of his hedge fund meeting. Regretfully, I only caught part of it — my body was sitting in the booth near the window, but my mind had wondered far away to the top floor of the RPH building…with Aiden Raine.

❧Chapter Three❧

"Okay, you've barely acknowledged anything I've said. What's up with you today?" Kellan asked.

"I'm sorry. I have a lot going on at work." I felt guilty for being less than honest, but in my defense, it wasn't a complete lie.

"From what I've gathered, that's the norm for you, so what's different now?" he asked.

"I'm trying to adjust to all of the changes." I could honestly say that much. I couldn't very well tell him I was adjusting to the fact that the guy who I'd been fucking—which was complicated enough when I thought he was my intern—was actually my multi-billionaire boss who'd blackmailed me into accepting a position as CEO and even now, he was still making attempts to get in my panties. And worst and most embarrassing of all, how could I tell him I was still weak for a man who'd deceived me every time he'd touched me?

It was going to be difficult to deal with the changes all right. That was certainly one way of wording it. I'd taken on a huge responsibility as CEO, and to add to that, I'd have to fight my natural instincts each time I was anywhere near Aiden. As disillusioned as I was with him, his brilliance and passion weren't something I could easily forget. I wanted to tell him to fuck himself, but on the other hand, I still wanted him to fuck *me*.

"Are you regretting your decision?" Kellan asked.

What decision? I never had one. Not really. "I'm not sure—I'm in the process of accepting some of the unexpected aspects of it, though," I said.

"Learning curve?" he asked.

"Exactly," I replied.

"In that case, I don't think you have much to worry about. Relax and enjoy your accomplishment. Everything else will take care of itself."

If it were only that simple, I wouldn't be worried about returning to my office. I didn't want to have another run-in with Aiden.

My phone pinged before I could reply. Glancing at the display, I saw it was a text from the one person I didn't want it to be. *Are you fucking kidding me?*

"Excuse me for a second, Kellan. This is work-related."

"No problem," he replied, as I scanned the message.

FYI, the company we discussed earlier will be absorbed into RPH by the end of the next quarter. Your placement there would make it that much easier. You should consider it. If you discover you're absolutely against it, we'll go with plan B. Although it's somewhat of a challenge, I'm always up for those.

I quickly tapped out a response.

There's nothing to consider. I'm not doing it. Besides I would hate to deprive you of the opportunity to undertake yet another challenge. We both know how much you enjoy those.

I resumed my conversation with Kellan, as much as I could, anyway. I was distracted, wondering how long Aiden would be in Boston. I doubted it would be more than a few days. If that were the case, I could arrange to work from home the remainder of the week. *Just great. Now I'm considering hiding from him. That's what that man has reduced me to.* Wait. Had Kellan asked a question? If so, I missed it and I totally didn't know how to respond.

Another ping sounded. I sighed as I checked my phone again.

It dawned on me that your lunch meeting is with that guy from St. Barts. What are you doing, Aria?

Aiden had the unmitigated gall to question *me*, even after everything he'd done!

Focus on your latest challenge and leave me be. Please don't text me again!!

"I'm sorry, what did you say?" I asked, looking up at Kellan.

"I was wondering if you'd heard anything from April…about Blaine," he repeated.

"Yes, I have. Lots actually. I think it's safe to say she's quite smitten," I replied, thinking fondly of my friend. I was so happy for her. She, unlike me, had always been open to relationships; however, she tended to finagle her way out of them when the guy wasn't as perfect as she'd initially thought. That typically took about a month. I wondered what she would have done with someone like Aiden. She hadn't come across anyone like him. He was a game changer—he'd ripped away my defenses and pretty much revamped all my Fuck Rules—something that still bothered me, because until him I'd always been a stickler for doing things my way or no way at all. Someone like April, who was less inclined toward walls and rules, wouldn't stand a chance with Aiden. She'd be putty in his hands. I'd often thought I was much the same when it came to him. He was the artist, and I was the canvas, and he painted the picture to fit his desires.

"Good, because Blaine has it pretty bad. I'm starting to worry about him," Kellan added, laughing.

"No need to be—from the sounds of it, they're both on the same page." I was inwardly relieved by Kellan's admission. I didn't want to see April get hurt.

Kellan and I had met during my vacation with my best friend, April Jensen. We'd ventured off to St. Barts in August and stumbled upon Kellan McClane and Blaine Davis. April and Blaine had quickly connected and had gone as far as making plans for a weekend get-a-way soon after our return from St. Barts.

Things didn't click as quickly between Kellan and me. When we met, I wasn't in a place to fully appreciate him, because Aiden had suspiciously appeared on the island at the same time as I. I'd been too absorbed with Aiden to give much attention to Kellan, which I'd regretted both then and now. But Aiden's arrival had done crazy things to my head. I was drawn to him and I didn't want to be. So most of my time in St. Barts was spent one of two ways — thinking of Aiden willingly and thinking of Aiden unwillingly.

I did manage to have a couple of dates with Kellan during my short stay on the island. And after spending only a small amount of time with him, I knew I would've enjoyed getting to know him better, but Aiden's presence halted anything that could have developed. Before leaving St. Barts, Kellan and I exchanged additional contact information, which was something I never did on those escapes from my real world. But the nagging feeling I could be excluding something potentially great made me bend yet another rule. This was one I hadn't regretted.

Within the last couple of weeks, Kellan and I had exchanged numerous texts and emails. We'd also enjoyed several extended phone conversations. My end-of-day routine had become one of working out and talking to Kellan. He was in town for the next few days on business, so of course, we'd planned to spend some time together. Yet here I was again, straining to maintain focus on him.

"So how was your morning? Signing any new deals? Changing the world?" he asked.

I laughed. "Nothing as monumental as that, but we're rolling out a few new projects that I'm pretty excited about," I replied.

"Such as?" he asked.

"It's top secret. If I told you...well, you know how the saying goes."

"Yeah, you'd have to kill me," he replied, smiling.

"I can tell you this. We plan to employ a multi-platform marketing approach, utilizing all forms of social media, so you'll hear about it soon enough."

"Sounds like something big," he said.

"It could be," I replied, smiling. This could utterly transform the publishing industry. I just needed to get Aiden to sign off on it.

Arriving at my office shortly after one o'clock, Raina gave me a strange look as I approached her desk.

Please...what now? I knew my serenity would be short-lived with Aiden lurking about. He seemed to somehow place a dark stain on every part of my day. I slowed my steps, but then decided not to ask. Instead, I would bask in the enjoyment of my time with Kellan a while longer. Although it had taken some time to remove Aiden from my thoughts, I finally did, and it was a huge relief because I'd started to feel like a first-class jerk for ignoring what was right in front of me. Kellan had a very soothing effect, in direct contrast to Aiden—who kept me on edge more than I cared to think about.

Upon opening my door, the look on Raina's face instantly made sense. My office had been slightly enhanced during my short absence. Orchids were everywhere. As I glanced around, I was immediately taken back to the day I arrived home from St. Barts to a similar scene—Aiden had arranged for the placement of orchids throughout my condo, along with the sweetest of hand-written notes. I remember having felt as if I was in the midst of a fairy tale. No one had ever done something so extravagantly sentimental for me before. I suppose they would have if I had ever allowed my relations with men to go beyond the physical—but I never had. But Aiden—he penetrated every barrier. It wasn't so much as I *allowed* him to break through—he just did. I rejected every attempt, some more adamantly than others, but eventually I succumbed to his every desire, and I was still paying the price for it.

I took in the many vases, each one a delicate crystal-style design overflowing with my favorite flowers. They were beautiful. I inhaled the sweet fragrance, and I was suddenly livid — this shit may have worked when I initially agreed to an arrangement with Aiden, but it would not work now! The largest vase was placed on the center of the work table with a white envelope propped against it. Marching over to the enormous bouquet, I snatched the note. Not bothering to read it, I crumbled it and tossed it into the trash.

I went directly to my desk, grabbed the phone and pressed the button for the receptionist's extension.

"Yes, Ms. Cason," she said.

"Bailey, can you please have someone remove these flowers from my office? Immediately," I added.

She was silent.

"Bailey, did you hear me?" I asked, irritated by her lack of response.

"Yes ma'am, but—"

"But what?" My patience was thinning.

"I'm sorry, Ms. Cason, but I've been given explicit instructions from Mr. Raine to not do that."

Tempted to slam the phone down, I inhaled deeply and replied as calmly as my current state would allow.

"Thank you. That will be all, Bailey," I said. My grip

tightened around the receiver as I fought the impulse to toss the phone across the room.

He was doing it again — manipulating me and everyone around me! If he wanted a reaction, he'd be disappointed because I wouldn't give him the satisfaction.

Raina walked into my office, and the look on her face verified my suspicions — that she, too, had been instructed to not touch the flowers.

"I'm sorry, Ms. Cason. Bailey said you called, and you sounded upset."

That was stating it mildly. I shook my head, knowing she couldn't do anything to assist with this.

"Raina, can we just get to work? I need to make some changes in my schedule this week," I said.

Dr. Grist's office called to inform me that she would be going on vacation and needed to reschedule my annual exam or I'd have to see the on-call physician, which I didn't wish to do.

"Can you move the first two appointments around for me on Thursday?"

I didn't want to miss that appointment. Having decided several years ago that I didn't want children, I wanted to discuss some permanent options with my doctor. I'd actually broached the topic a few years ago, but she was insistent upon my waiting until I was older before making such an irreversible decision. She asked that I give it at least five years, and this month marked year five.

"Yes, ma'am," Raina replied. I could see she was uncomfortable, given the flower ordeal, but this simply had to stop. We couldn't allow Aiden to set the tone for our work day.

After a two-hour meeting with Raina, my mind was where I preferred it remain...on work. The tension of my earlier encounter with Aiden had subsided, thanks in part to a text from Kellan extending a warm wish for the remainder of my day.

Looking up at the Phal Sogo Rose orchids, my heart started to sink because I was pulled right back into that forbidden Aiden zone. This display proved what I suspected — a relationship with him was too much of a distraction. Why was he making this so difficult for me?

Aiden had invoked feelings I never imagined possible, emotions I'd never experienced. Every day with him had been a new adventure. But in the end, he was a liar, and I no longer trusted his intentions. Yet here he was, again attempting to lure me back into his web. As sexy as the thought of being stuck to a web that was spun by that man, I knew there was much more behind his gorgeous green eyes that I didn't want. He needed to move on and so did I...somehow.

≫ ≫ ≫ ≫

By four o'clock I was so over this day. Anxious to leave before anything else came up, I shut down my computer, grabbed my purse and headed out of the office. Just as I was about to open the door, I released the knob and traipsed back over to the trash, retrieving the note from Aiden. I didn't want to do it, but the part of me I didn't like — the part that was having a hard time letting him go — wanted to know what he'd written. I wanted to open it, but for some reason, I couldn't bring myself to read it just yet. I let out a sigh as I placed it in my purse and stepped out of my office, contemplating the evening I'd be spending with Kellan.

Aiden had left several sweeping spaces in my life, and one of those vacancies had been filled with Kellan. I often wondered if I was using him as an emotional buffer between myself and thoughts of Aiden. As badly as I didn't want to believe I'd treat Kellan or anyone else that way, I knew I wasn't on the same page as he was where a relationship was concerned. Did that mean I should back away? Even if the answer was yes, I knew I wouldn't. I didn't want to. I really liked him, and I felt at ease with him. It was relaxed, and it was natural.

Kellan lived in New York and would be flying home tomorrow. We'd planned to meet for dinner this evening, and despite my initial reservations about his visit, I was looking forward to it. I knew from our lunch together that I could unwind, free from thoughts of Aiden. At work, he was on my mind because in a sense he *was* RPH. At home, he was there, too, not just because of the grand piano that captured my attention every day, but because he was the only lover that had been to my home.

Lover? Even in my head that sounded wrong—like something I would never have. Looking back on everything, it was as though all through our time together I'd been a sex-crazed teenager—full of hormones and ignoring obvious red flags. Why hadn't I inquired more about Aiden's background? I'd never had cause to dig into anyone's past for personal reasons before, which was likely why I didn't think to take a closer look at Aiden's. Actually, the fact that all of this constituted a *first time* was even more reason to have checked. If I'd known more though, would it have changed anything? He'd said he wouldn't have stood a chance with me. Was that true?

I was looking forward to spending the evening with one man, but I was driving home thinking about the other. Aiden had taken up residence in my head, and he wasn't leaving anytime soon. I sighed as that truth sat in. I wanted to forget him, but I knew that would never happen. A change of jobs wouldn't change that, so it was pointless to even consider leaving Raine Publishing.

I loved RPH, and I honestly didn't want to resign because of issues with my boss. Although I'd been pressured to take the job, I was happy and excited about my new position. I couldn't have asked for a better transition than what I'd experienced as I took on my new role. There had been little to no resistance in the new hierarchal structure. I don't quite know if I'd expected any, but I was pleased all the same. I'd hoped that Aiden would back off and allow me to truly appreciate this experience without his interruptions and finagling; so far that hadn't been the case, so I couldn't help but wonder what was next.

❧   ❧   ❧   ❧

Kellan and I were sitting on the sofa in my condo. We'd started a second glass of wine when the sound of a Skype call interrupted our laughter. My only callers were typically one of my family members, April or Kellan. I grabbed my tablet from the table and saw that it was my mother.

"Hi, Mom," I said, greeting her with a cheeky smile.

"Hello, Aria. How was your day?"

"It was okay," I replied.

"Just okay? Is something wrong?" she asked.

"Not really. I'm not in complete agreement with my boss on a few things." It killed me to think of Aiden that way. "But that's typically the case for anyone working for *the man*," I added, smiling. "But things will work out. How was your day?"

"Pretty great actually. I'm working on some gifts for you and your sisters for Christmas."

"Already? You're getting a great head start," I said.

"Well, I think I should've started sooner because I actually don't know what I'm doing. I'm attending a quilting class."

"Wow! You're making quilts for us?" I asked.

"Yes, and I wanted it to be a surprise, but since I need to get more information on your favorite colors and such, I needed to check in with you," she said.

"That sounds amazing. I can't wait to see it."

I totally forgot Kellan was sitting next to me until he grabbed a strand of my hair. "I'm being rude, Mom. My friend, Kellan is here," I said, turning the screen to include him.

"Hello, Kellan," Mom said.

"Hello ma'am, how are you?" he asked.

"I'm well. This is a special treat. I rarely meet any of Aria's friends," she mused.

I rolled my eyes as I thought about the reason she'd never had a chance to meet any of my friends. For one, she was never in any condition to socialize until very recently, and two, I didn't have any friends, except April.

The intercom buzzed, interrupting the nearly awkward conversation. I was sure it was the food delivery. Although it was more my idea than Kellan's, we'd decided to skip the restaurant and stay in for dinner. I foolishly hoped that introducing new memories into my home would flush out the others.

Passing the tablet to Kellan, I told Mom I'd be right back and rushed to the door. After paying the delivery guy, I placed the bags in the kitchen and headed back to the sitting room.

Kellan's laughter caught me by surprise as I entered. I heard Mom laughing, too. I wondered what that was all about.

"That was dinner," I said, looking at Kellan and then at the monitor. "So, what did I miss?" I asked.

"Nothing that you don't already know," Mom replied. "I was telling Kellan about your first school play — you know, the one where you had the hiccups."

I didn't respond. I wanted to smile and not place a damper on the moment, but that memory belonged to a time when we were all together as a family, and while I was making great efforts to reconnect with Mom and my sisters, I hadn't yet opened the door to the room that included my dad.

I looked over at Kellan, who was still grinning.

"You two are about to have dinner so I'll check in with you later… more than likely tomorrow, because I really want to get started on the quilt swatches."

"Okay, Mom. But did you want anything else?" I asked.

"No, I just wanted to see your face and hear your voice. I love you, Aria."

"I love you too, Mom."

"It was nice talking to and meeting you, Kellan," she added.

"It was nice meeting you too, Mrs. Cason," Kellan replied.

"It's Costanzo. Her last name is Costanzo," I blurted out. My surname was different because I changed it to Mom's maiden name before I graduated from college. I didn't want my dad's name to follow me around for the length of my career... another attempt to distance myself from him and my memories.

"Sorry about that, Mrs. Costanzo," he corrected.

"Kellan, it's nothing to apologize for; it's a logical mistake," Mom said. "Goodnight you two. Enjoy your dinner."

"Thanks, Mom. Goodnight."

The video disconnected.

"Your mom seems nice," said Kellan.

"Yeah, she's great," I said, smiling at him.

"I'm glad I had a chance to meet her. Virtually anyway," he said.

"So am I," I replied.

"I'm starved," Kellan said, reaching for my hand.

I looked at our intertwined fingers, startled by the ease and comfort of his touch. "Me, too," I replied, as we headed toward the kitchen. "Why don't you have a seat while I prepare our plates?"

"Do you need any help?" he asked.

"No. I think I have what it takes to remove food from a bag and scoop some onto our plates," I replied, smiling.

"Are you sure? From what I hear, that can be kind of tricky."

"I think I recall reading that someplace myself, but I'm up for the challenge." I regretted those words as soon as they escaped my lips. *Up for the challenge...* those were *his* words. It seemed no matter what I did or who I was with, Aiden was there with me.

Over dinner, Kellan and I talked about one thing after another: his college years, his family, his job. And surprisingly enough, I even gave him more of a glimpse into my life.

"Hey, I was thinking," he said. "Blaine was talking about going to Barbados with April. Maybe we could plan a trip for the four of us."

"That sounds amazing, but I'll have to check my schedule," I said. I hoped my response sounded natural. I wasn't sure I was ready for a couples' trip, especially one with Kellan, which would undoubtedly send the wrong message. He didn't seem to think anything about my putting him off. We easily dove into other topics of conversation — it was comfortable and I found myself talking to him as if we'd been friends for years.

The night ended much too quickly — before I knew it, we were at the door saying our goodbyes. After giving Kellan a hug, he leaned down for a kiss, but it was awkward when he placed his lips on mine. They weren't familiar...they weren't Aiden's lips. I stepped back from Kellan, ending the short kiss and hoping I did so in a way that didn't offend him. I didn't know what was happening with Kellan, but *something* was developing...although it was more for him than it was for me.

"I'll be in Boston next month," he said, lingering in the

doorway, "right around the time of that charity event you mentioned earlier."

Over dinner, I'd told him about the Raine Industries event for the American Academy of Arts and Sciences.

"If you don't already have a date, I could escort you."

"I actually don't have a date, so I'd like that," I said, agreeing before considering the possible problems. But the moment I closed the door behind him, I realized I might have made a huge mistake. If Aiden attended and saw Kellan was my date, I didn't know how that would turn out. Not only that, what if Aiden had a date, also? How would I react to seeing Aiden enter with a woman on his arm?

❦Chapter Four❧

Relieved to hear Aiden would be heading to Los Angeles the next afternoon and wasn't scheduled to return to RPH any time in the foreseeable future, I felt as though I was finally able to completely exhale. His absence would allow me to not only relax, but focus on my job, specifically my new proposal—I had back-to-back meetings all morning to fast-track research on the project.

Earlier, I'd felt the vibrations of either texts or calls but failed to check until now, so I skimmed over them as I sat at my desk. After placing my phone in a drawer, I looked at my schedule, noticing I was much too busy to schedule any time out of the office, so that meant a working lunch today—and for the next several days actually.

Waking up my computer to check my email, I saw a message from Aiden. Although I was sure he wouldn't send an email of a personal nature on RPH's server, I hesitated to open it. I double-clicked and braced myself.

Aria,

I'll be in Los Angeles for the next several days. I'll be traveling to New York afterward and from there to Chicago. Brooklyn is coordinating my schedule to accommodate my attendance at the Raine Industries sponsored event for the American Academy of Arts and Sciences. In the off chance I'm unable to attend, I would like for you to serve as the keynote speaker. There are a few important mentions I'd like you to include in the speech; please see the attachment.

This would be an excellent opportunity for your first public appearance as the new Raine Publishing House CEO. Should you have any questions, please contact either myself or Brooklyn.

Regards,
Aiden W. Raine
Chief Executive Officer
Raine Industries
875 North Michigan Avenue
Chicago, IL 60611
Website: www.ri.com
Email: awr@ri.com

Maybe I'd jumped to the wrong conclusion about the flowers and the note yesterday. Could they have been an apology for the kiss? I never did read his note. Reaching for my purse, I pulled the crumbled paper from the side pocket. I smoothed the wrinkles before opening it—an obvious delay tactic. After looking at it for several nervous seconds, I once again decided against reading it. I'd wait until later. Maybe when I was home. Yes, that seemed the better idea. I'd read it after my workout—the endorphins would enable me to swallow his words that much easier. I shoved it back into my purse when Raina entered with my lunch.

"Thank you, Raina," I said.

"You're welcome. Do you need anything else?" she asked.

"No, this will about do it."

She offered a polite smile and walked out of the office.

I needed to do something special for her. Reaching for my phone, I entered a reminder to do just that. In doing so, I saw Mom had texted about the quilt. After adding a note about Raina's gift, I started my lunch, eating in a hurry so that I'd have time to call Mom.

"Tell me more about Kellan," she said immediately.

"Not much to tell. He's a great guy, and we're getting to know each other." It was still weird talking to her about a guy. Maybe it was commonplace for most moms and daughters, but other than speaking with her about Aiden, this was a first for me.

"I like him. Very handsome. But I don't know if he's the one."

"Mom, I'm not looking for *the one*. He's just a good friend. Besides, how can you tell from just one meeting and a conversation that lasted all of five minutes?"

"A mother knows these things, Aria," she replied, as though it was scientific fact.

"Well, you can put your sixth sense back in your box of mom tricks because he and I are just friends. I really like him, and that's that."

"Are you sure that's all it is?" she asked.

"I think so…but there are times when I'm not sure what I want. It feels very natural with him. It did from the moment we met."

"Just take your time and make sure it feels right. If it doesn't, don't lead him on, Aria."

"Mom, I wouldn't do that." Would I? Is that what I'd been doing? There was that kiss and the discussion of a trip to Barbados. But that was just as friends…right?

"Are you still at work?" she asked.

"Yes."

"I don't want to keep you. I'm headed to the fabric store this afternoon so give me the rundown on your favorite colors, patterns, hobbies…basically anything you like that I could add to the quilt."

"How about I text you? Then you can have it all on your phone."

"That's a good idea. But do it now, Aria."

Pushy much? "Okay Mom," I said, laughing.

"Okay. Love you."

"Love you, too."

Ending the call, I started on the text. She was becoming more and more like the mom I remembered. I really hadn't thought much about my favorite things enough to compile a list, but I needed to hurry before she called back. After thinking for a few moments, I tapped out a short list and sent it to her—already excited to see the finished product. I wondered if I should go with handmade gifts, too. I hastily decided that I would. Well, I would at least try.

As I started prepping for my two o'clock meeting with the IT and marketing teams, Raina popped in to review some other pressing matters before they arrived. Once we'd finished, she placed portfolios at each attendees' seat. The excitement for this project was already building—I only needed Aiden to give the thumbs-up and we could move full-speed ahead in preparation for launching it next quarter. It would've been great to work on a project like this with him. We'd worked well together when we were at RPH under different circumstances. I kicked myself for going there, but it was true nonetheless.

"Dane Patrick is on line two, Ms. Cason."

I stopped short. It had been weeks since he was at my office. I'd met Dane on one of my trips with April. We'd had a good time that was supposed to have been left in Venezuela, but I'd recently learned he was married, and his wife had learned of our brief indiscretion. I'd hoped their silence meant they'd worked things out.

"Aria Cason," I said, speaking into the receiver.

"Hello, beautiful," he said.

"What do you want?" I asked.

"Why so rude? I don't recall you being this way in Venezuela."

"I don't care to revisit anything that occurred on that trip. Haven't I made that clear?"

"Crystal."

"Then tell me the purpose of this unpleasantness," I said.

"If I were more of the sensitive type, my ego would be crushed," he replied.

"Dane, you have thirty seconds before I hang up."

"It's about Tiffany, my soon to be ex-wife."

"I don't believe that's any of my concern," I said.

"Unfortunately, it is."

"How so?" I asked.

"She's filed for divorce on grounds of adultery, and she's seeking a vast abundance of my assets. Assets she doesn't deserve, but will receive if she can prove anything."

"And this concerns me how?"

"You know how, Aria. I know she's been in contact with April. I also know she plans to speak with you."

"As I've said, this has nothing to do with me so please keep me out of it!"

"And again, you're incorrect. She needs someone to substantiate her claims and you, unfortunately, are that someone," he replied.

"Dane, surely there's something you can do to keep this quiet."

"There's only one thing that will make this go away, and that's money. And I don't intend to just give her everything I've earned."

"Okay, what exactly are you saying?" I asked.

"You need to tell her that nothing happened between us. Corroborate my story."

"The hell I will. I'm contacting my lawyer; I don't intend on being a part of this at all."

Glancing up, I saw Aiden standing in my door. Fuck. Had he heard my conversation? I totally checked out on the phone call and stared at him. Surprisingly enough, he didn't approach me— he just stood there— his eyes squinted as he studied me. Dane was mumbling something about a subpoena, but I only heard a word here and there. Aiden didn't say anything— he simply turned and walked away.

"Dane, you can't keep bringing this shit to my job," I whispered into the receiver.

"My wife wants you to testify in our divorce. If you do that and give them what they want, you may not have that job much longer, so we need to do whatever's necessary to protect ourselves."

"I need to consult with my attorney and figure a way out of this crap. In the meantime, give me your number and I'll contact you, not the other way around."

After adding Dane's information into my phone, I told him I would call him in a few days. Once I'd ended the call, I noticed my hands were trembling. I needed to pull it together and prepare myself to do whatever was necessary to make sure this didn't affect my job.

Exiting my office, I headed down the hall as I sent a quick text to April, updating her on the latest and asking if she'd heard from Dane's wife. I wasn't looking where I was going and bumped right smack into Aiden, dropping my phone.

"Note to self—don't text and walk," I said, as he passed the phone back to me.

"Everything okay?" Aiden asked.

"Yes, why wouldn't it be?"

"I don't know. You tell me," he said. "Who was on that call?"

"That's none of your business," I replied, moving past him before he could say anything else.

❧ ❧ ❧ ❧

Having a few more minutes before my meeting and since she hadn't returned my text, I called April.

She answered on the third ring. "Hello."

"Hi, April. Did you get my text?"

"Yes, I was planning to call you later," she replied.

"Are you okay?" She didn't sound like herself at all.

"Yes, I'm fine. What's up?"

She sounded like a sad child, and that worried me. April was rarely anything but upbeat. "It can wait. Why don't you tell me what's wrong?"

"Aria, it's nothing I can't handle."

"Well, you can tell me anyway."

She sighed. "It's Blaine."

"I thought things were going well with you two," I said, confused.

"They were, until his girlfriend appeared."

"Girlfriend? I didn't think he was dating anyone." Kellan hadn't mentioned anything about Blaine seeing anyone else.

"They were having issues when he and I met so she never came up in our conversations. Things sort of just grew into something with us. Then his girlfriend...well, you know how it is when the other person senses you're no longer interested."

"So, she reached out to try to fix things with him when she

saw he was slipping away. What does that mean for the two of you?"

"It means we're pretty much done. He wants us to remain friends, but he's trying to work things out with her."

"What the fuck?" I had the good mind to call Blaine and let him have it.

"I know, right. They'd been in a relationship for three years so I can understand that he wanted to exhaust every effort before throwing in the towel."

"I'm sorry, April." This was one of the many times I wished we lived closer.

"Thanks, but no harm; no foul. It was only a couple of months, and knowing me, I would have found a way to end it anyway."

I tried to console April as best I could in the remaining time I had before my meeting. I didn't mention the situation with Dane to her at all — it could wait for now. My best friend needed me.

❧Chapter Five❧

Over the next few weeks, I didn't hear a peep from Aiden.
Going M.I.A. was obviously his M.O. I should've been relieved,
and part of me was, but the other part wondered. Why did he
make such grand gestures and then…nothing? At least his
extended silence allowed me to manage the disarray he'd left
behind, and, oddly enough, I was starting to heal, thanks in part
to Kellan. He was fast becoming a constant in my life, one that I
valued very much.

I no longer wondered as much about Aiden, but there were
days when my thoughts of him lingered more than I cared for.
Today was one of those days. He was expected to attend the
charity gala this evening, but there had been a last-minute change
to his schedule so his appearance was still in question. I hoped
that whatever was keeping him away persisted. It's sometimes
easier to abstain when your addiction is nowhere in sight. That
was especially true in regard to Aiden.

As he'd instructed in his email, I'd prepared a short but
heartfelt speech that I was quite anxious to deliver to the
benefactors and other attendees, especially since this was my first
event as CEO of Raine Publishing. However, my preparation
would be for nothing if Aiden graced us with his appearance. I

didn't want to be caught off guard, so I'd asked Raina to check in with Brooklyn, but she'd been unable to confirm his attendance — which meant I had to wait and see.

Stepping out of the shower, I sat at the vanity to do something with my hair. After a few moments of lifting and brushing it from one side to the other, I'd decided on a strawberry swirl, which would accentuate my neck, given the cut of the dress I'd be wearing. Sweeping my hair to one side, I tied it into a low ponytail, twisted it toward the end and folded it back against my head. I tucked the ends of the fringed section into a floral bun, and I was done. I surveyed my work, smiling at my small feat.

When I glanced at my phone, I noticed it was nearly time for us to leave. Kellan had slept in one of my guest rooms because the hotel in which he was booked had lost his reservation. When he'd arrived in Boston late last night he wasn't able to coordinate with his company's travel assistant, so he'd called me asking for hotel references, and I'd offered to let him stay at my place.

We'd only shared a short kiss up to this point, and as much as I thoroughly enjoyed sex, Kellan and I had yet to broach that area. Much to my surprise, I enjoyed spending time with Kellan despite the absence of the physical, and Virginia was apparently just as content. She'd barely voiced an opinion on anything since things with Aiden had ended. It would seem both of us were learning to play it safe — or maybe both of us only lusted for that one person who'd turned our worlds inside out.

Sex with Aiden was intense—it was like receiving a concentrated dose of endorphins. When his skin touched mine, I lost all sense of self and gravitated to another place deep in my psyche—a place where he was the master and I was the student. I didn't resurface until he released me—and that release came in the form of orgasm after orgasm, each one more extreme than the last.

Having shared such intimacies with a man like Aiden, to abruptly stop required some regrouping, and, of course, that applied to the sexual aspects as well as the emotional.

One of the aftereffects of my affair with Aiden that I'd quickly discovered was that I could enjoy a man for more than sex. Though, this was in a lesser, but still significant, degree due to Kellan. I'd sensed from only a few conversations with him in St. Barts that he was a great guy. Of course, I couldn't take anyone at face value—I'd asked my attorney to run a background check. Given the financial aspects of our relationship, my request was warranted.

Kellan was a Senior Hedge Fund Analyst, and I was his firm's most recent client. A thorough review of his firm's credentials was actually a suggestion from my attorney. I'd added the *extra* request, explaining to my lawyer that I'd be working exclusively with Kellan, therefore I wanted to run a check on him as well. I was less paranoid about both Kellan and his firm after receiving the all-clear. I didn't want another Aiden-size secret popping up and knocking the air out of my lungs.

After taking one last look in the full-length mirror, I walked out of my bedroom. I'd selected a Maison Rabih Kayrouz bias-cut red charmeuse one-shoulder gown. It had a draped panel that extended from the shoulder to the asymmetric hem at the back. There was a high asymmetric slit in the back of the dress as well, which showcased the results of the extra time I'd put into my leg workouts. The red Giuseppe Zanotti lace-up pumps I'd chosen would not be very supportive, so I was hoping the amount of standing and walking this evening would be minimal.

"Wow! Just when I thought you couldn't possibly look more beautiful. You look amazing," Kellan marveled as I entered the sitting area.

"Thank you. You look quite amazing yourself," I replied. Kellan was a very handsome man and was quite dapper in his dark blue suit. His light brown hair was cropped short. He had chocolate brown eyes, strong arched brows and prominent cheekbones. His chin and nose were well-defined, as were his lips. I had a thing about guys' lips, and although Kellan and I had only shared the one kiss, his mouth captured and held my attention quite often.

"I thought we'd have a drink before we headed out," he said, extending a glass of wine to me.

"Thank you," I said.

"When are you going to play something for me?" he asked, looking at the piano.

"I'm not very good, but I may be able to play a little something."

"Okay, let's hear it," he urged.

"Now?" I asked.

"Why not?"

"Okay, but don't say I didn't warn you." We walked over to the piano and I took a seat as Kellan stood behind me.

"What is that?" he asked.

"What?"

"That." He pointed at the inscription.

I suppose that was a natural question from anyone who saw this piano.

"The piano was a gift," I started, not knowing how to explain the rest. "And this inscription was sort of an inside joke."

I sensed he wanted to ask me something else, but was relieved when he didn't.

"Any requests?" I asked, jokingly.

"How about—"

"I can only play five songs so it needs to be one of those five," I interrupted.

"Well, in that case, you choose," he replied, grinning.

"If you insist," I said, and dove into my favorite of the five. When I finished, I looked up to see him smiling.

"What? You look surprised," I said.

"Honestly, I am. I thought the piano was more of a decoration piece. That was amazing."

"Really?" I asked. I'd never played for anyone besides Vincent, my instructor, so I was nervous. "I'm too excited to be offended by your décor crack."

"You can crack a joke on me later to make up for it."

"You can count on it, mister."

"We should get going," he said.

After grabbing my pashmina and clutch, we left the comfort of the condo behind us, heading out to what promised to be a very interesting night.

Kellan and I were among the first to arrive, so I easily spotted Raina and Zoe in the midst of the small crowd. Walking over to join them, I offered a cordial greeting and then introduced Kellan. A look of shock passed over Raina's pretty features when she recognized Kellan as the guy I'd rushed out of RPH a few weeks ago. And since I'd never attended a business function with a date before, I expected Raina's expression to be one of the many I'd encounter over the course of the evening.

We were knee-deep in discussion about the charity, Kellan, and work when a sudden uproar near the entrance halted our conversation. Turning toward the source of the hoopla, my heart nearly jumped out of my chest when I discovered the reason for the excitement. It was Aiden…and he wasn't alone.

Raina's eyes darted to mine, and wanting to appear untouched by Aiden's arrival, I forced my wry version of a smile. Raina looked on, mimicking my gesture with a tight-lipped one of her own. Hurriedly cutting our exchange, I returned my focus on the entrance. Seriously, how could anyone not stare at that gorgeous man? He was born with the charisma that commanded the attention of everyone in his path.

As if for more of an effect, he paused, allowing everyone the chance to soak him in before stepping from the threshold. Photographers snapped pictures and reporters flung questions, but it was though they were invisible — he ignored them all. After shaking hands and nodding a few hellos, a member of the wait staff appeared to escort him to his table — which I noticed was much closer to ours than I would have liked.

I wanted to look away, and I knew that I should, but my eyes wouldn't cooperate; they were glued to him as he strolled into the room. My gaze slowly moved over his tall, powerful, and incredibly gorgeous frame. He was so hot he could make a pussy come just by looking at it. And there on his arm, enjoying the company of one of the most eligible bachelors in the world, was a stunning redhead. There was a unique beauty about her, and she wore the same air of affluence as the man whose arm she clutched.

Allen and Michelle Lane were also in close proximity — they were friends of Aiden's parents, so it wasn't a surprise to see them. Skimming his entourage, I looked for his mother or father — who was reportedly on the mend and working part time in the Chicago office. I wondered what that meant for Aiden. Would he retain his current role? He certainly couldn't resume his alias now that his undercover probing into Raine Industries had been made public. You'd have to practically live under a rock to not know what had transpired.

Looking away just as Aiden spotted me, I realized I wasn't the only one getting an eyeful — Kellan had been watching my prolonged survey of Aiden. I turned away from his inquisitive eyes and scanned the room, pondering how I'd possibly manage this night.

Conversation resumed, the orchestra began playing, and several splendidly dressed couples made their way to the dance floor. Waiters circled the room taking orders and distributing drinks. I definitely needed one…possibly two. My subliminal message must have been loud and clear, because one of the waiters approached our group. I noticed Raina eyeing him, too. I was about to reach for a drink, as was she, but I stopped short when her expression changed. Following her gaze, I saw Aiden was headed our way. He'd barely been in the room five seconds, and he was already strapped and ready to cause problems.

No way would I let Aiden disrupt what had barely started. Turning to Kellan, I asked him to dance. Although caught off guard by my abrupt request, he accepted, leading me away from our group. He and I merged with the small crowd already on the floor, and were soon gliding along with them, moving fluidly to the gentle sounds of Franz Schubert's *Serenade*.

Everything felt awkward now and I didn't know what to say. Should I ignore Kellan's curiosity, or should I address what I knew he was piecing together? My gaze darted about the room — glancing at the other dancers, the orchestra, and the waiters — anything but Kellan. I felt his eyes burning into me. I knew I'd eventually have to answer his questions if I wanted an honest relationship with him.

"Mind if I cut in?" came a voice from behind Kellan.

I was so lost in my thoughts of how to avoid Aiden that I hadn't noticed his approach.

"That's up to the lady," Kellan said.

"Aria, will you do me the honor?" Aiden asked. He noticed my hesitation. "I promise not to bite," he said.

I sighed. "Fine, but just one."

"Whatever you want," he replied, as he reached for my hand.

I placed my palm in his, and his touch literally sent chills throughout my body. This was a bad idea. I looked toward Kellan, offering a silent plea for his rescue, but Aiden tactfully moved me from Kellan's reach.

"You're starting to make running from me a new art form," he said, peering down at me.

"I'm certain I don't know what you mean."

"And I'm certain that you do," he replied. "It's just a dance, Aria. Nothing to be afraid of."

I knew all too well that nothing was that simple when it came to Aiden.

"Don't flatter yourself — at least not any more than you already do. There may be a few things I fear, but you're certainly not one of them."

He leaned down toward me, drowning me in his rich scent, "Are you sure about that?" he whispered.

And just like that, Virginia awoke from her hibernation, the gentle throbbing between my legs nearly causing me to stumble. "What happened to this being just a dance?" I asked.

He responded by sweeping me into his arms, taking my breath away — I was still apprehensive, but Virginia was elated by his proximity. We slid easily across the floor, his graceful movements taking me on an enchanted flight. Being in his arms like this felt right somehow — I was more comfortable than I would've liked. Conflicting emotions consumed me. I craved his touch, yet it hurt to be this close. I wanted to run, yet I wanted to melt into him.

"I heard good things from Chicago," Aiden said, changing the subject.

"Did you expect anything less?" I asked.

"I can't say that I did, but in the future, you should take heed of my suggestions and trust that I know what's best."

"This is my job — not yours, and I will not go along blindly with everything you say. I'm not one of your corporate neophytes who think you're all-knowing."

"It would appear I struck a nerve. That was not my intent. I only want what's best for you. You know that, right?"

"Aiden, can we just dance in silence?"

The last time I'd danced with him, it had ended with him fucking me against the wall of a dark room on a yacht. When he didn't answer, I looked up, prepared to denounce anything inappropriate he may have had in mind, but my determination floated away when my eyes locked with his. They were as breathtaking and spellbinding as a thick blanket of stars, bewitching anyone who fell under his gaze. And just like his temperament, his eyes were strangely mercurial. At times, they were of a brilliant emerald, inviting you into his amazing world. At other times, they were hooded with lust as they morphed into two dark, smoldering pools of liquid green. And then there were the times when they were angry, spitting jade bolts of flashing fire.

He smiled as he looked down at me, the light bouncing from his chiseled features. His only blemish was that his brows too often knitted in frustration, at least when it came to me. When I'd last seen him, he was sporting that sexy stubble, but tonight he was clean-shaven. And thanks to Virginia's prodding, I wasn't thinking with a clear head—I had the insane desire to lick the side of his face. Yes, dancing with him had been a very bad idea.

"You're nervous. Don't be. What do you expect me to do in a room filled with hundreds of people?"

Torture me. You seem to enjoy that. My thoughts again flashed to what happened on the dinner cruise.

I replied bitterly, "Well, one never knows with someone as immoral as you, Aiden."

"I suggest you drop the attitude, Aria…and maybe go one step further and give the pretense of getting along," he scolded.

"Is that an order, Mr. Raine?" I asked.

"If it needs to be, then yes."

"Do you get a perverse kick out of exerting control over your employees?"

"Aria, you should really watch what comes out of your mouth," he warned.

"Professionally, I intend to, but privately, what comes out of my mouth isn't something you will ever control," I said.

"What about what goes into your mouth?" he asked with a smirk.

"There's nothing of yours I want in my mouth."

"So, no pineapple? And here I thought you wanted to corner the market on that commodity."

"Oh, I did until I found I was highly allergic, so I've moved on to something that won't give me cause for concern."

Our private joke about the taste of his come whisked me back to the playful and sensual moments we'd shared, but I quickly pushed those thoughts to the side.

"So, it's back to the battery-operated boyfriend, I presume. That's not enough for someone as sensual as you, Aria."

"Presume whatever you wish."

"You're so very beautiful," he said. "Does your B.O.B. tell you that? Does it kiss you or tell you how sweet you taste? Does it whisper the dirty things I know you like to hear as it plunges deep inside that tight cunt of yours? I know how very wet you get when I tell you how hard I want to fuck you. And I'm certain your pussy is seeping for me right now. Tell me it's not."

Virginia's quiet murmurs became pounding throbs. "Will you

please stop?"

"I can't."

"You mean you won't."

"No, I mean just what I said. I can't. You're a hard woman to forget."

We stared at each other in silence. Now that I was engulfed in his aura, my mind was fluttering. He was a hard *man* to forget, but no way would I tell him that.

"Enjoy your evening, Aiden," I said, when the song ended. As I turned to leave, he reached for my arm, pulling me back to him.

"Can you at least give me a minute?" he asked.

"You just had several, so that would be a no."

He placed his hand at the small of my back and pressed me forward. I reluctantly walked alongside him. As soon as we were away from the glare of prying eyes, he stopped and turned to face me.

"What is it?" I demanded. "What do you want, Aiden?"

"You know what I want. I want you."

"Is your *date* aware of that?" I asked.

"You're the woman I want to be with, Aria."

"You say you want me now, when you're with me, but as soon as you walk out the door, I have no idea of what you're thinking, what you're feeling, what's real, what's not…I can't do that with you again."

"Aria, you need to know that I feel the same way about you, whether I'm in your presence or not. But I have responsibilities. I can't devote all my time to us. I don't know if I would if I could. That's just not who I am. But you really need to trust me and trust my feelings for you."

"Are you done? I don't have the time or inclination for a relationship, especially with you. Besides, your timing sucks. This conversation is several weeks too late."

"It doesn't have to be."

"What we had is over," I said.

"It isn't for me, and I know it isn't over for you, either, so stop with the bullshit, Aria."

No, it wasn't over for me. But it should be. I needed it to be. Being here with him like this, the flood gates were opening, and all those feelings were threatening to be unleashed.

"I know I ruined it," he said. "But it wasn't because I didn't love you...I did. I still do. I just went about all of this the wrong way."

"All of this doesn't matter now," I said, shutting out his words so I wouldn't weaken.

"But it does. I'm asking for a second chance—a chance to make this right," he said. The impassioned plea of his smoldering gaze was almost tangible. But that didn't matter, not after all he'd done…what he was still doing.

"A second chance?" I asked. "Is that why you came here with the redhead draped all over you?" This man had nerves of steel.

"I can explain that. It's not what you think," he replied.

"Aiden, I can't do this with you now. Please."

"Well, tell me when."

"There's not going to be a *when*. Why can't you accept that?"

"I won't accept it," he said, an unyielding determination in his eyes.

"Well that's just too damn bad," I replied.

"And this guy you're with tonight…what are you doing with him?"

I hated that Kellan was now mixed up in this. "I would imagine the same thing you're doing with your date."

"She's just a friend."

"Same here," I replied.

"I don't think friends look at each other the way I saw him looking at you. I don't like it."

"Do you even hear the words that are coming out of your mouth?" I asked.

His eyes narrowed. "Are you reverting to your old ways? Is that why he's here?"

My eyes widened as I shook my head. "My old ways? Aiden, he's here because I want him here."

"And the other part?" he asked.

I crossed my arms. "That's none of your business."

"So, I'm right. You're doing this for kicks? To avoid being hurt," he said.

"You have no idea why I do anything, so don't pretend as if you do," I replied.

"I know all too well. You said it was for control, but we both know there's more to it."

"I'm so done with this. I'm tired of you trying to figure me out. You don't know who or what I am."

"I don't think you do either," he shot back.

"That may very well be true, but I do know one thing, I'm not about to let you finish the job you started," I said, walking around him, only to have him pull be back.

"I'm not your dad or your mom or any of those fuckers that agreed to the bullshit you offered them. I legitimately care about you. And I won't let you do this."

"Do what? Protect myself?"

"I know how hard this is for you. I know it's easier to put walls up or to deal with men only for sex, but you can't go through life like this, Aria."

"It's what I like," I defended.

"Oh, so you like being treated like a piece of meat?"

I winced— his words tore through me like a knife.

"Fuck you, Aiden," I said, again turning to leave, but he blocked my way. His eyes were two angry emeralds shielded only by the evening dusk.

"Don't you think you deserve more than that?" he asked. "Stop with these antics and go after something that's real."

"With who? You? Why? So, you can make me fall in love with you? Make me need you?"

"No, because you deserve to be loved."

There was that word again, the one that had caused all of this, the one I'd run from for years. "The one time I had a love that I thought I could count on, it was taken from me, and there was a hole in my heart that grew every day — every day that Dad was gone and every day that I watched Mom suffer because of it. I finally found a way to close the hole, and it's worked for me up until now. And I'm scared — I'm not willing to take the chance that it *may* work out."

"Love is risky, but sometimes you meet someone who is worth the risk."

I glanced past him. "I'm not in a position to take a risk like that."

"Does your friend know that? I know he wants more than friendship, Aria. Are you planning to take a risk with him? Surely you know, I won't allow that to happen."

I stared at him, wide-eyed. "I don't know who you think you

are, but you don't have that type of control."

"You have no idea."

"You're a fucking bully. You bullied me into that job, you bullied me into fucking you, and you bullied me into this discussion. I am done, Aiden. You will not continue to treat me this way."

"He wouldn't be here if he didn't want you." It was as if he hadn't heard shit I'd said. "It makes me wonder if you want him, too," he said.

I eyed him. "If I didn't know better, I'd think you were jealous."

"Is that so outside the realm of possibilities?" he asked.

"For someone such as you, yes," I replied.

"Let's not put that theory to test. At least, not tonight."

What did *that* mean? "What are you saying?"

"What I'm saying is obvious." He inhaled and closed his eyes. When he opened them, the passion of his gaze nearly took me away. "I don't want anyone touching you but me."

"I would never have thought you to be delusional, but it seems you are," I replied.

"I know you want me. I can see it when you look at me, and I'm sure that friend of yours sees it. Do us both a favor and let him know that you're taken, because whether you want to admit it or not, you are...and I'm not going to share you," he stated.

"I'm not taken, and you needn't worry yourself about sharing me because I'm not asking you to."

"Then what are you doing?" he asked, searching my eyes.

"I'm doing what I do best. I'm doing me," I replied, and walked away.

❧Chapter Six❧

Rejoining the others at the table, I found Kellan making polite conversation with the ladies in our group. Raina excused herself as soon as I arrived, and Kellan focused his full attention on me. I felt uneasy looking at him after what he'd witnessed earlier. And now I had to add the dance with Aiden to the list of uneasy topics.

"So, that's the guy? The one who has your heart?" Kellan asked.

I hadn't expected that question and I didn't want to acknowledge it, especially not to Kellan — the man who'd become my refuge from a world that had been turned upside down.

"What makes you say something like that?" I asked, knowing exactly why he'd said it.

"It doesn't take much to see that something's there. And now I totally understand his reaction to Blaine and me in St. Barts, and again when I came to your office for lunch. The tension that surrounded you two — it was extreme. I would guess that whatever you two shared is over, but even now, he seems very protective. He's not letting you go, is he?"

"Protective? Well, I don't know if I would use that word." More like possessive. "It doesn't matter if he's let me go, because I've let him go."

His brows lifted. "Have you?" he asked.

"I don't want to spend any more time talking to or about Aiden. I need a drink. Would you like one?"

He looked at me as if expecting more. He deserved more, but not here.

"I promise to tell you everything later, okay?"

"I don't want to pressure you into doing something you're not ready for," he said.

"And I don't want to leave your questions unanswered."

He studied me for another moment, and then nodded his acceptance...of more than my offer of a drink. "Sure. I'll have a scotch."

"Great. I'll be right back," I said, excusing myself from the table. I went to the ladies' room first and then to the bar, where I ordered our drinks and turned to people watch as I waited. One of those people was approaching the bar; it was Aiden's date. I wanted to yank her fucking hair out.

"Hi, I don't think we've met. I'm Nadia Lane," she said, smiling like she had the juiciest of secrets.

So, this was the *no one important* Aiden didn't wish to talk about. Nadia Lane. Wait. Was this the same Nadia who was mentioned a few months ago when I attended Allison's ballet? The one that Michelle Lane had said would be happy to see Aiden?

"Hello. I'm Aria Cason." Though I sensed she already knew who I was.

"It's nice to meet you, Aria," she said, then beckoned the bartender. She ordered a drink and turned toward the crowd as I had.

I looked over at Kellan talking to Zoe and then glanced toward Aiden's table. He was never alone. Someone always wanted a piece of him, including Ms. Thing standing beside me.

"He's an intense guy, isn't he?" she asked, having followed my gaze.

"Excuse me?"

"Aiden. He can be very intense…both in bed and out. Don't you agree?"

What the fuck? Who *says* that to someone they just met?

"Nadia, I don't particularly care for your assumptions, nor will I engage in conversation with you as a means of substantiating them." She needed to know right off that I wasn't about to play this game with her.

"I wasn't implying—"

"Oh, I know exactly what you're implying, and I know what you're hoping to accomplish here, and sweetheart it ain't working."

"I was simply making conversation about a man we both seem to appreciate—I don't see it as any reason to be impolite."

"So, my refusing to validate your statement is impolite, but what you said is considered casual conversation?" I asked. "Listen, I won't be party to whatever type of game you're attempting to play, and I'm no threat to whatever it is you're trying to accomplish with Aiden, so I suggest you direct your phallic rage elsewhere. Enjoy your evening." I grabbed the drinks and headed back to my table, but I didn't make it there before running into Allison.

"Hi, Aria. You look beautiful," she gushed, reaching out to hug me, careful not to jostle the drinks in my hands.

"So do you. I didn't know you were here. It's so good to see you!" I exclaimed. I really liked Allison, and seeing her reminded me of a much happier time.

"I saw you speaking with Nadia."

I rolled my eyes. "She seems to be a piece of work."

"I'm guessing that means your conversation was nasty."

"It was what it was," I replied, waving it off.

Allison winced in sympathy. "She saw you and my brother dancing earlier," she said. "She watched the entire time, and when the dance ended, she saw Aiden pull you away. And that's when she asked me if I knew you. I had a feeling she would say or do something horrid. In case you didn't pick up on it, she has it bad for him. I'm sorry you had to deal with her."

Aiden had said she was just a friend. He'd failed to mention that his *friend* had feelings for him. How interesting that he glossed over that tidbit during his anti-Kellan speech.

"Allison, she's the least of my worries, and if her intent was to warn me off, she wasn't very effective. If anything, she's shown her desperation."

"I knew there would be some craziness when I realized Aiden had feelings for you, and I don't want this to be an additional reason for you to have an issue with him. I'd really hoped you two would've figured it all out by now."

"Some of the *craziness* could have been avoided, but what's done is done." I was certain she knew that I was referring to the lies surrounding his identity.

"I agree. And I'm sorry I haven't been in contact with you. I wanted to call, but Aiden forbid me to reach out to you. He said you needed time. He's such an idiot. I told him time is exactly what you *didn't* need."

"It's okay, Allison. I know how he can be when he wants his way."

"He can be such a jerk. But Aria, he's really an amazing guy and I'm not just saying that because he's my brother. I know he wants you. And I can tell you're still into him," she added, smiling.

Choosing to contradict her last statement, I said, "Some things just weren't meant to be, Allison. But I would love it if you kept in touch. Don't let Aiden boss you around."

"I won't." She grimaced. "But don't mention it to him. I don't want to upset the only sibling I actually get along with."

"I don't plan to discuss anything personal with him, so you have nothing to worry about."

"So, who's your date? He's a hottie," she said, glancing toward Kellan.

"A friend. He was in town on business, and since I had to be here, we made a date of it."

"Are you sure he knows he's just a friend? You should let him know you're taken before he falls for you."

"Allison, you're just like your brother… relentless."

"Where do you think I get it from?" she asked, laughing.

"I'd better get back to him; I don't want to be rude. I hope to hear from you soon."

"You will — I promise," she said, giving me another quick hug. "I'm still rooting for you and my brother," she said and she was off before I could tell her not to hold her breath.

I finally made it back to the table. If I'd known it would be such an ill-fated trip, I would have stayed put. I was more than ready to put a cork in this night.

Kellan sensed my unease and suggested we get some air, so we escaped to the terrace. Having grown tired of all the small talk, I was relieved to see we were alone. Normally a night like this would have been perfectly fine, but the mind games with Aiden had more than exhausted me.

"Looks as if you're ready to go," Kellan said.

"Is it that obvious?"

"Just a tad," he replied, grinning, his dazzling smile accentuating his dimples.

"Seems we keep bumping into each other," Aiden said, having joined us on the terrace.

Oh shit. Will it ever end?

"I don't think I caught your name," Aiden said, approaching Kellan.

"I didn't catch yours either," Kellan replied.

Aiden smirked. He was accustomed to everyone bowing down to him when he put on the Raine Industries CEO face; Kellan apparently wasn't doing that. This would be interesting.

"Aiden Raine," he said, extending a hand.

"Kellan McClane," he replied, shaking Aiden's hand.

Why was Aiden doing this?

"You've met, so you can go now," I said.

He continued as if I hadn't said a word. "Are you affiliated with McClane Funds and Investments?" Aiden asked.

"One in the same," Kellan confirmed.

"Hmm," Aiden replied.

"Whatever you're thinking...don't," I said, glaring at Aiden.

He looked back at me, all innocence. "Aria, Mr. McClane is in the business of hedge funds, and I'm thinking he could possibly do some work with Raine Industries."

"Since when?" I challenged.

He returned his attention to Kellan. "How long are you in town? Maybe I can drop by your hotel and talk some numbers before I head out tomorrow," Aiden suggested.

"I'm not at a hotel," Kellan corrected. "I'm staying at Aria's place."

And there it was. The one thing I didn't want him to know.

Aiden's eyes froze. He looked as if he wanted to hit Kellan.

"Come again," he said, stepping closer to my date.

Kellan didn't flinch. If anyone was in the market for a bottle of fresh testosterone, they could definitely get it here. This was fucking crazy. I'd gone from having no man in my life to having two who were staring each other down like they wanted to pulverize each other.

"Aiden, what are you doing?" I asked, stepping between them. "Unless you're planning to be tomorrow's headline, I suggest you walk away."

"Aria, look around you. There's absolutely no way this will go any further than the three of us." It was as if a switch had flipped; his voice was ominous, and his eyes blazed with anger.

I looked around to see that there was security detail standing near the terrace entrance. No one would be coming out here. He'd made sure of it. "So, you came out here looking for a fight?" I panicked as I considered how this could end.

"I actually needed to make a call that required privacy. Why are *you* out here? Did you have a need for privacy also?" Aiden insinuated.

"I suggest you watch how you speak to her," Kellan said, his voice low and controlled, but I could see that Aiden's question made him angry.

"And I suggest you back the fuck off," Aiden threatened, directing a stabbing glare at Kellan.

"Aiden, isn't it almost time for your speech?" Allison asked, appearing at just the right time.

Aiden didn't move. Neither did Kellan.

"Aiden, don't do this. This is not a good idea," Allison said, tugging her brother's arm.

He looked down at Allison, and she shook her head, silently warning him. He hesitantly stepped back and cast an angry glare at me.

"Aria, if you think this is over—" he began.

"Aiden, stop it…let's go," Allison urged.

Aiden looked back at Kellan, his temper still flaring. He then turned his fury towards me. I was all too eager to return his murderous glare. Who the hell did he think he was?

"Just go," I said to him.

Aiden took a few steps back and turned, walking away, leaving Kellan and me alone.

With ashamed eyes, I looked up at Kellan. "I'm sorry. I've never seen him like that."

"Why are you apologizing for that jerk? Don't worry about that. But you need to let me know what's going on. I don't want to be in the middle of something that you two obviously need to work out."

Staring into Kellan's eyes, I could see that he knew. He knew why I wasn't able to kiss him, why I was complacent with our platonic relationship.

I let out a sigh. "That's just it. I thought it had all been resolved."

There was no way around it — I had to tell Kellan about Aiden, and then allow him the chance to decide if he wanted to remain in my life. Fucking Aiden! If he thought he was going to parade around with that pretentious bitch while he destroyed my friendship with Kellan, he was dead wrong!

It was time for the keynote speaker, and in the midst of everything, I'd completely forgotten to ask Aiden if he would be delivering the speech. I looked around the room for him and spotted Nadia's red hair. I knew I would find Aiden close by, and he was. That somewhat angered me, and I decided I wouldn't worry about the speech. It was his company—his charity event— he could give his own damned speech.

I had to admit Nadia was beautiful. I watched her smile and touch Aiden in the most intimate of ways. I wondered if he'd whispered to her—as he had so many times to me—that she was beautiful. Would he be able to keep his hands off her? Would he whisk her away to a dark room and do unspeakable things to her, as he'd done to me, or would he wait and take her back to his penthouse and fuck her into the wee morning hours?

I was ready to go. I'd done my part. Now that Aiden was here, he could handle the rest.

"I think I'm ready to call it a night," I said.

"I thought you were scheduled to speak."

"That was a contingency in the event Aiden couldn't make it. As you can see, he did—so my presence is no longer necessary," I said.

"Well in that case, sure."

The night had been everything I'd feared tossed in with so much extra shit that I could barely think straight. I was sure I hadn't heard the last of it, but at this point, I just didn't care.

✎Chapter Seven✎

Despite the less than stellar evening at the R.I. event, the following morning started with a surge of excited energy. After escaping last night's gala, Kellan and I came back to the condo and vegged out like two carefree teenagers. We watched sitcoms, drank wine, and in the midst of cracking silly jokes, we created a make-shift meal from the various leftovers in my fridge. How weird was it that I was enjoying a sleepover at my age? This clearly indicated my need for an active social life.

Kellan was pouring a cup of coffee as I walked into the kitchen. "Hey, do you want to work out with me?" I asked.

"Sure. I'll get changed and meet you in the gym."

I trotted down the stairs with a silly grin on my face. I was in a great mood. Things weren't just as I would have wanted, but they weren't as bad as they were during the gala last night. Walking into the gym, I flipped on the lights and swiped through the control panel in search of a workout playlist that I hadn't heard in a while. I made a mental note to create a few new ones. Turning toward the exercise equipment, I decided to take some time with the tread climber.

Kellan walked in, sporting shorts and a T-shirt. Allison was right—he was a hottie. It wasn't as if I hadn't already known that, but I had a difficult time picturing him as anything more than a friend right now. But with a body like that, I was sure he could do some serious damage in the bedroom.

Aiden's accusation about my having shallow relationships still echoed in my head—he wasn't completely off track, because I was typically all for detached sex. But even that seemed less than appealing now. I was looking at so many things with fresh eyes…reevaluating my views on relationships, friendships, and even sex.

Kellan looked around. "What do you recommend?" he asked.

"Anything that allows me to fixate on those amazing muscles," I replied, smiling.

"What? These things?" he asked, flexing his arms and flashing a sexy, dimpled smile.

"How often do you work out?" I asked.

"Typically, three to four times a week. What about you?"

"The same. Maybe more if I'm stressed."

"You seem to have it all together. I can't imagine you having much stress. Well, at least I couldn't until last night."

"I honestly didn't until recently. But I thought we'd agreed to put last night behind us?"

"We did and we have," he replied.

I watched as Kellan stretched, his muscles contracting as he reached one hand over his shoulder. He was somewhat more muscular than Aiden. I never understood how these magnificent specimens were still single. Kellan was a dream—totally hot, successful, great sense of humor, and easy to talk to. He was definitely single of his own choosing because no way in hell would any woman who had the chance to get close ever let him go.

"Hey, you didn't have a tattoo in St. Barts," I said, inspecting the impression on his bicep.

"Nope, I didn't. A few of the guys had the crazy idea of getting tattoos the night before the wedding," he replied.

"A group of wild drunken guys doing God knows what the night before a wedding. I'm sure there're stories there."

"One could say that," he laughed.

"So, how was your friend's wedding? Did it go off without a hitch?" I asked.

"Yup, as far as I could tell. I don't remember much—I had a massive hangover."

"Typical," I said, shaking my head. "Your tattoo, what does it mean?" I asked.

"It's the Japanese calligraphy for strength."

"Oh. I recognized the symbol, but not the interlinked embellishments. I like it. I may get one myself."

He lifted a brow. "Seriously?" he asked.

"Yes. Does that surprise you?"

"Sort of," he said, his eyes gliding down my body. "I don't figure you as the tattoo type."

"There isn't a type," I said.

"Sure there is," he countered.

"Are you the type?" I asked as I increased the incline on the climber.

"I have a tattoo, don't I?"

"What type am I, if not the type to get a tattoo?" I asked.

"Do you really want to know?"

"Of course," I said. "I asked, didn't I?"

"That you did." He grabbed a couple of free weights and then straddled the weight bench. "Okay. The person I'm getting to know seems to be very careful and methodical; people like that don't normally get tattoos," he said, as he started pumping the iron.

"Is that all? You made it sound as if you were about to insult me. Maybe that's the person I was but no longer wish to be," I said.

"That remains to be seen," he replied, breathing through his reps.

He was right; although I was joking, there was some truth to my statement. I no longer wanted to be that safe, careful girl. I wanted to live in the moment…enjoy my life. Make real memories.

After a few more reps, he stepped on the treadmill, and within a few strides, he was jogging. I studied him from head to toe. He was a very appealing man, and under different circumstances, he and I would have already been going at it. And although I still welcomed the daydream, Aiden's naked body appeared and blocked out everything else. Would I ever be able to have anything sexual with another man, or was I destined to an eternity of one B.O.B. after another? That reminded me—I needed to get a couple of new friends. *Guess I'll be scrolling on my favorite sex toy site tonight.* I sighed and started to move on the elliptical. Damn you, Aiden!

Kellan left for New York shortly before six o'clock that night, with the hope of seeing me when we all met up in Barbados. I wasn't sold on the idea yet. April had texted saying she thought it was a great plan, which was surprising considering she and Blaine had called it quits. Being a third wheel wasn't her style, so more than likely, her goal was set on scouting out some fresh meat. As the saying went, the best way to get over one man is to get underneath another.

Over the rest of the weekend, I enjoyed several talks with Mom, Lia, and Bianca. It wasn't without its awkwardness, and I did sometimes pull back, but we were starting to feel more at ease with each passing day. I was hoping to get some idea as to what I could make for them as Christmas gifts. Like Mom, if I wanted to allow time for error, I needed to get started on it as soon as possible.

Work, however, was my first concern. A last-minute schedule adjustment left Aiden in town for the next three days, meeting with different teams — meetings in which I had to be included. I wasn't as nervous about it as I would've been before I'd accepted a couple of realities.

Reality number one: Despite my distaste for his domineering attempts to re-insert himself into my life, I still had strong feelings for him. I'd fully accepted the depth of my emotions, but I didn't plan to do anything beyond letting time do its thing. I'd employed the methods that worked previously — minimal eye contact and absolutely no personal conversation. That worked to a point, but he was consistently inconsistent, and that worked against me.

Reality number two: I wanted to fuck him…repeatedly. He was always Mr. Fuck Me — that went without saying — but there were different versions. He was mesmerizing, humorous and even playful at times. Then there were those times when he was in total billionaire CEO mode, and that was the version of him I'd started to see more often, the version I didn't like, the one that made it easier to stand my ground. But not today. Today, his display of power and confidence was pulling me to him. It was an aphrodisiac I hadn't accounted for.

It was day two — Aiden's last meeting was with me. I waited until we'd reviewed every item on our agenda before I proposed the idea I'd been working on for the last few weeks. We would conduct a contest similar to the TV show "The Voice." It would be ninety-five percent virtual in our case, hosting a writing contest for a different genre each quarter. The contestants would be required to submit specific pieces that were forwarded to all editors of that genre. The editor would bid on a contestant, and the contestant would be paired with an editor of their choosing, who would mentor them and provide content and developmental critiques. At the end of the quarter, one author would be chosen for a book deal. After the conclusion of the first year, we'd have a new author's book released every quarter, possibly more.

"I like this idea," Aiden said. "It's actually brilliant. Of course, we would have to get the appropriate checks in place — R and D, legal, marketing."

"That's already been taken care of. I've been meeting with the teams for a while now."

"So, I'm the only holdup?" he asked.

"It would appear so." I was shocked he agreed so easily — not only that, he actually loved the idea.

"If you'd come to me with this sooner, we could have already had this in place. Was there a reason for the delay?"

"I was still on the fence regarding my decision to stay here."

"And why is that?" he asked.

Was he fucking kidding me? I stared at him as he feigned innocence. "The first few weeks upon my assuming this position, I was forcefully immersed into the storm that was Chicago Brown every fucking day, and then as soon as he left, you were back in town. That type of oversight doesn't exactly reflect the confidence I thought you had in me when you strong-armed me into taking this job. If you felt I needed to be watched every day, why do I have this position?"

"Aria, I don't feel that way at all. I think you misinterpreted the situation."

He sounded almost apologetic—*almost*—but I wasn't buying it. He was a very intelligent man, and he was very much aware of his actions and how they affected those around him.

"Whatever, Aiden. I eventually decided if I couldn't lead RPH in the manner that I saw fit, I should leave this company, regardless of your ability to restrict me from working elsewhere."

"So, you're still pouting over that?" he asked.

"Pouting? Is that what you think I'm doing? Do you really expect no reaction from people when you bulldog them? Obviously, you're accustomed to having *everything* your way."

"Not with you, it would seem." He strolled over to the bar and poured a drink. "Would you like one?"

"No, thank you," I said.

"I'd like nothing more than to have my way with you. Right here in your office. But since you're clearly opposed to that…" He walked back over and took a seat.

And how I would love to let him. It was mind-boggling how we diverted conversations to terribly inappropriate topics and then bounced right back into business. I so desperately needed an orgasm that I damn near jumped from my chair and demand he do just what we both wanted. But what would follow? I didn't want to find out, so responding to his offer was a terrible idea.

"I'm surprised you didn't come to me sooner with this. Certainly, you know that whatever it is you *think* I'm doing to you, comes second to a sound business decision."

Oh asshole, I don't think *you're doing it. I* know *you're doing it.*

His phone rang before I could issue a reply. After pulling it from his pocket to see who was calling, he answered. Holding up a finger, he excused himself as he stood and walked away from the meeting table. I busied myself with some notes for *The Writer* as I waited.

At the conclusion of his conversation, he assumed the seat across from me. "I'm afraid we'll need to table our meeting until later this evening. Brooklyn's set up a video conference that I need to be in on. I would like to tie this up before I leave tomorrow so if you can get the appropriate papers and background information to me, I'll review it with you tonight over dinner at my place."

Huh? I couldn't have heard that right.

"Let's say seven o'clock."

I opened my mouth to object, but he turned and walked out of my office. Dinner at his place? Why couldn't he and I have a video conference as well? Did we have to be face to face to *tie this up*? I considered alternatives for a few moments, but realized he wasn't going to agree to anything but his own plan. Fuck it. I'd go. I'd get in and get out within thirty minutes or so.

Rushing home after work, I started on my plan to repel any non-business tactics Aiden may attempt during our meeting. Maybe I was overdoing it, but the ends would justify the means. I'd planned it all. What I'd wear. What I'd say when he opened the door. Where I would suggest we sit. All of it. And I'd be damned if it didn't all go out the fucking window as soon as he opened the door to the penthouse.

"Good evening, Aria. Come in," he said, standing in the doorway. His undiluted scent enveloped me when the air from the motion of the door sashayed its way to my nose.

"Hi," I said, and followed him inside.

He was barefoot, wearing jeans and a snug black T-shirt that showcased his sculpted arms. He looked amazing. I, on the other hand, looked just the opposite. I'd scrubbed my face clean of all makeup, thrown on some sweatpants and tossed my hair into a messy bun, all part of my plan to get in and get out…untouched.

"Would you like a glass of wine?" he offered.

"Yes, please," I replied on instinct. Oh fuck, that should've been a no. "On second thought, I'd better not."

He spun around, shocked by my change of mind. "It's just wine, Aria. It's not as if I'm asking you to strip off your clothing and allow me to pour it over you and lick it off. However, if that's a scenario of which you have interest, I'm sure we can work something out."

"You bastard." I knew he'd do this, but I didn't expect it as soon as I walked in the fucking door.

"What? I offered you something to drink. I hardly think that justifies name-calling."

"If I were any other person, you wouldn't have said that," I said.

"But you're not just any other person."

I looked into his intense green eyes, and I knew I needed to run.

"I thought a drink would put you at ease. You've been wound pretty tight lately. I was merely attempting to help," he said, shrugging it off.

He was his most charismatic in situations like this, and the part of me that enjoyed the game we once played gave in. "Let's forget it."

"Consider it forgotten. So, what about that drink? Shall I pour you a glass?" he asked.

"Sure, why not?"

"Good," he said. He took in my appearance, then smirked as he turned away.

Yeah, soak it all in, asshole. This is all for you.

I grasped the strap of my carrier bag and pulled it over my head. I then reached for the wine he extended and took a sip. "I know you wanted to do this over dinner, but I'm really tired. If we could just finish this up so I can get home, that would be great," I said. That was part of the plan—to tell him I was tired so we could move things along without any weirdness.

"Well, I'm really starved, and I need to eat."

Well, shit. That *wasn't* part of the plan. I didn't want to react to the double meaning of his words—experience had shown it was best to just ignore it. "Okay, well, food it is. Let's do it," I said, turning toward the kitchen.

"Actually, everything is set up in the dining room. Come," he said, motioning for me to follow him.

It would appear he had some strategies of his own. I followed him to the opposite side of the penthouse, my bag clutched to my chest as I reconstructed my plan.

"May I?" he asked, taking my bag and offering a chair to me.

I sipped the wine as he moved toward the head of the table,

taking his seat. "This is a really nice wine," I said.

"I thought you would like it," he replied as he studied my face.

What was he looking at? Was he appreciating the effort I'd placed in my appearance?

"I don't want to keep you any longer than necessary so let's see what you have for me."

You've already seen what I have for you. Stop it, Aria. Focus.

"Well, you reviewed most of the material today," I began.

As we started to eat, I completed the proposal, reiterating some of the critical components. "The other information you'll need is outlined here." I passed him the portfolio from my bag. He skimmed over it as he ate. I watched him. I couldn't help it. He was an insanely handsome man.

Looking up from the papers and finding me studying him, his lips curled into a smile. "Yes?"

"Nothing. I'm a wee bit anxious to hear the final response," I lied.

"In that case, you have nothing to worry about. As I said earlier, this is brilliant. I say we get moving on this, first thing."

"That's exactly what I wanted to hear," I replied, smiling. I was so excited that I was damned close to bouncing up and down in my seat.

He smiled again at me, and our eyes momentarily connected.

And then something in the air shifted, our smiles gradually fading as we stared at each other. Sensing I should break our eye contact, my gaze fell to the half-eaten food on my plate.

After a small window of silence, I swallowed the discomfort between us and asked, "Anything you think we missed?"

He only had a few modest suggestions, and then we fell into another stretch of quietness. It was intimate, yet it felt like two strangers with so many questions that neither would ask, such as, why he and I couldn't seem to shake our intense attraction for each other, and what we should do about it, and why he freaked out on Kellan at the charity event.

"Thank you for dinner. I need to head home. Now that you've given the green light, I have tons to do tomorrow."

"It was my pleasure. And again, excellent work. I expect great things, Ms. Cason."

"And great things you shall have, Mr. Raine," I said, copying his formality.

I was inwardly breathing a sigh of relief. He didn't do or say anything inappropriate over dinner, and he was allowing me to leave without any other advances.

"I'll walk you out," he said, pushing away from the table. "After you," he offered, gesturing me ahead of him.

I was almost out of there. I grabbed my bag and headed toward the exit. He walked quietly behind me. This was crazy. I felt so on edge. Once I reached the door, I turned to say goodnight. He was staring down at me like a predator eyeing its prey, and my heart rate soared, rapidly fluttering as I shielded my chest with the bag, clutching it as though it could protect me from his advance.

"Are you okay?" he asked, reaching out to me, and tracing a finger along my cheek. "You look adorable, by the way."

So, he liked me even when I tried to look like crap. I shrugged his hand away. "Yes, I'm fine."

"Are you sure?" he asked, stepping closer, until he was mere inches from me.

"Yes, I'm sure," I replied, swallowing the lump in my throat.

His gaze lowered to the rapid rise and fall of my chest. "Then why has your breathing accelerated?"

"Because you're pissing me off."

"I suspect there's more to it than that," he said.

"Well, you're wrong. I'm upset because in a span of five seconds, you spoiled what I'd considered a nice evening."

"I think you're upset because you want something you're afraid to ask for," he said.

"And according to you, I want you?"

"It's okay. Don't be afraid. Ask. I'll give it to you," he said. His voice was pure sex.

"Of course, you'd think that. You make everything so much

more difficult than it has to be. You frustrate the hell out of me," I said.

"We all have frustrations, Aria. It's how you resolve them that makes the difference. In regard to you for instance — you have frustrations with me. Take them out *on me*. Fuck me," he said, his tone deep and laced with honey. "I'll surrender total control. You wanted that at one time, right?"

"Is that what this has reverted to?" I asked in disbelief.

"Only because you've made it that way. And if that's the only way I can have you, I'll take it…at least for now."

"What about your paramour? Is she on board with your sexual propensities toward other women?" I probed.

"Paramour?"

"The insecure twit who was with you at the charity event," I said.

"Aria, I've told you on countless occasions, you needn't focus on irrelevant people — focus on me."

"I don't want to focus on you, Aiden, and I can certainly do without the headache of dealing with you again."

"Okay, no headaches then…you've dissociated sex and emotion before. Do it with me."

"What?" He was confusing me, and he'd obviously read and shredded the hell out of my plan long before I'd arrived, because this shit had gone terribly awry.

"You heard me."

If I could actually do that with him, it would be the best of both worlds.

What are you? Crazy? Say yes, bitch! Virginia just had to come bursting out of her cave. Of course, she wanted me to say yes. Kingston was all she wanted.

I sighed. I could make it easy and just fuck the shit out of him. But nothing was ever easy with Aiden. I opened my mouth to say no, but somehow Virginia spoke for me. "Just sex? Our secret? No expectations? No emotional bullshit?"

"That's what I'm offering."

"In that case, I accept." I knew I was lying to myself even before I said the words. As badly as I needed to, I couldn't shut off my feelings, but I wanted to fuck him so badly that the lie didn't matter.

Aiden pushed me against the door, his eyes filled with lust as they linked with mine. "Do you have any idea how long I've wanted this?" he asked, as his thumb traced across my lip. In the next second, his lips covered mine and his tongue was rediscovering my mouth. Losing sense of everything except the feel of him, my bag fell to the floor and my hands were in his hair, fisting handfuls as he raptured me. Aiden grabbed my hands and forced them above my head as he went for my neck…uncontrollably sucking, licking, and kissing, his hungry mouth devouring me. He was as starved for me as I was for him.

Releasing my wrists, he turned me so that I was facing the door. And then he pressed his rock-hard frame against mine, nipping my ear as he reached beneath my shirt, and then his hands were traveling along my body. In one swift movement, he had my sweatpants and panties at my ankles, and then he was on his knees, spreading my cheeks apart, his tongue spearing into the puckered tissue. Reaching behind me, I grabbed his head and arched toward his tongue, rotating my ass in his mouth, and moaning as his tongue prodded the tight hole.

He stood and scooped me into his arms, our lips and tongues tousling as he carried me to the bedroom. Severing our kiss, he placed me on the bed, our breathing labored as our arousal transcended into an excruciating need. I couldn't stand it a second longer. With anxious hands, I reached for his waist, rushing to unbutton his jeans. Before I could grasp the zipper, he pushed my hands away and I watched as he pulled out his big, beautiful cock. A small gasp escaped my lips upon seeing the vastly satisfying image I'd been fantasizing about for months. Not removing his pants, Aiden shoved me back onto the bed and pushed my legs apart. In the measure of a beat, his long, thick cock pushed into me, delving deep into my core.

"Ahh," I cried out, digging my nails into his back as he plunged deeper. God, he felt so good inside me.

❧ ❧ ❧ ❧

Awaking hours later, I noticed we were spooning. Aiden's breathing was steady, his face buried in my hair. Glancing at the bedside table, I saw that it was five o'clock. I hadn't planned on sleeping at his place. I didn't want to blur the lines of an already abstruse relationship. Spending the night was not part of the plan, not now and not for any future romps. This was sex. Nothing more.

Easing out of bed, I turned back to look at Aiden — he was gorgeous even when he was asleep. He was uncovered and gloriously naked. His arm lay above his head and his face was turned toward the cup of his elbow. His hair was mussed and his body was…well, I could get myself off just by looking at him. His chest revealed magnificently sculpted pecs and his stomach boasted just about the most perfect abs I'd ever seen, let alone touched. His thighs were muscular; not overly so, but just that right amount to suggest intense power behind every movement. After covering him, I watched a few moments more as he slept. I thought back to the conversation we'd begun after we had fallen onto the bed, exhausted from multiple incredibly satisfying orgasms.

"I'm perfectly fine with the arrangement of sex and nothing else, but you will want more."

"Oh? And why is that?" I asked.

"I'm going to make you want it," he said.

I slipped out of Aiden's bedroom and closed the door behind me. I'd see him later at RPH for one final meeting this morning before he left town. After dressing in the hallway, I went in search of my bag, remembering it had fallen near the entrance last night. It was still there, lying beside the door. I picked it up, tossed the strap over my shoulder and left the penthouse.

ঔ ঔ ঔ ঔ

I walked into the RPH building shortly after eight o'clock. I was certain that Aiden would have texted about my slipping out by now, but nothing. At the very least, I expected to hear from him in his effort to maintain momentum in wearing me down. I walked into the conference room, and he was already there, ever the consummate professional, in total business mode. He barely looked up when I entered.

"Good morning, Ms. Cason," he said, and returned to the papers in front of him.

"Good morning, Mr. Raine," I replied, confused as to the chill in his tone. It was as if he hadn't been inside me a few hours ago. I should've been relieved he wasn't behaving differently this morning, but I wasn't. That's when I admitted to myself that he was right. I couldn't do the *just sex* thing with him. I just couldn't.

The meeting was productive, but it went by in a blur thanks to my conflicted feelings about the man leading it. Then almost abruptly, it was over and Aiden was standing to adjourn.

"Excellent work everyone. I trust you all can iron out the remaining details. I have a tight schedule over the next week, so I need to leave earlier than I'd anticipated. Should you need anything, please contact Brooklyn." And with that, he stood and walked out without even so much as a glance at me. Was that his idea of making me want more? I fucking hated him.

Pouring myself into work over the next few weeks, I successfully shut out most of my thoughts of Aiden. It was the week before Thanksgiving, and I was bringing a close to my day. One more day and I would be out of the office for eleven consecutive days, nine of which would be spent with my family. I opened my desk for my phone just as Raina popped in.

"Mr. Raine asked that I personally deliver this to you," she said, passing me a sealed envelope.

What is it this time? I thought with a sigh.

"Thank you, Raina," I said, taking the envelope and placing it on my desk. Once she closed the door behind her, I opened the small package — it was a piano-shaped flash drive. Looking in the envelope, I found a small piece of paper.

Call me once you listen to this.
-A.

Our communications over the last few weeks had been strictly professional, so of course I was intrigued. I briefly considered listening to whatever it was, but ultimately decided against it and placed the drive on my desk. I had too many loose ends to tie up before the holiday to get caught up in his shenanigans.

Mom, Lia, and Bianca were flying to Boston tomorrow afternoon. I was so excited to spend the Thanksgiving holiday with them. I certainly didn't need Aiden's black cloud hanging over my head while they were here. I finished my last email and powered off my computer, eager to focus on my renewed connection with my family.

❧Chapter Eight❧

My family would be arriving later in the afternoon. I had a full itinerary for pretty much every day of their visit, starting with today. Hoping they wouldn't be exhausted from traveling, I made plans to show them around Boston and for dinner, I'd made reservations for one of the best restaurants in the city. Tomorrow we'd organize our Thanksgiving menu—each of us were to be assigned one entrée to cook individually, and the other foods we'd prepare together. I'd also planned a trip to the Whole Foods store Raina suggested.

We were all excited— anticipating a wonderful time as a family, as evidenced by the increase in calls and texts over the last few days. This was an important milestone for us—not only was it my first holiday with my family since college, it would be our first holiday where it actually *felt* like a family in years.

My phone rang as I stepped into my office. Glancing at the screen, I saw that it was Lia. I smiled and tapped answer on the display.

"Hey, little sister. Are you guys at the airport? I'm so—" I stopped mid-sentence. It sounded as if she was crying. "Lia, what's going on?" I asked.

"Aria, something's happened."

"What is it?"

"I have awful news," she said, her voice fading in and out. "It's Mom. She's…she's…"

As her sobs became louder, I couldn't make sense of her words. Had Mom sunk back into her depression? My heart fluttered as I considered the possibility.

"She's what?" I asked. Lia was muttering something in between sobs, which I couldn't make out. "Lia, I can't understand what you're saying."

I closed the door to my office as she attempted to explain, but again I couldn't understand anything. A sinking feeling of panic swept over me. "Lia, where's Bianca? Can you give the phone to her please?"

There was a brief silence, followed by rumbling in the background. What the hell was going on?

"Aria?" It was Bianca.

"Where's Mom?" I asked, frantic for answers. "What's going on?"

"Aria, I don't know how to say it," she said.

"What is it?" A sense of dread churned in the pit of my stomach. "Is Mom okay?"

She sniffed and replied quietly. "Mom's gone."

"Gone? What do you mean gone? Is she missing?"

"No, Aria, she's…dead."

I froze. Dead? Had I heard her correctly? That couldn't have been what she said. I stopped breathing. "What did you say, Bianca?" I asked, my mind racing. I plopped down at the meeting table, feeling as though I was having an out of body experience. Lia was bawling in the background as Bianca's quiet sobs started to resonate through the phone. No. No. This wasn't happening. This couldn't be right.

"There was a car accident, and it was really horrible. The police were chasing someone in a stolen car — the driver skipped lanes and crashed into Mom. Her car flipped, and there was an explosion." Bianca was silent for several seconds. "When the firemen finally arrived to the scene it was too late. She'd been trapped in the car."

I heard the words, and I tried to make sense of them, but it simply didn't come together. This couldn't be happening. Mom couldn't be gone.

"Maybe there's some type of mistake. Are they sure it was Mom? If there was an explosion…" I said, desperate for another possibility.

"They were able to get the vehicle identification number and locate our address. The officer just now left the house after giving us all the details of the accident."

No. No! I sat there, trembling like a leaf, as the worst news a daughter could hear started to register. Bianca's sobs transitioned into the same cries I heard of Lia, but I didn't have any words of comfort for my sister. I was crying along with her, tears streaming down my face as I replayed Bianca's two life-altering words…*Mom's gone*. There would be no Thanksgiving. There would be no holidays at all. Ever. It was over.

"Aria. Are you still there?" Bianca finally asked.

"Yes, I'm here. I'm just…this doesn't seem real. This *can't* be real."

"We don't know what to do, Aria," she said, her voice breaking again.

Mom had said how mature the twins were for their age but no child, regardless of age, can handle something like this, especially my eighteen-year-old sisters. Mom was all they'd had for most of their lives. They needed me now more than ever. I had to put my own feelings aside for now and be the person — the sister — they needed me to be.

"Don't worry, sweetie. I'm on the next flight to Dayton. Is there someone from the church you can call to come over and stay with you until I get there?"

"Yes. Mrs. Warner."

"Okay, call her, and I'll be there as quickly as I can. I love you."

"I love you, too. And Aria?"

"Yes?"

"Please hurry. We really need you."

"I will. I promise. I'll see you soon, okay?"

"Okay," she replied.

The phone went silent. I wiped my eyes and called Raina.

ço   ço   ço   ço

I felt as though I was lost in the darkness of a nightmare. How did this happen? *Why* did this happen?

After speaking with Bianca, I rushed home and threw some things in a bag and headed to the airport. Raina managed to get me on the next flight out and I had only a few minutes to get to the airport in time to get through security.

Beyond the tears I'd shed on the call with Bianca, I was too much in shock to really cry. Instead I was immersed in regret for all the lost years. The last few weeks had been the most heart-warming moments I'd had with my family in ages. We'd been so happy and hopeful. Now we had nothing.

After getting settled at the boarding gate, I pulled out my phone and called Kellan. He answered on the second ring.

"Kellan?" I didn't recognize the raspy voice. "Is that you?"

"Yes, it's me."

"You sound different," I said.

"I'm dealing with a terrible bout of the flu."

That explained why he sounded so horrible. "Oh, I'm sorry."

"Are you okay?" he asked.

"No, I'm not. My mother…" I trailed off. I just couldn't say it.

"What is it, Aria?" he asked.

I took a deep breath, choking back the tears. "My mother was killed this morning in a car accident." I said the words and I felt as though someone had squeezed the air from my lungs. I keeled over in pain.

"Aria, I'm so sorry. Is there anything I can do?"

"Thank you. I'm at the airport now. I'm flying to Dayton to be with my sisters."

"I'll be there in no time. What's your Mom's address?"

"Kellan, no. I can't ask you to do that. If you feel anything like you sound, you need your rest."

"I'm fine, Aria. I can deal with a few sniffles," he insisted.

"No, don't. If you come sick like that, it'll only give me more to worry about. Thank you so much for wanting to be there for me. I'll call April, and I'll have my sisters. Take care of yourself, okay? I have to run now because they're calling for us to board."

"Call me when you land and—" He couldn't finish because of the terrible stretch of coughing that ensued. He sounded much worse than I'd originally thought. "Call me anytime, okay?"

"I will. Thanks, Kellan. I hope you feel better soon."

The flight to Dayton was horrible. There was so much turbulence that my focus was more on the pilot's experience with flying in bad weather than the sadness that awaited me in Ohio. Actually, I thought I was too afraid to let the reality of mom's death sink in. Could something like that ever sink in?

As the plane descended into Dayton International, I powered my phone on to see a text from April. She was on the next flight out of Pittsburgh. I would need her more than ever. I didn't think I could face this alone.

I hurried from the terminal in search of the rental car kiosk. Raina was truly a godsend — she'd arranged everything right down to researching funeral homes and scheduling an appointment with one of them for me.

Tossing my belongings into the car, I prepared myself for the daunting drive to my childhood home. When I reached into my purse for my phone, I saw the flash drive from Aiden. I picked it up, turning it over and over between my fingers until finally placing it in the console. I sent a text to Lia and Bianca, letting them know I'd arrived safely and I was on my way to the house. I also sent a text to Kellan.

As I merged onto I-70, memories of my younger years permeated every part of my brain. I took a few deep breaths as the chills rolled through me. I didn't want to be here, but I knew I needed to be. I was overwrought with pain and this new layer was more than I could handle. It felt as though I were being torn apart from the inside out. I pulled off to the side of the road as I turned onto Austin Boulevard. I was so close to the Winding Creek subdivision, but I wasn't ready. Not yet.

Needing something to momentarily derail my thoughts, I reached for the radio. The display flashed and there was a mini-setup tutorial. *Geez!* My gaze dropped to Aiden's flash drive. I grabbed it, removed the cap and then slid the drive into the port. Within seconds the car was filled with the soft sounds of a piano. Then I heard Aiden's voice crooning the words to one of my absolute favorite songs—Sam Smith's *Lay Me Down*.

As the last notes of the song faded into nothing, I silently wept. The significance of that song—of those words—touched the very essence of my soul. Aiden knew I loved Sam Smith, and this song...well, it was enough to bring me to my knees. I couldn't do this anymore. It was all too much. Mom was gone; Dayton was clawing at me, and now this song from Aiden. I knew this wasn't random—he'd chosen it specifically for me. For us. And at this moment, there was no one I wanted by my side more than him.

The phone pinged and disturbed the gravity of my admission. It was Bianca.

Is everything okay?

I should've known they'd be worried, given the circumstances. Had I not stopped, I would've been there thirty minutes ago. I tapped a quick reply to her.

Yes, just got stuck in traffic. Should be there in ten minutes.

Okay. I love you.

I love you, too, B.

I crept onto the street, my heart in my throat as I choked back tears. As I approached Winding Creek, one childhood memory after another flashed before me — walking to the bus stop, hanging out on the corner with classmates, playing in the yard with my sisters, sitting down to dinner with *all* of my family. That was all gone now. All that was left were memories and remorse.

Turning down Cobble Brook Drive, I glanced at the familiar houses, finally crawling up to the one I'd run from all of my adult life. I pulled into the drive and pressed the button to turn off the car. After taking a deep breath, I grabbed my purse, and opened the door.

I still had my key to the house, which I'd always kept on my key ring for some odd reason. I didn't feel comfortable using it, though, so I reached for the doorbell. Before I could ring, Lia opened the door and rushed into my arms, followed by Bianca. Broken and disheartened, we stood in the threshold weeping and consoling each other as best we could.

Glancing up, I saw Mrs. Warner standing in the doorway, and released the girls to greet her.

"I'm so sorry, Aria," she said.

"Thank you, Mrs. Warner, and thanks for sitting with Lia and Bianca."

"There's no need to thank me. This is where I should be. I watched you all grow up, and Melena was a very dear friend. I will miss her very much."

Mrs. Warner hadn't aged very well. She'd also put on a lot of weight. Everyone had their way of dealing with loss. I wondered if Mrs. Warner used food as a means to deal with hers. Her husband died several years ago, around the time Dad left. Before that, she was really health conscious. In fact, she'd actually pulled Mom and Dad into exercise regimens.

"Let's get inside and get you settled," she said. "I made some tea and coffee a few moments ago, if you'd like a cup."

"Tea would be great. Thank you," I replied, as we walked into the living room.

I took in my surroundings—not much had changed since my last visit several years ago. The short walk from the foyer to the living room still greeted me with a string of pictures on the walls. The living room was just as I'd remembered—a small cozy space with two chairs on either side of the fireplace that caught your eye as soon as you entered. The memory of Mom and Dad seated on either side of the hearth flashed in front of me. In the winters, Dad would light a fire, and he and mom would often sit in the chairs beside the fireplace reading the paper. And there was one Christmas that I'd taken a picture of them seated there dressed as Santa and Mrs. Claus.

I shook it off and looked at the mantle, which displayed even more family pictures. Stepping closer, I saw a picture of me from a charity event I'd attended two years ago. How horrible was I that my family had to get pictures of me from online? There was another picture of my sisters, and one of Mom and Dad on their wedding day. There were two others of us girls—I was in high school. I cringed as I looked at my hair—a curly style I wouldn't dare attempt again.

I continued looking around—there was a sofa facing the fireplace and a coffee table with an oval rug underneath. The furniture was different, but the setup was the same as it had been when I'd lived here so many years ago.

Looking toward the window was another memory. That very window was the one that had showcased our Christmas tree year after year. We'd spend hours decorating and laughing, with Christmas music playing as we attempted to sing along. We were allowed to open one gift on Christmas Eve. Then on Christmas Day, we'd all gather around the tree taking turns opening presents.

I walked back toward the foyer. Its walls held several pictures and certificates, some dating as far back as my days in grade school. There was also one from my first day of high school. I looked miserable. Dad was gone by then. I didn't think Mom had taken that picture. Maybe Mrs. Warner had come over that morning to help celebrate my first day. I couldn't clearly recall — I was in such a state during that period that I'd blocked out many memories.

My heart squeezed as I swept my eyes over the room again. There was nothing fancy about it. It probably resembled the living rooms of millions of houses. But this was more than just a cozy area. It held fragments of my past. It held memories that were specifically meant for me — memories of the time when I had a complete family. The many nights we played board games and snacked on popcorn as I watched Mom and Dad cheat to win. They both had been very competitive, a trait I picked up from them. There were also memories of the time when my family was broken, when we all finally realized Dad wasn't coming back. I remember the day Mom told us he was gone. It broke my heart, and that was a mild break in comparison to the desolation that his absence had caused within her.

I looked up and noticed Lia and Bianca were watching me. They looked much like I felt, broken into yet another piece.

"It's been a long time since you've been here. Not much has

changed, though," Lia said.

"Here you go, Aria," Mrs. Warner said, walking in with a tray of tea and cookies.

Reaching for a cup of tea, I said, "My assistant, Raina, has scheduled an appointment for us to meet with the funeral director later this evening."

"I'd rather not go, if that's okay," Lia said.

"That's fine, I understand. Is there anything special you'd like to have done?" I asked.

"I don't know anything about funerals. I trust you to do what's best," she said, and rushed upstairs.

I placed the cup on the table. "I need to check on her," I said.

"I'll do it," Bianca offered.

"All right, but if you need me, I'm here."

As we neared the time to leave, the girls decided they would both stay home. Mrs. Warner offered to come with me, and I was relieved because I had no idea how I was going to get through it all alone. She chatted the entire car ride to the funeral home. I didn't have very much to add to the conversation, but she filled me in on how Mom had slowly come back to herself. Mom had even convinced her to start working out like they did so many years ago.

We made the funeral arrangements in just under an hour—actually Mrs. Warner did most of the talking as I listened with the occasional nod. The funeral director explained that the service would be closed-casket, due to the condition of my mother's body. He also requested a picture and some other details about Mom for the obituary. When he asked for a date for the service, I decided on the day after tomorrow. I didn't see the point in dragging this out. Mom didn't have many close friends, but there were a few church members who would attend the service, and there was no need to wait on family to fly in. Mom hadn't spoken to her side of the family in decades. They disowned her when she married Dad. My parents were a mixed-race couple so I'd assumed the issue had to do with race, but when Mom told me that my grandparents were an interracial couple themselves, it put a hole in that theory. And since Mom never explained much more than that, I'd never understood why they'd turn their backs on her.

Arriving back at the house, I found Bianca and Lia were having a very difficult time. I didn't quite know how to comfort them, but I figured talking was good, so that's what I did—I kept them talking. We'd decided they'd move to Boston with me and attend Boston State next fall. I hated to pull them out of high school during their senior year, but I honestly didn't have any other viable options. We decided to sell the house and invest the money to start a trust for them. I'd already contacted Kellan to help with that, I'd even contacted a realtor to get the house on the market. With relative ease, I'd handled all of those types of arrangements, but how was I going to handle being a *real* big sister again? How was I going to handle being without my mother?

✄   ✄   ✄   ✄

Holding onto my sisters, I watched as the casket was lowered into the ground. This was the end of my mother's journey. She was gone and I'd never see her again.

After the service, some of the church members, most of whom I didn't know, extended their condolences. I'd asked April, Bianca, and Lia to ride home with Mrs. Warner, explaining that I would be along shortly. I wasn't ready to say goodbye to Mom just yet.

After a while it was just me — everyone had left, but I couldn't seem to. I watched as the cemetery attendants covered the grave with the pile of dirt. I wanted to scream out to them to stop, but I knew that was ridiculous. This was it — the closest I would ever be to my mother again.

Once the attendants left, I stood there staring at the freshly covered grave. I desperately wanted my mom. I never wanted her as badly as I did at that moment. I should have been here. I should have been in their lives, but I was so determined to prove myself, to prove that I didn't need anyone, to prove that I wouldn't let anyone break me.

Forcing myself to step closer to the grave, I said, "Mom, I'm sorry. I'm so sorry I wasn't the daughter you needed, the daughter that I should have been. I'll never forgive myself for not being there. I don't understand why this happened. We were finally becoming a family again, and we had so many more talks and laughs left to share. Now we'll never have the chance." I looked up at the sky, trying to suppress the tears that I knew were waiting. Lowering my gaze, I looked at the temporary headstone. The attendants had already placed it at the head of her grave. I walked closer and leaned over, trailing my fingers across the letters of the epitaph.

Our Hearts Are Forever Touched
Aria, Lia & Bianca

"Mom, I promise to be there for my sisters. We're going to make you so proud of us. We're going to be so close…the way you would have wanted. I promise. I love you. I love you so much."

After several tear-shed minutes, I looked up from the grave and saw that I wasn't alone. There was a man standing there watching me. My gaze continued upward, from his polished shoes to his creased pant legs, finally resting on the tender green eyes of the one person I didn't expect to see.

❧Chapter Nine❧

My vision blurred. I blinked, attempting to focus on Aiden's face. It was really him. He was *here*…in Dayton. I was suddenly dizzy—I made an effort to shake it off, but my legs had a plan of their own. They could no longer support my exhausted body. My knees buckled, and I was on the ground.

My besieged fortress came tumbling down—I couldn't hold it in anymore. My emotions overcame me, and I began to weep. Aiden's arms were suddenly around me, and I leaned into him. I needed the strength that his embrace provided. I needed him to give to me what I couldn't give to myself at this moment.

There, at the edge of my mother's grave, I knelt sobbing into Aiden's chest for what seemed like forever. I cried for the lost years I would never get back, for the hugs I would never feel, for the voice I would never hear, and for all the memories I never made. And Aiden was there the entire time holding me, whispering reassuring words in my ear, stroking my hair, letting me know he was there, that he would always be there until I sent him away…and even then, he would still be there. And at that moment, I believed him.

The tears eventually came to a messy halt. Lifting my head from Aiden's soaked jacket, I accepted the handkerchief he extended. After I dabbed my eyes and wiped my nose, he stood and pulled me up, supporting me.

"I came as soon as I could. Words can't express how sorry I am for your loss, Aria."

"Thank you," I replied, looking at the grave. "I thought you were out of the country."

"I was. Once Raina called with the news of your mother, I rushed back."

Raina had come to the funeral, but she didn't mention having contacted Aiden. Since her first day of working with me, she somehow knew what I needed even when I didn't know myself. Like how I didn't know it until this very moment how much I needed Aiden to be here.

I looked back to Aiden, and he, too, was looking at the grave. "I didn't have the chance to get to know your mother very well, but I did have the opportunity to meet her once," he said, his voice solemn.

"What? How?" I asked, confused.

"I suppose I should say I *created* the opportunity to meet her. It was the day I left your office...after you told me you were done. I wasn't prepared to let you go, and I wasn't going to. At least not without one hell of a fight. I knew you needed time, so I wanted to give you that. I called April and told her everything—and that you were having a hard time and that a visit from her would be ideal as you sorted through your feelings. She was unable to leave due to her work schedule, but she assured me that between her and your mother you would have all the support you needed. As you can imagine, I was shocked because you'd last told me you hadn't been in contact with your mother, at least not on an intimate level, for years. April went on to explain that you had been making amends with your family and how happy you were about it. So, I left Boston a day early and flew to Dayton to meet her."

I shook my head. "Neither of them said a thing," I said in disbelief.

"Well, that took some convincing on my part. They were both extremely worried about you. You in a relationship—that was something as foreign for you as being in someone else's skin. They wanted to be there, but they didn't want to be in your face about it."

They'd both been great, checking on me every day. Mom even sent chocolates…more than once. She also had some for herself, and we ate them together as we Skyped.

"I'm not upset. I'm touched by all of it, actually. Even you, going as far as you did to make sure I was okay."

"Your mother was very nice, and I was looking forward to getting to know her better. She loved you so much, Aria."

"But I was so horrible to her," I said, ashamedly.

"She didn't blame you for any of that. She was so proud of you."

"I'm sure I'll be angry at you later, but for now I'm happy you had the chance to meet her and give me another piece of her — another memory."

"I'm pretty sure you'll be angry later, too, but that's okay. I'm not going anywhere. And that's exactly what I told your mother."

"Oh, did you?" I asked. "And how did she respond to that?"

"She liked me. As a matter of fact, she said I was quite handsome," he said with an exaggerated lift of his brow.

"Did she?" I asked. Only he could make me smile at a time as dismal as this.

"She sure did," he said, grinning. "It made my day. She told me not to give up on you, and that you were very stubborn. But I already knew that."

"Thank you, Aiden."

"For what?"

"For being here — for being overzealous enough in your pursuit of me to meet my mom behind my back."

"What can I say? I'm a man who knows what he wants."

I reached up to hug him. He pulled me close, enveloping me. It felt good to be in his arms. It felt like home. This was where I wanted to be — where I needed to be.

"Come. Let's get you home," he said.

After sliding into the car, the driver closed the door after us. The ride home was quiet. I rested my head on Aiden's chest as he stroked my hair, every so often a tear falling onto his jacket. When we arrived at the house, we were greeted by my sisters and April. They all rushed over to hug me.

"Where is everyone?" I asked.

"The last of them left a few minutes ago," Lia said.

"Oh," I replied. "What time is it?"

"It's almost five o'clock," said April.

I hadn't realized how long I'd been at the cemetery. "I'm sorry I wasn't here for you guys," I said, looking at Bianca and Lia.

"It's fine, Aria. We knew where you were. Aiden called and explained," Bianca said.

"So, it would seem you already know this guy," I said, looking at him.

"Yes, we do. Thank you for coming, Aiden," said Lia.

"I'm going to get out of these clothes. Aiden, have a seat," I said.

"Do you need me to come with you?" he asked.

"Thanks, but I'm okay." I smiled. He was really worried about me. I saw it in his eyes and in the way he was still holding me, almost as if he thought I would fall without him there to support me.

"She'll be fine, Aiden. Are you hungry? We have tons of food," April said.

"Sure, that would be great," Aiden replied, as he slowly released my hand and followed April to the kitchen.

Walking upstairs, I stopped at Mom's bedroom. I stood at the door for several moments and then peeked inside. Everything was neat and in place. It didn't look to be the room of someone who was no longer in this world. I took a step over the threshold and closed my eyes. Once I felt steady enough, I willed myself to take a few more steps, and then surveyed her room.

The picture of the four of us at Disney World was on her nightstand. I crept closer and picked it up. She was a beautiful woman. She looked so unlike the mother I'd grown to resent. There was light in her dark brown eyes and a happiness that had been absent since Dad left. I looked at my goofy smile and the silly expressions on the faces of my sisters. We looked so happy. We all shared the same rich shade of mahogany hair — ours was slightly darker than Mom's, though. Mom typically wore her hair in a ponytail, but not in this picture.

Lia and Bianca were still running around with pigtails when I left for college. Now they could have passed for college students themselves. I was still getting used to the maturity of the two sisters I'd left behind. They were so much alike, yet they weren't the carbon copies of each other I'd thought them to be as children.

They were both petite and wore the same hairstyle, flowing in waves around their glowing, café au lait skin. Although you couldn't discern from this picture, they both had bright amber eyes. Bianca was gregarious and more apt to surround herself with friends while Lia, much like me, enjoyed her moments of solitude. I'd noticed that hadn't changed at all. I'd been surprised when I met Lia's boyfriend, though. I would have expected Bianca to have a guy, but she insisted she liked to date rather than have one guy who would inevitably bore her to tears. Suspecting there was more to it than that, I briefly entertained the thought of her having some of the same issues with men and relationships that I had. For her sake, I certainly hoped not.

Holding the picture against my chest, I compared the happiness of the day in Disney to the sadness of this one. Then I looked around Mom's room, remembering the nights, so many years ago, when I would crawl into bed with my parents, unable to sleep. Dad would tell me a story that led me to dreamland, and the next morning I awoke in my own bed. I walked over to the dresser, and beside Mom's jewelry box, was a picture of Dad. I found myself staring at it—he was so handsome. He and Mom had made a beautiful couple. I stroked my fingertip across the image of his face, and for the first time in years, I wanted my dad.

Turning around, I looked at Mom's bed and then walked over and sat on the edge as I stared at the picture of us. I was emotionally exhausted. Pulling my feet up in the bed and laying back, I curled into a ball as I clasped the picture tightly to my chest. I started to cry as the reality of the loss hit me again. I must have cried myself to sleep because I awoke with a bolt…screaming. Aiden was beside me in no time — holding me, rocking me in his arms, telling me it was going to be okay.

"April, can you sit with her for a second? I need to make a call," he said.

I didn't want him to let me go. I tightened my hold on his shirt, clutching it in my fist, but he gently pried my fingers away.

"I'll be right back, Aria," he said, peering into my eyes.

Did he see the loss and bewilderment I was feeling? I reluctantly released him as April came over to assume his spot near me on the bed. I watched Aiden — relieved he didn't leave the room. He pulled his phone from his pocket.

"Morgan, this is Dr. Raine. Please contact Dr. Grist to obtain information on any possible allergies or contraindications for Aria Cason for alprazolam. You have access to all of the necessary information they'll need for a release of information."

How did he know my doctor's name? Were they colleagues? He shouldn't have access to my medical information either way…but then again, he was Aiden *Raine*. I hadn't yet adjusted to the power the Raine name afforded him.

"Call in the prescription. I'm headed to the jet now so I need this handled immediately."

Was he leaving? I panicked—I needed him with me.

Aiden glanced at me and then the others. "I'm taking her back to Boston. She can't be here," Aiden said, as he returned his phone to his pocket.

❧Chapter Ten❧

"What do you mean? We need her here with us," Bianca exclaimed, her eyes darting from Lia to Aiden.

"Look at her. Have you ever seen her like this?" Aiden asked.

Bianca cast her gaze toward me, and replied, "No."

"Exactly. Being here will only make matters worse. I'm taking her home—end of story."

"But—" Bianca began.

"I don't mean to offend either of you, but you haven't been around her enough to know what's best for her."

Both of my sisters looked at April for confirmation.

"I'm inclined to agree. I don't think being here is good for her," April said, her face apologetic as she echoed Aiden's assertion.

I wanted to be anywhere but here, but I didn't say anything. I didn't have anything left—I was numb. I watched and listened as they discussed me as if I weren't in the room.

"I would like for the two of you to come also. We'll buy whatever you need once we arrive. April, of course, you're welcome to come. I think she'll need you," Aiden said.

"I think so, too. I'd planned on being here with her for the next week or so," April said.

"Can one of you grab her things and meet me downstairs?" Aiden moved toward me in a rush, kissed my forehead and then lifted me from the bed. He carried me downstairs and we were nearly out the door.

"Where's the quilt? I want the quilt," I whispered.

Aiden looked down at me, confused. "Are you cold?"

"No, I'm not cold. I don't want to leave without the quilt," I replied, as fresh tears began streaming.

"I'm not sure what you mean, Aria. What quilt?"

"I know what she's talking about. I'll get it," Bianca volunteered.

"Everything's going to be fine, princess. Bianca's getting the quilt for you."

He settled me in the back of the limo as my sisters and April hurriedly grabbed some items and secured the house.

"What about the rental car?" Lia asked.

"I'll have someone take care of that," Aiden replied.

"Here it is, Aria," Bianca said, passing me the quilt.

I reached for it and pulled it to my chest. One of the appliques was of a book and another of music symbols. Mom had used my list of favorite things and started the quilt, just as she'd promised. I sat in silence, my eyes glued to my Christmas present as the others clambered in.

Within a few minutes, the others were all settled, sitting

quietly in the limo as the driver stowed our luggage.

As we pulled away from the house, I felt another part of me being left behind. I stared out of the window watching the landscape twist and turn, recognizing nothing. Everything seemed distant. I felt Aiden beside me, and as necessary as his presence was, it wasn't enough to diminish the pain I was trying to process.

Arriving at the airport, the limo stopped a few feet from the Raine Industries jet. Aiden kissed my forehead, like before, and excused himself.

Turning to watch him, I saw him talking to a woman who passed him a small white bag, and then he returned to the car.

"The pilot has confirmed we're ready to go. You all can board now. Aria and I will be directly behind you."

Aiden reached for me, securing me in his arms and carrying me from the car. I protested that I was fine to walk, but he insisted. Once at the steps to the jet, he set me on my feet and assisted me inside, ushering me to a seat and buckling me in.

"Mr. Raine, is there anything I can get for you?"

I looked up, following the voice, to see a statuesque blonde standing above me. Her name tag read Kelly.

"Biscotti, chai tea and a glass of water for Ms. Cason. Nothing for me."

"Yes, sir. Can I get something for anyone else?" she asked,

turning toward April and my sisters.

"Just water, please," Lia said.

"Same for me," said Bianca.

"I need something stronger than water. What do you have?" April asked.

"I'm sure we can accommodate any request, ma'am," Kelly replied.

"In that case, I'll have a French Seventy-Five."

I looked at April. That was our signature drink for our getaways. She looked stressed. Now that I thought about it, she'd appeared that same way the day she'd arrived at Mom's. Something was wrong—something more than her concern for me. I made a mental note to check on her when we had some alone time. I didn't know how much help I could be—all things considered—but I would definitely try. And maybe listening to April would give me something to concentrate on other than my own grief.

Aiden was on the phone. From the sound of it, he was speaking with Brooklyn. Lia and Bianca were sitting quietly, taking in the luxurious interior of the jet. It boasted a simple design with clean lines and a minimalist color scheme. There were white leather arm chairs towards the front and a matching white leather sofa to the rear. It was tastefully decorated with oil paintings and Waterford crystal lamps. It was as if we'd stepped into a lavish hotel suite. I suppose if you were planning to travel, this was certainly the way to do it.

Looking down at the quilt again, I studied one of its appliqué patterns. Curious, I unfolded it to see what other arrangements Mom had added. But as I sifted it through my fingers, I realized the quilt wasn't finished—she hadn't had a chance to complete it. "No!" I cried.

"Aria? What is it?" Aiden asked, alarmed by my outburst. He shoved the phone into his pocket and pulled my hands into his. "What's wrong?"

"Mom…she didn't have a chance to…to…" I stuttered, my lips trembling.

"To what?" he asked.

"To finish the quilt," I replied through my sobs.

Aiden remained calm, cradling my face between his hands. "Aria. Look at me. Look at me, Aria."

I tore my attention from the quilt and lifted my tear-blurred gaze to meet his.

"It's okay," he whispered. "Shh, it's okay."

"No, it's not okay. It's not okay, Aiden," I insisted.

"Aria, we can finish the quilt for you. We can all help. We'll finish it," he said, his eyes locked with mine.

Kelly returned with our drinks, and Aiden reached inside his jacket. I watched as he opened the prescription bottle.

"Take this, princess," he said, lifting the pill towards my mouth.

I looked at him as he urged me with a nod of his head. I opened my mouth, and he lifted the glass to my lips. After I'd taken a few sips, he placed the water on the table to his left.

Glancing up, I saw Lia, Bianca and April staring at me. I closed my eyes and reclined in the seat. Aiden pulled me toward him, molding me to his chest.

I must have drifted off. When I next opened my eyes, Aiden's hands were at my waist, removing the seat belt. "We're home Aria, back in Boston. Everything's going to be fine."

His words, although soothing, were a harsh reminder of reality. My mother was dead. I would never have the chance to make up for the years I'd lost with her. I hadn't been there to help her get better. I'd run, leaving her to struggle with years and years of depression. I'd been a horrible daughter. I looked up at Lia and Bianca and the guilt moved through me in gushing waves, filling me with remorse and shame. Did they blame me? Was this my fault?

The urge to cry pulled at me, but it was as though my tear ducts were frozen. It must have been the medication. I felt like a zombie. Shaking my head, I tried to resurrect the Aria that was strong enough to shelter herself, but she refused to surface. She simply sat there, under the buffer of medication, weighted down by the enormity of grief.

Rising from the seat, Aiden was close behind me, offering his strength because he knew I had none. I turned to look at him, wanting to say something, but the words wouldn't come.

He smiled at me, his warm eyes melting the chill that had been with me since hearing the news of my mother's passing. "Is something wrong?" he asked.

Shaking my head, I turned to face the others. April rushed over and hugged me. I didn't deserve their sympathy. Lia and Bianca — they deserved it — but not me. In my nearly catatonic state, I couldn't offer any type of solace to either of my sisters. I looked at them, watching me with sad eyes as April and Aiden fussed over me.

Brooklyn, Aiden's personal assistant, was there. Did she ever take a break?

"Mr. Raine, the car is waiting, and I have Kinsley with me. She'll take some quick measurements for Ms. Cason's sisters and have some clothes and other essentials sent over to the penthouse within the hour. Will there be anything else, sir?"

It must have been nearly midnight. Where would they get clothes at this hour? Knowing Aiden, someone had been awakened to meet his every request.

"Were you able to cancel the two meetings with Dasani Software in the morning?" he asked.

"Yes sir," Brooklyn replied.

"And what of Nicholas? Is he prepped to step in for the Japan meetings?"

"Yes, he actually flew out three hours ago," Brooklyn replied.

"Good. Forward my itinerary, and I'll review it to determine what other meetings I can either reschedule or have Sloan cover. She's been shadowing my recent acquisition of Soshibi, and she should be ready to take the lead on that project."

"I've already been in contact with your sister, and I scheduled a teleconference with your legal team tomorrow, as well," Brooklyn said.

"Sloan isn't equipped for that. Move it to the first of next week. I'll have to take that one on myself."

"Yes, sir. How shall I respond to the Pier Five proposal?"

"We can't restructure the deal at the eleventh hour. It stays as is. They either agree to the terms or we absorb the company."

"I'll take care of it first thing, Mr. Raine."

"That's all for now, Brooklyn."

"Yes, sir." Her eyes fell on me. "I'm sorry for your loss, Ms. Cason," she said, somberly and sincerely.

I acknowledged her condolence with a tight smile as Aiden guided me toward the exit.

We were in the limo waiting for Lia and Bianca when April's phone rang. She looked to see who was calling and frowned as she silenced the ringer then placed the phone back in her purse. I wondered if that had to do with what I saw on her face earlier.

Lia and Bianca soon joined us and settled in. I felt horrible for them. I felt horrible for all of us. I wanted to be the sister they needed. I wanted to be a real family. Of that, I was sure, and I'd do everything I could to make that happen.

Again, I'd fallen asleep, only to be awakened by a gentle kiss on my cheek and the soft whisper in my ear that we'd arrived. I opened my eyes to the deep green gaze and worried expression of the man who'd rescued me. We were outside Aiden's penthouse when it dawned on me that I would prefer to be in the comfort of my own home.

"Aiden, I think I want to be at my place," I said.

"What about the decorator? Isn't your house out of sorts right now?"

How the hell did he know that? I'd hired an interior designer some time ago, but she hadn't been able to get me on her schedule until now. "Yes, but—"

"I'll have Brooklyn get everything situated as quickly as possible so you can get home, but until then, you'll stay here," he said, as he slid out of the car.

We all quietly exited the limo and headed toward the building. Aiden held tight to my hand, tracing his thumb back and forth across the top, a sentimental gesture I hadn't realized I'd missed until now.

Entering the penthouse, memories of the last time we were here as a happy couple popped into my head. Aiden and I had awakened at my place that morning, full of playful banter after a night of crazy hot sex. We later joined his family here for breakfast, which had gone surprisingly well. After the meal however, Aiden and I had a fight, after which he'd disappeared for weeks.

A stranger opened the door for us. "Hello, Mr. Raine."

"Hi, Dianna." Aiden greeted the woman with noticeable affection in his voice, then turned to me and explained, "I've called Dianna in to assist with anything you may need. She can show you to your rooms. Make yourselves at home, and if you need anything, please let her know."

I looked at Dianna as she introduced herself to my sisters and April. She was a petite, curvy woman who looked to be in her mid-fifties. Her hair was light brown with several strands of gray, and pulled back neatly in a bun. She had a kind face with rounded cheek bones and full lips. Her almond-shaped eyes were a warm brown, and I immediately pictured her as a sweet, loving grandmother.

"I didn't know you had a housekeeper. I thought you didn't go for that sort of thing," I said.

"I don't, but due to the circumstances, this is best. I don't want you to have to do anything but rest. The same goes for your sisters."

It was a little after midnight when we settled near the fireplace making casual conversation, so I was surprised when the doorbell rang. Dianna appeared a few moments later notifying us that a representative from Bergdorf Goodman had arrived with clothes for Lia and Bianca. They excused themselves, following Dianna out of the room.

"Thank you for everything, Aiden. I can't begin to say how much your being here means," I said.

"No need to thank me. And don't worry about RPH — that's all been taken care of, too. Just focus on you and your sisters."

RPH hadn't crossed my mind since having received Lia's call about Mom, which surprised me, because it was typically never far from my thoughts.

"I think you should try to get some sleep," Aiden said, reaching for my hand. I rushed over to hug Lia and Bianca when they returned, and told them I would see them in the morning.

Aiden and I walked into his room, and my eyes fell upon the vast bed in the center. Our most recent encounter — when we attempted the guise of fuck buddies — flashed before my eyes. I'd been angry with him for not reaching out to me afterwards, but perhaps he'd kept silent because of his own anger for my slipping away as he'd slept.

"Would you like to take a bath?" he asked.

"No, I think I'll take a shower."

"Okay. I need to make a couple of calls. I'll be here when you're done," he said.

"Who could you possibly call at this hour?" I asked.

"It's mid-morning on the other side of the world," he replied as I walked to the bathroom.

I'd forgotten he'd been out of the country, and I was sure that his quick departure to be here with me had placed a huge wrinkle in his schedule.

Stepping into the massive shower, I adjusted the spray settings as the gentle stream of hot water began to flow over me, soothing my raw nerves. This day didn't seem real. My mother was dead, my sisters were now my responsibility, and my father…well, who knew where he was or if he was even alive. And here I was standing in Aiden Raine's shower.

I'd shunned Aiden for weeks and most recently slipped out of his bed without a word, yet here he was providing comfort for me and my sisters, without my ever having to ask. I burst into tears, the crippling waves of despondency drowning me. I wept for it all—the lost time, the broken relationships, and my remaining family. The tears eventually ceased—I wasn't sure how, because the feelings that triggered them were still there. Looking at the drain, I imagined my tears escaping—taking the despair of this day with them.

That fucking pill was obviously not working. Or maybe it had just worn off. Either way, I needed another. I finished showering and grabbed a towel from the warmer, and wrapped it around my body, not really drying myself. Grabbing another towel for my hair, I stepped out of the bathroom, too exhausted to think of anything but flopping into bed.

As I entered the bedroom, I expected to see Aiden, but he was gone. The bed had been turned back, and there was a black silk gown lying across the pillow, along with a note.

I'm sure you don't want to deal with unpacking your things tonight, so I asked Kinsley to have some items sent over for you, also. I'll sleep in one of the guest rooms tonight. Sleep well, princess.

-A.

I looked at the gown lying on the bed and was instantly filled with so many warm thoughts of Aiden. Honestly, I hadn't given any thought to the sleeping arrangements, but now that I was aware, I was slightly disappointed. I didn't want to be alone.

I haphazardly dried myself and slipped on the gown, appreciating the soft feel against my skin. After wrapping my wet hair in the other towel, I glanced around the room. Beside the bed was a tray with a water decanter, a glass, and my medication. Aiden had scribbled another note.

Take one if you start to feel overwhelmed. If you need me, my phone is near, so text or call and I'm there.

-A.

Sliding into bed, I pulled the covers around me, curling my body into a grief-stricken ball. I was dealing with more heartbreak than I could fathom—I didn't want to think about anything. I wanted to feel better. I wanted to forget, at least for the night.

Turning over in bed, I looked at the prescription bottle, but I knew what would both make me forget and feel better…and it wasn't a pill. I reached for my phone and typed a text.

Are you asleep?

No, doing some work so that I can be available however you need me tomorrow.

I know I've already said this, but thank you for today. I'll never be able to say how much it means to me.

I'd do anything for you, Aria. I hope you realize that.

Where are you?

In the study. Why?

I don't want to be alone.

Stay put, I'll come to you.

Within a couple of minutes, the bedroom door opened. Aiden stood in the doorway wearing only pajama bottoms, with his cell phone in hand.

"I'm sorry for bothering you," I said as he closed the door and walked toward the bed.

"It's no bother, Aria. I'm glad you're allowing me to be here for you," he replied, as he glanced at the bedside table. "Did you take another pill?"

"No. I don't like the loopy feeling," I said as I sat up in bed.

"But if you need one —"

"I know. I know. I'll take one. I promise," I said.

"Good. You try to do so much on your own, but you don't have to," he said.

He glanced at the top of my gown then returned his gaze to my eyes.

"Thanks for the gown. Perfect fit," I said, smiling, and thinking back to the first time he'd bought clothes for me. "That reminds me, you never did tell me how you knew my bra size."

He grinned and sat on the edge of the bed. "In med school,

we had to learn to determine breast size by touch, and let's just say I had a lot of practice."

That sounded insane. I looked at him, my brow rose skeptically, waiting for him to continue.

"You know that's total bullshit, right? I actually guessed," he said, grinning again.

"Really?"

"Yes and no. I had a picture of you, and I showed it to the sales person, and she helped me out."

"You're such a liar," I said, smiling.

"So, it's back to the name-calling? That's a sure sign you're feeling better."

"If I am, it's in huge part thanks to you," I said.

"I'm here for you, as long as you need me."

I needed him, especially now, and it was much more than I could dare tell him.

❦Chapter Eleven❧

Aiden had lain in bed with me until I'd fallen asleep. I'd asked him to talk to me about anything that would take my mind elsewhere. He dove into stories about his kid sister Allison, the amount of trouble she'd gotten into as a child, and how no matter what, he tended to always cover for her.

Aiden absolutely adored his sister. And they were much closer than I'd originally thought. I would have that type of relationship with my sisters—I was sure of it. I must have dozed off around the time he was spinning the tale about Allison skipping school to host a party in the servants' quarters, because I don't remember how that one ended. Aiden had taken my thoughts away from the present, away from the city of Boston, and away from the sadness. His beautiful velvet voice was a sexy melody that had taken me away from it all.

It was a little after ten o'clock when I awoke. My first thought was of Mom…then my sisters…then the reason I'd awakened in Aiden's bed. It was because my mom was gone. It was because I'd totally lost my shit yesterday. I let out a sigh and glanced at the prescription bottle, hoping I could make it through the day without taking a pill.

Figuring Aiden wouldn't be too far away, I scanned the room, and was disappointed when I didn't see him. What I did see, however, was a large bag on the chaise at the foot of the bed. There was a balloon attached, with my name written across it. I pulled the sheets back and crawled toward the bag with a goofy smile on my face. Looking inside, I spotted Aiden's calling card — a note.

You seemed very comfortable in these, so I've purchased you a new set. Don't be surprised if your flair for fashion starts catching on.
-A.

What the hell did that mean? I pulled the clothing out of the bag and burst into laughter. It was a gray sweat suit like the one I'd worn to his place when I was hoping to discourage his advances. At the bottom of the bag were sneakers and a scrunchie for my hair.

Bundling the clothes under my arm, I headed to the bathroom to wash my face and brush my teeth. I didn't bother with makeup or hair. After I'd dressed in my new designer swag, I grabbed the scrunchie for my messy bun—a silly grin on my face the entire time. I felt a tinge of guilt for this small moment of happiness. Was it okay to smile, or have my thoughts pulled from the sadness of my mother's death to a lighter, happier place?

Everyone grieved in their own way and maybe this was the way for me…not to grieve at all. I didn't want to mope around, burying myself in all the horrible things I was thinking yesterday. I wanted to honor Mom's memory, and I wanted to solidify a close relationship with Lia and Bianca. Mom would want that, too. She wouldn't want me to sink into a pit of despair like the one that consumed her when my father left. If I fell in, it was quite possible I would never emerge. I wouldn't go there. Instead, I'd try my best to be the person she'd want me to be.

She'd said I was strong, and I was—not as strong as some may have thought— and not as strong as I was even a few months ago. But I wanted that person back, and she was going to come back. She may stumble a little, but she was definitely coming back…sooner rather than later.

I stepped from the bathroom just as the door to the bedroom opened, and in walked Aiden…dressed exactly like me.

"You," I accused, pointing at him and doubling over in laughter.

"What?" he asked, feigning innocence.

"You're ridiculous, you know that right?" He was better for me than any pill could ever be.

We smiled at each other for a few quiet seconds.

"I need to check on Lia and Bianca," I said, ending the awkwardness of our silence.

"They aren't here," he said, walking toward me.

"Where are they?" I asked, worried something was wrong.

"I had Allison fly in this morning, and she and April are out with them. I figured someone as buoyant as Allison would be great for your sisters right now."

Actually, Allison was the bolt of energy we *all* needed. Aiden never ceased to amaze me. "Tell me again, how is it that you're still single?" I asked, making light of something I realized I shouldn't have as soon as I'd said it.

"Because the girl I want doesn't want me," he replied, his gaze soft on my face.

"Clearly, that girl's insane," I said, hoping to lighten the weight of his words.

"I couldn't agree more," he replied.

"Either insane or afraid," I said, reflecting aloud.

Thankfully, he ignored my last statement and gave me a quick onceover. "This look works on you."

"Are you kidding? I look hideous. This look doesn't work for anyone," I replied.

"I don't know about *anyone*, but it works for you."

"Whatever," I said, waving him off.

"It got you fucked, didn't it?"

"I don't even know how to respond to that," I said, laughing.

"Are you hungry? Dianna's prepared pretty much everything you can think of for breakfast."

"You know, I think I am ready to eat something," I said,

surprising myself. I wasn't sure when I'd last had food.

"Good, I'm glad you have an appetite. Shall we?" he asked, motioning toward the door.

"You know...I was wrong," I said, following him. "This look is totally working for you. I could honestly have *you* for breakfast."

"So back to the pineapple? Last I heard, you were allergic."

"I can't believe I said that to you," I replied, remembering that night. It seemed like a lifetime ago.

"Hell, I can. You have quite the smart mouth."

Aiden's jokes and off-handed remarks were the perfect antidote to pull me from the recesses of my mind. But there was nothing that could dull the ache for long, not even him—a truth that hit me hard and heavy as I retracted into the thoughts I'd hoped to suppress.

Flashes of the past few days popped in and out of my head: the news of mom's accident, the trip to Dayton, my sisters, the funeral, Aiden showing up to liberate me from it all. If I had to isolate a single moment of joy, it would be the moment I learned that Mom had met and approved of Aiden. Other than that, it had all been a devastating mass of hopelessness.

"Are you okay?" he asked, when I became quiet.

Would I ever really be okay? "Yes, just thinking about everything. It hurts, Aiden. It hurts so much," I said, as my eyes started to water.

"I know. I know," he replied, walking around the kitchen counter and pulling me into his arms.

"I think you should take an alprazolam with breakfast. What do you think?" Aiden asked, after the sobs subsided.

"Yeah, I think so. I was hoping I wouldn't need one, but I guess I do."

"I'll get it," he said, releasing me from his embrace. "I'll be right back."

Wiping my face, I watched him leave the kitchen. I didn't want to feel like this. My self-pep-talk this morning was apparently unsuccessful. Trying to skip some of the stages of grief wasn't going to work. There was no shortcut. It would take time. I knew that—but I simply didn't want it to.

"Here you go," Aiden said, passing the bottle to me once he'd returned.

"Thank you," I said. "So, tell me more about this crazy girl who doesn't want you. Maybe I can talk to her for you…make her see the light."

"Could you?" he asked, grinning.

"After all you've done for me? I'd be happy to speak to her on your behalf."

"I don't know. She can be quite obstinate," he said.

"Do you think she's worth it? She's probably a real bitch," I said.

"Now that you mention it..." he started.

Dianna walked into the kitchen, her entrance halting our wacky conversation. "How are you feeling this morning, Ms. Cason?" she asked.

"As well as can be expected I suppose," I replied. I could feel Aiden's eyes on me. Was I that much of a mess? Looking up, I saw the worried look in his gaze. He smiled, attempting to cover his concern, but I could see it. I didn't want him looking at me like that. I looked down at my food before the tears spilled over.

We finished breakfast and I took the medication, Aiden watching as I swallowed it.

"How about a game of chess?" he asked.

"What makes you think I play?"

"You were staring at the board on the jet last night, so I just figured..."

I had only played chess with my father. Yet another sad, missing piece of my life. Now that both my parents were gone, all I had were memories, most of which I wanted to seal away in a box I never wanted to open.

"Did I say something wrong?" Aiden asked.

"No. It's just...I used to play with my dad," I said, shrugging.

"We don't have to play," he said. "We can do something else."

"No, it's fine. I want to." Maybe it would be therapeutic.

"Are you sure?" he asked.

"Yes, Aiden I'm sure," I snapped. "You don't need to keep fussing over me and watching everything I do or say as if I'm going to lose it!"

I felt like shit as soon as those words escaped my lips. "I'm sorry. I don't know what I'm feeling. Everything is all jumbled up."

He didn't say anything. I expected some type of disapproval, but his expression revealed only sympathy and patience.

"I'm being a bitch… just like that girl you like, huh?" I asked, embarrassed by my outburst.

"I plead the fifth," he said, smiling.

"Are you ready for me to kick your ass at chess?"

"You can try," he said, leading me to the study.

We played two games—he was a formidable opponent, but I didn't expect anything less. I won the first game and he won the second. Just as we were about to start the third, a knock sounded from the door…followed by the entry of the four other houseguests. I laughed as I took them in—they were each dressed like Aiden and me.

I looked at Aiden. "What happened to your messy up-do?"

"Look at this," he said, pointing at his hair. It was slightly disheveled, but he was still seriously hot, so that didn't really count.

"We still don't know why Aiden insisted we all dress alike," Allison said, frowning at her brother.

"He thinks he's funny," I replied. "It's more of an inside joke."

Aiden winked at me and flashed a mischievous grin as he watched me attempt an explanation. His phone rang, and he sighed as he walked to his desk.

"Hi, Allison," I said, as she wrapped me in a hug. "Thanks for coming."

"Of course, Aria. And I'm so sorry for your loss."

"Thank you. So, what did you guys do this afternoon?" I asked.

Aiden looked up from the file on his desk, explaining, "It's Nicholas. I need to take care of this. Something's gone wrong with the Japan deal."

We took that as our cue to leave, so I followed Lia, Bianca, April, and Allison out of the study. Allison announced they were headed to the theater room to watch a movie. They decided on a comedy I'd seen before, but it was a pretty good one, so I grabbed some popcorn and joined them. Two movies later, Dianna announced that dinner was ready.

Aiden was still behind closed doors. I could only imagine the strain my presence was placing on his schedule. He was making too many adjustments for me. I'd check with the designer later in the day to see how much longer we'd have to wait before going to the condo.

Over our salads, the girls filled me in on their day, and it seemed Lia and Bianca had really connected with both Allison and April. Aiden walked in as we started the main course. He appeared troubled by something. He rarely looked anything less than steely and controlled, so I wondered if our presence was complicating things for him. I felt I should hurry to get out of his hair, but I wasn't ready to leave.

I didn't know what to expect when my sisters and I went to the condo—a home that had been *mine*, a home that was now *ours*—but I was sure we'd all be uncomfortable for a while. As I watched Allison chatter with my sisters, I realized we hadn't had a chance to speak alone yet. I'd make sure I took some time to check on them tomorrow. I was also still in the dark in regard to what was bothering April.

Aiden took the seat across from his sister. He was quiet for the most part. I would imagine he was thinking of a way to juggle his schedule to allow him more time here with me. Allison later asked him to join us for another movie. His initial response was no. After some prodding, he finally agreed. I didn't say anything, but I wanted him with us, too. His presence had become necessary for me. Odd how the one person who typically placed me on edge, was now my source of calm…but then again, maybe that was the medication. Either way, I was feeling less crazed—a little loopy, but definitely less emotional.

৯৹ ৯৹ ৯৹ ৯৹

Halfway through the movie, I found myself struggling to stay awake. Aiden nudged me and asked, "How about a bath before you go to bed?"

"I'd like that," I said, as we rose from our seats, slipping out unnoticed.

Once we'd shut ourselves off from the rest of the world, Aiden went directly to the bathroom. Seconds later, the sound of water filling the large, opulent tub drifted around me, instantly relaxing the bundle of nerves I'd become. A sense of guilt crept over me again as I stood in the doorway watching him—he was spoiling me.

After adding a pouch of bath salts to the water, Aiden pressed a button on the wall—giving life to a soft, relaxing playlist. He then walked over to me and reached for my sweatshirt. I raised my hands as he lifted it over my head and tossed it to the floor. With the warmth of his eyes focused on mine, he reached behind me and unclasped my bra. His hands were then at my waist, lowering my sweatpants and panties. Stepping out of them, I walked over to the tub and settled in—forgetting everything and losing myself in the soft melodies of the room.

Hozier's *Like Real People Do* was playing in the background. The lyrics took me to my mom's grave and then back to the person who'd rescued me.

After checking to see if I needed anything, Aiden left me alone, closing the door behind him. A half hour or so later I stepped into the bedroom, and found him sitting in a chair near the terrace, reviewing something in a folder that bore the Raine Industries logo. The guilt surfaced again as I thought about the sacrifices he was making for me.

He looked up from the file. "How was your bath?" he asked.

"It was nice. Thank you," I replied, stifling a yawn.

He placed the folder on the table beside him and rose to meet me. "Looks like it's past someone's bedtime."

"I didn't think I had one."

Aiden grasped my hand, and led me to the bed. "You do now," he said, as he tucked me in. Leaning down, he placed a soft kiss on my cheek and then turned to leave. "I'll let you rest."

"Aiden," I said, once he'd stepped away.

"Yes?"

"I don't want you to go just yet," I whispered. "Can you hold me, please?"

He didn't reply—he simply walked back to the bed and climbed in beside me, pulling me close. I rested my head on the contours of his chest, inhaling — taking in a concentrated dose of his unique scent.

As we lay in silence, my mind started to wander. I thought about my being here, and about my sisters and, of course, about my mom. I could feel the tears forming, and I absolutely didn't want to cry. I was so over the crying. I wanted to forget the pain. I wanted to forget the tears.

Touching the side of Aiden's face, I gently turned him toward me and pressed my lips to his. It was a soft and tender kiss that slowly transitioned to one of quickened heartbeats and exploring hands.

Reaching inside his pants, I moaned as I started to stroke his manhood. I wanted him inside me. I wanted his skin on my skin. I wanted his touch to erase everything else, if only for a short while.

Aiden groaned as he broke our kiss. "Aria, are you sure about this?"

"Yes. I need this," I pleaded. "I need you."

His gaze swept over my face, searching my eyes, and seeing my dire need for him. He lowered his head to my anxious lips and kissed me again, but then he suddenly pulled away. Reaching up, I drew his mouth back to mine, but he resisted.

"Aria, no. Stop. You're trembling. We aren't doing this. As much as I'd love to be with you like this again — not this way. I want you lucid. Tomorrow, if you're okay without the medication and if you still want this, then we'll make it happen."

"But Aiden—"

"No buts," he said, his voice firm.

I let out a sigh. There was no way I'd be able to sway his decision. "Will you at least hold me until I fall asleep?" I asked, hoping for a compromise.

"Now that, I can do."

He pulled me toward him and I placed my head on his chest again. He drew me closer, surrounding me with the warmth and comfort that only he could provide. I took a deep breath and sighed. Closing my eyes, I allowed the erogenous pheromone to penetrate my senses.

We were both quiet. My raging thoughts soon calmed as I listened to his heartbeat. It was a soothing cadence that carried me to the edge of unconsciousness. My last thought before I dozed off was that, tomorrow I wasn't taking any medication…not even aspirin.

❧Chapter Twelve❧

"Good morning, sleepy head."

"What time is it?" I asked, my voice a scratchy whisper.

"Shortly after eleven," Aiden said. He was seated at the large table near the window, drinking his morning coffee, and reviewing what looked to be some work-related documents.

"Geez, I never sleep this late," I said, sitting up, not quite ready to leave the comfort of the king-sized bed.

"I was starting to worry, but then I saw you stirring a little while ago," he said.

It was probably that freaking medication. No way would I bother with those pills today. "What's all this?" I asked, looking at the tray of food on the bedside table.

Aiden looked up from the files he was placing in a briefcase. "I helped Dianna prepare something special for you."

"Something you helped with?"

"Yes. What? Are you surprised?" he asked, walking over and kissing the top of my head.

"Everything about you surprises me."

"Is that so?" he asked, as he straightened his tie.

Why was he in a suit? Had his time with me come to an end? "Are you leaving?" I asked, bracing myself for the response I didn't want to hear.

"I need to sign some papers and meet with a few key people at RPH. I don't want to lose momentum on the roll out of *The Writer*."

"Hey. That's my project. Everything has gone just as I've planned so far, please don't slap your Aidenisms on it."

Aiden scrunched his brow. "What the hell does that mean?"

"I'm sure you can figure it out," I replied.

He considered my unyielding expression and asked, "These Aidenisms...when did you come up with those and how many are there?"

"They kind of just appeared, I guess. And there are several," I answered.

"Do any of them have a positive connotation? Because your reply a few seconds ago leaned more toward the negative."

"Of course, there's positive, but there are also a few I'm not particularly fond of," I replied.

"I don't want to hear about those," he said, placing the tray across my lap and sitting on the bed beside me. "Tell me the others."

"Yeah, you would want to hear any and every thing that inflates that monstrous ego of yours."

"That's not it," he said grinning. "I want to make sure I understand, is all."

"Nothing to understand. An Aidenism is simply the term I apply to your attributes or to your way of doing things…like you posing as Aiden Wyatt, or your tendency to control everything."

He frowned. "Cute, Aria. Real cute," he said.

"Don't be that way. Those are just the bad ones. Would you like to hear a good one?"

"If you can manage to scrape one up, sure."

I laughed. Was his ego so easily bruised? "It's not like that. There are some Aidenisms that take my breath away."

His brow lifted. "Such as?"

"Your surprises…like the flowers after I arrived home from Belize. Your hand-written notes. The way you take care of the people you love. Your way of handling business matters…I don't frown on all of them, you know. Your weird sense of humor. Your strength. You have this graceful, but dominant demeanor — it's sexy as hell. And you have this thing with your eyes…they're kind of spell binding. I could go on, but I think you get the idea."

"Humph," he said, considering what I'd revealed, looking content, but not really surprised.

"Why do I get the impression you somehow know all of this?" I asked.

"Maybe not *all* of it."

"What do you mean?"

His lips pulled into a lop-sided grin. "Do you know you talk in your sleep?"

"What?"

"You talk in your sleep," he repeated. "Not all the time, but you have on a couple of occasions."

"Really?" I knew I did as a kid, a *lot*, and I did a time or two in college, according to my roommate. I hadn't slept with anyone else besides April, and she never said anything, so I hadn't considered the possibility that it was still happening.

"Don't be too self-conscious," he said. "It's mostly undecipherable gibberish."

"What have I said?" I asked, hoping it wasn't some of the shit I'd thought about him.

"You mentioned my eyes once — that's all. And before you ask, no…I don't watch you sleep. I've awakened a few times before you, and I heard you mumbling, so I listened. Granted, I didn't know it was an Aidenism at the time," he replied, smiling.

"So, you've never watched me sleep?"

"Nope," he replied.

"Well, I've watched you."

"You do that all the time anyway," he said, shrugging. "So, I'm not surprised."

"You jerk," I replied, tossing a pillow at him. But one would have to be crazy not to stare at Aiden. He was beautiful. I was beginning to see more and more that his outward beauty mirrored what was on the inside.

"Eat, and I'll see you shortly. You're going to make me late."

"Seriously, Aiden, I don't — "

"Relax, Aria, I understand and share your vision. I won't do anything that's not in line with that. You have my word."

"Okay, but if you make even the slightest of modifications — "

"I won't. There will be no unapproved Aidenisms added to your project. I promise. Now eat."

Escaping the seclusion of Aiden's bedroom, I stepped into the hallway, intent on spending time with my sisters. I found them in one of the guestrooms — their heads together researching colleges. I was astonished as to how well they were coping, seemingly moving forward amid their heartache. They were so independent, just as I was at their age. I suppose we had to be, with a Mom who was more focused on the past than her children. I promptly chastised myself for thinking ill of my mother. But for so many years, my disdain was instinctive — an inclination that now seemed disrespectful.

I'd assumed Lia and Bianca were on board with my suggestion they attend Boston State, but apparently, they had ideas of their own. They missed their friends, and they missed their home and, of course, they desperately missed Mom. We discussed the possibility of counseling and ultimately leaned toward no, but decided to leave that door open. They were very comfortable at the penthouse and totally adored Allison and April. As for Aiden…well, I could see Lia was crazy about him, but Bianca wasn't as accepting. She appreciated his support, but she wasn't sold on him. All things considered, they were in a good place, much better than I'd anticipated.

"There you are," April said, as I was walking out of the guestroom.

"I was actually about to look for you," I said. "We haven't had a chance to talk. Are you okay?"

"I should be asking you that. Not the other way around," she replied.

"I'm actually coping pretty well. Thanks in large part to Aiden."

"Yeah, he's great. He's so good for you, Aria," she said with a sigh. Her words didn't match her expression.

"Now, are you going to tell me what's wrong?"

She looked at me with sad eyes and said, "It's Blaine. It's officially over."

"What happened?" I asked, and motioned for us to head to her room.

"Things were amazing. I mean, we totally hit it off in St. Barts, and we couldn't seem to get enough of each other once we were back in The States. I was all in, and I've never been that way with a guy before."

Stepping into the bedroom, I closed the door behind us once April sat on the bed. "I know. I don't get it—Kellan said Blaine was crazy about you."

"Everything was awesome, and then all of a sudden he was different—distant, you know. He started pulling away, and we argued about it, and then one day he finally told me about his girlfriend."

April was near tears—I'd never seen her like that over a guy. I felt bad for my friend. I sat on the bed beside her. "What an ass. I'm sorry."

"To be fair, they weren't together when he and I met."

My best friend had finally found someone that made her want to stick around but he had baggage she hadn't accounted for. "Would you be okay if I tried to get some details from Kellan? Because something doesn't add up here."

Kellan had been checking in with me every day since Mom's death, but I missed our funny texts and nightly chats.

"I know all I need to know, but thanks for the offer," she said.

I leaned over to give her a hug and somehow, we both ended up crying—for two very different reasons.

It was late afternoon. Having been inside all day — my sisters, April, Allison and I had become somewhat restless. Allison suggested we try our hand at pool — an idea to which we all agreed — so we ventured to the game room. Not long after a brief introduction from Allison on the rules of eight-ball, were we teasing and laughing at our pitiful attempts to execute a shot.

Although I was enjoying the time with everyone, I'd started to miss Aiden. No sooner had the thought popped into my head, did he stroll into the room.

"Be careful. Allison cheats," he said.

"I do *not* cheat."

"Oh yeah? Have any of you won?" he asked, surveying the room.

"Now that you mention it, no," said Lia.

Aiden and Allison exchanged jabs about her history of cheating when they played billiards at the family home. When she'd finally had enough of his snide come-backs, she challenged him to a game, which he accepted. Aiden grinned at his sister as he loosened his tie and removed his jacket, still taunting Allison as he rolled up his sleeves and approached the table.

The siblings were unable to finish their dual. Before they could determine a victor, one of Allison's friends called and invited her to dinner. She, in turn, asked us all to join them. As I was about to accept, I caught the subtle shake of Aiden's head, so I politely declined her invitation. The others were raring for any excuse to leave the house, so they bid us farewell as they rushed off to shower and change.

As the room emptied, Aiden walked over to me and traced a fingertip along my cheek. "I thought they'd never leave," he said, reaching down to pick me up. I wrapped my legs around his waist as he brushed his lips across mine, slowly introducing me to a deep, exploratory kiss. After what seemed like too soon, he pulled away and lowered me to my feet.

"Did you arrange that?" I asked, referring to the dinner invite.

"Yes," he replied, grasping my hand and leading me out of the room.

"Why?" I asked.

"To fulfill your request, of course."

After a short bath, I slipped into the black silk gown and removed the clip from my hair, letting it hang loosely past my shoulders. My insides were a mix of heat and butterflies, as I reached for the door.

"Where's your cell?" Aiden asked, as I stepped out of the bathroom.

"In there," I said, pointing to the bedside table.

He lifted the phone out of the drawer, powered it off and then returned it. He then pulled out his own, powering it off as well.

What was he doing?

"This is going to take some time, and I don't want to be interrupted," he said, replying to my thoughts.

In that instant, the aura of the room changed. Hunger, lust, and anticipation hung in the air, washing over us like a hot, summer breeze.

"Come here, princess," he said, his voice a velvet whisper.

Aiden captured me in his arms and pressed his lips to my neck. "You're so beautiful," he said, as his mouth trailed lower. "So very beautiful."

He lowered his lips to my collarbone, his touch sending shivers all over my body. My hands moved across his back, gripping his taut skin as his mouth found mine. His kiss was a soft caress, and his hands were grasping my curves, pulling me closer and melding my body to his.

Breaking our kiss, his large hands cupped my face as he searched my eyes.

My heart pounded in my chest as the beauty of his dark emeralds held my gaze. Was he seeking affirmation? He had it.

"Tonight is about us, and I don't want to focus on anyone else but us," he said. "I want to spend the entire night showing you how much you mean to me."

Aiden unhurriedly lifted the silk garment over my head and then he stepped away. Sitting on the edge of the bed, his eyes darkened as they devoured my nakedness—his gaze lingering on my lips, my breasts, and the heated area between my thighs.

I stood before him, bare and unashamed as he savored and coveted every inch of my body…the body that was his, the body that only he could tame. His focused attention stirred the heat between us, my nipples hardening—my sex pulsing.

My eyes fell to the tenting of his silk pajama bottoms. Anxious to see him in the flesh, I stepped toward the bed and tugged him toward me. I looked up at him as my fingers loosened the drawstring, letting his pants fall to the floor, and displaying the object of my desire. Aiden Raine—naked.

His penis was beautifully erect—already demanding my undivided attention, so I gave it. Curving my fingers around his length, I started to stroke his hardness, moaning as he grew even more beneath my touch.

Aiden groaned and stepped closer, his lips again, finding my neck, placing soft, endless kisses along my nape as I continued stroking his arousal. I leaned into his hard frame, shuddering as his tongue swept softly across my skin.

"It would appear someone is quite anxious," he said, a satisfied smile tracing his lips. He scooped me into his arms and gently placed me in the center of the bed. He was making me wait—drawing this out until I begged for it, something I was extremely close to doing.

Aiden stood at the foot of the bed, watching me as I beheld the beauty of his naked body. His lean, muscular frame was truly a sight to behold. My gaze traveled from his rounded shoulders, to his biceps and then along his broad chest—pausing briefly to admire his pecs before resuming my lascivious tour. My mouth fell open as my gaze held the tight band of flesh on his abdomen which led to a well-defined V of muscle. *People Magazine* had it wrong—Aiden Raine was the sexiest man alive.

I sucked my lip between my teeth, watching him as he placed a hand on either side of my legs, his biceps flexing as he leaned forward, their tone and definition accented by the thick veins coursing down his forearms. Lowering his head, he kissed the top of each foot before starting his sensual progression upward, planting soft, sweet kisses on my legs. When he gently pushed them apart, I wanted to scream. This was torture at its best. A deep moan resonated around us as he bestowed slow kisses along my inner thighs, moving closer to my sex and finally settling comfortably between my legs.

His fingers were on my lips, spreading me open and blowing the warmth of his breath over the wet flesh.

I squirmed, eager to feel the wet heat of his tongue. Tenderly, he moved his fingers over my anxious center and planted a soft, lingering kiss there, his tongue teasing as he kissed.

"Mmm..." I moaned, as my fingers found his hair.

Aiden's lips covered my clit, lightly sucking the sensitive bud. He flicked his tongue on the extreme tip and suctioned and my body convulsed as the gentle sting of his teeth pulled me to my orgasm. He didn't stop. He continued kissing and sucking – licking deeply inside my pussy, taking my juices and making them his. My desire for him exploded as my body quaked, releasing my lust for him and demanding more.

I wanted Aiden inside me. I wanted the fullness. I wanted the connection.

He moved his body over mine, grabbing my wrists in one hand, placing them together above my head. His soft lips settled on my neck, as his fingers slid in and out of my core. Endlessly, I whimpered as he reduced my body to a limp mass beneath his skilled touch.

"I want to make love to you, Aria. I want you to feel everything I'm feeling." Placing his knee between my legs, he spread them farther apart and I felt his manhood at the entrance of my sex. Aiden's eyes were lost in mine, exposing the depth of his feelings, revealing the ravenous desire that so very much echoed my own.

Moving the head of his shaft up and down the wet slit, he

eased inside me. His eyes were focused on mine, absorbing my reaction to his girth — to the stretching of my core.

Fuck, he was so big. I cried out as he pushed in deeper. I peered into his smoldering green eyes, and our connection was as immediate as it was intense. He lowered his head to my lips, his mouth molding mine.

Aiden's kisses moved to my neck — they were light, passionate touches that trailed to my breast. He clutched my nipple between his teeth, and I arched into his mouth as he gently moved in and out of me. The unfamiliar feel of the gentle plunges into my essence was as deep as it was emotional. I felt the depth of his connection with each tender push into my tightening walls. As my orgasm started to take hold, he pushed deeper, his pelvis rotating into me, still stretching me, making me feel with his body what he conveyed with his eyes.

"You're so beautiful, Aria," he said as he looked down at me. "I love being inside you." His kisses and his words flowed over me, washing me with the depth of his passion.

Aiden's tongue snaked across my bottom lip before pulling it into his mouth. Each thrust moved him deeper, the heat of our mingled breath fueling our desire. Releasing my wrists, he buried his face in my neck as he expertly moved in and out of my over-filled center. "Aria, you feel so good," he breathed.

Every touch engaged a part of me that only he had discovered and now only he could sate. Every stroke was focused, targeting that spot that released all my control to him. He gave every part of himself with each slow drive. The essence of his being was utterly transferred into me with each tender thrust. He had control of a part of me I didn't know existed, that only he could touch, a part that lusted for him, ached for him, needed him.

"Aiden, please don't stop," I panted, as the fierce beat of my heart resonated in my ears. I was connected to this man in a way I couldn't understand — a way that defied logic. Each gentle invasion took me higher and higher. I was floating above Boston, above all the pain and uncertainty of this world. The feel of his skin on mine was electric and I was about to explode.

My mind was free, and my body was his. Closing my eyes, I fell deeper into the world in which he'd taken me, soaring above the clouds in a place where only he and I existed.

"There it is, princess. Come for me."

And I did. Crying out as I let go, my back arched into his chest and he sealed my mouth with his, effectively absorbing my moans. Our tongues danced as my hands tightly clutched his back, Aiden still moving in and out, his intense plunges tender and deep. He was giving all of himself to me in a way he never had before. Each kiss had a different meaning. Each slow thrust was an emotional journey to the center of my soul. Each touch expressed the depth of his desire.

Aiden guided me onto my stomach and planted soft kisses on my back before lowering his hard body onto mine, spreading my legs.

"Ah," he groaned as he sank into the tenderness of my sex.

I grasped the sheets as he went deeper.

"Does this feel good?" he asked.

I was breathless. "Yes."

His skin was hot and wet against mine. Reaching under my chest, he grasped my shoulders, pulling my body to meet his thrusts, and touching every part of my being. I didn't want this to end. I wanted time to stand still.

Guiding me on my back, I was again pinned beneath his hard frame. He reached for my hands, interlacing our fingers above my head as he gently inched into my core. My fingers tightened around his as he hit that spot, the one that made me lose myself.

I stared into his eyes, his gaze hot on my face, as he filled me with firm, dexterous strokes. He was gentle...careful...and sweet, caressing me as if I were a delicate flower. He was making love to both my mind and body — he was making love to my soul.

I felt loved. I felt adored. I felt complete. I was overwhelmed by the flood of emotion that accompanied the delicate worshipping of my body. Tears rolled down my cheeks as this beautiful man made love to me. My eyes focused on the dark intense allure of his, watching his reaction to my silent cry, his eyes searching mine until understanding crossed his handsome face. He softly kissed away my tears. We both knew this moment sealed our fate—I was his and he was mine. "I love you, Aria," he whispered as our lips met.

Aiden pushed into me—so deep that he made us one.

"Oh. God. Aiden." I whimpered as my body released my essence around him, my frame trembling beneath him as the intensity of the orgasm tore through me, touching every cell in my body. His manhood expanded, and then he let go, exploding inside me.

Releasing my hands, he cradled my face and stared into my eyes, his release pulsing rhythmically. As his climax ended, he adorned my forehead, cheeks, and lips with soft, chaste kisses, and then finally rolling over and cradling me to his chest. The soft music that had seemingly faded, now enveloped us as we both lay there in the afterglow, surrounded by the sensual aroma of sex.

"What are you thinking?" I asked.

"How special you are to me...how special this moment is," he said. "If time could stand still, I'd choose this moment."

We both lay quietly, each listening to the other's breathing, content after our lovemaking, and as if the universe heard our pleas, Enya's *Only Time* filled the room, enclosing us in its embrace. For those brief moments, time really did stand still for us...two lovers finding their way and growing in love.

It was the first time I'd ever made love, and it was a feeling, an experience, that left me speechless, that left me raw. I felt cherished and worshipped, and so much love from him in this moment. Every wall, he'd knocked down. Every part of me, he'd explored. There was no going back. I was forever changed. Forever touched.

❧Chapter Thirteen❧

"Aiden, don't leave," I said, as I bolted awake from the recurring nightmare.

"Hey. I'm here," he said, wrapping me in an embrace. "Are you okay?"

I hugged him tightly, hoping his presence would force the visions away. "Yeah. Just had a bad dream," I said.

"I'll never leave, Aria."

"Yeah, I've heard that before," I mumbled, more to myself than to him.

"What?" he asked.

"Nothing."

He released me and grasped my chin, forcing my eyes to his. "What did you say, Aria?" he asked again.

"I've heard that before," I repeated.

"That I'll never leave?" he asked, confused.

"Not from you specifically. From my dad." I shrugged. "It's nothing. Let's pretend I didn't say it, okay."

"Tell me," he said.

"But—"

"Aria, I want to know," he insisted.

I let out a sigh. "When I was younger, I guess I was about

nine or ten, my friend's parents divorced and her dad left, and she rarely saw him after that. One night Dad was tucking me in and I said to him, 'Promise you'll never leave.' And he promised…and I believed him. But I was just a kid so why would I not believe him, right? I went to bed that night feeling sorry for my friend, but I was happy because I still had my father. I was convinced that what happened to her would never happen to me…because Dad promised."

And here come the tears. I could feel them building—but I refused to cry, so I choked them back and said, "In the end, he left anyway…and he never looked back. He didn't care if we needed him. Even now, he doesn't know if we're dead or alive. He doesn't care to know."

I hated feeling like this, especially after having shared such a beautiful experience with Aiden, but that dream—that ridiculous dream—it wouldn't let me go.

"I don't have either of my parents, and I have two sisters to take care of now. I don't know how I'm going to do this, Aiden. Each time I look at them, all I see is what I no longer have."

"Aria, you—"

"I don't want to talk about it," I said, climbing out of bed. "I'm taking a shower."

He didn't push the issue, but I knew he was going to make me talk about it, and I would…but not now.

"Hurry and get dressed," he said, following me to the bathroom. "After breakfast, we're going out. Allison has the day planned for us."

"I'm almost afraid to ask what Allison has in store," I said, stepping from the closet.

"Nothing too '*Allison*,' he said, grinning. "Just the Skating Club and lunch at Bronwyn. Do you like German food?"

"Sure, sounds good. But that doesn't sound like the entire day."

"She wants to show your sisters around a bit and then head to The Sinclair for dinner and live music."

That's when I smiled.

"I thought you'd like that," he said.

"I do. Very much."

Walking out of the bathroom and dressed for bed, I decided it was time to tackle something that had been brewing in my mind. "I know the timing is less than ideal, but I think we need to determine what's happening."

"What do you mean?" he asked.

"Between us."

"Oh…that," he said.

"Yes, *that*," I replied. "Why so dismal?"

He let out a sigh. "Because I'm not prepared to say goodbye to you."

"You're so sure that's where this will lead?"

"I know it's highly probable, considering you wouldn't be here had you not lost your mother."

"That's true. But my loss has forced me to think about some things—things I can't continue running from, and I think we should talk about it."

"I didn't want to be insensitive, so I've not said anything, but I agree—we need to talk," he said. "But as much as I want to solidify things between us, I want to be considerate of what you're going through. This conversation can wait."

"Thank you, Aiden, but I'm fine to talk about it now."

He tugged me toward him, his finger stroking my cheek. "Are you sure?" he asked, perceptible concern in his green eyes.

"Yes. But first, I'd like to express my gratitude. You've not left my side since all of this happened. You've gone over and beyond anticipating my every want and need—hell, even things I didn't know I wanted until you'd done them for me. You stepped in and made everything better. My sisters are crazy about you…well, maybe not Bianca," I added, smiling. "And from what they've told me, Mom had some type of cougar crush on you."

"A cougar crush, huh?" he asked, clearly amused by my choice of words.

"Yep," I replied.

"Aria, there's nothing to thank me for. I'm where I should be, where I want to be...where I hope you'll allow me to stay."

I considered his words, anxious to tell him what he wanted to hear. "You know a little about my relationship issues, but I want to give you more insight," I said.

"Aria, I know all I need to know."

"That very well may be, but I want to say it. You need to know what you're signing up for."

"I already know what I'm signing up for, Aria," he replied. "But since you're determined to warn me off, go for it. Tell me."

Moving from his embrace, I stepped toward the rear of the bedroom and settled Indian style in the brown leather sofa. "I've dealt with so much heartache in the last few months," I started. "And as a result, the part of me that was beginning to open started to close again. Before losing Mom, I'd convinced myself it was for the best because it would reduce the likelihood of unnecessary pain."

Regret washed over Aiden's face. "I know I haven't said it aloud to the extent you deserve, but I hope my actions have spoken for me. I'm deeply sorry for my deceit, and for the pain

I've caused you. I've been kicking myself in the ass every day. Even when things were going well, I was battling with myself about telling you everything, but I couldn't risk losing you," he said.

"Part of me is still struggling with that, to be honest…the deceit. If you could conceal such a huge part of your identity, how can I ever trust in anything you say or do?"

Aiden took a seat across from me and said, "Although I understand why you see it that way, I wish you didn't."

"You hurt me…more than you realize."

"Aria, I know what—"

"Wait. Let me finish. That hurt allowed me to have something I wouldn't have had otherwise—time with my mom. I can't regret that. Amid the craziness, there were some very happy times with my family…and with you."

"It's good that you can acknowledge that. I'm happy for you—that you had that time with your mother. And I hope you keep your heart open to more times like that, regardless of whether it's me you choose to be with."

I couldn't imagine even *attempting* this with anyone other than him. "When I left my family so many years ago, I left a way of life and I had no intention of going back to it. Ever. I left with two thoughts: I would never be hurt by it again, nor would I allow a man to do to me what my father had done to Mom. So, I buried all feelings and avoided all situations that might lead to those possibilities—no meaningful relationships with men and breaking some of the ties to my family."

Escaping his probing eyes, I walked toward the window, looking at the darkness and the small sprinkle of stars as I continued. "I felt guilty for leaving. I knew they needed me. I heard them screaming out to me—to come back, to help them—and I tried. I tried, but I couldn't. I couldn't do it anymore," I said, turning to face him.

His face twisted, feeling the pain in my words.

"Every day I was at home was miserable. I'd hoped Mom would snap out of it, but those hopes became day after day of disappointment. I needed her…and she just wasn't there. When it gets to a point when all you expect from someone is to be let down or bailed on, it changes you. It created a fear of embracing anyone—of allowing anyone to get too close."

"I'm so sorry, Aria," he said. "No child should have to endure that. And believe it or not, I can understand your need to protect yourself because of your past. But disappointment and pain are a part of life. We all face those same possibilities."

"Life…yeah. I've seen this life take what I love, like the wind snatching away a leaf. Life blew it all from my reach, and there was nothing I could do but sit and watch. It was out of my control. That's when I decided maintaining control was the only way to accommodate the need to protect myself. I wanted to pull the strings—never giving it a chance to get to a point where I could get hurt. I walked around every day with my guard up, thinking that someone was going to hurt me and keeping everyone at arm's length. At the end of the day, I had exactly what I wanted—nothing and nobody. That solution wasn't foolproof, but it was effective...until I met you."

"Sorry for throwing a monkey wrench in your program," he said, lightening the moment.

"I know you're kidding, but that's exactly what you did," I said. "And I didn't want any part of it."

"And there was nothing about me that made you want to at least try? Like the feelings I know you have for me? You've never said the words, but I know you love me. And that had to have had some effect," he said.

"Aiden, when your heart's been broken in a million pieces, you're not able to recognize the feeling of love, especially if you've never had it in a romantic sense. And when your love found a way to filter through one of the tiny cracks, it felt intrusive and very disconcerting. And now that I know who you really are, I find myself with yet another dilemma—fitting into your world. Considering a relationship with any man to this degree would be a challenge, but with someone like you, it's added additional layers of complexity."

"Aria, you needn't worry about that. That shouldn't be the reason—" He broke off and said with conviction, "As a matter of fact, I will not *let* that be the reason we don't give this a try, especially considering we're obviously to a point where the other obstacles are being pushed away."

"That's easy enough for you to say, but it's much different for me," I said.

"Explain."

I didn't feel comfortable unveiling another insecurity to him, but I knew I had to if this discussion was to be of any use. I recalled Raina telling me Aiden was a fish out of water when it came to me. I'd been too hurt and angry to give that any consideration, but I saw now she was right. He and I both were trying to find our way through unchartered waters.

"I never felt as though I fit in anywhere. I think it started when my father disappeared. He and I were very close, and when he left there was no one at home I could identify with. My sisters were too young, and Mom...well, you know. Soon after that, I started to feel as though I didn't fit with my friends, which is probably the *real* reason I only have one. Then there's the fact that I'm biracial. When people look at me, it's as if they're trying to figure out who or what I am. Funny thing is, I do the same thing, and to this day I still don't know. Until you entered my life, I really *thought* I knew, but when I look in the mirror now, I see a stranger staring back at me. I feel as though I morph into someone different with every situation. I don't know who I am. What I find so surprising is that I don't even know who I *want* to see in the mirror anymore."

Aiden had that look I'd seen once before when I'd opened up about myself. He felt sorry for me. I hated seeing that in his eyes. I looked away so I wouldn't have to. "Don't look at me like that."

Turning me to face him, he forced me to gaze into his beautiful green eyes. "You do fit…in more ways than you can imagine, princess," he said and cradled my cheek. "Don't you understand that you're perfect? Wherever you are, you fit perfectly. No matter whom you're with, or where you are, you belong, and you need to know you belong." A silly smile crossed his perfect lips as he stifled a laugh. "As for feeling sorry for you…give me a break. If anything—and I may lose my man card for saying this—I've found you to be intimidating at times."

I couldn't believe anything or anyone intimidated him. "Well, that goes both ways," I replied.

"Princess, what I *do* feel is admiration for the success you've become despite the pain and hurt that could've led you to a *very* different path. You're like the missing piece of a puzzle…at least for me. I've walked around for as long as I can remember, feeling as though there was something significant missing from my life. I had no idea what it was until I met you."

My heart melted as I looked into his eyes, seeing the truth he'd placed in his words. He was making it difficult to stay on course, but knowing we needed to discuss everything, I continued. "I did a little digging into the Raine family after I'd learned who you really were. You all lead very different lives than what I'm accustomed, and you exist in circles in which I never would. Hell, your family has *created* most of those circles. And I've read articles about you and some of the women you've dated. I'm nothing like those socialites," I said, shaking my head. "Now I understand why Sienna and Connor weren't very accepting of me. I'm not the woman they would choose for you."

"Is that what you're worried about?" he asked. "It doesn't matter what my family wants. All that matters is what I want, and what I feel. Aria, I've dated women my parents approve of, but I never wanted any of them. I was just there — playing the role of the highly-respected billionaire's son. But when you came into my life, all of that changed. I awoke every morning exhilarated. I thought of you continuously throughout the day. I even hated to go to sleep because I knew my thoughts of you would be interrupted. When I found myself drifting off, my last thought was a hope that I'd have dreams of nothing but you. Granted, I wanted those dreams to involve fucking you," he said with a mischievous grin, "but still, only you. In the end, even though you gave the pretense of hating me, I couldn't stay away. I naturally gravitate toward you. I can't explain it, but for the first time, I feel full of life. It's the same feeling I have when I play music, but somehow, it's more than that. I love everything about you — the way you look, the way you walk, the way you talk. I love the way your eyes twinkle when you laugh. I'd bet you didn't know your eyes twinkled. I love your smile. It's a little crooked — your upper lip goes more toward the left a little bit, but I love it. I love all of you."

"Wow, you make me sound so incredible that even I want to date me," I said, smiling.

"So, do you understand, at least in part, why I want this to happen?"

"I do."

"Good," he said.

"So, I have a crooked, twinkly-eyed smile? I thought you said I was perfect," I joked.

"You *are* perfect — in every way. You're definitely perfect for me," he said, grasping my hand and tugging me onto the couch with him.

"You're amazing, you know that right?"

"Yeah, I do," he replied, a smug smile dancing on his lips.

"Ugh," I said.

"Let's just press restart," he said.

"What?"

"Either that or pick up where we left off the morning of the breakfast with my family."

"So, those are my only options?" I asked.

"Quite frankly, yes."

"And what if I don't like either of those choices?"

"Let's not entertain crazy notions, Aria. If I could go back and do things differently, I would, but I can't. I know I lied to you from the very beginning. I didn't go to RPH looking for anything like that to happen. I expected it to be just as it was when I went to any of my father's companies. I know I broke your heart, and I'm sorry. What I can do is make up for it, but you have to be willing to let me do that. I want this. I want you," he said, the conviction in his eyes mirrored his tone. "You make me different, you make me better, and I know I do the same for you. I'm asking for the chance to put your heart back together. I know how to love you. I can give you everything you want—everything you need. That's what I'm offering."

The fiery passion of his eyes urged me to fall into his arms, but if I did, how long would it last this time? I couldn't bear the thought of accepting the hope of him only to have it disappear again.

"Just say you're willing to give us a chance."

There was a hint of desperation in his voice that both scared and compelled me. "What if I get hurt again, Aiden?"

"No one can promise that you won't, but if you continue to isolate yourself from the mere possibility of love, you imprison yourself. Why can't you see that, Aria? You can't live your entire life with loneliness and isolation because of the fear that you might get hurt."

"I know that...now. It's just very difficult, especially when it comes to you. You're the first person to see me for who I am—the first one to know the woman behind the mask. Every day I saw that little something in your eyes that let me know you were seeing the person I kept hidden, and it terrified me because it gave you an edge over me. And I had no idea of how to get it back. I still don't."

Aiden was quiet. He closed his eyes and sighed. When he opened them, he said, "I have something for you. I wasn't sure when would be the right time to give you this, but now somehow feels right."

"I'm not sure I understand," I said, confused.

Walking over to his briefcase, he opened it. His back was to me as he looked down at whatever he was holding.

"Aiden. What is it?" I asked, walking over to him.

As I reached to touch his shoulder, he turned and faced me, studying me as if trying to make a decision. And in his hands, was an envelope.

"This is from your mother," he said, passing it to me.

I stared at him, confused.

"When I went to visit her, she wrote this for you and asked me to give it to you when I felt the time was right. I'm not sure what's in the letter, and quite frankly I'm a little worried about the timing, but for the most part, it feels right."

I stared at the front of the letter. It simply had my name. I traced my fingers over it, wondering how my mother was feeling when she wrote this. I wanted to open it, but I was afraid.

"If you would rather I held onto it until you feel ready, I will," Aiden offered.

"No, no. I want to do it now," I said, my fingers trembling as I opened it.

"Aria—"

"I'm okay, Aiden."

Unfolding the letter, I took an anxious breath as I started to read.

My Dearest Aria,

I'm sure you're surprised to receive a message from me in the form of a letter. It seems the art of handwritten correspondence has been lost on your generation. Your father and I wrote letters and small messages to each other the entire time we were together. They were one of the many joys of my time with him. I thought this particular message was worthy of something more than an email or text, and I'm hoping you will carefully consider its contents.

It you're reading this, it means you know I've met your young Aiden. Before you unleash your rage upon him for coming to me, I want you to know he's someone you should not treat with the same restraint as you have the other men in your life. Although I've only had a small amount of time with him, it was sufficient to see his heart, and to see that you have it. Some people enter your life for a season, and others enter for a reason. Aiden is not a seasonal entrance for you, Aria. He's going to be your world, as I know you'll be his.

I remember when my dear friend, Constance Warner, lost her husband to cancer after more than twenty years of marriage. She swore she would never marry or fall in love again because Bryan had been "it" for her; he had been "the one." At the time, I thought it foolish. How can you live the remainder of your life on mere memories? Not until losing your father did I understand. He was the love of my life, Aria. I know you think otherwise because he left, but he loved me in a way that all women deserve to be loved, cherished, and worshipped. Once you've experienced that type of love, nothing else will ever do. There is no substitute.

I understand that now. Constance didn't want a substitute. She only wanted the real thing, and once it was gone, she was done. I'm sure you realize by now that the same applies to my feelings for your father. Sweetheart, I don't want you to have a substitute. Aiden isn't a place holder, he's the real thing. Aiden is to you what Matteo was for me. It may hurt to read these words, but that doesn't make them any less true. Aiden is that person for you. I saw it in his eyes. I heard it in his tone *when he spoke of you.*

I know I haven't been there to help you learn or sort out these things, but I've always wanted the absolute best for you. You deserve nothing less, Aria. Follow your heart. Don't settle. And if Aiden is the man I'm certain he is, he will not allow you to.

You're very headstrong, and when you set your mind to something, you stick to it, even if it's to your detriment. Don't let your stubbornness blind you to your reality. Fall in love, let it fill you, and let it give you all the joys that accompany it.

I love you more than you can possibly imagine,
Mom

A steady stream of tears started as soon as I'd read the first line. I rubbed the back of my hand across my face, staring at the words until fresh tears blurred them again. I reread the letter, holding firmly to the last communication I'd have from my mother, trying to imagine her voice saying those words to me. I was overcome with emotion, questions and even more regret. It became too much and suddenly, I was too weak to stand — my legs could no longer support me.

Aiden caught me, lifted me into his arms, and carried me to the bed. Placing me on the edge, he looked at me in silent concern as I tried to accept the truth of my mother's words. Mom had told me once that Kellan wasn't the one. Was her judgment based in part on the time she'd spent with Aiden? I wondered why she never said anything to me. Had she wanted me to make up my mind myself? She must have known I wouldn't, which was why she wrote the letter. Did she somehow sense I couldn't get past my stubbornness and hurt to see that Aiden really was the one for me? I'd never know her reasons, except that she loved me.

The words in her letter about Dad...*loved, cherished, and worshipped*...those were the exact words I'd used last night to describe how Aiden made me feel. That couldn't be a coincidence. It was as though she were here—guiding me to the place I belonged— to the man who was destined for me.

Aiden sat beside me, holding me as I wept. When the tears finally stopped, he pulled me into his lap. "Are you okay?" he asked.

"Yes." I kissed his cheek. "Thank you."

"For what?"

"For meeting my mom. For giving me this letter."

"I want to say you're welcome, but I don't feel I should, given your reaction to it," he said.

"No, it's okay. It was a beautiful letter, and the timing was perfect." I didn't want to run anymore. I did love him...and there was nothing I could do about it and it was so powerful that I couldn't ignore it. "I think I'm ready to finish our talk."

"Okay, but only if you're sure."

I was sure and I jumped right in and asked, "Why did you have Raina spy on me?"

"I needed to know how you were, and I needed to make sure no one else was of any interest."

"Why not check on me yourself?" I asked.

"Because I knew you'd have questions, and maybe it was my paranoia, but I thought you'd get enough information to make you wonder and possibly piece it all together, and I didn't want you finding out who I was in that way."

"As opposed to the way I did find out?" I asked.

"When Raina and I had last spoken, it was clear that she'd be telling you before I arrived. I had no idea she hadn't had the chance to do that."

"But you were still fine with me finding out from her and not you?"

"No. I hated placing Raina in that position, but she wanted to do this for you, and since I was going to be there the same day, I thought...well, I'd hoped I could make you understand."

Allison was right — men are stupid.

"Raina knew who you were before I did. I felt so foolish."

"But you were open to talking things out— even then," he said.

"Yes, I was. You'd sent me a very sweet text saying how much you missed me and you were eager to talk. I was about to reply that I'd missed you, too, but that's when Raina told me everything. And it verified what I grew up learning, that you can't trust anyone—that no one is who they say they are. As soon as she left my office, I sent you that text telling you to fuck off."

I looked down at the letter in my hands and continued. "My heart broke a little more every day because I missed you more each day. I wanted it to stop, but it didn't. I realized all of it was out of my control. You'd grabbed a piece of me I couldn't get back."

"You've grabbed a piece of me that I don't *want* back, Aria. I regret how this all played out. Business decisions are second nature to me, but this relationship with you…I'm learning as I go, and I've made some mistakes that have caused you pain. I can't undo that, but believe me, if I could, I would. By the end, with not knowing if my father would live, my mother being hospitalized, and assuming leadership of the company…I barely had time to think. I was basically reacting. I'm not excusing anything I did, but I hope you'll at least consider my position."

"Why did you do it—get involved with me without telling me who you are? Why did you think it was okay?"

"I never said it was okay," he replied. "I didn't expect this. It took on a life of its own. Hell, it still is running its own course. I don't plan with you, I just *do*. And back then all I wanted was you. I didn't look beyond that. But once you told me a little about your past, I knew I needed to explain, but I also knew you'd feel betrayed, and you'd run, so I didn't want to take that chance. It was challenging as hell to get you to bend *without* a lie between us. I knew I'd lose whatever we had if I told you…so, I didn't. I couldn't risk it."

"And the other part? Why even do the *Aiden Wyatt* thing…ever?" I asked.

"Aria, if you'd been in my shoes for the past twenty-eight years, you'd understand. When I'm Aiden Wyatt, I garner respect based on my achievements and contributions—not because of my last name. That's important to me. I resent so much of this life. This was the only part that was mine. It was based on me, not my father. It's important that I'm my own man, not just an heir apparent."

I might not quite understand, just as he might not quite understand everything that made me the person I was. But I did understand the tenacity to be the person you felt you had to be, whatever the reasoning. And he was right—when I thought he was Aiden Wyatt, I'd appreciated his shrewdness—he was brilliant, and it wasn't because he was a Raine. It was because he was Aiden.

I'd seen glimpses of some things I found odd for a rich guy, or at least my preconceptions of a rich guy, but I didn't know he resented parts of his life to this degree. In regard to me, I truly believed he thought he did the best he could, given the circumstances.

"I know you want this, and I know you're scared—and that's okay," he said.

I sighed and looked away.

"What is it?" he asked.

"You know, before you came along, I was all right. I had what I wanted."

"There was no purpose—there was no meaning to that kind of life, Aria," he said.

"But it was *my* kind of life, and I hated you wouldn't let me get back to it."

"Because I couldn't. I literally couldn't— and I can't now," he said.

"I don't want you to," I said, looking back at him. "I'd gotten so used to keeping guys at a safe distance that I didn't know how to behave when someone…when *you* got close. But I want to learn, and I want to do that with you, if you'll have me."

"You already know I'll have you—in every way possible."

There was so much passion in his eyes. I'd felt it when he made love to me. I felt it every time he touched me.

Tugging me from the bed, Aiden pulled me into his arms. I was his again. I'd always been his. He smothered my lips and cheeks with soft kisses and then stepped back, holding me at arm's length, his eyes filled with adoration. "You have no idea how happy you've made me."

The last time I'd agreed to any type of relationship with Aiden, he'd told me I wouldn't regret it. The part of me that was stepping into unfamiliar territory couldn't help but wonder if I would regret it this time, especially now that the stakes were much higher.

❧Chapter Fourteen❧

Our last night at Aiden's—my sisters and I would be going home tomorrow. We'd put it off long enough, it was time to start our new lives. Of course, Aiden objected to my impending departure, but I made him understand it was time.

He and I spent the better part of the day fine tuning *The Writer*. It was great to finally do something constructive, and it was that much better working alongside him again. He worked with such keen insight and vigor—it was fascinating to watch.

We'd made some pertinent modifications to the roll-out strategy, which I was anxious to share with the marketing team. Dianna brought our lunch to the study, and we continued to work as we ate. The day passed by much too quickly—Aiden and I were unaware of the time until Allison checked on us for dinner. We enjoyed a movie afterwards and when the credits began, I turned toward Aiden and found him watching me.

"You look tired," he said. "How about we get you to bed?"

I hoped by "bed," he meant "sex," because it had been all I could think about since we'd made love. I was sure I was using it as a diversion, but for now it would have to do. Rather that, than to walk around buried in grief.

Aiden and I said goodnight to the others and headed toward

the opposite side of the penthouse. Stepping into the bedroom moments later, Aiden dimmed the lights and then disappeared as I placed my phone on the charger.

"Aria, I've started your bath. Come," he said.

Smiling, I placed my hand in his. "You're so amazing, do you know that?"

"That's the word on the street," he said, as I followed him into the bathroom.

"Ugh. I forgot."

"Forgot what?"

"That I can't give you any compliments," I said.

"Why is that?" he asked as he unbuttoned my shirt.

"Because you don't take them well."

"Quite the contrary, I take them very well. I never disagree."

"Exactly, you react to them as if I'm stating the obvious. You're not *all* that, you know."

"Sure I am. A guy would have to be all that to capture your attention, princess."

Reaching behind me, Aiden unhooked my bra—a task he somehow managed to always complete with ease. I wondered how many of those he'd undone.

"I can undress myself you know," I said, as he unbuttoned my pants and reached for the zipper.

"I know, but I want the pleasure of doing it for you. You

wouldn't deny me that, would you?" he asked, placing his hands between my jeans and my thighs, and easing the denim down my legs.

I stepped out of the pants, and he looked up at me. "I love seeing you like this." He grasped the lace trim of my panties and slipped them off. "You're so beautiful, Aria," he said, his eyes fixed on the space between my thighs.

"Are you referring to me as a whole or just one particular part of my body?" I asked. The devilish gleam in his eyes made me wet — I wanted to pounce on him. But I sensed he had something special in mind for the night, so I was content to let things play out. Knowing Aiden, he would have made it happen per his plan anyway.

"Although my eyes were lingering on one specific area, yes, I do mean you as a whole. Now, let's get you in the tub."

The next morning seemed different than any I could remember. I was nervous, excited — and despite the grief — I was happy. I felt Mom's presence. I felt her approval of the choices I'd made as of late.

Aiden and I had finished breakfast and were in his study playing a game of chess before I headed home. It was my move.

Out of nowhere, I said, "You've explained why you weren't

forthcoming with your identity, but that didn't mean you had to conceal the fact that you were wealthy, so why did you?"

He grimaced. "If you're referring to the Raine billions, it's not my money, it's my parents'."

"Same difference," I replied.

"If you say so."

"But you know…when I think about a billionaire's son, you don't quite fit the bill. You're not at all what I'd expect."

"Oh. And just what did you expect? Perhaps I'm not doing it right," he said playfully.

"You're very down to earth, at least when you want to be. You're not as prudish as I would expect. You don't seem spoiled. Well, for the most part anyway. You're very domesticated and you're very, very dirty."

"Don't get me wrong—I do partake of some of what this life offers, but I don't consistently lavish myself with it. That's just not who I am."

"I love that about you," I said.

"I love lots of things about you. Wait—why do you say I'm domesticated? Is it because I can cook? It was just the one meal."

"And the breakfast," I said. "I recall you saying there was a story behind that."

"Sort of. We grew up with servants, so of course we had cooks and what not. As a child, I bored of everything quite easily, and I had a thirst for knowledge of any type. We didn't venture into the kitchen very much because our meals were always prepared for us, but I wanted to know how, so I was often in the kitchen observing and talking to the staff. And the fact that Mother scolded me—for consorting with the help, as she put it— well, that caused me to sneak in there even more, as a means of defying her if nothing else."

"So, your frequent kitchen visits…does that mean you can cook more than just the two meals?"

He smiled. "Yes."

"So, you've been depriving me of your skills all this time?"

"I can't agree with that, princess. The skills that keep you interested are never kept from you."

"You think it's the sex that keeps me here?" I asked teasingly.

"Hmm…yeah," he replied, laughing.

"It feels so good to laugh with you again. I didn't think this would ever happen," I said.

"I knew it would. I knew it wouldn't be easy, and I didn't know how long we'd be apart, but I always knew we'd find our way back," he said.

"I'm curious. Why did your family go along with the *Aiden Wyatt* charade?"

"It was an attempt to appease me. They tend to do that a lot. I haven't been as eager to take on this role as my father would have liked. We butt heads over it. Always have."

"Then, why do it?" I asked.

"I do what is expected of me, Aria," he said, his tone impassive.

"Even if it makes you miserable?"

"What makes you think I'm miserable?"

"You just don't seem to enjoy it. And if you fight your father on it, it's pretty evident, to me at least, that you don't want it."

"It's not that simple."

"Why?"

"I didn't really go to school for those degrees due to any passion for either of them. I thought that maybe, just maybe, if my father saw I had a noble profession — that I was helping people, actually making a difference in their lives — then he would release me from what he thought of as my family obligation. It didn't work out that way. He saw something in me at a very early age and he harnessed it. He wanted me to take the reins of the company one day. The fucked-up part of this is that you're right — I don't enjoy this, but I'm good at it. Even more so than my father — he even said as much."

Aiden was sacrificing himself for his family. I didn't know whether to hug him or cry for him. I could sense he didn't want to say anymore.

"You're delaying the inevitable," he said, changing the

subject with a nod to the game board. "You're not going to win," he taunted.

"You've been so accommodating with me and my family that I wanted to do a little something nice for you and let you win this one, Mr. Raine."

"Whatever. I'll win because I'm the better player. Admit it," he prodded, his face relaxing into a playful grin.

"Never," I replied, and made my last move, the one that ended it all.

"Check mate," he said, tossing my queen aside.

"When did you know you wanted this with me? Was it after the ballet?" I asked.

"I knew I was in trouble long before that," he said.

"Trouble? Me? I think you have that confused, but I'll bite. When?"

"The night I took you to Seducente."

I didn't quite know how to take that. "Are you saying that my submission—"

"No, it was actually when we came back to your place afterwards…when we were in the bath together."

That night had opened my eyes to quite a few things, about him and about myself.

"It was the first time you let your guard down. You gave me a glimpse of you. But I later got the sense you regretted that. Did you?"

"Yes, I did. It was confusing for me. I couldn't figure out why I was so comfortable with you."

"I was comfortable with you, also. And I knew you had a genuine interest in me. It wasn't for my money or my family, just me. Even now, you're interested in the person behind the name. That doesn't happen very often."

He sounded regretful. I couldn't imagine how it would feel to be him, even for a day. I saw the desolation in his eyes, and for the first time I could see why he wanted to escape the Raine name. "You were and still are an enigma."

"Oh, I am?" he asked.

"Yes, you are, and you know it," I replied.

"I could say the same of you."

"Perhaps, but that's a mode of protection for me, and now I can see it is for you, too," I said.

"I know what you've been through—I know why you felt the need to protect yourself from me. But you don't have to do that anymore," he said.

"Watching Mom slowly slip away every day…it caused me to make a lot of poor decisions, I guess."

"All of those decisions made you who you are. I like who you are."

"Why are you so good to me?"

"It's easy," he said. "You're every man's fantasy of what a woman should be."

I wasn't whole. I was broken. And looking into his eyes, I knew he realized that just as much as I did. But for some reason, he still wanted me.

❧Chapter Fifteen❧

Stepping into my condo, not only did it look different—it somehow felt different, too— as though I was walking into someone else's life. It was my first time back in my place since the funeral, and because of the interior decorator, I knew it wouldn't look quite the same, but I didn't expect it to feel so strange— almost as if it were no longer my home.

I found myself smiling as I showed my sisters to their new rooms. They didn't resemble the guest rooms I'd left, or even the guest rooms that were discussed with the designer—they'd been decorated to fit the girls. From the canopy of dim lights lining the veil above the beds, to the string of photographs above their desks—the rooms were perfect—each complete with a fresh bouquet of flowers, a computer and a framed picture from our trip to Disney World.

Their closets had been filled with designer clothes and the drawers were overflowing with everything they could possibly need and then some. I hadn't spoken to the interior designer in weeks, so Aiden must've had a hand in this—he somehow always got it right—down to the last detail.

Despite my attempts to reassure Aiden that I was okay, he was still in Boston, and it took some convincing, but he finally agreed to allow the girls and I some time to get settled before he came over. I'd urged him to get back to work—he'd put off his responsibilities long enough to console me, but it was like talking to my hand. When my sisters and I left the penthouse, I saw the worry in his eyes. He didn't think I was ready. And to be honest, I was worried as well. How would I become the person I needed to be for my sisters while also providing the comfort we *all* needed?

April had headed back to Pennsylvania first thing that morning, and Allison would be leaving later in the day. I really needed this time alone with my sisters. I'd actually spent more time talking *about* them lately than I had *to* them, and it was time to remedy that. I looked at their faces as they completed their inspection of what would now be their rooms.

"So, what do you think?" I asked, as we stepped out of Bianca's closet.

"I'm totally floored. I had no idea you were doing all of this," Lia exclaimed, looking excitedly from Bianca to me.

"I can't take the credit for it. This is all Aiden. I had no idea until I stepped in just now that he'd done all of this."

"He's been amazing! I can't believe you were considering letting him go," Lia said, looking at me as if I had two heads.

"You guys obviously spent a fair amount of time getting to know him over the last few days," I replied.

"We have," Lia said. "And Aria, he's totally in love with

you."

"He almost seems too good to be true," Bianca said, her voice low.

Lia and I both looked at her, surprised by her cynicism. Where had that come from?

"Sometimes when something or someone appears too good to be true, there's a reason," Bianca said and walked out of the room.

I couldn't help but agree, but I was puzzled by such a dismal view from someone so young. But then again, I'd been the same way at her age. We were all grieving and attempting to make the best of this new arrangement, but Bianca was obviously going through more than she'd let on, because her attitude was so different. It was as if she and Lia had switched personalities.

"Let me show you around. I want you both to feel at home, so if there's something you need, or don't necessarily like, let me know and we can find an alternative. That is, if it's not too drastic. I can't very well let teenagers redecorate for me—I don't think I want posters of boy bands hanging everywhere," I added, smiling at them.

The intercom buzzed.

"Lia, can you get that please?" I asked, walking toward the kitchen. It felt odd knowing I'd no longer be living alone. Had I made the right decision moving them here? Should I have moved there instead? I shouldn't second guess myself, but who was I kidding? I had a huge responsibility now — I'd be overthinking everything.

Aiden had also stocked the house with food. I guess he remembered that I didn't cook and my pantry was typically bare. He really did think of everything.

I took a seat on one of the counter stools just as Lia entered the kitchen with Dianna following closely behind her.

"Hello, Ms. Cason," she said.

"Hi, Dianna. Did we forget something at Aiden's?" I asked, looking at the two large bags in her hands.

"No ma'am," she replied. After placing the bags on the counter, she reached inside one of them. "Mr. Raine asked that I give you this. He said it should explain everything."

It was one of Aiden's signature white envelopes. A warm tingly feeling washed over me as I reached for it.

Lia let out a long sigh and I glanced at her. "So lucky," she said.

My sister seemed almost as giddy as I. Yes, I was lucky, but I hoped she knew Aiden wasn't all stars and rainbows.

Bianca strolled into the kitchen just as I was about to read the note.

Princess,

Since you insisted upon going back to your place, I've endeavored to make the transition as fluid as possible. I know Lia and Bianca will appreciate this, and I hope you will also. I spent a great deal of time talking to your sisters. They enjoyed cooking with your mother, especially your grandmother's Italian recipes. When I visited with Melena in Dayton, I joined them for lunch; it was homemade pizza. I've asked Dianna to deliver fresh ingredients and provide any other assistance you may need for a pizza lunch with your sisters. I thought this would be a great way to start you all off on the right foot.

I've decided to take you at your word regarding my return to work. Something has come up in the Chicago office that I need to handle, and I'll be heading to the airport within the hour.

Although you've been gone for only a short while, I already feel the absence. I'll be in touch before you have the chance to miss me.

-A.

"Well, it looks like we're making pizza for lunch," I said, looking at the girls and then Dianna. "Thank you for bringing this over."

"You're welcome. Is there anything I can do to help?" she asked.

"No. I think we've got it. I'll walk you out," I replied.

"Mr. Raine is very concerned and wanted to make sure I was available should you need anything. This is my contact information," she said, passing me a card. "Call anytime. Day or night."

"Thank you for everything, Dianna. I hope we weren't too much trouble."

"It was a pleasure. Your sisters are lovely girls, and you, well, you put a joy in Mr. Raine that I've never seen in all the time I've known him."

"And how long is that?" I asked.

"Since he was a child. I've worked for his family for years. I've been in Boston for a little over a year to care for my sister; her health was failing."

"I'm sorry. I hope she'll be okay."

"She's doing much better, and it looks like I'll be returning to Chicago soon," she said. "Well, I'd better be going."

"Thanks again, Dianna," I said as I showed her out.

Returning to the kitchen, I found my sisters removing items from the bags and realized I never really asked if they wanted pizza. "Are you guys even in the mood for pizza?" I asked.

"Sure," Lia said.

"From the looks of it, we're making the chicken and herb white pizza with garlic sauce," Bianca said.

"Mmm. That sounds yummy," I replied.

"That's what we made when Aiden visited Dayton," Lia added. "He loved it."

I was starting to think that Lia had a crush on Aiden.

We chatted and laughed as we busied ourselves with our

contributions to the meal. I hadn't made pizza sauce since high school, but as I added and mixed the ingredients, it seemed like it was just yesterday. Aiden and Dianna had left no detail to chance, including the pizza stone.

After Lia placed the pizza on the stone and slid it in the oven, we started on the salad. We were all quiet. I imagined we were thinking of what was and what could have been.

"Mom would have loved this," Bianca said. "She was looking forward to Thanksgiving."

Glancing up, I saw tears pooling in her large amber eyes. I rushed over to hug her and soon felt Lia's arms around us. We stood in the middle of the kitchen hugging and crying as the enormity of our grief came crushing down around us. Doubt seeped into every part of me. Why did I ever think I could handle this? Managing my heartache was one thing, but the three combined—how would I do it?

Our sobs gradually subsided and we finished the salad and set the table. "You know what? Thanksgiving is two days away, and I think we should resume our plans and cook dinner."

Lia and Bianca exchanged brief glances, but neither of them said anything as they headed back to the kitchen.

Following them, I said, "I know this is going to be difficult, but I think this will be a good, positive step for us."

"I think so, too. It's just hard to imagine it without Mom," Lia replied.

"I think you're right, Aria. We should do it. Mom would have wanted that," Bianca said.

The oven timer pinged and Lia removed the pizza. The exquisite aroma of Italian spices reached me just as my stomach growled. It smelled amazing—it smelled like those days back in Dayton. A quick image of our floured faces flashed in front of me—the five of us, so very happy. The girls were really young and couldn't help out much, so their job was to sprinkle on the toppings. Even that had turned into a colossal mess, but I'd gladly exchange that for what we were trying to work through now.

The pizza was fabulous. Lia suggested we have pizza night at least once a month, a suggestion to which Bianca and I quickly agreed. As we ate, we tossed some Thanksgiving menu ideas around. We leaned more toward the traditional entrées so we decided to stick with those.

After lunch, we made a quick check of the pantry. We really didn't need many food items thanks to Dianna and Aiden. After making a list, the girls went to the building's gym to look around. I was alone for the first time in days. And even so, I felt crowded—out of my element. Taking responsibility for my sisters would have been difficult no matter what, but it would have been an easier transition had I not shut myself off from my family for so many years. We were all feeling our way through a forced arrangement, and I didn't know what to do to make it easier. I guess only time would do that. I didn't want to push and bring too many feelings to the surface that could cause catastrophic consequences, but I needed to know they were okay—that they were managing.

We'd discussed counseling and decided to keep it as an option, but maybe we should take that off the back burner, or maybe I could be intentional about having in-depth talks on a routine basis. I really didn't know what the answer was. Maybe I was expecting too much too soon. I'd had several years to adjust to the idea of having a life without parents and coping without family. But they'd still had Mom and a small appearance of family life. So, this was much more of a dramatic change for them than it was for me.

Walking into my closet, I went to the corner I typically avoided and opened the bottom drawer in the far corner. I pulled out the forbidden box and waited a moment before working up the nerve to open it. Removing the lid, my attention was immediately drawn to the pink heart-shaped note that bore my mother's handwriting. I picked it up and trailed my fingertips across the two small but immensely powerful words. Mom constantly left notes like this in my room, on my door, or in my book bag. Two words in Italian. *Ti Amo*. Once Dad left, the notes appeared less and less, until one day they disappeared altogether.

I placed her letter on top of the note and put the box away.

A little later in the day, Aiden called to check in, and he also invited us to his home for Thanksgiving. Although grateful for his offer, I politely declined, explaining my sisters and I needed this time to be a family. I was pleasantly surprised when he didn't push. I didn't have the energy to debate, and he must have sensed that. He was being careful with me, and I really appreciated his efforts, especially since I knew his preference was to take control and make everything okay.

Despite my misgivings about the girls volunteering to handle the turkey, we made it through Thanksgiving without burning down the kitchen. We'd made a huge mess, but the dinner was delicious. A few times, we fell into uncomfortable silence, but we'd managed to muddle through.

The girls started class the following Monday at Boston Latin, and I went back to work. I'd checked in with Mrs. Warner regarding Lia and Bianca's car and I'd also hired someone to pack up the house. It was slated to be on the market within the next two weeks. We were donating the car to a charity and updating it to something more reliable. In the meantime, they had a rental.

We soon developed a routine, and we seemed to be handling the recent changes. Their school counselor suggested that, even though the girls seemed to be doing well, some counseling with her or with another professional outside of the school might be helpful. When I raised the subject with the girls that same night over dinner, they had fallen silent. But after the initial hesitation, they admitted they could see the benefit. I was secretly relieved they wanted to see someone outside the school system. The memories of my time with the school counselor who attempted to help me cope with the loss of my father were rather unpleasant.

Fortunately, unlike adolescent me, Lia and Bianca appeared to be adjusting well. They really liked Boston Latin and were quickly making new friends. Their core group from Dayton, along with Mrs. Warner, constantly called to check in on them. I knew they missed Dayton and their home, so as a surprise, I made plans for them to visit soon.

I was also looking forward to my upcoming alone time with Aiden. He'd been out of town for the last week, and I missed him terribly. Due to the vast difference in time zones, texts and emails had become our primary means of communication. I'd be seeing him soon, though. Work was going well and the girls were doing pretty good…either I had a way better handle on this than I thought, or any minute now the other shoe was going to drop.

❧Chapter Sixteen❧

My world had become total chaos. With so many alterations to my life in such a short time span, it felt as though my head was literally spinning. Everything was different—my career, my family, my household, my relationship status. I was a strict creature of habit. If it wasn't written down or planned, then it simply wasn't happening. I'd found comfort in that. I no longer had that comfort, and I hadn't processed how I was managing without it.

There was a time, in the very recent past, when I would have eagerly rushed to the familiar comfort and isolation the condo provided, but not today. I longed for a distraction from what had become my new normal. The one and only distraction I craved came in the form of one extremely hot and sensual man...and thankfully I would be seeing him later in the afternoon.

My sisters had left for Dayton earlier that morning, and in dire need of some deep relaxation, I'd spent the better part of the afternoon at the spa. And now I was counting down the minutes until I would see Aiden. I only needed to drop by the condo to grab some clothes and then head to the penthouse.

As I unlocked the door, my phone pinged. I figured it was Aiden texting a reminder about meeting at his place, but I was wrong—it was Kellan. Although I was extremely happy he and I were maintaining a friendship, my heart dropped a little when I saw his name on the display. It was the guilt—I felt as if I'd once again tossed him aside for Aiden.

Aiden filled one part of me—a part I now accepted as something I *needed*. And then there was Kellan, he added something very different to my life. Something I *wanted*, but couldn't quite explain. The question of the hour: should I go with the want or the need? I didn't want to sort that out, and I figured I didn't have to because I was keeping them both. Should I have felt some type of remorse, for holding onto two men? Sure, but I didn't. I couldn't control my feelings…nor would I bother with the pretense of doing so as I'd done in the past. I was doing the one thing Aiden had asked of me on several occasions—I was *going with it*. I knew Aiden wouldn't like it, but I wanted Kellan in my life. I didn't want to say goodbye to him, nor did I feel I should.

Skimming Kellan's text, I saw his news about the recent hedge fund development. He was on track to becoming a portfolio manager. I tapped a reply, congratulating him, and then dashed to my bedroom to pack a bag.

Within the next hour, I was standing outside the door of the penthouse. Aiden had barely opened the door before I was flying into his arms. He laughed, twirling me as I wrapped my legs around his waist.

"Hi, princess," he said, with a grin.

Forgoing a hello, I pressed my lips to his. When his mouth opened, I slid my tongue inside, stroking it against his. Our tongues were soon dancing to their familiar tune as our breathing became heavy and labored. My hands were in his hair, my fingers twisting. I wanted him closer. Fuck, I wanted him naked. Reaching for his buttons, my fingers rushed to undo one, and then another before Aiden pulled my hands away.

"What's wrong?" I asked, panting as I looked at him.

"As far as homecomings go, I couldn't have asked for anything better, but I think we should close the door first," he said, smiling. "And Dianna's here. She dropped by to pick up some things before she heads back to Chicago so..."

"Oh," I said, embarrassed.

He placed me on my feet and then reached in his pants to readjust himself.

"Let me do that," I offered.

"Damn, you really want to be fucked, don't you?"

"What can I say? Virginia knows a good thing when she feels it. Besides that, I've missed you."

"I've missed you too, princess," he replied. "As for Virginia, well..."

"I think this is everything," Dianna said, entering the room.

"Let me get that for you," Aiden offered, grabbing a box from her.

"Hello, Ms. Cason," she said, smiling sweetly at me. "It sure is nice to see you again."

"Hi, Dianna. It's nice to see you, too."

"I'm flying back to Chicago today," she said. "Since my sister is on the mend, she's given me my walking papers."

"That's wonderful news," I said.

"It certainly is. Well, I'm sure I'll see you at Mr. Aiden's birthday party in a few months. Take care, Ms. Cason."

Party? Aiden's birthday was five months away. "You too, Dianna." My reply was a bit automatic as I watched Aiden help her out with the box.

"I'll be right back. Make yourself at home," he said, following Dianna out the door.

A little hurt he hadn't mentioned the party to me, I walked further into the room and took a seat near fireplace. As I waited, I began ticking off the reasons Aiden may have for not telling me.

"You're having a birthday party?" I asked when he entered the room.

"Apparently," he replied, walking closer, pulling me into an embrace that I resisted.

"What's wrong?" he asked.

"Why was I not invited?"

"I just learned of it this morning, Aria," he said shrugging it off.

"What do you mean?"

"Mother," he said.

"I don't understand." I'd met Aiden's mother, and I wasn't too impressed. To be frank, I didn't like her, and I knew the feeling was mutual. So, if she was spearheading this, I was sure my invite was *lost in the mail*.

"I'll show you. Give me a second," he said and walked toward the study.

My phone rang just as he stepped from my view. It was a call from a number I didn't recognize. I considered not answering, but Lia and Bianca were traveling, and I didn't know whose phone they could be using so I pressed answer. "Hello."

"Is this Aria Cason?" the caller asked.

The voice was unfamiliar. "Yes. To whom am I speaking?"

Silence.

"Hello," I said again.

"Yes, I'm here. I thought I was prepared to hear the voice of the woman who slept with my husband, but apparently, I was wrong."

"Excuse me? Who is this?" I asked.

"If what I previously said doesn't clue you in, then you've obviously made a habit of fucking married men, so let me narrow it down for you. This is Tiffany Patrick."

You've got to be kidding me. Now? She picks now to call me with this crap. I choked back what I really wanted to say, because I needed to keep this situation contained. "Tiffany, the only reason I'm not replying to your insult in the way it deserves is because we both were victims in this. But if you continue to speak to me like that, I have no problem letting you know exactly what I think of you and this bullshit."

"If you're biting your tongue, it's not because we're both victims. It's because I have the upper hand. I can blow your little house of cards down with one phone call," she replied.

I stepped into the foyer, hoping I was out of Aiden's hearing range. "Don't pretend you know shit about me."

"I may not know you, but I know women *like* you."

"Women like me? Oh, you mean women who've been lied to by men married to horrid bitches like you? Maybe this is how you get your kicks, but I have better things to do with my time, so I suggest you drop the insults and get to the point of this fucking phone call."

"I'm sure your friend explained that my attorney is planning to subpoena you," she said.

"No, she didn't. Your marriage...or divorce rather, has nothing to do with me."

"Isn't it too bad you didn't feel that way before you had my husband's dick inside you?"

"This is my last time telling you to watch your fucking mouth."

"What's going on, Aria?" Aiden asked, having stepped behind me.

I spun around to face him. "Nothing. Can I have some privacy please?" I asked, hoping he hadn't overheard anything.

Taking another step toward me, he asked, "Who is that?"

He wasn't exactly overflowing with patience.

"No one important," I replied, as I pressed end on the call. I was sure I hadn't heard the last of Tiffany. She would definitely call back later.

"What?" I asked, scowling at Aiden.

"You already know what. I'll ask once more. Who was that?"

"And I will tell you one time, it's of no concern to you." I pushed past him and switched my phone to vibrate. Aiden was on my heels. He was not going to let this go. Sitting on the couch, I watched him pull his cell from his pocket. He keyed something in, and then snatched my phone. I tried to grab it back, but he held it out of my reach.

"Run a trace on this number and let me know exactly who it is," he said, speaking into the phone as he watched me. "Yes, as soon as possible," Once he ended the call, he held my phone out to me.

"How dare you!" I said, grabbing it from his hand. "If I wanted you to know who I was speaking to, I would have told you."

"If you speak that way to anyone, it's because they've stepped out of line with you, and I won't allow anyone to do that."

"You step out of line with me on a regular basis," I said.

"That's because I'm allowed," he stated, matter-of-fact.

"Like hell you are."

"Aria, I'm not going to argue about this. I'll have the information I need soon enough."

"Please stay out of this, Aiden," I pleaded. It was humiliating enough without having him know the details.

Before he could reply, his phone rang. "If you'll excuse me," he said and answered the call. "Yes. Anything else?" he asked. He listened to the caller and then replied, "No. That will be all." He ended the call and coolly slid his phone back into his pocket.

"Why is Dane Patrick's wife calling you?" he asked, stepping toward me.

I tried to bluff my way out of something I didn't wish to reveal. "What are you talking about?"

"You know exactly what I'm talking about. What's going on, Aria?" he demanded.

"Why don't you just pick me up and shake the details from

me, Aiden? You can't just insert yourself into matters that do not involve you."

"Is there something you need to tell me?" he asked.

"You sound as if you already know. And you can't continue to invade my fucking privacy!"

"Can we forego the dramatics, Aria? Just once? What the hell is going on?"

He already knew enough, and if I didn't tell him now he would know within the next twenty-four hours. I'd rather he hear it in my words than from one of his hired hands. And quite frankly, I was worried. What if I couldn't keep this mistake quiet?

"You can tell me now or not," he said. "Either way I *will* find out."

"Fine!" I replied. I exhaled my reluctance and began explaining the entire situation to him. I paid close attention to his expression. I didn't want him to judge me for this. Had this come up a few months ago, I wouldn't have given his reaction a second thought—I didn't care what anyone said about the way I chose to live my life. Now that I had Aiden…what he thought of me mattered. I found myself feeling embarrassed, but I knew I needed to tell him everything.

I explained how I'd met Dane and what happened in Venezuela. I told him that I'd later learned that Dane was married and was going through a divorce. I went on to tell him that Dane had shown up at RPH out of the blue and had contacted me again recently. I further explained that Tiffany had called April some time ago, but her first call to me was the one he'd just interrupted. Both Dane and Tiffany presented a threat, but each of a different type. Dane pretty much wanted me to keep quiet or lie, and Tiffany wanted me to shout the truth to the mountain tops. Either one could be damaging for my career…and Raine Industries. I had no idea how to handle this effectively, yet quietly. I'd been in contact with my attorney, but when I hadn't heard anything from Tiffany, I placed it aside, figuring they had resolved their differences without involving me.

"And that's everything," I said, concluding the story.

His jaw hardened as he shoved a hand through his brown waves. "I'll take care of it."

"What do you mean?" I asked.

"I mean, I'll take care of it," he said, and disappeared into the study, closing the door behind him.

"Oh, shit," I said and started pacing the floor.

Ten minutes later Aiden strolled back into the room as if nothing had happened. He went directly for the bar, poured two drinks then stepped toward me.

"Have a drink," he said, extending the glass and taking a seat on the couch.

What just happened? Was he upset with me? "Aiden, what's

going on?"

"Nothing I can't handle. Now drink. You need to relax."

I reached for the glass and sipped as I waited for him to reveal the details of how it was being handled. After a few seconds, I realized he didn't plan to divulge anything.

"What's this?" I asked, looking at the glass.

"It's apple cider cognac."

"So, are you planning to keep me in the dark?" I asked, taking another sip.

"I assure you the situation with the Patricks will be resolved. And as soon as there's an update, you'll be the first to know. Now, let's set that aside for the moment and focus on us."

What had he done? How was he handling this?

"Stop worrying," he said, and took a swig of the alcohol.

I needed to know what was going on. What was he planning? Did he think poorly of me? Would this affect his feelings for me? I couldn't handle the not knowing — it was sending me into a panic.

Placing his drink on the table, he turned to me, cradling my face between his strong hands. "Stop it, Aria," he said.

"Aiden, you can't just —"

"Look at me," he commanded. He wasn't playing fair. I unwillingly stared into his dark green irises. "Stop it," he whispered, leaning in, placing a kiss on my cheek. He moved his lips back and forth across mine and then softly kissed me, the taste of cognac on his lips.

His alcohol-laced tongue mixed with the intoxicating scent of just him…it was overkill. I was done.

"Is this what you came here for? To argue?" he asked, moving to my neck and planting a kiss below my earlobe.

I leaned into him when he began gently sucking. "You're the one keeping things from me, so maybe it's you who wants to argue. Is that what you want?" I whispered.

"You know what I want. What I always want," he purred as his tongue traced the hollow of my neck.

Yes, I knew what he wanted, but I wanted to hear him say it. Virginia wanted to hear him say it. "Tell me. What do you want, Mr. Raine?"

He placed my glass on the table beside his and gently tugged me from my seat. Turning me away from him, he moved so his body was flush with mine. His hand was under my skirt, moving between my thighs to palm my sex. "I want this," he whispered, his lips grazing my earlobe.

"Then take it, baby," I replied. "It's yours."

"Gladly…but first I need to take you up on your earlier offer to assist Kingston," he murmured.

Facing him, I fell to my knees, my hands at his crotch, unzipping his pants. Seconds later, his thick cock was falling heavily into my hand.

"Mmm. It's beautiful." And I wanted it everywhere — my mouth, my pussy…my ass. I lightly kissed the head as lust engorged his manhood, evidence of his desire flowing from the tip. My tongue fluttered across the wide crown, hungry for his sweet taste — and it was exactly that…sweet, pure ambrosia. I could've literally sucked him dry. Curving my fingers around him, I stroked his length, fisting him from root to tip, eager for his sweet pineapple taste. At the first glimpse of more of his liquid delight, I licked it away and then took him into my mouth, moaning as I slid my lips over the large head. I swallowed as much of him as I could — until his rod touched the back of my throat. Then I began moving faster, stroking him with my mouth, my head bobbing frantically as I sought his climax.

"Ah, shit…suck it…just like that," he breathed as I pleasured him, rapidly moving his big cock in and out of my mouth. "You're going to make me come, Aria."

His words evoked a steady wave of violent clenches. I reached down and massaged my throbbing clit as I hollowed my cheeks and sucked harder. With both hands, he grasped my head and began thrusting deeper, grunting as he fucked my mouth, gagging me with each jab. "Ah, fuck!" he shuddered, as a sudden burst of semen filled my mouth.

Aiden groaned as his release continued, spurting long and in deep vicious waves. At the last pulse, he let out a deep breath and pulled me up to him. He pressed his lips hard against mine, tasting himself as his tongue slid into my mouth. The salacious disregard of his essence on my lips heightened my desire—I was aching for him. I needed his dick inside me.

"Fuck me, Aiden," I said, severing our kiss.

He positioned me over the side of the couch and lifted my skirt. Then he pulled my panties down and pushed his hand between my legs, moving his fingers over my sex.

"You're so deliciously wet, princess."

He pushed a finger inside me and slowly eased it back out. Why was he teasing me?

"Do you want more?" he asked.

"Yes. Please," I begged, as he pushed a second and then a third finger inside me.

"I need to fuck this pussy."

"Then do it. Fuck me," I moaned, as I grinded flagrantly on his fingers, desperate for his hardness.

Aiden removed his fingers, and then I felt his cock on the lips of my pussy, just before he shoved his big dick into me.

"Fuck, you're so tight," he murmured, rotating his cock inside me, stretching me. "Your pussy feels so good, baby," he said, his voice a sultry whisper as he began moving in and out.

I cried out, moaning as his slow pushes became rhythmic blows. I moved with him, meeting his forceful plunges. "Ah fuck, it hurts…don't stop." He was so hard I didn't think I'd ever adjust to it. "Don't stop fucking me, Aiden," I panted.

He growled, his grip tightening around my waist as he continued his brutal drives into me.

I could feel my climax building as my center contracted. "I'm going to come, baby," I whimpered as the ferocity of my orgasm ripped through me, my nails digging into the couch as his violent blows continued bolting me forward.

"Fuck…ah shit, Aria," he grunted, as I felt him harden. His dick jerked, forcing his seed into my depths as his final strokes subsided. Aiden collapsed atop me, his hard frame covering mine. Our ragged breathing gradually calmed — our heartbeats slowed. He kissed me lightly on the neck and scooped me up into his arms, tossing me over his shoulder and then smacking my behind.

I squealed with laughter as he made his way to the bedroom.

"Let's shower," he said. "I want you clean and well-fed, because I'm not nearly done with you."

After getting dressed, I went in search of Aiden. I found him in the kitchen setting the table. "Did you cook?" I asked.

"No. Delivery."

"Oh," I replied, noticing the way he was eyeing me. "Why are you looking at me like that?"

He frowned. "I'm not looking at you as much as I'm looking at your attire."

I looked down at my jeans and shirt, not understanding. "What's wrong with it?" I asked.

"There's a rule for sleepovers," he said.

"Since when?" I asked.

"Since now," he said, devouring me with his eyes.

"Okay, so what's the rule?" I asked.

"No clothes allowed."

"So, we walk around in the buff?" I asked, intrigued by the thought of seeing him completely naked for the next few days. Virginia, although already sore, was eager for such a rare treat.

"Not *we*. You," he replied.

"That's not fair," I complained.

"My house. My rules. So take them off."

"And why should I go along with this rule? I could just leave," I teased.

"Sure, you can try."

"So, not only will I be naked, I'll be your captive. You have a twisted mind."

"And you love it. Now strip."

"Now?" I asked.

"Yes, now."

"Can we wait until after dinner?" I asked.

"No. You're here until Monday, and I want you naked…all day, every day."

I considered denying him, but I knew that would lead to one of our tug-of-wars. "Fine, I'll give you what you want. But are you going to help me?" I asked.

"I'm going to instruct you," he replied.

Oh fuck. This man was going to make me his sex slave — the mere thought of his eyes on my naked body made me instantly wet. He was a walking, breathing vessel of seduction. He only needed to step into a room and panties would drop. Mine were certainly about to.

Aiden pressed a button on the control panel in the center of the island and the sounds of Jhene Aiko's *The Pressure* seduced me further. "Take off your shirt…slowly," he said.

I slid my fingers down my top, unbuttoning it as his gaze held mine. Shrugging the shirt off, it fell to the floor.

He took a sip of his wine. "Now the jeans."

My pussy was already throbbing. I could have melted right there into a puddle of hormones on the floor. I unbuttoned my jeans and slowly eased the zipper down. As I grasped the waistband, he said, "Wait. Turn around. And bend over as you pull them down." The velvet whisper was as sensuous as the look in his eyes.

Fuck, fuck, fuck. I was so close to shoving my fingers in my pussy and masturbating right there in front of him. I turned and did as he instructed—bending over as I slid the jeans down my thighs and stepping out of them.

"Damn, Aria. I want that ass, baby."

Turning to face him, I saw his hand sliding over his crotch. His gaze had transitioned into the dark green that sent shivers through me. My gaze shifted, focused on the bulge in his pants.

"Take off your bra," he said, his eyes hooded with lust.

Tearing my eyes away from Kingston, I unhooked the clasp. My fingertips slid beneath the straps, lifting them from my shoulders and allowing the bra to drop at my feet. He was making me so hot for him. My breasts were already heavy and tender, yet my nipples hardened even more under his heavy-lidded glare.

His tongue slid over his bottom lip as he took me in. "What are you waiting for? Take off the panties."

My hands were at my hips, preparing to do as he'd instructed, but he shook his head. "Turn around and bend over," he said, his voice low and husky.

Following his instructions, I faced the opposite direction as I grasped the top of my panties. Moving in time with the slow seductive beat, I peeled them off, bending over as I did so, giving him what he wanted. I heard his sudden intake of breath and smiled, reveling in his torture.

Stepping out of my under garment, I turned around, and

tossed it to him.

Aiden reached up, coolly catching the red lace as he took another sip of wine. A slow smile played about his lips, as he looked at the panties—they were already wet. He lifted them to his face and inhaled, and then with his eyes still on mine, he licked the traces of my essence.

Holy fuck! Did he just do that? This man gave a whole new meaning to the word seduction.

Aiden smirked—fully aware of the effect of his gesture. "Have a seat," he said, as he sat at the table, and tossed the panties in the pile with the other clothes.

At a loss for words, I walked to the table and sat across from him. Needless to say, we didn't finish dinner...

The time passed much too quickly. In line with his *rule*, I was naked all weekend and I finally persuaded him to at least give me the pleasure of seeing him in his boxer briefs and one of the snug T-shirts that perfectly accentuated his physique. I lost track of the number of orgasms he'd given me. I was sore as hell and each step reminded me of that—a reminder I relished as Monday approached and Aiden prepared to leave town. Although he wouldn't be gone as long this time, I already missed him.

❧Chapter Seventeen❧

Lia and Bianca adapted to life in Boston with relative ease, having forged new friendships while also staying connected to their friends in Dayton. They'd even considered joining a few of the school clubs. I'd also overheard them discussing an upcoming senior trip, but from the sound of it, neither of them wanted to go. I didn't want to push, but I thought it would be a good experience, so I interrupted their conversation. It was a hard sell, but I ultimately convinced them it was important they grasp everything life had to offer, even something as simple as a high school trip. They eventually agreed and were actually headed to Aspen with some friends for the weekend, leaving me at home alone, impatiently awaiting Aiden's visit. I was surprised when I received a text instead.

Meet me at RPH within the hour.

You're here? I didn't expect you until Friday.

Something came up.

What?

Just meet me, Aria. I'll see you soon.

Well, fuck. What was that about? It was after four o'clock. Since I hadn't undressed yet, I grabbed my purse and headed back to the office.

Once inside the elevator at RPH, I pulled out my phone to text Aiden.

I'm here. Where are you?

In the 30th floor conference room.

Slowing my steps, I surveyed the four-person security detail posted outside the door. What the hell was going on?

"Mr. Raine asks that you come right in," one of them said, holding the door open for me. Aiden looked up as I entered. I immediately noticed a difference in his demeanor. He was gorgeous as ever, but there was a distance in his eyes.

"Hello, Aria," he said, standing to greet me.

He didn't call me princess. Although I'd asked him to refrain from his use of my pet name at work, I was surprised. One would think since we hadn't seen each other in nearly a week, I would receive something more than his almost formal greeting.

"Hi," I replied meekly.

"Have a seat," he said, motioning to the chair beside him.

"Aiden, what's going on?" I asked, confused by his aloofness.

"The Patricks. They're here," he replied.

"What are you doing? This is my problem, not yours."

"Aria, it's *our* problem and I'm handling it. You're here because you should be privy to the conversation, but beyond that, I want you to remain silent," he said, his voice firm.

I didn't take kindly to his directive and as I was about to counter his reproof, he shook his head. "Aria, today is not a day to go head to head with me. Just do as I say, please," he said, the hardness of his gaze muting my words.

Not awaiting a reply, he pressed a button on the side of the table, and the security detail filed into the room.

"Everything has been handled per your specifications, sir," said one of them. "We've checked for all electronic devices and any possible wires."

"Show them in," Aiden said.

"He's ready," the man said, speaking aloud into a headset.

The door opened and another one of the security personnel, then Dane, a woman—obviously Tiffany—and a final security member filed into the office. Tiffany wasn't at all what I expected. She was a curvy woman of average height with platinum blonde tresses flowing down her back.

"Have a seat," the man said to them, motioning toward the

chairs at the end of the table.

The Patricks assumed the chairs they were offered and nervously, they glanced around the room until their eyes rested on me. Dane was expressionless. What had been going through my head when I hooked up with him? Alcohol had certainly played a part in that decision. He was sporting a light mustache and stubble. He was a good-looking guy. His facial features weren't outstanding, but there was still something alluring about him.

"I trust you know who I am, and the purpose of your visit," Aiden began, drawing their attention to him. His voice was different. It was cold…hard.

"Yes," they replied, almost in unison.

"Good. We can dispense with the preliminaries and cut to the chase. First, I don't make a habit of interruptions to my schedule such as this, so this is already a very unpleasant part of my day. However, I felt it necessary to articulate my intent in person to ensure there are no misunderstandings."

"Mr. Raine, I—" Tiffany started.

Aiden held up his hand—silencing her.

"You're not here to speak, you're here to listen," he said, his tone was cutting.

She looked toward Dane and I followed her gaze. If she was looking for support, she wouldn't get it from him. He was like a robot—no emotions. I couldn't read him at all. His eyes were focused on Aiden, who at that moment was quite frightening.

"It's been brought to my attention that you're experiencing marital difficulties, and you're forcefully soliciting Ms. Cason's assistance to further your ends. Unless the laws have changed— which they often do, but I highly doubt they have in this case—a marriage is between two people. Ms. Cason is not married to either of you; therefore, she will have no part in your sordid divorce."

The entire scene had me on edge, so I could only imagine what the Patricks were feeling. Aiden, on the other hand, was the epitome of calm and control.

"You both have the same goal—money. Based on reports I've obtained on your assets, there isn't much of any significance, and if you want to keep what little there is, you will do exactly as I say."

"Mr. Raine, Dane should pay for what he's done to me—to our family. My attorney feels Ms. Cason's testimony will more than make my case," Tiffany pleaded.

"Did I or did I not specify that you are not to fucking talk?" he asked, his voice laced with venom.

Tiffany's eyes widened and she sat back in her seat.

My heart was racing; I wasn't prepared to see this side of Aiden. His eyes were rolling flames of molten green. I swallowed the lump in my throat and glanced back toward Tiffany.

"You'll resolve this predicament without the inclusion of Ms. Cason or anyone, anything, or any entity that is affiliated with Ms. Cason. Let's be honest here, you didn't request Ms. Cason's assistance; you threatened her…and that was the worst mistake you could've made." His tone was chilling and I, like the Patricks, was hesitant to do anything more than listen as he continued.

"Whatever drove you to this place in your relationship is of no significance to Ms. Cason, and she's therefore not a player in this game of yours. I don't anticipate any further communication from either of you, nor does Ms. Cason. If either of you do as much as utters her name, I'll know. And I assure you, the outcome will not be to your liking. I don't make futile threats. I can target anyone, anything, and anywhere — and I say that with every possible connotation."

Tiffany — who looked as if she was about to pee herself — responded with a nod. I knew Aiden was a force to be reckoned with, but this was different — I hadn't witnessed this side of him before. His tone was menacing and his expression was downright lethal. Even I was afraid to speak…and that was saying a lot.

"I trust there is no ambiguity as to how I expect this to evolve. Now, if you'll please leave, my team will return your devices and escort you to the airport."

Dane looked at Tiffany, a small smirk on his face. Of course, this suited him perfectly — it gave him the result he wanted all along. He didn't want his wife to stake claim to his holdings, and from the sounds of it, she wouldn't…well, not through any involvement on my part at least.

"Mr. Raine, this is giving Dane exactly what he wants," Tiffany protested.

"Perhaps you're confused. This meeting is over. Don't test my patience, Mrs. Patrick."

Looking toward the security personnel, Aiden gave a slight nod — his prompt for them to escort Tiffany and Dane from the room. "See that they're logged in on the list for our special guests," Aiden said, eyeing them distastefully.

"Yes, sir," one of them replied, and then they all exited the room, leaving Aiden and me alone.

I didn't know what to say.

"I'm late for a dinner meeting. I'll call you later," Aiden said, standing and leaning towards me. He planted a kiss on the top of my head and then he was gone.

What the fuck just happened? I sat there, motionless, replaying the scene, and a sudden chill ran through me. Was this the way he dealt with people who pissed him off? Was this the way he handled business? I didn't know whether to be relieved, terrified, or turned on. I think it was a mixture of all three.

Aiden was incensed by the Patricks' disregard for discretion, and I couldn't help but wonder if he was upset with me also. Was that the reason he'd left so abruptly? Or why he'd been so distant? He was fine — or seemed fine — when I initially told him about this. Was *hearing* it so different from *dealing* with it? I would imagine so. Hearing about Nadia was more abstract, but seeing her and knowing she'd been intimate with Aiden made me want to vomit, so I could only imagine how Aiden felt dealing with Dane.

Of two things, I was sure — that was the last I'd hear of Dane or Tiffany Patrick and secondly, my recent decision to change the way I lived my life had been long overdue. I'd thought I had all the answers and that I'd made logical choices by taking certain measures to protect myself, and it had worked for a while, but the recent backfires verified the need for a different approach.

Men! Even when you gave them *only* sex, they still managed to fuck you up somehow. I'd wanted the detached sex, but I never wanted to be someone's mistress or break up families. Turned out, that's exactly what I'd done. I truly felt bad for Tiffany because I had a strong feeling I hadn't been the only one Dane had cheated with.

It was almost six o'clock when I traipsed back to my office. I walked slowly to my desk and sank into my chair…thinking about Aiden. Were we okay? Should I have handled the Patricks on my own? I had so many other questions, but I feared I would never get the answers.

I glanced at the picture on my desk. It was the one Mom had sent of the four of us in Disney World. When I was younger—and even after we'd reconnected—she'd always made a fuss over everything, large or small. She'd wanted it all to be special. Everything had been significant to her. When I'd told her of my promotion, she was so excited for me and extremely proud. She'd even remembered that my favorite flowers were orchids and had a beautiful bouquet delivered. A card had also been included— one that I intended to take home. Opening the desk drawer, I pulled the card from the envelope and read it.

Congratulations Aria!

I'm very proud of the woman you've become, and I'm happy I have the opportunity to celebrate your success. You've ventured out on your own and created a wonderful life for yourself. You've always been strong and tenacious—I love that about you. I pray that you continue to make wise choices and that you have every happiness life has to offer. That's all a parent can ask for. I know I'm far from perfect, but when I look at you and your sisters, I know I got something perfectly right. I love you for all that you are, for all that you have been, and for all you are yet to be.

Mom

I placed the card in my purse—wanting to add it to my box of keepsakes. Glancing at my phone, I saw it was almost seven o'clock, and Aiden had yet to call. Maybe he was taking some time to cool off after dealing with Dane and Tiffany — he was obviously more upset by this than he'd let on. I didn't know if I liked him fighting my battles, but, fuck, was he ever good at it. I was constantly seeing sides of him I didn't know existed. Clearly, we had some things to discuss.

℘Chapter Eighteen℘

It was nearly midnight and still not a word from Aiden. I'd considered calling, but I didn't know what state of mind I'd find him. And I didn't want to take the chance it was a bad one. I flipped through the TV channels, too antsy to settle on any one program, then eventually gave up and headed to bed.

I'd finally settled in when my phone pinged. As expected, it was a text from Aiden.

I'm downstairs. I'm coming up.

There wasn't any point in replying. I was convinced his visit was meant to inform me of his need to re-think our relationship. At least this time, he had the decency to deliver the news in person. With a wave of nausea in the pit of my stomach, I climbed out of bed to let him in. There was a knock just as I reached the door. I opened it, and there he was…the gorgeous, sexy, intimidating CEO of Raine Industries.

The coldness I'd seen in his eyes earlier had thawed, giving way to the salacious gaze he reserved specifically for me.

"Hi," I said, my voice low.

"Hi," he replied, pulling me to his chest and sealing his

mouth over mine, his tongue expertly exploring as his body pressed tighter against me. All my worries vanished as he moved us inside, closing the door behind him. Within the measure of a minute, we were both naked…moments later he was shoving his huge cock inside me.

ی۔   ی۔   ی۔   ی۔

In the kitchen the next morning, I was preparing tea as Aiden reached for coffee. Neither of us had mentioned the Patricks. I wanted to know more, but I was hesitant to raise the subject.

"I'm flying home for the weekend. I would love for you to come with," Aiden said.

"What?" I asked, startled by the suggestion.

"Come home with me," he said. "I have a charity event, and I'd like for you to see where I grew up."

I smiled, picturing a cute little green-eyed Aiden. I wondered if he'd been as challenging as a child as he was as an adult.

"Can I take that smile as a sign that you'll be joining me?" he asked.

"No, you can take that smile as a sign that I think it was kind of you to offer, but I would like to decline."

"And why is that? Give me one reason."

"I'll do better than that. I'll give you two — your mother and your father. No, wait, I'll make it three. What's going on with us is supposed to be a secret, remember? At least to the public. If I start taking trips to the family home…let's just say it would raise a few eyebrows, and I definitely don't want that."

Aiden sighed and pulled me toward him. "About that. I only went along with it because…well, to be honest, I would have agreed to pretty much anything if it meant I had a second chance with you. But I'm not doing this anymore. We're together, and I don't give a damn who knows it. And it's about time you didn't either."

"I'm not ready for the complications of making this public," I said. Once our status was revealed, I'd be harassed, scrutinized, critiqued and picked apart. That's the world Aiden was a part of, but I simply wasn't in the market for that.

He grinned. "Typically, the woman I'm dating wants the universe to know, and here I am with a woman I'm crazy about who wants to keep me as her dirty little secret."

"Well, I don't think the universe is ready for my revelation of just how dirty you are, Mr. Raine."

"What about you? Are you ready for me to get dirtier with you, Ms. Cason?"

"Baby, I'm dying to see what's next."

"Let's make a deal. You come home with me, and I'll give you a very generous taste of what's next," he said, a hint of mischievousness in his eyes.

"I don't know." I'd love to see where he'd grown up, but that would mean being around his parents, and the thought made me nauseous.

"What's not to know? I can show you around Chicago. We can go to the Navy Pier and the Chicago Theater and we can visit the Museum of Contemporary Art and the most motivational reason of all—I can fuck you in my childhood bedroom."

"Well, you should have led with that," I said, laughing.

"I forgot I was dealing with a sex-crazed woman."

He was making this sound like an offer I couldn't refuse. "It does sound fun, but your parents will be ogling the entire time. What if I use the wrong fork or sip water from the finger bowl?"

"I won't let you." He ran his fingertip over the worry line that I was sure had touched my face. "Stop worrying—you know I've got you."

"But your parents—"

"Let me deal with my parents. You deal with me. Now come here. Kingston is begging for your mouth."

And just like that, the tranquil air floating innocently around us changed—his prurient invitation adding a layer of lust and hunger to the already sexually charged ambience. Aiden tugged me closer, pulling me to his chest and trailing his finger along my cheek.

"How about a warm up?" he asked, sliding his finger into my

mouth.

My insides tightened — anxious and greedy for something much larger that would soon replace his finger.

A slow smile shaped his beautiful pink lips as he stared at my mouth and made light circles on my tongue. He removed his finger and then placed a barely-there kiss on my lips. Grabbing my hand, he guided it down his body, releasing me once I'd reached his erection.

I unzipped his pants and grasped his beautiful length, my arousal heightening as I watched him grow longer and thicker. I lifted my gaze to Aiden's, and his sultry eyes urged me forward. Dropping to my knees, I kissed the plush head, and then opened wider as I took him in, and gradually eased to the root. I allowed my jaws to adjust to his girth, moving slowly at first, but the thick, hard flesh moving in and out of my mouth was driving me crazy, causing me to suction my cheeks and suck faster, anxious for his release and desperate for his taste.

"Ah, fuck," he growled, grabbing the top of my head as I continued worshipping his cock. When I moaned around his dick, his breath hitched and his fingers ran through my hair, cradling my head, as his hips met me with strong, solid thrusts, fucking my mouth hard and fast, and forcing me to take him deeper. "Ah, shit…I'm coming," he grunted, as his dick hardened and jerked — spilling into my mouth.

ॐ   ॐ   ॐ   ॐ

We sat in silence, holding hands and toying with each other's fingers as we headed to the airport. As the driver came to a stop, Aiden turned to me. "Just a little warning. The lifestyle my parents lead is nearly a direct contrast to mine," Aiden said.

"What do you mean?" I asked, glancing up at him.

"I've told you I don't partake of all the luxuries that being a Raine affords."

"Yes. So?"

"My parents do. They rarely drive themselves. They have several servants, gardeners, stable hands and groundskeepers. You name it—they have it. I attempt to do as much as possible without all of those trappings. I always have, and they've always frowned upon it."

"Then why not just follow suit?"

"It just never felt right, especially when I saw how the other half lived. It's excessive."

"In St. Barts, Sloan said you've always been the challenging one of the bunch. Is that the reason she said that?"

He laughed. It was a rich, guttural sound I loved. "It's one of them, so yeah, I suppose you could say that."

"You know, it's actually quite awesome to think of it the way you do. It's impressive all things considered," I said.

"Don't get me wrong, I do call in favors or do what I need to when the time calls for it."

"Oh yes, I've observed that a few times, and I've found it to be quite impressive, and also a little intimidating."

"So, I still intimidate you?" he asked.

"You're atypical. It would be difficult to find someone who wasn't intimidated by you, especially when you have that *don't fuck with me* thing going."

"What?" he asked.

"Dane and Tiffany come to mind."

"Did that bother you?" he asked, his eyes cautious.

"No, not really. I was just taken aback. I didn't know what to think. It made me wonder more about you."

"You don't need to wonder," he said. "Just don't leave, and you'll have a chance to know anything you want."

"In that case, I think I'll hang around."

"Good," he said, lifting our intertwined fingers and placing a kiss on the back of my hand.

Becoming quiet again, I thought about the pieces of information I'd sorted out about his family. Finally, I said, "You know, it sounds as if you long for normalcy."

"More often than not," he said wistfully.

"It also seems as if you'll never have it."

"Yes, I suppose that's true, too. But you…you make me feel

normal."

"How?" I asked. I was happy to hear he felt that way — that I added something to his life.

"You don't treat me like I'm some prodigy or this greater than life rich guy. You don't really take my shit."

"Yeah, well, you don't take mine either." He was wrong, though. I did take a lot of his shit, more than I had ever taken from anyone. But I supposed he wasn't accustomed to any resistance at all. I was glad to know he saw me as not succumbing to him as others did.

"We're good together, Aria, and we could be so much better if you really let me in."

"I have." I'd let him get closer than anyone — how much more did he want?

"Not completely," he countered.

The last time I thought I'd let him in, it fucked my world pretty badly. I wanted to take it a lot slower this time around, but that was rather challenging with a man like Aiden. He really *was* this greater than life guy — whether he chose to buy into it or not — and he was the kind of man that would make the most sensible and controlled woman lose her shit.

"I know, Aiden, but you've got to let me do this at a pace that is not so terrifying for me."

"I will, but only if you promise not to run again," he said.

"I promise."

৯৹ ৯৹ ৯৹ ৯৹

The Raine Industries jet landed in Chicago shortly after eleven o'clock. Aiden and I stepped into a beautiful autumn morning. The brisk wind blew harshly against my face as I looked up, smiling at the sky's brilliance. The clouds, having engulfed an enormous helping of the cool Chicago air, were happy and full. They were cheerfully bouncing on the perfectly-painted baby blue backdrop. And the sun was shimmering brightly, casting its stamp of approval on our day.

I kept happily in step with Aiden as he pulled me alongside him, leading us to the car awaiting us on the tarmac. I stole a glance at him to find he was smiling at me, his brown hair slightly tousled by the wind.

As Aiden and I enjoyed the short drive to his home, we discussed our afternoon plans. I couldn't help but smile at him— his excitement was tangible. I wanted to bottle it and keep it under lock and key for those days when this part of him was hidden. The only thing that could place a damper on my day was Aiden's parents.

I didn't know how his family would react to my intruding on their weekend, so I was nervous. I wanted them to like me. I wanted this to be easier for both of us this time. Aiden had promised it would be fine, but I found his assurance to be of little to no comfort.

After thirty minutes or so, the car turned down a long tree-lined drive and stopped at a towering, formal, gated entry. The gate crawled opened, and we continued down the drive. I looked out the window and gasped. Although I'd seen an online photo of his home, it hadn't properly prepared me for this. The mansion was enormous. I couldn't help but wonder what social dramas had occurred within the walls of this massive estate.

Its opulence was intimidating and beautiful — two words I had come to associate with Aiden.

"It's quite large," I said, stating the obvious.

"Yes, that's a word for it," he replied, frowning.

"Do you not like it?" I asked.

"I didn't say that. I grew up in this house, so as you can imagine, it's quite different for me than it is for someone seeing it for the first time."

"I just can't imagine what anyone would do with so much room," I said, again glancing out the window. "Exactly how large is it?"

"Five stories, fifty or so rooms," he said.

"Or *so*?" Wow!

"It changes as they feel the need for additional wings. A couple of years ago, a beauty salon and an additional screening room were added," he said.

"And the other rooms?"

"To be honest, I tend to stick to only a few, so I'm not sure, but there is an assortment of rooms—home offices, workshops, libraries, solariums, sports courts, game rooms, entertainment dens, wine cellars, butler pantries, three kitchens, sauna retreats and staff quarters. I'll show you around when we get settled."

His list of rooms made me think of the story of his mom running him from the kitchen as a child. I was anxious to see it, and hopefully meet the person responsible for his culinary skills.

The limo stopped in the crest of the circular drive, and Aiden, still holding my hand, assisted me from the car. With entwined fingers, we walked up the steps to the vast double entrance.

He looked down at me and asked, "Are you ready?"

"I suppose," I replied, nervously.

He planted a chaste kiss on my lips and then opened the door.

Stepping inside, I gasped as I took in the palatial elegance of the Raine family home. Aiden glanced at me, a reassuring smile gracing his lips. He continued to hold my hand and led me to what I imagined was the drawing room. It was massive; there was enough space to easily host the social event of the year. My attention was immediately drawn to the flames dancing in the ornate carved fireplace in the middle of the room. Several feet to the left, was a grand staircase that spiraled toward the uppermost section of the second floor. Beautiful mosaic-tiled floors encased the stairs on either side. The room was embellished with sharply arched windows that led to a vaulted ceiling from which hung an elegant crystal chandelier.

"Aiden!" his mother exclaimed as she rushed in and quickly embraced him. Her dancing eyes froze as they rested upon my face. "Aria, I didn't know you were joining us. Hello, dear," she said.

I coaxed a smile into making an appearance. "Hi, Mrs. Raine," I replied.

"Please call me Sienna. *Mrs. Raine* is Connor's mother," she said with a brittle smile.

"If you'll call me Aria instead of *dear*, I'll call you Sienna."

Her smile faded and Aiden looked at me, obviously surprised by my ultimatum.

"Your name is as beautiful as you are," I added, in an attempt to soften my request. Despite my disdain for her, I had to admit she was a beautiful woman. Her hair, the same dark brown as Aiden's, made her appear younger than her years, undoubtedly the handiwork of a very expensive stylist. Her green eyes weren't dark like Aiden's—they were an icy green, and they were agleam with delight as she doted on her son. Her thinly plucked brows were perfectly arched. She was exquisitely dressed, the embodiment of distinction and beauty.

Sienna's eyes were fixed on me, most likely cursing me to the high heavens. When I didn't flinch from her evil glint, her gaze flashed back to her son's. "Your father is resting in the study. He'll be pleased to see you." She then turned to address a man who'd appeared. "Clark, can you get their bags. You can place Aiden's things in his room, and Ms. Cason will be in the guest room closest to the stairs on the second floor," Sienna instructed.

"Hello, Clark," Aiden said.

"Hello, Mr. Aiden," he replied, with a nod.

"You can place Aria's things in my room, too," Aiden said, refuting his mother's instructions.

"Yes, sir," he replied, and looked at Sienna for approval.

"Thank you, Clark. That will be all," she said, as she glanced between me and her son.

Shit. Way to add more fuel to the fire, Aiden. "It's fine. I can stay in the guest room," I said, flinging a warning look that Aiden ignored.

"Aria, I want you to be comfortable. You and I both know you would be most comfortable with me. Besides, my mother knows I'm an adult who does adult things, which means she is more than aware we've seen each other naked by now."

Did he just say that? As if she didn't have enough reason to dislike me. Why would he do that?

"Aiden! Don't be crass," Sienna exclaimed, reproving his openness.

He smiled at me and laughed at Sienna. "Mother, please assure Aria that her sharing a room with me is fine."

"Of course. I didn't want to assume, but now that Aiden has more than verified the state of your relationship, I'm somewhat embarrassed," she said, looking at me, the iciness of her eyes mirroring her cold demeanor.

"I'm sorry. If Aiden had told you I was coming, we could've avoided the awkwardness," I said, tossing daggers his way. Sienna was probably thinking I couldn't control myself five minutes without jumping Aiden and us fucking like rabbits. Well…that was true when it came to her son. Even still, I didn't want her thinking any less of me than she already did.

"I thought I heard voices out here." Aiden's father appeared in the doorway. "Well, hello, son. And Ms. Cason, so happy that you're here. It gives me the opportunity to congratulate you on your promotion—and to also apologize for my part in the deception regarding Aiden's identity."

"Thank you on both counts." I studied him, curious about the things I'd heard. Granted, I didn't really know him, but he didn't seem like the person Aiden had described.

"Dad, the identity thing is water under the bridge, so do a favor for your son and don't mention that anymore. You have no idea the amount of torture I endured at the hands of this gorgeous woman. I practically threw myself at her feet, beseeching her forgiveness."

"I can certainly understand that," Connor said, looking at me with approval in his eyes. "Consider it forgotten."

I smiled at him, noting his obvious resemblance to his son. Between Sienna and Connor, I couldn't tell to whom I should most attribute Aiden's beauty. Connor had distinct cheekbones and an angular jaw, though his skin was rather pale, perhaps due to his recent illness. His curls were dark brown with a touch of gray at the edges and the crown of his head. You could easily see that at one time he'd been in excellent shape. I doubt it ever rivaled Aiden's, however.

"I also wish to extend my condolences for the loss of your mother," Connor said.

"Thank you very much. It's been difficult," I replied, looking at Aiden. I would never be able to thank him for stepping in the way he did. "Aiden has been a very strong shoulder. I don't think I would be standing had it not been for his support."

"Don't underestimate yourself. You're far stronger than you realize," Aiden said.

"If there is anything we can do, you'll let us know?" Sienna asked.

"Yes, thank you." She seemed genuinely sympathetic.

"I was a child when my mother passed, and I understand how heartbreaking it is to lose someone you love, especially someone as precious as a mother," she added.

"I'm sorry, Sienna," I said. She was right—I was heartbroken over the loss of my mother, and I didn't wish that on anyone. Her statement brought the guilt to the surface—the guilt that would walk with me every day for the rest of my life. For so many years, I didn't regard my mother as the precious part of my life that she was.

"Thank you, dear...I mean Aria," she corrected with a smile. I appreciated her effort even though it was more for Aiden's benefit than mine.

"Son, let's have a drink. Nicholas and Sloan are roaming around here somewhere."

Sienna said, "They're at the tennis courts. They've been out there for a while—I would have thought Sloan would have embarrassed Nicholas enough by this point that he would have cut his losses."

"Isn't it too cold?" I asked.

"The courts are enclosed," Aiden explained.

We were in the study enjoying a drink when his siblings burst in, full of vivacious banter.

"Well, look who decided to grace us with his appearance," Sloan said, walking over to hug her brother.

"Don't start, Sloan," Aiden cautioned.

"Whatever you say, brother," she mocked. "Hi, Aria. It's wonderful to see you," she said, walking over to greet me, her eyes twinkling with an intriguing mix of blue and green. I easily sensed the sincerity in Sloan's words. I knew instantly that I liked her. It appeared she'd cut her hair since St. Barts. It was tucked behind her ears, but it looked as though it was chin-length now. It was the same dark brown as Aiden's.

"Hi, Sloan, it's great to see you, too," I replied.

Nicholas surprised me, picking me up and twirling me around. "Hello, Ms. Aria," he said, grinning.

"Put her down, Nicholas," Aiden warned.

"Geez, bro, just being friendly. Take it down a notch," he replied, smirking at his brother.

Aiden's reply was a narrowing of his eyes as his jaw hardened.

I motioned for Nicholas to release me.

"Don't let him turn you into a fuddy-duddy like him, Aria," Nicholas joked, as he placed me on my feet.

"He couldn't even if he tried. It's good to see you again, Nicholas," I said.

"It's even better to see you, darling," he replied, flashing a megawatt smile.

I would imagine he was quite the charmer. Nicholas

resembled his brother. His hair was a shade darker than Aiden's, almost black. His eyes, closer to the light green of his mother's, were framed by graceful brows. He had the same prominent jaw as his father and Aiden. I could easily see his dashing personality went hand in hand with his smile.

"Why don't we let the men catch up, Aria," Sloan said, grabbing my hand pulling me away, attempting to diffuse a situation that could have easily escalated.

She sensed my hesitation. "They're just kidding around. Don't worry about them. They do this to each other all the time. Believe it or not, they're actually quite close," Sloan assured me.

I looked back at Aiden—he and Nicholas were laughing as Connor looked on approvingly. As Sloan and I walked out, she offered to show me to the bedroom to unpack.

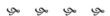

Aiden later pulled me from his bedroom to visit the Museum of Contemporary Art. It was wonderful being with him like this, away from the tension of his family. It was subtle, but it was constant tension nonetheless.

We arrived back at his home in time for dinner. The Raines were on their best behavior, and I was surprised business never entered the conversation. Well, unless you included the countless accolades to Aiden. I watched as Conner and Sienna showered

Aiden with praise — all three siblings seemed slightly uncomfortable.

After dinner, Sienna, having complained of a headache, excused herself to retire for the evening. The men returned to the study to discuss more Raine Industries business, while Sloan and I grabbed our glasses and strolled to the living room.

"I'm surprised you're still here," Sloan said.

"Why would you say that?" I asked.

"My parents typically disapprove of Aiden's relationships with anyone they haven't hand-selected. They always have. If he does involve himself with someone that's not of their choosing, they tend to…steer that person in a different direction."

I could see she was trying to choose her words carefully. I didn't know quite how to respond to her disclosure — it seemed she wanted to say more, so I held my tongue.

"Not that he's had a ton of relationships or brings many women home, but there have been one or two in the past," she added.

"Why are you telling me this?" I asked.

"I like you, and I want you to know what you're getting into, especially since my brother hasn't."

"How would you know what Aiden has or hasn't said to me about your parents?"

She took a long sip of her wine and then said, "Because if he'd told you the truth, you wouldn't have come."

Damn. Were they that much worse than I'd imagined?

"But don't worry, I want to help in any way I can. I see how Aiden brightens when you come into a room," she said, crossing her legs. "I think you're good for him."

"But your parents don't, so you thought they would make that known, and I'd run for the hills?" I asked.

"Something like that. But since you're not the typical woman that Aiden would date, I suspect they'll be handling it a little differently. Honestly, I can't say if they like you or dislike you, but the fact that you're someone of Aiden's choosing is a red flag," Sloan said.

"I don't understand."

"Their preference—well, they actually see it as more of a necessity than a preference—is for Aiden to be with a woman who knows her place, who'll be fine sitting patiently on the sidelines, leaving Aiden to assume the responsibilities they feel he should. I get the sense you're not the type that's going to sit by and just wait for him to find time for you."

"Exactly what responsibilities do they feel he should assume?" I asked.

"Oh, so you haven't noticed?"

"Aiden doesn't like to talk about it very much, and I'm somewhat the same when it comes to family matters, so I've respected that," I said.

"Raine Industries. They want him to maintain leadership…indefinitely. And they don't want anyone in his life that could be a distraction," she said.

"And you think I'd be a distraction for him?"

"You already are." She took in my expression and attempted to rephrase. "I wouldn't necessarily term it as a distraction. But that's how my parents will see it."

"I don't get it. You and Nicholas are involved with the company, and from what little Aiden has shared with me, you're both extremely capable, so why place all of this on Aiden's shoulders?"

"Aiden has always been treated as though he was the golden child. He's very intelligent and he really does have a knack for business. That, and the fact that he's been, for lack of a better word, brainwashed into thinking he has to assume the responsibility that he has."

I didn't like hearing all this. I actually couldn't see Aiden being brainwashed by anyone.

"Nicholas and I get to pick up the scraps. I'm resentful, as you can obviously tell, but I honestly hope you're able to hang in there because Aiden is different when he's with you. You really make him happy, and he deserves that. He deserves a chance at a normal life, or at least as normal as it can be for anyone with the

Raine name."

Just great. Not only was I feeling my way through, I had to fight with these lunatics to keep a man that I was quite frankly concerned had already complicated my life more than I would have preferred.

"Judging by your expression, I probably should have kept this to myself. But I think you need to know what you're up against. Like I said, I like you, and I get the sense you appreciate Aiden for who he is and not for everything that comes with who he is. And he needs someone like that. On a selfish note, I think your presence in his life will also level the playing field so that Nicholas and I will no longer be regarded as the dispensable ones. We want to contribute equally to the company."

"That's understandable. And thank you, Sloan, for sharing this with me," I said, though I was unsure whether I was really grateful or not.

"You're welcome. Hey…you know Allison will be here tomorrow. Maybe we can have a girls' outing, excluding Mother of course," she added.

"That sounds like fun." Although I liked Sloan, Allison had found a place in my heart almost the instant I'd met her, and her presence would certainly make this trip much brighter.

Sloan and I were discussing the launch of *The Writer* when her phone rang and she excused herself. I had a feeling she'd be a while, based on her expressions as she listened to the caller. I sat quietly in the room watching the flames dance in the fireplace as I sipped my wine and considered what I was in for. I was committed to being with Aiden, which meant I had to accept everything that being with him implied.

ᔓ   ᔓ   ᔓ   ᔓ

Having grown bored, I went in search of Aiden. I was walking by the study — I had no intention of eavesdropping, but the words rang out.

"You're me now…have you accepted that?" Connor asked.

"You've given me no choice," Aiden replied, bitterly.

"Aiden, when will you stop with this resistance?"

"One son resists, but you force it on him. The other is eager to assume the role, but you spit on him," Nicholas said.

"I don't know why you bother, Nicholas," Connor stated.

"Because I'm your son. Obviously not your favorite, but I *am* the one who really wants this. I don't treat it like a burden as Aiden does," Nicholas replied.

I could hear the resentment in his voice.

"And you feel that entitles you to what, exactly?" Connor asked.

"A position of authority…a chance."

"Nicholas, I know you think I favor your brother to you. That simply isn't the case. I'm doing what's best for the viability of Raine Industries, and son, you don't have the foresight or the aptitude to be at the helm of this company."

"Why the hell do you think Aiden does? Because you've groomed him for years while Sloan and I sat on the wayside."

Nicholas was clearly furious — nothing like the happy-go-lucky guy who'd flirted with me before.

"Nicholas, calm down," Aiden said.

"This is bullshit, Aiden, and you know it as well as I do," Nicholas replied.

"I built an empire from the ground up, but it means nothing if I can't pass this on to someone who can do it justice. Who can carry on the family name and the family tradition. Both of you — hell, this entire family — has known for years that Aiden is that someone," Connor said. He'd started to raise his voice.

"Dad, Nicholas is right. I've seen him lately, and he's become quite the businessman," Aiden said. "I'm very impressed, and if you'd take the time to truly review his contributions, you would be also. You shouldn't so readily dismiss his abilities."

"I've received glowing reports on both Nicholas and Sloan from you, Aiden, but you…you have responsibilities to the family, to the business. I've been more than understanding of the goofing off with these other businesses of yours, but I need you here. I need you to stop playing around."

"Playing around? Those companies are important to me. But you wouldn't know it because I've *delegated* all of my playing around, as you put it, so that I could take the reins of this company. This was to be temporary, but you insist on making it permanent."

"You speak as if this is news to you, son. You knew this was coming, yet now you reject it. I can't help but think you're resistant because of the other distractions in your life."

"Just say it. You're referring to Aria. She's off-limits in this discussion," Aiden warned.

"Just as I suspected," Connor replied.

"I'm not your only offspring. Nicholas is anxious to take over, and hell, he'd date and possibly marry someone of whom you would approve. So would Sloan, for that matter."

"Son, you're getting off track here. That's not what I'm saying. I don't need to approve of who you date, but I would prefer it be someone who doesn't disrupt your obligations to this family."

I didn't want to hear anymore. Walking upstairs, I headed toward Aiden's room to ready myself for bed. I wanted to go home.

ço   ço   ço   ço

A light kiss on my cheek awakened me. I opened my eyes to

the face of my handsome king. Sitting up in bed, I noticed I'd fallen asleep fully dressed.

"You did it," Aiden said, smiling at me.

"Did what?" I asked.

"Survived a night at my family home," he replied.

I wasn't so sure I had. I was exposed to more than I'd expected. I'd carefully observed Aiden's interactions with his family, and their affection for each other was apparent, but so was the careful hierarchy. Months ago, when he'd attempted to explain his reasons for deceiving me, he'd said I didn't understand the burden of the Raine name. At the time, I'd had no empathy. I'd felt his issues with his privileged life were inconsequential. But after today, I was sympathetic to his ordeal. I was damn close to understanding how he must have looked forward to escaping his identity.

"I cringed when Dad brought up the *Aiden Wyatt* thing. You know that, right?"

"I figured as much, but it's okay, Aiden. I'm past that. *We're* past that."

"You really mean that, don't you?"

"Yes, I do. Why do you sound so surprised?" I asked.

"Because I know what it cost you. I know what wounds it opened."

"Yes, it did. It was horrible for me. It took me to a place I couldn't share with anyone, not even April, which was odd because I used to tell her everything." I was starting to see that I didn't have to place everything into one person. April would always be a great friend, but I could now see that we had both been crutches for each other. I wanted a friendship based on the simple desire to be friends, not one in which we were place holders until something or someone came along to make one of us not need the other as much.

"How did you forgive me? How did you get past it?" he asked.

"I realized that what you *did* is not who you *are*," I replied.

Aiden took me into his arms, holding me. I sighed and rested my head against his chest. This felt good. It felt right.

"I don't think your parents want me here," I said.

"I told you, don't worry about them."

"That's easy for you to say. They actually *like* you," I said.

"I know you don't think so, but they do like you, Aria. I wouldn't have brought you here otherwise. They just want what they want, but once they see they aren't getting it, they'll come around."

"Will it always be so hard? Will we have to always fight everyone to be together?" I asked.

"What? You don't think I'm worth the fight?" he asked.

"Worth the fuck, without a doubt. But the fight? Eh, I don't know," I replied.

"You and that mouth. It's lucky for you it's good for much more than foul language and smart comments, or you'd be in trouble."

"Maybe I like being in trouble. Maybe I want to be punished," I said.

"Maybe you should be punished," he replied, sitting up. He grabbed me and tossed me face down on the bed. "Don't move."

Looking over my shoulder at him, I said, "Hey, I was only kidding."

"Well, I wasn't."

"Are you really going to punish me?" I asked.

"Do you really question if I'm worth the fight?"

I refused to reply.

"Just as I thought. After a little reminder, you'll never question if I'm worth the fight."

Aiden reached over to pull at my pants, lifting me up to access the button and zipper. He had me out of my jeans in one swift tug. He positioned me on my knees and before I had a chance to take in what was happening, he smacked me hard on the butt.

He *was* worth the fight, and he knew it as well as I did, but no way would I tell him that and further contribute to his monstrous ego. Besides, why deny myself a punishment that resulted in a playful and delicious night of indescribable sex with Aiden Raine?

❧Chapter Nineteen❧

The following morning, I awoke snuggled next to the man who'd taken extreme pleasure in rendering his own special version of punishment. My penance was delivered in the form of an extremely erotic spanking, one so intense that my insides tightened just thinking about it. And lying here now, hours later, nestled in the strength of Aiden's arms, I could still hear the grunts that met each blow and the sweet sting of his palm as it repeatedly made contact with my ass.

Our sexual endeavors consistently surpassed my every expectation. They were mind-blowing — *he* was mind-blowing, but I'd discovered there was so much more to Aiden. More than his talents in the bedroom, more than what met the eye, more than what was expected. He'd said he hoped I would stick around to get to know more about him, and despite some of the unpleasant parts, I was glad I had. He needn't worry. I wasn't going anywhere.

A happy sigh enclosed us as his arms tightened around me.

"Good morning, princess," he said, touching his cheek to my neck.

"Good morning, Mr. Worth The Fight," I said, grinning.

I felt his smile on my skin.

"See, you can be taught," he said.

"My backside tends to agree with you, sir."

"You're okay, right?" he asked, his voice full of concern.

Turning over to face him, I said, "Yes, I'm better than okay. I was making one of those smart comments I've become famous for."

He frowned. "You know I don't like when you joke around about that shit, Aria."

"I'm sorry. I don't know why you get so touchy about it." Geez, he sure wasn't worried about it *during* the act.

"Because I don't want to do anything you're not okay with, and I especially don't want to hurt you. When you make comments like that, it puts me on edge."

"When you spank me, it puts *me* on edge… in a good way."

He planted a small kiss on my cheek. "Let's get showered and dressed. We're expected downstairs for breakfast."

Sitting up in bed, I moaned at the thought of spending another day with his family.

"I know, I know. But look on the bright side, it's only one more day," he said, kissing my hair. "I'm glad you're here with me. It makes it almost bearable."

"Can I ask you something?"

"Anything," he said.

"Why does your family treat you so strangely?"

He laughed. "What do you mean?"

"I don't know. It's weird. It's as if you're the second coming or something."

He sighed and I could see the tension my statement caused. "I've told you. They expect a lot of me. They always have."

"Yes, but why? It's not as if you don't have siblings, two of whom would gladly ascend to the throne."

"What?" he asked, his brows scrunched. "Why do you say that?"

"Sloan and I had a talk yesterday, and she sort of clued me in on some things."

"Sloan needs to keep her damn mouth shut," he replied, as he walked past me.

What the hell was that? I followed him to the bathroom, entering just as he stepped into the shower. Considering his abrupt change in mood, I didn't know if I should get in with him or just wait until he was done.

I contemplated my dilemma as I surveyed him through the glass. From head to toe, Aiden was visual overload. It wasn't long before an uncontrollable pull overtook my reservations, and I stepped into the shower behind him.

As I positioned myself below the second showerhead, Aiden turned toward me, his gaze gliding over my nakedness. When his eyes connected with mine, they'd shifted to their darkened shade of green, coveting me and revealing the salacious thoughts behind them. Raking a hand through his wet hair, he stepped closer and pressed my body flush against the marble wall. Then his mouth was on mine, assaulting my senses with a deep probing kiss as his hand cupped my sex. He positioned his leg between my thighs and pushed two fingers inside me.

I broke our kiss, my mouth still partially open as I breathed through the rhythmic strokes to my core. "Ahh. More. Give me more," I panted.

He touched a sensitive spot and I shuttered — my body falling prey to the delicious wickedness of his skill. Stepping back, he watched as I started to lose control.

The things this man did to my body should have been illegal. I closed my eyes, my head pressed against the wall as I focused on the in and out. His touch was electric, like heated bolts of lust penetrating my skin.

"Look at me," he demanded.

My lids slowly opened to meet the darkness of his emerald eyes. They were molten pools of lust, and I watched with fascination as his pupils dilated more with each passing second. His irritation had morphed into a desire that held me at his mercy — right where he wanted me — but I didn't care. The only thing that mattered was his fingers violently fucking my pussy, and the sensations that flowed through me. My body tensed, and within seconds I was coming—panting and moaning as I stared into his eyes.

Aiden dropped to his knees, placing my leg over his shoulder and giving my pussy his full attention—licking and sucking, going at it like a starved man. At this rate, we'd be exceptionally late joining his family for breakfast, but no way in hell would I ask him to stop.

ᔓ   ᔓ   ᔓ   ᔓ

"How many other women have slept in your bed?"

"Why would you ask me something like that?" he replied, not looking at me.

I could hear the irritation in his voice, but I still wanted to know. "Are you going to answer?"

"No," he replied.

"Why?"

"You shouldn't concern yourself with things like that," he said, as he stepped into the closet.

I don't know why I asked him that ridiculous question. *Sloan…damn you.* I wish she'd kept all of her information to herself. It just raised more questions, and so far, I was batting zero when it came to getting answers.

Aiden pulled on a pair of jeans, so I figured I'd follow his lead, dressing in jeans and a white blouse. While he checked some messages on his phone, I went to the bathroom to do my makeup and hair. I considered wearing it loose around my shoulders, but I could see this wasn't going to be a good hair day so I lifted it into a ponytail high on my head, teased it to give it some volume and a messy texture and then pulled a few rogue pieces out around my face.

Aiden was on the phone when I walked into the bedroom. He held up a finger, asking for my patience, so I stepped into the hallway to look around as I waited. Each level of the five-story mansion offered delightful details that spoke to the Raines' massive wealth. I wandered down to the second floor to search for the room Sienna had intended for me. Most of the rooms on the floor were bedrooms, each with a theme for every taste, and the one she'd chosen for me was absolutely beautiful, decorated in a vibrant floral motif. It could have been featured in any luxury home magazine. Hell, it probably had.

Aiden found me wandering about and led me downstairs for breakfast. I felt self-conscious, suddenly worried everyone had heard us last night. Or this morning.

"What's wrong?" Aiden asked.

"Nothing."

"Then why do you look like that?" he asked.

"Like what?"

"Like something *is* wrong," he replied.

"It's silly, actually. I feel as though everyone, especially your mom, heard us last night. I was quite loud."

He grinned.

"It's not funny," I said, slapping his arm.

"I told you to keep quiet, but I guess you couldn't help yourself. That's what happens when you get good cock."

"Ugh. You ass!" I said, laughing.

Walking into the dining room, we encountered the Raine matriarch. "Good morning, you two," Sienna said.

"Good morning," we replied in unison.

"How did you sleep, Aria?" she asked.

Not at all. Your son fucked me all night. "I slept very well. Thank you." Did she know? Had she really heard us? I looked up to see Aiden grinning, and I wanted to die.

"What's so funny, Aiden?" Sienna asked.

"Just thinking about something I heard last night, Mother."

He was really enjoying this, much more than he should, so I decided to ignore him. I was excited to see Allison had shown up. She rushed over to embrace me and her brother. My excitement was mingled with a tinge of upset when she mentioned the Lanes were expected later — they were flying in for tomorrow's charity event.

"Where's everyone?" Aiden asked, as he helped his mother with her chair.

"Something on the news caught their attention. They should be here any second," she replied.

As if on cue, the remaining members of the Raine family strolled into the room. They were chatting amongst themselves about one of their company's investments. As we started to take our seats, Aiden joined their conversation. This was obviously a huge deal because it monopolized most of the breakfast conversation. Not that I was complaining, because it meant less interaction with Sienna.

After breakfast, I went to the restroom to wash up and then returned to see Michelle and Allen Lane had arrived. I didn't see Nadia, so hopefully she wouldn't be coming. We exchanged pleasantries and when the subject of the charity event came up, Aiden pulled me aside.

"How about we go for a tour of the grounds," he suggested.

"Sure, let me grab my jacket and phone first." I'd generally always kept my phone with me, but even more so now, in case my sisters needed me. I walked upstairs and opened the door to Aiden's bedroom, and the darkness of the room startled me. Why would the black-out curtains be closed this time of day? As I reached for the light switch, someone spoke.

"I was hoping you'd gotten my message."

Flipping the lights on, I found Nadia lying naked in Aiden's bed. "What the hell?"

"What are *you* doing here?" she asked.

"I think that's a question I should be asking you," I said, stalking towards her.

"Aria, change of plans. How about a ride before—" Aiden entered the room and stopped mid-sentence upon seeing Nadia lying on his bed. "What the hell is going on?" he demanded.

Nadia directed her attention to Aiden, her eyes gleaming with salacity as they roamed over him. I watched Aiden's reaction to her. His frustration with the shameless redhead was obvious. Walking past me, he tossed her the robe that was lying near the foot of the bed. "Cover yourself," he ordered.

When Nadia reached for the robe, Aiden turned to me. "Aria, can you give us a moment?" he asked.

Was he serious? Hell no, I could not give them a moment. I gawked at him...enraged by his request. "I can give you the entire fucking day. I'm going home," I said, walking past him and grabbing my purse. I knew he was upset, but I didn't give a damn, because so was I.

"Aria—"

"Aiden, don't," I said.

He grabbed my arm and I tried to shrug him off, but he held tightly.

"Let go," I demanded.

"Why? So you can run? You're not going anywhere." He

ushered me outside the door and closed it behind us.

"Please let go of my arm."

"Will you stay if I do?" he asked.

"Hell no. All things considered, whatever you need to say to her can be said in front of me."

"I know that, Aria. It's just that she and her family have been very close with mine for years. I'm sure she's humiliated at this point, and I was hoping to avoid embarrassing her further. I thought it would be easier if she didn't have an audience."

"Oh, so you're concerned about making it easier for her? Are you fucking kidding me?" This was more than his being tactful. I'd been too intimate with him not to be able to tell something more was going on here.

"It's not like that, Aria."

"Then why don't you tell me how it is?" Something didn't add up. Why would she think it was a good idea to lie naked and wait for Aiden in his bed?

"How can I, if you're planning to leave?" he asked.

I sighed, hating that he had a point.

"Will you stay?" he asked.

He saw the stubbornness in my eyes. I was not backing down.

"If talking to her together is the only way to remedy this, I'll do it. Just don't leave."

"Fine, I'll stay," I replied, letting him hear my reluctance.

Aiden breathed a sigh of relief. "Why do you fight me on everything?" he asked, leaning over to kiss me softly on the lips. He grasped my hand and opened his bedroom door.

I was surprised to see Nadia at least had the decency to put on the robe. She was sitting cross-legged on the edge of the bed. For someone in such a precarious situation, she appeared overly-confident, but when her gaze dropped to our intertwined fingers, her cheeks reddened.

"Nadia, I'm not sure what you expected to happen, but I thought I made it clear you and I are just friends," Aiden said.

"It's fine, Aiden," she said. "No need to hash out the dynamics of our relationship in front of her."

My fingers tightened around his. I knew he sensed I was about to let her have it.

"Nadia, you know how important Aria is to me. I've made no secret of that. And I'm pretty sure you know she's here as my guest, and your display was very disrespectful to her. I'm not asking that the two of you get along, but you will respect her. Are we clear?"

"I'm sorry, Aiden. And, of course, you too, Aria. I wasn't aware you two had transitioned to more than business associates," she said. "Well, as fun as this has been, I think I'll run. I do hope I get the chance to speak with you in private, Aiden. Unlike you, I think this is between the two of us." She stood, tossed a hateful look at me, and walked past us.

I yanked my hand from Aiden's. "What. The. Fuck? Are you going to let her just waltz out of here saying shit like that?"

"Aria, I can't control what she says any more than you can," he replied, angrily shoving a hand through his hair.

"And it's so fucked up that she's even here," I said.

"I can't very well tell her not to come to a home that's not mine."

"And I don't think this was some random act of lust on her part," I continued.

"What do you mean?" Aiden asked, walking over to close the door.

"You know what I mean. I'm asking if you had sex with her."

"Aria, I don't want to discuss Nadia," he said.

"Did you fuck her?" I couldn't believe how calm I sounded.

"Aria, don't be absurd."

He was being suspiciously evasive. "Answer my question."

He closed the distance between us and said, "It's not like that, Aria."

"Then how is it?" I asked, moving away from him.

"Nadia and I were a couple at one time, but that was years ago. So, of course we've been intimate."

"You know damned well I'm not referring to your past with her. Did you fuck her recently, Aiden? This is my last time asking." I knew the answer even before he said it, and my stomach was in knots as I looked at him.

"The night of the gala," he said, looking at me, absorbing my expression and bracing himself for my reaction.

I felt as though someone had punched me in the stomach. I turned away from him — I didn't want to see his face. She'd touched him, and he'd wanted it.

"Aria, let me explain," he said, his hands on my shoulders.

I recoiled from his grasp. "Get away from me."

"I couldn't get you out of my head, and I was furious that you were with that fucking Kellan guy."

The thought of Aiden touching her naked body, knowing she'd enjoyed it…it sickened me. I sat on the bed and immediately stood back up, remembering that only a few moments ago, Nadia was in the exact same spot…naked.

"I wanted *you*, Aria," he said.

"So, you fucked her instead. Yeah, that makes perfect sense." The images of him inside her made me want to vomit.

"I wanted it to be you, every touch…I wished it was you."

"Oh, so you *used* her, then? Should I feel some sense of comfort in that?"

"Aria, stop it, okay. Nadia's a big girl, she knew what she was doing, and despite her comment about you and me being only business associates, she damned well knew how I felt about you."

"Is that supposed to make me feel better?"

"Aria, look…the fact of the matter is, you pushed me away. I made repeated attempts to make things right with you, but you wanted nothing to do with me. I always felt we'd find our way back, but how was I to know *when* that would happen? Was I supposed to stop living?"

"I did."

It was as if I'd slapped him solidly across the face. His expression twisted, mimicking the torture I was feeling.

"Aria, do you have any idea how badly I feel knowing I let that happen?" he asked, his tone pained.

"Is this why you wanted to speak with her alone? You were worried she would let your recent jaunt slip? Although I'm sure it would have given her great pleasure to share that tidbit with me, considering how she enjoys raving about your skills in bed," I spit out.

"What are you talking about?" he asked.

"The night of the gala, when she'd made a point of welcoming me to the *I've Fucked Aiden Club.*"

"Aria, I'm sorry. I'll speak with Nadia. I'll make sure she doesn't approach you with anything like this again," he said.

"Didn't you just say you couldn't control what she says? Besides, I'll fight my own battles, Aiden. I'll handle Nadia, my way."

"Aria, there's no battle here. I'm with you, and I don't intend on that changing," he said, adamantly. He was worried I was going to run. I could see it in his eyes.

He was right—he didn't have to explain or justify anything to me. I had pushed him away…repeatedly. And we had found our way back to each other, and I was happier about that than I thought possible, at least until we'd come to Chicago, where one thing after another kept tearing away at that happiness. Would I have to keep fighting everyone and every situation to be with this man?

"The thing with Nadia has nothing to do with us now, and it doesn't touch anything I feel for you. You know that. You *feel* that. Let's not let this ruin our weekend."

"The thought of her hands anywhere on your body is utterly repulsive." I was so pissed at him, and I needed to go—I wanted to run. But I couldn't be without him, so that meant we'd have to deal with this and everything else as it came.

"I know. I feel the same about you. I don't want anyone to look at you, let alone touch you."

Aiden walked over to the phone and pressed a button on the base. "Can you have the staff change the bedding before we retire for the evening?" he said, speaking into the receiver.

He must have read my mind because there was no way I would even touch that bed after that naked bitch had been sprawled across it.

"Come here," he said, as he placed the phone receiver in its cradle.

I walked over to him, and he pulled me into an embrace. "Don't ever doubt my feelings for you. Trust me when I say my thoughts are only of you. There's no one else. If my mind isn't on work, it's on you," he said, cradling my face. "Do you believe me?"

"Yes," I whispered, lost in the yearning in his emerald eyes. I did believe him, and as much as it hurt, I could see why it had happened. He'd done with Nadia the exact thing I'd *tried* to do with Kellan. He'd wanted a small measure of relief from the longing—from the pain.

He softly touched my lips with his, pulling my top lip into his mouth, gently sucking before sealing his mouth over mine. He pulled me closer as his tongue sought its entrance, and our kiss deepened as he lavished my mouth with slow, deep licks. His kiss was soft and gentle and full of the love I knew he had only for me. I was pulled back in, just like that, and all thoughts of Nadia evaporated.

❧ ❧ ❧ ❧

Aiden and I headed back downstairs to find the family had scattered.

"I'm not sure where everyone has gotten off to, but I'd followed you upstairs to suggest we go for a ride."

"You mean cycling?" I asked.

"Horseback," he replied, gauging my reaction.

"Err — I don't think so," I said.

"Why not?" he probed.

I'd only ridden a couple of times, and I wasn't very good at relating to horses. "I don't have riding clothes." That was just as good of an excuse as any.

"We have extra in the tack house," he said.

"I'm sure you don't have my size."

"You and Sloan are similar in size. If all else fails, you can wear hers."

I frowned. "You have an answer for everything."

"Don't I always? Any other opposition?" he asked.

"Um — I'm afraid not," I replied.

"Good. Let's go," he said, grasping my hand and tugging me alongside him.

We stepped outside to the crisp autumn day. My gaze crawled over the grounds, attempting to take in everything. The property was massive and, of course, exquisitely landscaped. I could only imagine how beautiful it would be in the spring.

Aiden suggested we take the scenic route to the stables, but quite frankly, every inch of the grounds possessed a picturesque allure. Our path took us through one of his mother's conservatories. Some of the flowers appeared especially delicate, as if they would be forbidden to touch. I walked closer to one that was familiar, admiring the vivid orange color. Looking up from the flowers, I saw Aiden contently watching me.

"I'm glad you're here. I'm somewhat surprised you agreed to come."

And after what I'd experienced so far, I could see why. Sloan was right — Aiden did need me in his life. These people were fucking crazy. I wanted to run for the hills, but I could tough it out for one more day. "Why is that? We've been making progress. Don't you think?"

"I do," he said.

"But...?" I could see there was more.

"We need to clarify a couple of things," he said.

"Such as?" I asked.

"When we agreed to the sex with no emotions a couple of months ago, you'd made it clear you wanted it to remain private — a secret if you will."

We'd recently discussed this. Why was he bringing it up again? "What are you saying?"

"I'm saying that things have changed since we first agreed to keep our relationship hidden."

"Yes, but the reasons for keeping it hidden haven't," I replied.

"I don't care what anyone thinks or says, Aria. I'm not doing the behind-closed-doors thing. The situation with Nadia could have been avoided had she known. And that guy, he needs to know. Either you make it clear to him or I will."

"I highly doubt anything would have diverted Nadia's plans, and as for *that guy*, I'll make it as clear to him as you made it to Nadia," I said.

"Aria, don't compare—"

"I'm serious, Aiden. Kellan's become a good friend. I'm not going to just toss him aside. He's really a great guy."

"Yeah, a great guy who wants to fuck you."

"It's not like that."

"It's exactly like that, Aria. Have you ever looked at you? What guy wouldn't want to fuck you? Hell, even my dad salivates when you walk into a room, and I've never seen him do that." He grasped my hand, leading us out of the conservatory.

"Just so you know, Kellan already knows about us. But as I said, he's a friend, and I'm not going to push him out of my life."

Aiden didn't say anything, but I knew he didn't like it, and I knew this wasn't the end of the matter, but I steered the conversation away for now. "Okay, what's the next area that requires clarification?"

"I need to know how you feel, Aria."

"If my being here hasn't made that clear, then I don't know

what else to say."

"Your feelings aren't as clear as they could be."

"Why is that? Because I haven't said it aloud?" I asked.

"That's typically how feelings are communicated. Are you afraid?"

I squeezed his hand. "Other than my father, you're the only man I've ever had such raw emotions for. And yes, that's a scary thing for me, Aiden, to even open that door. I actually wanted to say it when you made love to me, and it wasn't because I was caught up in the moment. I wanted to say it because it was how I felt."

"*Felt?*" he asked.

I swallowed my nerves. "It's how I still feel, but I've shied away from saying it or even thinking it because of the implications. But I love you, Aiden." I couldn't believe I'd said it—I'd finally voiced what my heart was feeling.

He was quiet for a few moments and then a slow smile appeared on his perfect lips. "Finally," he said, picking me up and twirling me around.

"Say it again," he urged.

"No. Once is enough," I replied, laughing.

"There's a lake out near the stables. Say it again, or I'll take you there and toss you in," he threatened.

I laughed. "You'll do no such thing."

"Say it," he said, still spinning me.

"You're making me dizzy," I squealed.

"Say it and I'll stop."

"I love you—you big jerk."

"Louder."

"I love you!" I yelled. He stopped twirling me, and I looked down to see a triumphant smile on his face. Easing me down his body until our lips met, he gifted me with a sweet kiss and then gazed into my eyes for long seconds before finally placing me on the ground.

"Now everyone is going to think I'm crazy," I said, looking around to see if anyone was in earshot.

"No one heard you, but I wouldn't care if they did," he replied.

That was a good thing, because someone was standing on the third-floor balcony watching us. "Who is that?" I asked, nodding toward the house.

Aiden squinted as he looked at the figure. "It's my mother," he said.

I wondered how long she'd been there. When she saw us looking at her, she turned and walked inside.

"What's that all about?" I asked.

"I'm not sure," he replied.

I was sure we'd soon find out.

Aiden continued with the tour as we walked towards the stables. Everything was no less than I expected — absolutely beautiful. There were several flower and vegetable gardens, conservatories, and a gardener's cottage. Aiden pointed out one of Sienna's award winning flower gardens, explaining how much she loved to work in them, although her time to do so was limited due to her charity obligations. I recalled her telling me that in Boston. Even now that I'd seen the garden, I still found it difficult picturing her being one with nature.

It was starting to get cold so we chose to postpone the horseback riding for a future visit. I was secretly relieved because I wasn't particularly looking forward to embarrassing myself.

We entered the house all smiles, our fingers interlaced. Everyone, including the Lanes, was sitting around the fire having what appeared to be a very boring conversation. They looked up as we entered, and Connor asked to speak with Aiden in private. The playful energy Aiden had exuded all morning instantly vanished. I felt it as soon as it happened — he was no longer the Aiden *Wyatt* to whom I'd confessed my love — he'd shifted into Aiden *Raine*. He released my hand and followed his father to the study. I stood in the middle of the room as everyone looked at me. I wanted this day to be over, and it had practically just started.

❧Chapter Twenty❧

Somehow, I'd managed to survive another night at the Raine house. It was a very beautiful home, but I'd been anxious to leave almost as soon as I'd entered it. And thankfully, Aiden and I would be returning to Boston later in the afternoon.

"You don't seem particularly enthused about the polo match," I said, as I watched Aiden dress for the Raine Industries annual equestrian event. The way he looked in those riding pants had to be a sin. They molded perfectly to him, showcasing his muscular thighs and his taut backside.

"It's a family obligation," he replied, solemnly.

Although I suspected he wanted to come off as impassive, I sensed his reluctance. "That doesn't really confirm or deny my statement."

His beautiful lips curved into a smile.

"There it is...the smile that lets me see the real you."

He lifted his brows. "Real me?"

"You hide so much of yourself from the world. You're particularly inhibited when you're in the presence of your family."

"Is that what you think? Maybe I present different aspects to different people. Everyone does that," he replied.

"I suppose," I said, considering his response. "You know, the only time I've seen you less subdued is when you're playing the piano. I've also noticed you're less reserved when you're with Allison, and even then, it comes and goes. Quite frankly, you never seem really happy unless you're alone with me."

He pulled on his riding boots and said, "Well, if that's true, it's only when you're not being difficult."

"What you really mean is doing what you want me to do."

"No, I mean cooperating," he said. "My powers of observation are extremely acute, and I've noticed you're partial to cooperating with me."

"Oh, am I?"

"Yes," he said, as he coolly raked his eyes over me. "Come here."

I did love cooperating with him, because it usually meant extreme pleasure for me. "Is there something you want?" I asked, as I sauntered over to him.

"You know what I want."

"I'm afraid I'm at a loss," I said. "You'll have to tell me just so I know we're on the same page."

Placing his hands at my waist, he pulled me closer and touched a soft kiss to my neck. "I want your pussy," he said, his voice a velvet whisper.

"Mmm. Do you?" I asked.

"Very much so."

"Well, it's yours for the taking…however, whenever."

"See this smile?" he asked, pulling his lips into a silly grin. "This is the smile of a man with a very cooperative woman."

We both laughed, and then he kissed me chastely on the lips.

"Unfortunately, we don't have adequate time to give that perfect cunt of yours the fucking it deserves," he said, his large hands traveling to my ass, grasping it firmly. "But tonight, be ready."

"Why tease me like that?"

"As if you never tease me," he countered.

"I don't," I replied.

"Oh, so it's nothing out of the ordinary for you to bend over in front of people wearing nothing but a towel?"

"I don't know a thing about bending over in front of *people*, but I'm sure if I bent over in front of *you* like that, it was because I must have dropped something on the floor," I said, feigning innocence.

"Yeah, okay. If you want to play that game, I'll join in."

"Join in how? I see the wheels turning. What are you planning?"

"I'm not *planning* anything," he said. "I'm just making it known that I may do things that sexually stimulate you…unintentionally, of course. You know, somewhat similar to how you unintentionally exposed yourself when you bent over in front of me to pick up something. I'm sure you didn't give any thought to the fact that I would see little Miss Virginia when you did so."

"So, that's your plan? More torture?" I asked.

"Torture?" he repeated.

"Yes. Torture. You do that quite well, and you know it," I said. "So if you plan on increasing your level of torment, I can guarantee this is going to be painful for one of us. And just so you know, women don't get blue balls."

"Is that your way of saying you're going to tease me and then not deliver?" he asked. "If so, you've done it before and I survived."

"No, I'm not saying that at all. I'm just following your lead and making it clear that I may do things—unintentionally of course—that could arouse you."

"How I love your competitive spirit, princess," he said, kissing the tip of my nose. "But just so *you* know, the next time you get my cock, it will only be after a very significant amount of begging."

"Begging will be involved, but I won't be the one pleading, baby," I said.

"Okay, princess. I can't wait to see how this plays out," he said, stepping from our embrace.

Fuck. What had I done? How the hell was I going to win this game? I was already turned on by his words a few moments ago…and that was just his *casual* conversation. No way would I be able to hold out if he unleashed the full heat of a seduction. Obviously, I'd need to come up with a few tricks of my own to ensure he caved before me. I'd just started a sex war with Mr. Fuck Me, but I wasn't prepared to lose.

After tucking in his shirt, Aiden crossed the room and opened the door. Glancing over his shoulder, he saw I hadn't moved. "Are you coming?" he asked, a hint of a smile emerging. "Or are you contemplating a way to back out of this little war? If you ask nicely, and if you suck my cock really well after the match today, I just may let you off the hook."

"Oh, I'm coming," I said, grabbing my purse. "And if you must know, I was thinking about which B.O.B. would best suit me tonight. You know how wet I get, so I need one that can take care of my pussy the way it deserves."

"Is that how you're going to play this?" he asked, extending his hand. Ignoring it, I brushed past him. He laughed aloud. I couldn't help but smile, but he didn't see it.

"Let the games begin, gorgeous," he said, as he followed me down the stairs.

❧ ❧ ❧ ❧

We landed in Boston late Sunday evening and went directly to my place. I was confused by the mass gathered near the entrance of my building. Stepping closer, we discovered they were reporters. As Aiden and I maneuvered the crowd of flashing cameras, questions were hurled in rapid succession.

"Ms. Cason, is it true you flew to Chicago to meet the family before the engagement is announced?" asked a voice from the crowd.

"Mr. Raine, how long have you and Ms. Cason been a couple?"

"Ms. Cason, did your relationship with Mr. Raine begin before or after your promotion to CEO?"

Aiden grabbed my hand and pulled me through the mob. He didn't say anything, but I could see he was angry. As soon as we stepped in the elevator, he was on the phone. "I pay you to handle this type of shit. If you value your job, ensure Ms. Cason never has to deal with anything like this again." He pressed the phone off.

"I'm sorry. You shouldn't have come home to that," he said.

"It's not your fault," I replied.

"Yes, but our intimate display at the match earlier didn't help matters. I'm sure it's what spurred this."

"Well, no more secrets—the entire world knows now," I said. This was what I'd worried about. I suppose I didn't mind the world knowing we were a couple, but I didn't anyone to cast doubts on my abilities to succeed as my own person. And even more, I didn't want strangers zeroing in on parts of my life that were meant just for me.

Opening the door to the condo, we saw Lia and Bianca sprawled out on the floor with Jade and Addison—a couple of friends from Boston Latin. I was still getting used to the idea of having teenagers around. I didn't think I'd ever *really* get used to it, though. I loved being closer to my sisters, but I was already looking forward to them heading off to college next fall—I valued my privacy and the only time I really had any now was within the walls of my bedroom.

"Hi guys," I said.

"Welcome back," said Bianca.

"I could say the same to you. How was the ski trip? Tell me everything," I said.

"Addison and Jade, this is my sister's boyfriend, Aiden," Lia said, introducing her friends.

"Hi," they chimed, gawking at Aiden.

"Addison, Jade—nice to meet you," he said, as he removed his jacket. Aiden and I settled in, and the girls dived into details of their trip. It was good to see them happy. I smiled as I thought of how pleased Mom would have been to see us together like this.

After a while, Aiden and I left the girls to themselves and

disappeared into the bedroom for the remainder of the night. True to his word, Aiden didn't touch me, but his sexual innuendos really did a number on my libido.

∾ ∾ ∾ ∾

Everyone filed out of the conference room after we laid out plans for *The Writer*, leaving Aiden and me alone. He reached for the button that locked the door and then slid his chair closer to mine.

"How do you think they took the news?" he asked.

"I think it was well received. Don't you?"

"I'm not sure about Adam. I've questioned his loyalty since Blake's departure," Aiden said.

"I think you worry too much. Adam is on board with this."

"Stand up for me, princess," Aiden said, changing the subject.

"You aren't supposed to refer to me by that name at work, remember?"

"Stand up for me, Ms. Cason," he corrected.

"That's better," I replied, sliding my chair back and moving in front of him.

As the silence surrounded us, Aiden eased my skirt up my thighs and sat me on the table. And then, moving my panties to the side, he slid his finger inside me.

I bit my lip as I stared into his gorgeous eyes, and moaned

aloud when he added another finger.

"I do so love the sound of this wet pussy, Ms. Cason," he said, his eyes focused on mine.

I concentrated on the rhythmic entry and exit of his long, talented fingers. I was soon lost in the invasive sensation that was taking me closer and closer to a climax. My breathing accelerated as I neared my forbidden release, and that's when he stilled.

I clenched my fists as he eased his fingers out of me. This asshole!

With his gaze hot on my face, his thumb slid between the wet slit, moving up and down and then adding the slightest bit of pressure to my clit. He removed his thumb and then surveyed the ocean of wetness he'd caused. I was certain his mouth was next, but was disappointed when he slid my panties back in place, lifted me from the table and lowered my skirt.

I glared at the beautiful man sitting in front of me. He was trying to prove a point. Did he want me to ask for it? Damn if that would ever happen. I severed our connection and with absolute professional etiquette, I excused myself—headed to my office to finish what he'd started.

Have you seen this?

It was a text from Aiden. Clicking the link in the message, I was directed to an article about Aiden and me. As I was reading it, Raina's voice came over the intercom announcing a call for Aiden. I was confused why she'd tell me that, but a moment later he stormed into my office with fire in his eyes.

"There's a call for you," I said, eyeing him.

He picked up the phone. "Yes. I see. The point is I shouldn't have to tell *you* about an editorial in the paper. The journalist made a very strong point, and it's your responsibility to counter that. I hired you for that. If you can't do it, I'll get a PR firm that can!" He slammed down the phone and collected himself before turning toward me. "I'm afraid I'm going to have to cancel lunch."

"But we only have a few more hours before you leave tomorrow," I said, trying not to pout.

"I know. But I promise to make it up to you," he said.

I smiled as I considered how he would do that.

"I see where your mind went, and I hate to disappoint you, but it's not what you think...unless you've given up," he teased.

"Ugh. Just go. I'll see you later at my place."

Aiden chuckled and sauntered over to plant a kiss on my cheek. He smelled so good that I had to restrain myself from grabbing him.

"I'll see you around six o'clock," he said, and strolled out of my office.

I watched until he was out of sight. He was as alluring going as he was coming. How the hell was I going to get what I wanted without asking for it?

❧Chapter Twenty-One❧

The toys weren't going to make the cut tonight. I needed the real thing—I needed Aiden. Other than the stunt in the conference room, he'd all but abstained from any sexual acts with me—and of course, I'd returned the favor. Well, it was more of a challenge than a favor. Obviously, neither of us would back down from this silly little game. Tonight would be especially difficult because he was leaving in the morning for a week or longer on a business trip. I'd teased, talked dirty and made all sorts of suggestive gestures, but nothing as overt as I knew would be necessary tonight.

Lia and Bianca were sleeping over at Jade's, so Aiden and I had the place to ourselves. He was sitting in the living room reviewing business proposals and I was sitting in the bedroom…plotting. This standoff had to be killing him just as much as it was me, but he seemed content on waiting me out. As bizarre as this was, and although I was dying to, I wouldn't back down—I was determined to make him break before I did.

I needed a catalyst—something he couldn't wave off as easily as he'd done with my off-handed remarks. Thinking I had just the thing, I opened the bottom drawer of my bureau in search of my favorite ratty T-shirt—the one with holes and a rip near the collar.

Smiling like an evil genius when I finally came across it, I dropped my towel and slid the shirt over my head. The T-shirt was snug and super short. I wouldn't need to bend at all for Aiden to get an eyeful of what I knew he couldn't refuse.

The next piece of clothing was underwear. Panties, boy shorts or a thong? Which would better serve my purpose? Considering the need for exposure, I chose the thong, slipping it on as I pondered a reason to casually walk past Aiden.

As luck would have it, I was thirsty — more for his essence than water — but the water excuse would have to do. Before I walked out of the bedroom, I shimmied out of the thong. Since I strolled around without panties when Aiden wasn't around, why not do the same when he was here?

Walking into the sitting area, I found Aiden still busy with work, his brows furrowing as he stared at something on his laptop. I looked away and strolled past him, focusing on my destination.

"What are you doing, princess?" he asked, glancing up from the screen.

"I'm thirsty," I tossed out casually. "I'm getting water."

"Water, huh?" he replied, laughing.

"What's funny about water?" I asked, turning to face him.

"Nothing," he said. "Nothing at all."

"What are *you* doing?" I asked.

"Reviewing some reports. I need to prepare for my meeting tomorrow."

"I recall a time when you called me the worker bee. Seems the tables have turned," I said, heading toward the kitchen.

When I stepped back into the living room, Aiden's eyes were still adhered to the laptop. Damn. Was he really going to make me wait? This was ridiculous, but I'd exhaust one final effort before throwing in the towel. I opened the water bottle, and managing to somehow miss my mouth, a fair amount of it fell to my T-shirt.

Aiden looked up at me again, a smile spreading over his lips.

"Are you thirsty?" I asked.

"As a matter of fact, I am," he said, his eyes falling to the exposed area between my thighs.

"I was referring to the water," I replied.

"I know what you meant," he said, standing up and placing the laptop on the table.

He wasn't wearing a shirt, so my eyes did their own thing — taking in every delicious aspect of his torso. Fuck, he was hot.

"Your body is…"

"What?" he asked.

"It's very distracting," I said, as he stepped in front of me. "Maybe you should put on a shirt."

"Maybe you should put on some panties," he countered.

"Never mind," I said, pushing against his unyielding frame.

"You're in my way—can you step aside, please?"

His arms crossed over his broad chest, his stance firm as he eyed me.

"Your time in the gym is very well spent," I said, my gaze still marveling his physique.

"Indeed, it is," he said, with a cocky grin.

"You're so fucking arrogant."

"Seriously, Aria, I only come off that way because you're hell-bent on applying that label to me."

"So, you don't toot your horn to everyone, then? Just me?"

"I didn't think I needed to 'toot my horn,' to you," he said.

"Trust me. You don't."

"And in case I haven't made it clear, your body is unbelievable, too, princess," he said. "Why do you think I can't keep my hands off you?"

"I just figured you were a man whore doing what man whores do," I replied, backing away, placing several steps between his body and mine.

Aiden smiled and closed the distance between us. Before I could object, his large hand was beneath my shirt, seizing my breast.

I gasped as he pulled me closer.

"What do you want, Aria?" he asked, his voice a sultry whisper.

This wasn't working the way I'd hoped, and as expected Virginia's craving was becoming impossible to ignore. Unwilling to submit to Aiden's aggression, I took a sip of water as I contemplated a clever, but seductive reply.

"Look at me," he ordered.

Ignoring the inner warning, I reluctantly met his gaze, the dark beauty of his eyes instantly claiming me.

"I asked you a question. What do you want, princess?"

"I want you to fuck me." The words escaped my lips almost involuntarily.

"How?"

"What do you mean?" I asked, my heart already racing.

"You know exactly what I mean. Now tell me, how do you want me to fuck you?"

"I want you to fuck me like the dirty girl I am." Was that Virginia talking or me? It was definitely something Virginia would say.

"Where do you want me to fuck you?"

"My mouth," I said.

"And?" he asked.

"My pussy."

"Where else?" he urged.

"My ass."

And there it was—a triumphant smile on his beautiful lips.

He'd gotten what he wanted. So maybe I'd asked first, but that didn't mean he couldn't do a little groveling of his own. I reapplied my game face and said, "Just because I want it, doesn't mean I'll go along with it."

"Oh really?"

"Unless you *ask* for it," I said.

"Is that so?"

His hand was still on my breast, rolling my nipple between his thumb and forefinger, and weakening me with each tug. As badly as I wanted him, I couldn't be the one who gave in, but I knew I was fucked—Virginia had been teased to the point of delirium, and was throwing up the white flag, waving it like crazy. Not knowing what else to do, I took another sip of water.

"Give me this," he said, reaching for the bottle. He took the top, twisted the bottle closed and dropped it on the floor. "Now, answer my question."

"Yes, it is, asshole," I said, angry that he'd forced me into a corner.

Aiden's hand abandoned my breast, his finger traced to the top of the T-shirt, and then in one swift movement, he ripped it apart.

I gasped. "What are you doing?"

"I'm doing what you want me to do," he replied.

"I fully expect you to reimburse me for this shirt," I said, pulling the two sides together, and covering my breasts.

"No problem. How do you want to be reimbursed?" he asked, playfully.

I didn't reply.

"Let go of the shirt, Aria," he said, all traces of his smile gone.

When I didn't move, Aiden grabbed my hands and jerked them away. Then he went for my hair, grasping a handful and pulling—gaining access to my neck. With the softest of touches, he pressed his lips to my nape and then his tongue was tracing a wet trail to my ear.

"When I ask you to do something, I expect you to do it," he said, yanking my hair harder.

"Ahh," I cried out.

He wrapped a lock of my hair over his fingers, securing his grip, as his other hand began its descent. He moved tortuously slow, barely touching me as his fingers traced their way to their throbbing, wet objective. When he finally reached the apex of my thighs, I squeezed them together, denying him access.

Aiden's grip on my hair tightened. "Open your legs, Aria," he ordered.

"No," I said, too obstinate to give in to his demand.

"You want me to beg for what's mine. That isn't going to happen, sweetheart." Lifting me from the floor, he tossed me over his shoulder. And then his palm came down on my ass…spanking me, punishing me for my stubbornness.

Holy hell, what had I done?

"What did I tell you about my expectations?" he demanded, striking my behind again.

Biting my lip, I suppressed a scream—no way in hell would I give him the satisfaction. If he was hoping to spank me into submission, I would have a very sore ass by the time this was over.

Aiden had smacked my ass—ten times, at least. After the first few, I lost count, my focus swaying from my defiance to the pain. Pulling me from his shoulders, he lowered me to the floor. He was rough, pushing my legs apart and ramming two fingers into me.

I gasped, panting heavily as he moved in and out of the hot flesh.

"Shit, you're so wet," he groaned and then his mouth was on my clit, sucking hard as he slid a third finger inside me. I clutched the back of his head, forcing his mouth closer to my aching, throbbing need for him.

Aiden feasted on my pussy like a man who'd been deprived, ravishing me as only he could, drawing my orgasm to the surface...and with one last pull on my clit, I climaxed, coming hard as impassioned trembles rolled through my body. I pushed him away, unable to withstand anymore, but Aiden didn't stop, he continued to inflict delicious torment on my clit.

Once he was satisfied, he pulled his fingers out of me, and like a tiger about to ravage its prey, he moved slowly over my body, his eyes never leaving mine.

His emerald gaze became dark pools of lust as he reached for my mouth and forced it open, slipping his fingers inside, rolling them over my tongue and making me taste myself.

I was so hot—so crazed with desire for this glorious man that I completely relinquished the ridiculous notion of denying him my body.

Aiden stood—removing his pants and boxers—and was back on the floor within seconds, turning me toward his erection. "I have something special for you, princess," he said, as he rubbed his heavy cock over my face and then slapped it against my mouth. "Suck it. Make me come."

Before I could acknowledge his demand, Aiden drove his shaft into my mouth, rapidly moving it back and forth, as he held a firm grip of my hair.

My hand moved between my legs, rubbing my clit with wild circular motions as Aiden's plunges became more intense. With one final thrust, he pulled his cock away and inched closer, rubbing his balls across my lips, allowing me to flutter my tongue over them before taking one into my mouth. I moaned around his jewel, and his breath caught. Then his dick was back in my mouth, fucking it just as hard as before. His powerful drives were almost violent. I made a motion to turn away, but he clutched tighter…demanding I suck every inch.

"Ah. Fuck. Your mouth. I'm going to come," he grunted.

Feeling the soft throbs of his cock, I prepared myself to swallow his thick treat, but before he exploded, he pulled his shaft away and spurted the hot thick drops all over my face.

Panting and eager to taste of him, I opened my mouth as he rubbed his essence across my lips. I moaned with deep resonating pleasure, as he slid his dick back into my mouth, giving me more, allowing me to milk every bit of him.

"I know how much you love sucking my cock, but I have something else for you, baby," he said, pulling me up and removing my shirt. He wiped his come from my face and then tossed the shirt onto the floor.

I didn't know what he had in mind, but I didn't think I could stand much more.

Aiden positioned me on my stomach and then he straddled me, placing his knee between my thighs, spreading them far apart. "I need to give you what you've been begging for," he said, his voice husky. He traced my swollen lips with the head of his cock and within the next second, he was inside my pussy.

"Fuck!" I screamed. It was the first time I'd uttered a word since he'd started in on me.

"So that's what it takes to get you to say something?" he

asked, plowing deeper into me.

I screamed again as he pounded my tender cunt, making me feel every divine inch, each hard thrust pushing my body forward.

"Don't ever expect me to beg for what's mine," he said gruffly, slapping my ass as he slammed into me.

"Ah, shit" I cried out, my hands pressed hard into the carpet, desperate for something to hold onto for leverage.

With brute force, he pulled me to my knees, his hands firmly grasping my hips as he repeatedly and vigorously plunged into my core. "This pussy is mine," he growled, as he pumped harder and deeper. I could feel him swelling inside me—he was about to explode.

"Fuck," he grunted, as he started to spill himself. He pulled out, allowing the large drops of come to fall on my behind and then he made a mess of me—smearing his essence all over my ass.

My body was on fire for him. I wanted more. I needed more. I inched back toward his cock, begging him to fuck me again. Aiden shoved his dick into my soaking depths, and I gasped, overwhelmed by the fullness. He was so very rough, and it felt so fucking good. I needed this. I would beg for this. I wanted to fuck until we couldn't fuck anymore. The raw, uninhibited, stabbing lust he delivered with each forceful drive into me was pushing me further and further toward that dark place in my psyche, and my intense desire for him pulled me to a second climax. It tore through my body like a hot dark storm, washing over me with crushing waves.

"There you go, baby," he said as I screamed aloud, the orgasm possessing me. "You want me to fuck you like a dirty girl? I'm going to make you feel real dirty. I'm going to ruin this pussy," he said, as he rammed his huge dick back into me.

"Ahh, fuck," I panted. "Aiden." The rapid smacks of his thighs against the back of mine coupled with the wet, nasty mess he'd made of my pussy were driving me insane. He pulled his dick out, rubbing his come over the tight part of me that belonged only to him. Without allowing me to completely adjust, he slowly pushed his hard length deep inside my ass.

"Shit, Aiden…shit," I panted, as he started to move. Ah fuck, it hurt. I lifted my hand, pushing him back, but he didn't stop, and the punitive blows he delivered were no less intense.

"Your ass is so tight," he whispered gruffly. "Rub your pussy for me, baby."

Reaching between my thighs and gyrating my fingers over my clit, I focused more on my pussy and less on the discomfort of my ass. And as I adjusted to his girth, the sudden urge to come pulled at my core again. Fuck, how did he do this shit to me?

"Baby, I'm coming," I whimpered, as another wave of passion ripped through me, my body trembling as it weakened.

"Ah…shit," he roared. He clutched my backside, digging into my skin as he relentlessly pounded my ass. I felt him harden, erupting…spilling long and hard into me. He grasped my hips tighter as explicit words continued to escape his lips. As the last of his release pulsed, he loosed his grip on my behind, and we collapsed onto the floor.

We lay there panting — spinning in the aftermath of the hottest sex I'd ever experienced. I was pinned beneath his long frame, our bodies mingled with the sweet scent of sex as we fought to catch our breath. Several seconds passed before Aiden kissed my back and rolled over to the floor. I looked over at him — his skin was beaded with sweat, and he was wearing that sexy just-fucked look.

When our breathing finally leveled out, Aiden grinned and said, "Looks like you lost your little challenge."

"No," I replied. "That would be you."

"You asked for it, not me," he said.

"Liar," I said.

"I certainly didn't ask for it. I was preoccupied with work. And in you came, strolling through with your tits and ass hanging out. Did you honestly think you were going to parade around like that and *not* get fucked? You can't win them all, Aria. Just admit it — you begged."

The way I saw it, we'd actually both given in — and it was

well worth it.

Aiden stood, extended a hand and helped me from the floor. Oh, fuck. It hurt to move.

"I didn't say one word, so where did the begging come in?" I asked, inspecting the carpet burns on my knees.

"Maybe not verbally, but you begged just the same," he said, as I looked up at him.

"You were the one who—"

He planted a chaste kiss on my lips to shut me up, and then trailed his finger across my bottom lip. "You begged," he said, and then turned away.

"Asshole," I said, staring after him.

As we headed for the bedroom, he spun around to face me. "You're going to stop calling me an asshole," he warned.

I rolled my eyes. He can fuck me like a dirty whore, but I couldn't call him an asshole? Yeah right.

"Otherwise, each time you say it, I'll assume it means you want me to fuck you in yours."

"Well, in that case…asshole, asshole, asshole," I teased.

We laughed as he reached for my hand, leading me to the bathroom.

"Don't we look like the perfect, well-fucked couple?" he asked, looking at our reflection in the mirror.

"Well-fucked or well-beaten?" I asked, as I assessed my

appearance. My arms also had carpet burns and when I turned to look at my backside, I found it covered in imprints. I glanced at him, knowing exactly what he was about to say. "Don't joke about shit like that, Aria," I said in a deep voice, mocking him.

"That's not funny," he said, scowling at me. "Are you okay?"

"Why do you only ask that *after* the fact? If I wasn't okay, there wouldn't be anything you could do about it now."

"I could caress you and kiss you softly in the spots that hurt," he said.

My brow rose. "Are your kisses supposed to make it all better?"

"Don't they?" he asked.

I shook my head and waved him off as I started the bath. As the tub filled, we climbed in together and Aiden sat behind me, pulling me into an embrace. He kissed my neck and wrapped me tighter in his arms. "I love you," he whispered.

"I love you, too," I said. It was as automatic as breathing.

As the exhaustion set in, I became so relaxed I nearly dozed off.

"I don't know about you, but I've worked up an appetite," Aiden said.

My stomach woke up at the thought of food. "Me, too. I'm starved. I haven't been this hungry in ages."

We bathed, wrapped ourselves in towels, and made a mad

dash for the kitchen.

❧Chapter Twenty-Two❧

"I like this one," Bianca said, pointing to the huge douglas fir.

"I think I do, too," I replied.

"I say we get a small one," Lia said, eyeing the trees on the opposite side of the lot.

"That would look weird, Lia. One of those tiny trees in that huge room," Bianca said.

"Yeah, I guess. Well, it's two against one anyway, so you guys win. But I get to choose the topper," Lia said.

"That works for me. Bianca, can you go tell him which one we want? They can deliver it around four o'clock," I said. "We should be home by then."

"Okay," she replied, and strolled over to the lot attendant.

The girls and I planned to spend the day selecting ornaments and then later trimming the tree. We were looking forward to sharing another holiday as a family, but at the same time, we were saddened by Mom's absence. Lia reminded us to be happy—one of us seemed to always remind the others of that at the times we most needed to hear it.

After hours of shopping, we arrived home just in time for the tree delivery. A few days ago, in preparation for our holiday, Lia added a playlist to the sound system. And as soon as we stepped inside the condo, she flipped through the control panel and started the music, filling our home with the sound of Christmas.

In the kitchen, I busied myself with making home-made cocoa, smiling as I added an extra scoop of whipped cream to each cup. Of course, that meant adding more time to my workout, but it was so worth it. Grabbing a few candy canes, along with the cups of chocolate goodness and some cookies, I placed everything on a tray and then joined the girls in the living room.

Christmas carols surrounded us as we sang along and decorated the tree. I was enjoying this time with my sisters more than I'd anticipated, and judging by their laughter and silliness, they were having a great time, too. After Bianca added the last ornament, we stepped back to admire our masterpiece — it could have used a little more work, but for our first sister tree, we all considered it beautiful.

"Okay, Lia, do your thing," Bianca said. "Add the topper."

Lia moved the stepladder closer to the tree and placed the angel on top. It resembled the one we'd had years ago, in Dayton. I was sure that's what prompted Lia's choice.

"Perfect," I said.

Bianca pulled her phone from her pocket and said, "Let's take selfies."

As we captured silly photos in front of the tree, I passed my phone to Lia, asking her to take a picture of me that I could send to Aiden. His trip to Dubai had been extended and he wouldn't be home for Christmas. I was saddened by that, especially since he'd promised we'd have the holiday together. I knew schedule changes were unavoidable, but it was Christmas. Not only was I sad for me, I was sad for him. The life he'd been living was impossible and unfair. Why couldn't he see he was living for his family and not for himself?

In lieu of the handmade gifts I'd planned for Lia and Bianca, I went with something more practical…kind of. Passing a gift to each of them, I watched as they opened the tiny boxes that held their keys—I'd surprised them with brand new cars. They'd been sharing the rental vehicle since moving to Boston, so they were ecstatic to each have their own.

After test driving the cars, we headed back inside—the girls chattering excitedly as we sat around the fireplace, sipping our second cup of cocoa. I noticed Bianca nudge Lia and nod toward the tree. Lia glanced at me and I scrunched my brows, confused by their exchange. With a weird grin on her face, Lia went to the tree and grabbed the large box with the beautiful silver bow, passing it to me.

Reading the names on the gift tag, I saw it was a present for me, and that it was from Mom, Lia, Bianca and Aiden. Still somewhat bewildered, I opened it to find something totally unexpected — my quilt. And as Aiden promised, they'd finished it for me.

"Wow, thank you," I said. "It's beautiful."

"You're welcome," they chimed.

Unfolding the quilt, I examined the new additions, easily recognizing the mosaics that represented my sisters, as well as those that depicted Aiden's presence in my life. I smiled, easily picturing my mother on this day, her soft gaze observing as I surveyed the varied pieces of my gift. I was certain she would've been a mass of hugs and tears. Still smiling, I ran my fingers over the fabric and was soon bawling like a baby as I fell into thoughts of what could have been. Of course, my tears led to my sisters' tears, which led to yet another group hug.

Hours later, I was sitting in the living room, staring at the remaining boxes under the tree. They were my gifts to Aiden. Lia and Bianca had purchased something for him as well. Although Aiden wouldn't be back for several days, we decided to leave everything as it was, and celebrate a delayed Christmas when he returned. I let out a sigh. I missed him.

Christmas with my sisters couldn't have been more perfect. Of course, it was awkward at times, but all things considered, it was wonderful. With so much joy and laughter, it prompted me to wonder about the holidays I'd missed with my family. I'd wanted to ask Lia and Bianca to share their memories, but I was afraid it would make them uncomfortable. Had I been there with them, I wouldn't have to wonder…I would know. Sighing to myself, I pushed down the guilt and took in my sisters smiling faces. Despite it all, they were happy. I was happy. And that's all that mattered. We were going to be okay. And this Christmas was the start of something different, something new…something that would last.

❦   ❦   ❦   ❦

I was lying across the bed, ready to surprise Aiden during our video chat.

"What's that?" he asked, squinting at the screen.

"What do you think it is?" I asked, holding up the butt plug.

A wicked smile crossed his lips. "What are you planning to do with it?"

"You're not here to give me what I want, so a girl's gotta do what a girl's gotta do."

He cocked his head. "So exactly what is it that you want?"

"You already know," I replied.

"Let's pretend I don't."

I pulled the screen closer and whispered, "I want your cock in my ass."

"And my cock wants to be there," he assured.

"Does it?" I asked.

"Yes, but since that's not possible at the moment, why don't you tell me *how* you want it."

"Why?" I asked.

"So I can be prepared to give it to you per your specifications when I next have the chance," he said.

"Hmm. So, you're going to do it as I say?"

"Yes ma'am. However, I may embellish a little. You know, to keep things interesting," he said, a sexy smile gracing his lips.

"In that case, I guess I should tell you," I said. "But pay close attention."

"Of course," he replied. "I doubt I'll even blink."

I laughed as I moved away from the monitor to give him ample viewing room. "Can you see me?"

"Every gorgeous inch," he replied.

"Good. So, I think I'd like you to start by rubbing the head of your cock on my pussy like this," I said, tracing the toy along my sex. "Then when it's all nice and wet, I want you to spread my juices all over my lips, and then I want to feel that beautiful plush head of yours right here," I said, moving the plug over the puckered tissue.

"You're making my dick hard already."

"Let me see," I said.

Standing and unzipping his pants, Aiden reached into his boxers to reveal a very alert Kingston.

He had a very impressive cock, and I knew it was all mine, but seeing it on my screen made it seem unreal, as if it were something I wanted, but could never have. I licked my lips, my gaze fixed on his erection, as I rubbed the butt plug over my pussy.

Aiden sat down, stroking his large penis as he watched the screen. "What would you want next?" he asked.

"I'd want you to slide it in…just like this," I said, trailing the toy from my sex and pushing it in my ass.

Aiden's hand moved to the crown of his cock, pre-come glistening and spilling over the tip.

"Then I want you to go deeper and deeper, until I feel your balls on the back of my thighs," I said, moaning, as I pumped the plug into my tight hole.

He stroked the length of his dick, his hands moving faster. It was so hot watching him jack himself off. It was making me wetter — I was already about to come.

"I want to hear you growl my name as you start pounding my tight little ass," I said. "And just when you think I can't take anymore, I want you to grip me tighter, digging your fingers into my skin as you go deeper...and harder, punishing my hole. Pushing, pushing, pushing until I'm over the edge, coming so hard that my ass clenches around your hard cock. And then I want to feel you come inside me, exploding in vicious spurts, so much until I'm over full and your seed is running down the inside of my thighs."

"Shit," he grunted. "That's my nasty girl. You're making me come."

I watched as his thick shaft erupted, spurting and dropping along the sides and then trailing along his hand.

"Mmm. Fuck," I breathed, as I continued pumping the plug hard and fast into me. "Aiden, this is how I want your cock in my ass," I panted, my core shattering, coming apart as he watched me claim my release.

෫෮ ෫෮ ෫෮ ෫෮

I glanced up from the file on my desk and discovered I wasn't alone. Standing in the threshold of my office door was an immaculately dressed Aiden Raine. I let out a sigh and smiled, cocking my head as I surveyed his six-foot three-inch frame. He was wearing that hot CEO look—complete with the domineering stance and the expensive suit perfectly tailored to his sculpted build. His unexpected appearance was definitely the highlight of my day.

"Good afternoon, princess." He breezed into my office, closed the door and locked it behind him.

"Good afternoon, Mr. Raine. I don't recall seeing your name on my schedule."

"Some very alarming information appeared on my computer a few nights ago, and I wanted to investigate it personally," he said, casually strolling toward me. He stopped directly in front of my desk and slipped his hands into his pockets, peering down at me with a devilish glint in his dark green eyes. "Don't I warrant a proper greeting?"

Pushing back from my desk, I stood and moved toward him.

"Don't." Lifting his hand, he signaled me to stop. "Stay right there. As a matter of fact, step back toward the window."

I stared at Aiden, confused.

"Don't think about anything, princess, just do as I ask," he said.

Responding to his instruction, I moved a couple of paces closer to the window.

Aiden reached for a chair, placed it a few feet away from me and took a seat. "Have you missed me?" he asked.

"Yes. You know I have," I replied, still confused by his

request.

He leaned forward, his elbows resting on his knees. "And your body—has it missed my touch?"

"Of course," I said.

"Prove it."

I shrugged. "How would you like for me to do that?"

"I want to see how your body responds to my presence. Take off your clothes."

My eyes widened in disbelief. Certainly I'd misheard him. As I parted my lips to protest, he shook his head, silencing me.

"I need you to do exactly as I say," he said, as he sat back and crossed his ankle over his knee.

I looked behind me—the back wall was all glass. Was he insane? Anyone could see me. Was he okay with that? Hell, was I?

"I highly doubt anyone would see anything," he said, replying to my thoughts. "We're on the thirtieth floor. Stop procrastinating and take off your fucking clothes."

His demand, while forceful and daunting, sent a direct injection of lust to a very compliant Virginia. The fierce look in Aiden's eyes pulled at me, compelling me to go along with something I knew I could later regret.

With an unsteady heartbeat, I leaned forward, removing one of the six-inch heels, and then dropping it to the floor as I reached for the other. My fingers were then at my blouse, unbuttoning it, as his eyes burned into mine. I could feel the tension building inside me—the air between us electric as the scene started to unfold. Undoing the last button, I allowed my blouse to fall open. With a nod of his head, Aiden urged me to continue. I shrugged off the shirt, my eyes following it as it fell atop my shoes.

I paused, wondering if Aiden really wanted me to go through with this. He couldn't possibly. The flexing temples revealing his impatience was my answer. He wanted me naked.

I could do this, right? My office door was locked and as he said, no one would see. Reaching behind me, I lowered the zipper of my skirt and moved the fitted garment over my hips, stepping out of it as I considered which item to remove next.

Aiden's eyes fell to my chest, his perfect lips snaking upward into a smile.

Following his prompt, I fingered the center of my bra, unclasping it to free my breasts from the constriction of the white lace.

"Is this what you had in mind?" I asked.

"Not quite, but you're getting there," he replied.

Slipping out of my panties, I bunched them into a ball and tossed them over to Aiden. "I know how much you get off on smelling them," I said.

Coolly reaching up, he caught the panties and returned my mischievous smile with one of his own. He lifted my underwear to his nose, and then his lids closed, moaning as he inhaled me.

When his eyes opened, they were dark, the darkest green I'd seen of them, a strong indication of how badly he wanted me — of how hard he was going to fuck me.

"You're so fucking gorgeous," he said. "Grab your tits for me, princess."

Seduced by the sexy baritone of his voice, I palmed my breasts, squeezing as my fingers moved to the tips, and then tugging my nipples as I leaned forward. "See. I told you my body missed you. My nipples hardened at the mere sound of your voice, baby," I said, twisting my already tender buds.

"And Virginia, what does she do at the sound of my voice?" he asked.

"Hmm. I don't know. Why don't you ask her?" I teased.

"I want you to show me. Face the window and bend over," he said, his tone low and sultry.

Tearing my gaze from his, I did as he asked and turned toward the transparency of the glass wall.

"Now spread those beautiful cheeks for me. If I hear what I should, I'll know I've been missed."

I didn't think I could drag this out much further — my body was already aching for his. Continuing with his instruction, I grasped my curves and spread myself open. My fingers were clutching my skin and clapping my cheeks, the soaking wetness audible.

"Is that what you wanted to hear?" I asked.

"Yes, it is," he said. "Step closer to the window."

I did as he told me — moving forward, only inches away from the glass — waiting for him, anxious for him.

Aiden stepped behind me, his frame hard against mine, as he pressed my body flush to the window. The coldness of the glass met my nipples as Aiden grasped a lock of my hair. He swept it to the opposite side, and then touched his lips to my neck. "I've missed you too, princess," he said, as he reached for my hand, guiding it behind me and curving my fingers around his erection.

"Do you want that?" he asked, his voice a deep allure that clawed at my insides.

Virginia was throbbing — the clenches so intense I could hardly stand it. "Yes. I want it so badly, baby," I whimpered.

Aiden removed my hand, and sank to his knees, planting soft kisses on my backside. Palming my behind, his fingers curled into my skin as he spread me open. "What a very wet and very pretty pussy," he said. He kissed the taut hole once, then twice, before flicking his tongue over it, my body arching toward his touch as he voraciously lapped and prodded my anus with the tip of his tongue.

Aiden planted one final kiss on my backside and then his palms were gliding over my thighs, moving to my ankles, and then trailing his way up again.

The heat of his touch held me spellbound. His touch was all I wanted, all I needed — and the place and time became inconsequential.

"You're so beautiful, Aria," he said, as he lightly kissed and palmed each cheek, squeezing and then opening me. His breath caught when he saw the wetness he'd caused.

"You're such a naughty girl, aren't you?" he asked, smacking his palm across my ass.

"Ahh. Yes," I breathed.

"Lucky for you, I have the exact thing for a naughty girl such as yourself."

Aiden licked the firm hole and I responded, grinding my ass on his sinful mouth.

"Mmm. That feels so good," I moaned.

"Good won't do," he said. "Let's see what I can do to make it feel better."

He spread me further, obtaining access to my sex, and then his tongue slid over the wet folds, dipping between the silken slit as I panted, hungry for more.

Aiden then pressed two fingers inside me, plunging deep, stroking the hot flesh.

"Oh, shit. Do it harder," I whispered.

"I have something else in mind," he said, pulling out, tracing a finger to my ass and sliding the tip inside.

I immediately tensed.

"Baby, relax," he murmured. "Don't you like this?" As he teased my anus, his other hand paid tribute to my sex, his fingers stroking my core.

I tried to concentrate on the pleasure of the motions inside me, but the threat of the other finger was pulling at my mind.

He eased his fingers from my sex and gave his full attention to my ass, pressing deeper into my tight hole.

I worked to calm my breathing, but the more I focused, the more labored it became.

"Stop thinking about it, Aria," he said, his breath was warm on my neck as he reached to cup my breast.

How could I not think about it? How does one ever prepare for that type of entrance? Maybe it worked better when I wasn't prepared...like last time.

His finger inched forward, moving in and out, stroking deeper and deeper, as he softened his assault with wet kisses to my neck. His lips and tongue alone were enough to make me lose all muscle control, but when he slid an additional finger inside my ass, my breathing hitched and I tensed again.

"Baby, I want to fuck your sweet ass, but I won't be able to if you keep doing that. Don't you remember how good it felt before? I want to make it so much better this time," he purred. Don't you want me to fuck your ass, princess? Isn't that what you demanded a few nights ago?"

"Yes, but—"

"Shh. Then say it. Tell me."

"I want you to fuck my ass, baby," I said.

"There you go," he said. "Now tell me how you want me to fuck it."

Just like that, a switch flicked, I was so turned on that his fingers suddenly weren't enough. I wanted his huge dick inside my ass. "Hard," I said. "I want you to make it hurt."

His mouth was still on my neck, sucking, as his fingers worked inside me. With one final kiss, his fingers were gone, and then I heard his zipper. Seconds later, the head of his cock was at the entrance of the open hole. As he pushed his dick inside me, I held my breath, biting into my lip as his thick rod filled my ass— inch by inch, until it was all the way in. He held still, not moving, allowing me to absorb the fullness.

"Are you okay?" he asked.

"Yes," I breathed, having stifled the scream that formed in my throat.

He pulled out and then gently eased his cock into me again. On the third stroke, he picked up the pace, pushing hard and deep, the penetrating plunges forcing me against the window.

"Oh, yes," I cried out, as his cock pumped into my ass, filling me, stretching me.

Aiden's fingers curved around my throat, holding me in place as he continued the punishing blows. "There you go baby, take it," he said gruffly, releasing my neck and grabbing my hips, pulling me back to meet his lunges.

Holy hell. He was too big. How could something hurt and feel so inexplicably good at the same time?

"Ah...fuck, Aiden," I panted.

"Do you like this, princess?" he asked, grunting with each solid drive into me. "Do you like this big dick in your tight little ass?"

"Yes, baby. It feels so good. Don't stop. Please, don't stop," I begged.

My pleas prodded him to fuck my ass harder and I let out a scream. Aiden's hand clamped over my mouth, muffling my cries. "You said you wanted it, then stop the fucking screaming and take it," he said, his voice was low, his labored breaths, warm at my earlobe.

My blood was racing, and his vulgarity only made me that much hotter for him. When I nodded, he removed his hand, driving his hard length into my ass over and over, each solid thrust pressing my body onto the window. I reached for my clit, massaging wildly, torn between the frenzy of emotions — the indescribable lust, the fear of being caught, the control he exerted over me, and the delightfully painful blows into my ass.

The friction of his thick manhood bursting into me was submergence into that deeper level of my psyche. Each impassioned plunge was delivered with a skill that could only belong to this man. Placing both palms on the window, I braced myself, arching toward him, taking it all, offering it all. The possibility of someone watching no longer mattered. All I wanted was this. Him. Making me feel this way.

Rushing blood filled my ears as Aiden claimed my ass, moving faster and faster, filling me, owning me. The depth of each thrust sent carnal sensations to every nerve ending in my body. Desperate for a release, my core tightened as my orgasm grabbed ahold. Uncontrollable trembles possessed my body, quaking as my climax peaked, violently ripping through me, taking and taking until there was nothing left. My legs gave way and I fell back into Aiden's arms, his weight supporting mine.

"Ah…shit," he growled, as he met my release, his cock pulsing in my ass…spurting, jerking repeatedly as he filled me with his seed.

The harsh warmth of his breath brushed over my cheek as he gradually eased out of me. I felt so open—so exposed. As my erotic high subsided, and the pain from the assault of my ass set in, Aiden picked me up and carried me to the seat near the window—holding me—cradling me in his arms.

He pressed his lips to mine and our tongues finally reunited in a long, deep kiss. When he pulled away, he asked, "Is this what I'm paying you for?"

I tucked my head against his chest and smiled. "Maybe it's why I keep the job."

ᨄChapter Twenty-Threeᨄ

Tonight was my weekly scheduled piano lesson. Since Aiden was in town, he'd be assuming Vincent's role as my instructor. Nothing like receiving a lesson from someone as sexy and melodic as my very own pianist, boyfriend.

Aiden and I had seen each other only once in the last three weeks. Knowing I had him all to myself for three full days was like receiving a delayed Christmas gift—one I was looking forward to unwrapping, over and over again.

"I'm fascinated by your love of music," Aiden said, as I joined him at the piano.

Staring into his stunning green eyes, I said, "It's like another strand that connects us."

"I was looking forward to teaching you how to play."

"I know," I said, saddened by the look of disappointment on his handsome face. We were both thinking back to the time we'd been apart.

Remembering the day I'd walked into my condo and discovered his surprise, I said, "I never really properly thanked you."

"Yeah, you were pretty pissed at me."

"That's putting it mildly," I said. "But it's a wonderful gift. I love it. Thank you."

"You're welcome, princess." He leaned over and kissed my cheek. "So, let's see what you've learned."

I couldn't believe how anxious I was — my fingers were trembling.

Aiden stroked my back, encouraging me. "Don't be nervous. It's just me."

Just him? It was just him, which was why I was nervous.

I let out a breath, placed my fingers on the keys, and started playing. There were a few hiccups, but I attributed those to the nerves. When I finished, he caught me off guard by applauding. "That was wonderful, Aria."

"Really?"

"Yes, it was remarkable," he exclaimed. "Just think, a few months ago you could only play a few notes. Listening to you now, one would never know."

"That's high praise coming from such an accomplished pianist, so thank you."

Aiden turned his attention to my list of sheet music, his dark brows scrunching in disapproval.

"What is it?" I asked.

"I need to have a talk with Vincent. You're ready to advance beyond these."

"You really think so?" I asked.

"Of course."

Humph. Maybe I was doing better than I thought.

"Let me play something I know you'll love," he said, as his long fingers began caressing the keys.

As usual, it was absolutely amazing. He made it seem so simple. As he started to teach me, my stomach growled.

Aiden glanced at me and laughed. "Guess we should eat," he said. "We can do more after dinner."

"I'd love it if you'd sing that song to me later," I said. "From the night of the serenade."

"If that's what you want," he replied.

"That evening at the Esplande was like something from a dream. I think about it a lot. It was beautiful," I said, as we moved toward the kitchen.

"You needed to know what I was feeling, and I knew singing would resonate on a deeper level than anything I could say to you."

He was right. The lyrics held a special significance — something I hadn't realized until they were directed at me. I'd had a fervent love of music for as long as I could remember, and when Aiden sang to me, I was touched in a way I couldn't explain.

Songs were heartfelt expressions that spoke to my soul. Music always seemed to tap into that part of me that needed to be awakened. And that's what Aiden had done. He'd awakened something inside of me — a burning flame that could never be extinguished.

I grabbed a glass of wine as I started dinner. Aiden didn't think I could cook anything that included more than three ingredients. It wasn't that I couldn't cook, I simply didn't. In the midst of Mom's depression, I'd taken on many of the parental responsibilities, and one of those included cooking for all of us. So, when it was no longer a necessity, I avoided it — just as I'd avoided everything that reminded me of Dayton.

But now, I felt as though I was healing. Aiden's presence — his patience and his love — brought a depth to my life I hadn't thought possible. I was the happiest I'd been since...well, since before my father disappeared. The loss of my parents was something I needed to accept, but in a healthier way than I'd done in the past, and I was ready to do that.

Pushing down the Dayton memories, I busied myself with finishing our salads and checking on the main course. I loved Thai food, as did Aiden, so I was sure he'd enjoy the meal.

Aiden stepped behind me, wrapping his arms around my waist and burying his face in my hair. I leaned back into his solid frame.

"I like this," he said.

"What do you mean?"

"Coming home to you. You preparing a gourmet meal for

your hard-working man."

"Well, it's definitely not gourmet. And as for you being *hard-working*, I've never seen you do much more than harass your employees."

"Since we're being honest, I'm actually skeptical about the cooking. I was just trying to give you a vote of confidence," he said with a grin. "As for the harassment, you're the only employee I enjoy harassing."

Turning to face him, I pointed a finger as I accused him. "I knew it! I knew you did all of that shit on purpose."

"What?" he asked, laughing. "I had to do something. My normal tactics failed with you."

"What tactics?" I asked.

"Just showing up and flashing this smile usually works every time."

"What an ass," I said.

"You really should be nicer to me," he replied.

"Why is that?"

"Because I have a special after-dinner treat for you. If you don't behave, you won't get it."

"I have an after-dinner treat for you as well...with the same condition."

"Always challenging," he said.

"I do what I can," I said, using one of his lines. "Besides, I don't think you'd have me any other way."

"The hell I wouldn't."

"Really?" I asked, a little surprised by his response.

"Yes. Really."

With all of the laughter gone, the sincerity of Aiden's words became evident in his gaze. He would take me however he could have me—challenging or not.

"I love you, Aria," he said.

The first time he'd spoken those words, I'd rejected them with everything in me—I didn't want his love and I didn't want the responsibility of being loved. But now, seemingly eons later, I relished those words coming from his lips. His patience with me constantly surprised me. His actions, his words, even the way his eyes coveted me—it all left me in wonderment. But then there were those times he could be cold and detached. That was the part of him I couldn't quite understand—the part that kept me on guard.

"Now let's get me fed so we can start on these after-dinner treats," he said.

"Yes, let's do that, because you've piqued my curiosity," I said, grinning.

"As you have mine. But what if I were to tell you I wasn't hungry?"

"No, that's not working. I made a special meal for you, and

it's not going to waste." Honestly, I was tempted to skip dinner myself. I'd been practicing with B.O.B. in an effort to give Kingston the reverence he so richly deserved. I mean, when it came to cock, Aiden's should be in the Guinness Book of World Records. He had an incredible tool, and he knew exactly how to work it. I wanted to be as sexually fulfilling to Aiden as he was to me.

I had the highest confidence in pleasing him with Virginia. I loved seeing the look on his face when I was astride his beautiful body, rolling, squeezing, and grinding on his cock. His expression alone was enough to make me come undone, and it quite often did. However, I knew my fellatio skills could stand a little embellishing. I wanted...no, I *needed* to give him the best blow job he could imagine.

I'd watched a few videos for some pointers, and I'd also invested in a new toy. It was called the *natural* and it was as realistic as advertised—hard and huge. It was the girth and length of Kingston, and I'd enjoyed several practice sessions. It was quite large—in fact, my jaws and lips ached in much the same way they did when I was pleasuring Aiden, and when that happened, I gave myself a break—taking it out of my mouth to caress and spit on it. It felt raw and it felt dirty— two words that had come to describe Aiden and me.

I'd learned to relax my throat and breathe through my nose to avoid my gag reflex, but from what I'd gathered, the gagging noise was a huge turn on, so I wouldn't deny Aiden those orgiastic sounds. My end goal was to swallow him whole. Smiling to myself, I thought about how those sessions typically ended with the *natural* plunged deep inside me, and I always came…hard. When it came to amazing, self-induced orgasms, I could actually give classes.

Once dinner was ready, I escorted Aiden to the dining room. After placing the *Som Tum* and bread at both table settings, I took a seat.

"What?" I asked, confused by Aiden's furrowed brows.

He shook his head, smiling as he looked up at me. "Nothing. This looks good. I was considering asking if you really prepared this or will I go over to the trash and see delivery containers."

"Wow. Really?" I feigned an insulted expression.

"You've never cooked for me, so you have to admit it's suspect. This looks incredible by the way."

"I've never cooked for you — that doesn't mean I can't cook. And this may be the first and last time if you don't hush and eat."

I watched as he lifted his fork and started the salad. He gave a nod of approval and smiled. "This is delicious, princess."

"You really like it?"

He had a second forkful and then a third. "Hell yes."

I breathed a sigh of relief and started my salad as I watched him eat.

"Wow," he said, taking a bite of bread.

"Hot, huh?"

"Yes, but I love it hot," he replied, a mischievous glint in his eyes.

"Oh, I know. That's another one of those strands that connects us," I said, smiling.

If you were new to Thai cuisine, this would not be a dish to try — *Tom Sum* was a very spicy salad and the main entrée was *Tom Yam Goong*, which wasn't beginner level Thai food, either. There was nothing better than food so spicy it made you sweat…unless it was watching the gorgeous Aiden Raine eating it.

I focused on his mouth as he chewed, and when his tongue slid across his bottom lip, I nearly asked him to forget about dinner. Reaching for a glass of water, I took a sip and continued watching him, pleased he was enjoying the salad.

"You're doing it again," he said, and took another bite of the bread.

"Doing what?" I knew exactly what he was referring to. I was staring at him, but I really couldn't help myself. He was so good-looking, it was nearly impossible to believe. And he had this way of holding you with his eyes, where he wouldn't release you until he wanted to.

"As if you don't know," he said.

"Whatever," I replied, as I took another forkful of my salad. It *was* delicious—definitely restaurant quality—but who could mess up a salad? Before the girls came to live with me, I couldn't recall the last time I'd really cooked. I had to do so much of it as a teenager that I grew to hate it, but tonight was different. Instead of evoking unpleasant memories, the time I'd spent shopping for and preparing the meal had actually been exciting…because I was cooking for *him*. He made everything exciting. Each moment with him was an adventure. I never knew where the day would lead when he was involved.

"So how was your trip?" I asked.

"It was not without its challenges, but fortunately Brooklyn was with me," he replied.

Yes, how fortunate. "Seems like she's always with you."

"Yes, pretty much everywhere I go."

"Where is she now?" I asked.

"At the hotel. Why?"

"Just wondering." As much as it appeared to be necessary, I didn't like her being with him. She spent more time with him than I ever would—I hated that.

"Why are you wondering?" he asked.

"I thought maybe she was at the penthouse."

"Aria, I've told you. You're the first woman other than family that I've ever invited there. That hasn't and will not change."

"What about Nadia? The night of the gala?"

His temples flexed. "Aria, why are you doing this?"

I really couldn't answer his question. Why *was* I doing it? Things were going so well—maybe *that* was the reason. Because it all seemed too good to be true and I wanted to destroy it before it destroyed me.

"Forget it. I already know the answer." I knew Nadia was a family friend and she would've stayed there regardless of whether sex was involved. It just so happened, sex *was* involved, and although he and I technically weren't together when he'd slept with Nadia, it bothered the fuck out of me. I didn't want him to think I didn't trust him, but I did have a few trust issues when it came to anyone, regardless of gender. That was a scar I couldn't conceal, another by-product of my childhood. It wasn't fair to subject Aiden to my crap. I couldn't help but wonder when he would tire of it...of me. I'd never had a committed relationship with a man so, of course, I wondered about longevity. Did I have what it took? Did he? Was he even thinking along those terms?

This was an entirely new world for me, and no amount of reading or reviewing of reports could prepare me for it. I had to feel my way through this, and I hated the insecurity it evoked. I was always very confident and strong...but with Aiden, I was in a whirlwind, trying desperately to grasp something familiar to guide me. Only there was nothing familiar here. Even the sex, in which I was quite experienced, was beyond my comprehension. What he did to my body made me feel things I didn't think possible.

"Nadia didn't stay at the penthouse the night of the gala. I know how she feels about me, and I didn't want to do anything to encourage it, so I insisted she stay at a hotel."

And fucking her didn't encourage her? I could see he was agitated by my questions, but I was surprised and relieved to hear, at the very least, he hadn't fucked her in the same bed as he and I shared. I needed to put that aside and focus on what was directly in front of me. "I'm sorry. I'm being silly. You're away so much that it makes me a little irrational at times."

His eyes softened, but he didn't reply.

Rising from my seat, I asked, "Are you ready for the main course?"

"I thought you were the main course," he replied, letting me off the hook.

"Nah, I'm the dessert, baby," I added, bending to place a soft kiss on his lips. I grabbed his plate and headed toward the kitchen.

"Can I help with anything?" he asked.

"No. I've got it. Just stay where you are, and I'll be right back."

Grabbing the two bowls from the warmer, I reentered the dining room and placed the food on the table.

"This looks and smells amazing, Aria," he said.

"There you go—sounding surprised again—but thanks," I said, as I pulled my chair up to the table. "Let's see if the flavor measures up."

I watched as he picked up the spoon for a taste.

"If you continue cooking like this, we'll never eat out again," he said, smiling as he took another spoonful.

Tom Yam Goong had a fierce spiciness, to match the intense fieriness of the man for whom it was prepared.

I laughed. "No, thank you. I would much rather spend the little time we have together doing other things."

We continued talking over dinner about Raine Industries' most recent acquisition, and Aiden's plan to bring Sloan in to manage the project despite Connor's resistance. I was surprised, since he seemed to buy into his father's insistence he handle matters at that level. He explained that Sloan nailed the finishing touches of the Soshibi acquisition when he'd turned it over to her, to be with me after my mom's passing. I'd felt guilty about taking him from his work, but if it had given Sloan a chance to prove herself, that was a great end result. I knew how much she wanted to contribute to the company and share more of Aiden's responsibilities, as did Nicholas.

After dinner, we cleared the table and loaded the dishwasher. It was still so very odd watching Aiden do things like that. I never gave much thought to how a multi-billionaire handled domestic tasks like shopping or cleaning. Aiden insisted he wasn't rich — that his father was — but I saw it as one in the same. He was a man of great power and affluence, but at times he was so down to earth that it was easy to forget he was the brilliant force who dominated the business industry.

Aiden closed the dishwasher and turned to face me. "Come here."

I strolled over to him, and he grasped my waist, pulling me close. "Thank you for dinner — it was delicious."

"I'm glad you enjoyed it."

Lowering his head, he touched his full lips to mine, kissing me tenderly. I caressed his back and pulled him closer as he explored my mouth, instantly filling me with a yearning only he could satisfy. Unfortunately, he had other ideas, as he severed our kiss much too soon for my liking.

"Wasn't there some mention of after dinner treats?" he asked.

"You're like a huge kid."

"Yes, I am, when it comes to you," he said, his gaze warm on my face.

My insides melted as I absorbed the dark passion of his eyes.

"I believe I behaved properly, so where's my treat?" he asked.

"I want to give you mine later. So, you first."

"Okay." Grasping my hand, he led me from the kitchen and went to his bag, unzipping it and pulling out a long box.

"What is it?" I asked.

"Open it," he said, passing it to me.

It was too short for flowers. Taking it from him, I walked over to the couch. It was also too *heavy* for flowers. I removed the lid, and simply stared. What had he done? It was a bottle of wine with the name *Aria's Orchid* displayed on the label. The design was beautiful. It featured a grayish background with three red orchid petals in the foreground and a string of red orchid petals laced the top.

I looked up at him, amazed by such an unexpected token of affection.

"Do you like it?" he asked.

"What's not to like?" As usual, he'd left me at a loss for words. "This is incredible. *You're* incredible."

"No, that would be you. And you inspire me to make you happier than you've ever been."

"I am." Despite the loss of my parents, I was genuinely happy.

I looked at the bottle again, trailing my fingers across the label, shocked to see it was from the Raine Winery. "I didn't know Raine Industries had a winery." I was still in the midst of researching the many holdings of the vast conglomerate.

"Our hands are in a little bit of everything."

"So, was this one bottle made as a special surprise?" I asked. "If so, I'm never going to open it."

"No, actually it's one in a selective new line—the Aria Wines."

"Oh my gosh! You can't be serious?"

"I am. I told you. You inspire me," he said.

"I don't know what to say. You're going to make it impossible for me to ever forget you if we don't work out."

He frowned. "Don't say that. We're going to work out."

He was right—we were. I wouldn't let my fear spoil our relationship. It would definitely be a whirlwind, but I'd be damned if I didn't hold on with all I had. "I absolutely love it. How involved were you with this?"

"Very. I described the essence of what I wanted in terms of taste and design, and every stage of the process required my approval. I typically don't involve myself to such a degree with that division, but this was special to me, so it had to be as perfect as its namesake."

I placed the wine on the table and rushed into his arms. He picked me up, hugging me to his chest.

Peering into his eyes, I found myself unable to look away. It was as if we were connected—in a way I couldn't explain even if I tried.

"Kiss me," he said.

I lowered my head and met his lips. He walked us over to the couch, our tongues toying and teasing as he laid me down—his lean, strong frame covering mine. My hands moved over his back, grasping and clutching, frantic for more of him.

Aiden's lips were soft and gentle—taking my mouth in a deep probing kiss. I moaned, breathing him in as he broke our connection and traced his lips to my neck, gently nipping at my skin.

"Fuck, I've missed you, Aria," he whispered as his hand wandered to my breast.

"Not as much as I've missed you," I replied, as I reached for his manhood. I was so lost in him that I'd nearly forgotten my surprise.

"Hey, don't you want your treat?" I asked, as I gently pushed him away.

His arched brow was a silent protest to my interruption. He grasped my hand and brought it to his lips. "Yes, but can't it wait?"

"No, it can't. Do you want it here or in the bedroom?"

"Let's go to the bed. I have more room to do what I want to you there," he said, his eyes playful as he stood and scooped me up, carrying me to the bedroom.

"So, you'll enjoy my treat more if you were naked," I said.

"You certainly have my attention," he replied, as he started to undress. He unbuttoned his shirt, and my eyes rested on his muscular chest.

"Let me undress you," I offered.

"Be my guest," he said.

"Your treat is more along the lines of an oral gift. I hope that's okay," I said, as I rubbed my hand over his crotch.

"I'm partial to any gift that involves your mouth," he replied.

In a rush, I freed him of his slacks. Already aroused by the huge bulge in his boxers, I fell to my knees and lowered the front of his briefs, releasing him. My eyes rested on my beloved Kingston, beautifully erect and aimed straight for my mouth.

"Do you like my cock?" Aiden asked. His deep, velvet voice evoked beads of desire all over my body.

"Mmm-hmm. I actually love it. You have no idea how much I've missed it," I said, grasping his hardness and moving my hand up and down his length. I kissed the head and pulled it into my mouth, moaning as I eased down the still-expanding shaft. Another low moan escaped as the sweet taste of pre-come graced my tongue. I stroked the root, focused on the head, hoping for another taste of his pineapple essence.

Taking him from my mouth, I saturated his cock with my saliva, and then I looked up at him. "I want to get you nice and wet, baby," I said, caressing his dick as the hunger in his eyes pulled at my core. I took him into my mouth again, my head moving back and forth—letting his dick hit the back of my throat.

I eased back, grasping his erection and twirling my hand around the base. "Fuck...I love sucking your cock." I traced my tongue over his thick pole, licking the heavy veins that coursed his length as I palmed his balls, massaging them gently. Returning my attention to his dick, I started sucking like mad, clutching the back of his ass and pulling him towards me, taking in all of him.

"Ahh. Aria, that feels so fucking good," he said, his voice steeped with lust. Grabbing the back of my head, he urged me to continue. "Fuck," he grunted as I stroked his thick cock. I leaned down to lick his balls, taking my time with each one. "Shit, Aria," he murmured.

I loved pleasing him. I loved knowing I drove him as crazy as he drove me. I slapped his dick hard across my mouth and then rubbed the head over my lips, spitting and sucking before taking him back into my mouth, and swallowing his length.

"Ahh. Shit. Do that again," he said, when I drew back.

I took him in again—all of him—and then hollowing my cheeks, I started sucking, pulling on his cock like I was starved for his seed. I felt him harden, preparing to give me the object of my desire.

"Ah shit," he grunted, as the thick semen fiercely gushed into my mouth. I swallowed the first large spurt of the smooth rich fruit. I sucked and sucked, pulling the last of his load as he held my head, grunting as his cock jerked. Easing him from my mouth, I rubbed the luscious head over my lips, coating them with his come, licking it off as he watched.

Aiden lifted me from the floor and placed me on the bed. He removed my shirt, and grabbed at my breasts, peeling them from my bra.

"You like these tits, don't you?" I asked.

"Fuck yes, more than you know."

Aiden grabbed my breasts fully in his large hands, kneading and tugging as my body ached for more. He then slapped each one and I whimpered, absorbing the sensual torment. He pulled and twisted my nipples as he watched the burning passion on my face.

"I'm so hot for you," I whispered.

He leaned in to kiss my blossoming buds, flicking his tongue around the extreme tip of each, lavishing them equally with his hard sucking and biting.

"I want you to fuck me, Aiden. I want you to fuck me so hard that I beg you to stop, and even then, I want you to keep fucking me. I want you to own this pussy," I panted, the fervency of my need for him taking over.

"Is that what you really want, princess?" he asked, his deep, smoky whisper intensifying my hunger.

"That's exactly what I want," I replied.

He pulled me to the edge of the bed and lifted my legs, pushing them over my head, giving him full access to my sex. I heard the rip of my panties as he growled and placed his hungry mouth on my pussy. He savagely licked my wet, swollen lips, placing his hands on either side, spreading me open. His tongue darted inside the wet hole, skillfully sliding in and out of me, taking me on an uncharted journey of carnality. I felt my climax building and began urgently grinding my cunt on his tongue. With his mouth focused on my clit, he pushed his fingers into me, eliciting a torture that I could barely withstand.

"Slide your tongue in my pussy again, baby," I panted.

Aiden returned his attention to my sex, pushing his tongue into me.

I was about to come apart in his mouth. I grasped the back of his head, forcing his tongue in deeper as the dam of my arousal came bursting open, flowing through me in a violent spiral, repeatedly rising and falling.

My breathing was fast and harsh. My heart was beating outside my chest. My blood was racing. He stood and slapped his dick across my swollen lips and then with one powerful thrust he was buried inside me. There were no words to describe how he felt—I clenched my pussy tighter, squeezing every inch of him. I screamed out as he began repeatedly pumping into me, slamming his iron-hard length deep into my core. My center contracted—I was about to come again. He moved his magnificent body and his divine tool with the skill of a master, holding me in place with ease as he drove into me, expanding me, stroking me in all the right places, and commanding my body to respond.

"Ah...yes. Don't stop, Aiden," I cried out. I could feel him throbbing, hardening inside of me. He slammed deeper, the ocean of wetness resonating with each delve into my core.

"Fuck...Aria, I'm coming," he grunted and I was right there with him, coming hard on his cock as he ferociously emptied his passion into me.

Once we'd floated back to earth, Aiden carried me to the bathroom and set me on my feet in the shower. I pulled him down to kiss me, and I felt a smile on his lips.

"What?" I asked.

"It would appear someone's been practicing," he said, grinning.

"Were you impressed?" I asked.

"Fuck yes. So much so, that I want you to do it again," he said, as he guided me to my knees and pushed his dick into my mouth.

I looked up at him, turned on by the fierce, dark look in his eyes as I started to give him sample after sample of everything I'd learned.

$$\wp \qquad \wp \qquad \wp \qquad \wp$$

We spent every moment we could together, but it was like I blinked and days had passed. Aiden would be leaving first thing in the morning, and I wouldn't see him for another two weeks. The thought of his absence affected my mood even before he left.

"With all the modes of modern communication, we'll be fine Aria," he assured me.

"I know," I said. "I just hate it."

I reached up to kiss him. His lips were soft and smooth, moving over mine like a warm gentle breeze. He pulled me closer, crushing my body to his. My lips opened to him and his tongue moved deep into my mouth caressing mine, and reminding me how sweet our reunion would be.

❧Chapter Twenty-Four❧

Over the course of the next several months, my sisters and I had the opportunity to build bridges and form foundations for very solid relationships. They'd each applied for and been accepted to both Boston and Ohio State. I hoped they'd stay close by, but would understand if they didn't. Although I wasn't exactly playing the role of mother hen, I was very much involved in their lives, probably more than they would have liked. They were typical of most young adults at that stage—they wanted a chance to experience complete freedom.

While my sisters and I had more time together, my boyfriend and I had less. Aiden's life had become an endless stream of business trips, most of which placed us on different continents, which meant missed holidays and an over-dependence on virtual means of communication. Aiden promised it wouldn't be that way for much longer, as he was preparing Sloan and Nicholas to take firmer leadership roles within the company. But considering the conversation I'd overheard a few months ago in his father's study, I doubted that would go as Aiden planned.

Although the little time we had as a couple was filled with special moments, I was afraid it wasn't enough for either of us. Something had to change.

❧ ❧ ❧ ❧

"I'll need those reports by the end of the week. And cancel my trip to New York. I don't have time for that right now," I said.

"Yes, ma'am," Raina replied.

"On second thought, see if you can get Stephanie Landen to take my place."

"Will do."

"And get her all the information she needs for the presentation," I added.

"Yes, I'll attach it to the email with her itinerary."

At the sound of someone clearing his throat, I looked up from my desk and was immediately distracted by the gorgeous man staring at me.

Raina glanced that way, too, and then turned back to me. "Anything else?" she asked.

"No, that's all for now," I replied, my eyes glued to my man, virtually stripping him of his tailored suit.

"Good afternoon, Mr. Raine," Raina said, walking toward Aiden.

"Good afternoon. Ms. Cason isn't working you too hard, is she?" Aiden asked.

"No, of course not. She would never do that," Raina replied, with a hint of sarcasm.

Aiden smiled as Raina excused herself.

❧387❧

"To what do I owe the pleasure of a visit from my boss?" I asked.

"Who said anything about pleasure?"

"Oh, so does that mean I'm in trouble? Should I lift my skirt and get on all fours?" I teased.

"See, that's why I wanted you in this position. You're so intuitive." He closed the door and I heard the click of the lock.

I smiled as I rose from my chair and started toward him. He was on me within a few strides — his lips pressed solidly against mine. He pulled me closer, forcing his tongue into my mouth. "I've missed kissing you," he murmured. "I've missed your taste."

My office was saturated with the heavy breathing and uncontrolled passion of two lovers whose longing had exceeded its threshold. Aiden grasped my chin, holding me in place as he licked deeper into my mouth. Breaking our kiss, he turned me around, and with his erection poking me in the small of my back, he hurriedly walked me toward the desk. Guiding me over the edge, he lifted my skirt and moved my panties to the side. Without any delay, he shoved his dick inside me.

"Fuck!" I cried out.

Aiden placed his hand over my mouth, muting the cries of lust as he charged into me. His grasp tightened, pulling me back to meet the stabbing blows. They were fast and hard. We were both eager for the same thing — a quick release to tide us over until we had time to really go at it.

My climax was almost instant, as was his. I bit into his finger as my core released its wave of desire, my body shuddering as he held me firmly in place. His cock jerked inside me and then he was coming long and hard, his hot seed surging into me.

"Well, that's one way to say hello," I said as he loosened his hold and turned me to face him. I stood on my tiptoes and kissed his beautiful pink lips. "I've missed you like crazy," I said, as I headed to my office bathroom.

He followed me inside and I passed a towel to him. I watched as he wiped himself, and smiled. He just didn't seem the type to have an office quickie. Then again, neither was I...until him.

After cleaning up, I pulled my skirt down and returned to my office. "Have I mentioned this is one of my favorite perks of the job? You provide an excellent incentive for me to remain in this position."

"I do what I can, Ms. Cason. I like to keep the employees' morale up," he replied, grinning.

"So, if another employee asks?"

"It would be inappropriate. I only give office fucks to the RPH CEO. I think that's in the contract."

I simply adored him. "So, this contract...are there any other items in fine print I might have overlooked?"

"As a matter of fact, there are several. I didn't want to

mention those just yet because you're still getting your feet wet, but since you asked…"

"I can't wait to hear this," I replied, giggling.

"I love your laugh," he said, sitting on the edge of my desk.

My phone pinged, and Aiden looked down and saw it was a text from Kellan.

"You're still in contact with that guy?" he asked.

"Yes, he's a close friend. And he didn't stop being a friend when you and I reconnected."

"Since when do you have guys who are close friends?" he asked.

"Since you."

"What does that mean?"

"A lot of things changed since having met you."

"This is one change I'm not in favor of," he said, a scowl on his handsome face.

"It's not as if you don't have female friends — like Nadia," I said, my tone bitter.

"That's different, and you're well aware of that," he countered.

"Don't you mean it's *complicated*?"

"I don't want to talk about Nadia," he said, growing surly. "It's only going to lead to an argument."

"But you do want to talk about Kellan?" I probed. "If Nadia is off limits, then so is Kellan."

"Now you're being childish," he scolded.

"Term it however you wish. He's a friend, and I've grown to care about him, and he stays," I said firmly.

"We'll see about that," he replied.

"Aiden, if you do anything to cause issues with our friendship, it will not sit well with me," I warned.

Rather than answer, he abruptly changed the subject. "Grab your things. We're going to my place."

I glared at him, hating that he was making me angry. I didn't want to fight with him. We only had so much time together, and I didn't want it filled with resentment.

"Well, aren't you bossy?" I asked. "You could try asking nicely and you just may get a *nice* reply."

"I've missed you, and I need some time alone with you," he said.

"I know. I feel the same, but I really need to tie up a few things. How about you let me finish here, and I'll meet you at your place in a few hours," I said.

I could see my reply frustrated him.

"That doesn't work for me," he replied.

"It's not all about you, Aiden. Everything doesn't just stop because you've decided to grace me with an appearance. I have work to do. And based on the amount of time and energy you pour into *your* work, I'm sure you understand."

"So, this is an issue of time?" he asked, glowering at me. "You obviously have time to text your *close* friend."

Oh fuck. Was he determined to make this a bad homecoming? "Aiden, it's not like that, and you know it."

"Do I need to call Raina and see when you can squeeze me in? Is that what I need to do to get on your fucking schedule?" he asked, his eyes already blazing.

"*My* schedule? Are you kidding me? I'm here. I'm always here. You, on the other hand…well, we both know how that works."

"That's nothing new, Aria, so don't make an issue where there isn't one. You were fine with my schedule before. What's changed? Is it that fucker you've been texting? Your fucking friend?"

"No, maybe it's *your* fucking friend. Maybe it's Nadia!"

"Yeah, well I'm sure she wouldn't have a problem with my schedule."

"What the fuck? Why are you behaving this way? You know what? I don't want to know. Get the fuck out. Go find Nadia. I'm sure you have her on speed dial. I don't need this shit from you!"

"And I don't need it from you."

"Good. There's the door."

I watched as he stalked out of my office. He was pissed. Oh

well, so was I.

Dropping into my chair, I resumed my review of the information from human resources on the RPH work-study guidelines. We needed to get those in place by the end of the week in order for the high schools to receive the information on time for summer internships. I called Lorraine to discuss some changes and then checked my email to see if Adam had finished the projections for *The Writer*. I was revising one report after another when my phone pinged. I grabbed it to see a text from Aiden.

I'm sorry for being an ass.

Instead of replying, I placed the phone in my desk and sent Adam an email regarding one final amendment. A few minutes later, my phone pinged again. Rolling my eyes, I pulled it from my desk.

Forgive me.

I still didn't reply. Within a few seconds, there was another text.

I miss you, princess.

I sighed and tapped a message to him.

I miss you too, Aiden.

❧Chapter Twenty-Five❧

Time with Aiden was practically non-existent, and it bothered me more than I cared to admit. I resented him for it, but I refused to think about that today. I planned to bask in every minute we shared—especially tonight—we were going on a date!

Although we'd technically been in a relationship for several months now, the act of dating was still a novelty for me, especially dating someone like Aiden Raine. The mere thought of him did crazy things to me, and tonight was no different. Although excited, I was oddly nervous about spending real couple time with him. I would have thought I'd be over that by now, but no such luck.

Aiden hadn't specified the dress code, but I was sure my apparel would fit any venue. I'd decided on a Lanvin black crepe maxi skirt with asymmetric draping. There was an oversized bow at the front with a high slit that provided an overly generous view of my upper thigh. My top was an eyelash-print tailored blouse with skin-baring black lace panels that revealed the curves of my breasts. A pair of Christian Louboutin Sempre Monica over-the-knee boots completed the look.

I was meeting Aiden downstairs at four o'clock, and I was sure he would more than appreciate my efforts. With a giddy smile, I grabbed my bag and said goodbye to my sisters.

As I was about to exit Bianca's bedroom, she asked, "Can you smile any harder?"

"Leave her alone. It's been forever since they've had any time together," Lia said. "Speaking of which, Aria...I've been dying to ask you something about Aiden."

I froze. Was she wondering about my sex life? No way was I prepared to discuss that with my kid sister. Sex with Aiden was damn near too explicit to even think about, let alone share with anyone.

"He seems so intense. That must be...err...how do you...well, you know what I'm asking," Lia said.

"Yes, I think I do," I said, relieved her question wasn't in line with what I'd thought.

"Well, are you going to tell me?" she asked.

"He *is* intense, very much so. And sometimes it's intimidating. And then there are times when he focuses all of that intense energy on me, and it's indescribable. It's like he sees no one else, like he wants no one else—I'm all that matters."

They were both quiet, gawking at me with their mouths agape.

"See, he has the same effect on you, and he's not even around," I said, laughing.

After saying goodbye for a second time, I headed downstairs.

Stepping from the elevator, I was greeted by Silas and his serene half smile. He was obviously in a good mood. Normally Silas was hard to read — his furrowed brows hinted at a constant state of deep thought. "Good evening, Ms. Cason," he said.

"Hello, Silas," I replied, as he held the door.

It was the end of April — there was a bit of chill in the air, but a long-sleeved shirt or light jacket would have sufficed. I emerged from the building expecting to see Aiden standing near his car, but was shocked to find his sexy frame straddling the body of a black motorcycle. He looked as if he belonged on the cover of *Motorcyclist Magazine*. It undoubtedly would be the hottest cover they'd ever have.

"Hello, princess. You look amazing," he said, biting his bottom lip as he assessed my appearance.

"Hi, handsome. Aren't you just full of surprises? I didn't know you had a motorcycle."

"As I've said many times, there's a lot about me you don't know," he said. "But I'm hoping you stick around to find out."

"As of now, that's the plan. But you know what they say about best laid plans..."

"Don't do that," he warned.

Fine. I wouldn't start with any of my qualms, but I still had my reservations. I was sure he had some of his own as well.

"I don't think I'm dressed to ride a bike. You could've given a girl a clue," I said.

"I didn't tell you for a reason. I want you to be more spontaneous."

"And what about what I want?" I asked.

"You want to be spontaneous, too. You just go about it the wrong way," he replied, with a smile.

"Oh, is that right?"

"As far as I can tell, yes."

"So…not really sure I want to ride this," I said, eyeing the bike. It was sleek and sexy, like the gorgeous man who owned it. It also had a hint of danger I was not at all eager to experience.

"Why?" he asked.

"Other than the obvious fact that I'm not exactly dressed for a ride on the back of a motorcycle? Not only does that thing look abysmally uncomfortable, it screams danger."

"I can quickly resolve both of those objections. As for your clothing, you can lift your skirt and straddle. I hear you're pretty good at that," he said, playfully.

I couldn't help but grin. I loved his mischievous humor.

"Secondly, there's no need to be afraid. I won't let anything happen to you," he said, dismounting the bike and strolling over to me. "I'm not debating this with you. Understood?"

"I don't have protective gear," I said, pouting.

Shaking his head, he turned away, walking toward the bike

and removing a backpack. He opened it to reveal a riding jacket and a full-face helmet.

"Anything else?" he asked.

As usual, he'd planned everything—anticipating and countering my objections.

"Luckily, you're already wearing boots," he said. "Now let's get you in your protective gear, as you call it."

As Aiden assisted me with the jacket, he placed a kiss at the nape of my neck, my skin tingling from the soft touch of his lips. It was amazing how every touch—even the casual ones—melted my insides.

A slow, sexy smile graced his lips. "You look like a sexy biker chick."

"We make a great pair, then, because you definitely have the look of a sexy biker dude."

After adding the helmet, Aiden stepped back, evaluating me and flashing a smile of approval. "Perfect," he said, and planted a chaste kiss on my lips before lowering the face shield and tugging me behind him.

He smoothly mounted the bike and then flashed a grin. "Hop on," he said, as he slid on his helmet.

"Easy for you to say," I mumbled, lifting my skirt as much as I could without flashing any passersby. I then placed one foot over the side of the bike and settled in behind him.

"Grab my waist," he instructed.

I wrapped my arms around his hard frame, inhaling as I leaned in. Once I was positioned, he started the bike and we were off. I was marginally worried, but less than I'd initially anticipated. There were no vibrations of any kind—I hadn't expected that. Resting my head on his back, I enjoyed the feel of his body enveloped in the rich-grained leather, and watched the scenery flash by as we exited the city limits of Boston.

We slowed, coming to a stop at a traffic light. Aiden reached behind him, moving his hand over my thigh. "Are you okay?" he asked.

"Yes, I'm fine." I smiled when I realized it was true. I didn't know where we were going, but the ride there was certainly a seductive one.

A few miles later, we slowed in an open area near a giant maple tree. My gaze swept over my surroundings. We were in the middle of nowhere. Several people were dressed in serving attire, standing dutifully beside a meal laid out on a picnic blanket, complete with a canopy and heated lamps. I clambered off the bike as gracefully as was possible and took off my head gear.

Once Aiden placed the bike on the kickstand and removed his helmet, he was in front of me, pulling me into a kiss.

"Did you enjoy the ride?" he asked, releasing me from his embrace.

Slow chills ran through me as I shook off the effects of his kiss. "I did," I replied, gauging his reaction.

"See. Spontaneity is good for you." He reached for my hand, interlacing his fingers with mine as we walked toward the canopy.

"Good evening, Mr. Raine," said the man dressed like a maître d'.

"Jason," Aiden replied, with a nod.

On the ground, was a large ascot picnic blanket embellished with a pile of oversized throw pillows. In the center was a bottle of wine chilling alongside a dinner that was much too elegant for a picnic. There was also a large tray of olives, crackers and fruit. The added touch was the soft music saturating the air and further complementing the afternoon.

"Sir, we've prepared olives in paprika sauce, gin marinated potatoes, Asian wraps with peanut sauce, lentil spinach salad, and the wine is a 2008 Bienvenues Bâtard-Montrachet Grand Cru," Jason said.

"Thank you. I appreciate your attention to my last-minute request," Aiden said.

"Of course, sir. Unless there's something else, we'll leave you to your privacy," he replied.

Aiden looked down at me. "Is there anything you need?"

"No, I think you've got us covered." He typically thought of everything—today was no different.

As the sun began to set, we finished our meal and Aiden stretched out, laying his head in my lap and staring up at me. I sighed, content with the simple perfection of the moment.

"So, I was thinking—would you like to drive us back?" he asked.

I laughed. "I know you're kidding, right?"

"Nope. You're a very quick learner. I can teach you in only a few minutes."

"And you would let me drive back—without reservation?"

"I trust you."

"I'm glad to hear that, but you shouldn't trust me with this, especially if you'd like to make it to your Denver meeting in one piece."

"Honestly, I was kidding." He grinned, still looking up at me. "But seriously, would you like to learn?"

"Hmm. I don't know. I never really thought about it."

"Don't think about it now. Just say yes. I'll teach you, and when you're comfortable, we could ride together sometimes when I'm in town."

I sighed.

"What is it?" he asked.

"I just don't like your being gone so much," I said, my voice small as sadness seeped into our evening.

"I thought we talked about this," Aiden said, sitting up, his gaze soft with concern. "You don't have anything to worry about."

"I know you've told me that, but it never seems that way when you're gone and I don't hear from you for days sometimes." It reminded me too much of the anxiety that tortured me for years as I awaited Dad's return. Then, there was the fact that Aiden had vanished once before. Although I'd forgiven him, his disappearance often crept into my thoughts during his long absences.

"That was then, Aria. You've explained how that makes you feel. I've heard you and I understand, so we're doing things differently. Let's not think about that right now," he said, resuming his place in my lap. "I want you to enjoy this day. Are you?"

"Yes…very much. This was wonderful. I love your surprises," I said, looking down at him, tracing my palm along his chiseled jaw.

"I hope to always surprise you. I can't have you losing interest."

If our dates consisted of us simply watching grass grow, I'd never lose interest. "Little chance of that happening, Mr. Raine. You're my pineapple juice supplier, remember?"

"Ah, yes. That's right. Speaking of which, why don't you do that thing I said you were good at?"

I stared at him, confused.

With the lift of his brow and a suggestive smile, his request became clear.

I looked around and noticed the staff had wandered off into the distance. "You can't possibly mean what I think you mean."

"Can't I?"

"That's not happening, Aiden."

"Come here," he said, sitting up and holding his hand out to me.

"Why?" I asked.

"Because you're too far away."

"I'm only a couple of inches from you," I replied

"That's too far."

Placing my hand in his — I allowed Aiden to gently pull me astride him as he looked up at me. As my eyes locked with his, a devilish grin traced his seductive lips. With his palms flat against my thighs, he traced his way upward, the heat of his gaze burning into mine when he reached my inner thighs.

I looked around, worried we were being watched. The wait staff was visible, but not close enough that I could determine what they were doing — and vice versa, I hoped. Aiden unzipped my boots and slipped them off. He continued his exquisite seduction, his piercing green eyes lost in mine as he reached higher beneath my skirt to pull at my panties, sliding them slowly down my legs.

I lifted each foot as he freed the scrap of lace and then watched as he bowed his head to his palm, inhaling. Dropping my panties, he placed his hands on my thighs and urged me down, so that I was straddling him.

"That's better. But not quite what I had in mind," he said, planting a soft kiss on my lips.

"Dare I ask what you had in mind?"

"I'm pretty sure you know," he said, sweeping my hair away from my neck and then leaning in to adorn it with sweet kisses.

"Mmm," I purred, savoring the artistry of his touch and the rich, carnal smell of his skin.

After a final kiss, and with his gaze fixed on mine, he lifted my panties to my face—his other hand guiding my head down to his palm. "I want you to smell what I smell," he said.

Fuck! I loved him dirty like this. His lascivious gesture had the exact effect I was sure he was hoping for.

"It's tempting, don't you agree?" he asked, as I inhaled my scent. He released my head and then he motioned me back, allowing him to unzip his pants.

The walls of my sex tightened when Kingston's plush head emerged, awaiting and eager.

"Have a seat, princess."

I positioned my pussy over the crown of his shaft and eased down.

Aiden groaned. "Fuck, you feel so good," he breathed, as I slowly sheathed his dick.

Sinking to the thick root of his cock, I moved through the pain, stretching wider for him. My eyes never left his face, observing his expression as my sex contracted around his girth. His sharp intake of breath and the dark, fluid movement of his eyes were my personal aphrodisiac.

"Do you like it when I'm on top, baby?" I lifted myself from him and then slowly eased down, partially sheathing him this time.

"Fuck yes, but don't tease me," he whispered, his eyes intense on mine. Moving his hands to my waist, he pulled downward, forcing me to take all of his hard length.

"Oh fuck," I panted.

"That's how I want it, princess. I want all of that tight pussy," he breathed. "I want you to feel all of me." He rolled his body into mine, rotating his hips, pushing his cock deeper.

"Isn't that how you like it?" he asked, his smooth, velvet voice clenching my insides.

"Yes, baby," I whispered.

I glanced around, hoping the staff wasn't watching.

"Don't worry about anyone seeing us. Focus on this," he said, as he guided me up and down, each motion expanding me.

I was already so full, but somehow each descent moved him

deeper.

"There you go, princess. Take it," he murmured, as he watched my lust for him take ahold. "Isn't this why you wore this skirt? Is this what you wanted?" he asked, his light whisper caressing my skin.

"Yes," I replied, my voice quavering as he moved me, forcing me to take it how he wanted me to have it. "You're going to make me come if you keep doing this," I said.

"That's what I want. To make you come. Don't you want to come for me, princess?"

"Yes," I breathed.

"Go faster," he said.

"No, I want you to take it how I want to give it," I said, taking over and grinding on his cock.

"Ah...shit, Aria," he grunted, his eyes rolling back in his head.

I loved seeing that—loved watching *him*, the man who dominated so much and so many, lose control beneath me. I arched backward, tilting my pelvis, and gyrating deeply—stroking him with the warmth and tightness of my clenched walls, feeling him in every part of me.

"Ah...just like that, baby," he breathed.

It was driving him insane.

His fingers curved around my waist, quickening the thrusts

and driving us both to that place that belonged only to us. The urgency of our releases escalated, pushing my inhibitions to the wayside. I no longer cared about who might be watching—I didn't care if the entire world saw us. I couldn't stop—the burning need to come was frantically tugging and pulling at me.

Placing the pad of his thumb on my clit, he rotated and teased the sensitive knot.

I was sure I'd go mad if I didn't get my release. I felt it building from the depths of my core. "Fuck, I'm going to come," I whispered. I closed my eyes, biting my lip, as my climax pulled at me.

"Open your eyes, princess. Look at me. I want to see you when you come. I want you to come with me."

His words were my undoing. "Ah, shit," I panted, as I unraveled like a mass of thread, my climax tearing through me, touching every cell of my being. It was blinding and loud, like lightning and thunder—flashing and exploding. I clutched his back, pulling him closer, his solid frame absorbing the violent shudders that coursed through my body.

He too, exploded—coming apart beneath me. "Ah... shit," he hissed, his teeth clenched as his cock jerked, shooting thick loads of his seed into me. He pulled me into a deep kiss as the final beats of his release pulsed. Aiden held me in place, our foreheads pressed together as we gradually settled from the relief of unbridled lust.

He was still inside me—his essence trailing along the inside of my thighs. I reached down to feel the wet, messy remnants of our arousal.

"Wow," I said.

"What?" he asked.

"We're really a mess," I said, looking around for a cloth.

We cleaned up as best we could and then reassembled our clothing. I was lost in thoughts of what just happened. I shook my head, smiling at our mischief. I couldn't believe the things he talked me into doing. Looking up at him, I saw him pull his shirt out of his pants—he seemed just as preoccupied as I.

"Are you thinking about how you've corrupted me?"

"Possibly," he replied, smiling. "And I think you like the way your pussy smelled."

"Why do you say that?"

"Because of the look on your face when you smelled your panties. Smells good, doesn't it?"

I didn't reply. I leaned down to zip my boot.

"It's okay, you don't have to answer. But I'll tell you this…as good as it smells, it tastes even better."

"Glad you like it, Mr. Raine."

"I know you've tasted yourself with me around, but have you ever done it alone? When you're getting yourself off?"

Hell yes, I had — on several occasions — and I enjoyed it immensely.

"Don't be coy now. Tell me, have you?"

"Maybe," I replied.

"I want to watch you do it. The next time we're alone…no, scratch that. The next time I *ask*, regardless of where we are, I want you to slide your fingers inside that delicious cunt of yours, finger yourself, and then taste."

Regardless of where we are? No way would I do that in public. But then again, he could seduce me into just about anything.

§   §   §   §

It was Aiden's last night in town. I was sitting in his bedroom, texting back and forth with Lia, when Aiden crossed the room, a sly smile on his lips.

"What are you up to now?" I asked.

He reached into his pocket, pulled out a box, and extended it to me. "Open it," he said, placing it in my hand.

As I removed the lid from the signature turquoise box, my heart smiled. An orchid drop pendant necklace was nestled amid dark red orchid petals. I lifted the platinum string from amongst the fragrant packing and traced it through my trembling fingers. It was lined with princess-cut diamonds and a single orchid-shaped ruby dangled from the center.

I looked up to see Aiden assessing my reaction. Did he think I wouldn't like this? I *loved* it.

"Aiden, it's beautiful," I said.

His lips curled into a smile, his green eyes twinkling with excitement.

"Let me put it on for you."

I passed the necklace to him and then lifted my hair while he placed the string around my neck and fastened the clasp. He pressed his lips against my neck, kissing it ever so softly.

I closed my eyes, freezing this moment—recording it all to memory—the feel of his lips on my skin, the joy in his eyes upon seeing my reaction, and the gift itself.

"Let's see how it looks," he said, turning me to face him.

"It's lovely, Aria," he said. "Go take a look."

I walked over to the dresser, Aiden following closely behind me. The necklace was absolutely stunning.

"I love it. Thank you, Aiden."

"You're welcome, my fair maiden."

I smiled as he bowed before me. "You constantly catch me off guard."

"I always will, princess."

"What's the occasion?" I asked.

"Looking a gift horse in the mouth, I see," he teased.

"No. I'm just curious as to what inspired this."

He traced a finger along my cheek. "You inspired it. I know what it does to you when I'm not here. Now, there will always be a piece of me with you when I'm not. Each time you start to miss me, touch the orchid and know that I'm missing you, too. You're always on my mind, more so than I would have thought possible."

My eyes welled up at his sentiment.

"My beautiful crybaby," he teased, looking into my tear-filled eyes.

"Stop. Don't call me a crybaby," I said, sniffling.

He pursed his lips, attempting to hide his amusement. "I'm sorry, princess," he said, enveloping me in his strong arms.

I held him tighter, not ever wanting to let go, but I knew he was about to leave for the next three weeks and the thought of his absence both hurt and frightened me. The necklace was his way of assuring me that we were connected even when we were far apart, but I had a feeling it would cause me to miss him that much more.

❧Chapter Twenty-Six❧

It felt like months instead of weeks. That's how long it had been since I'd last seen Aiden. He'd kissed me goodbye on the threshold of the penthouse, and then with an ache already in my heart, I'd watched as he walked away. Every day since then, I'd worn the trinket he'd given to me, hoping it would do as he'd said — remind me he was always close, even during those times when it felt as though he wasn't.

Today, he was finally headed back to the U.S., and flying to Chicago to celebrate his birthday. Lia, Bianca and I were scheduled to arrive at O'Hare later in the afternoon. I was thrilled the girls were joining us. They'd fallen under Aiden's spell and were almost as giddy about seeing him as I was.

"Aria, do you think he'll like our gift?" Bianca asked, her amber eyes beaming with excitement.

Lia had instantly taken a liking to Aiden, probably a little too much, but Bianca had been slow to warm up to him, so I was especially glad to see her enthusiasm. I was also relieved she wasn't as negative about relationships as when she first came to live with me. She'd been dating Landon, Raina's nephew, for about a month now, ever since meeting him at the RPH work-study interviews.

"I know he'll love it," I said, smiling at her. It was difficult shopping for someone like Aiden. He wanted for nothing, so a lot of thought had to be placed into his gifts. After crossing off this and axing out that, the girls finally came up with a great idea—a Jimi Hendrix guitar pick. It was quite an expensive find, but it wasn't about the money. I knew it would mean a great deal to him. But when my sisters came to me with their decision, I had no idea how difficult it would be to obtain it. We'd taken a day to travel out of town to attend an auction. It had been a battle to the bitter end, and we simultaneously sighed with relief when the auctioneer announced that it was ours. And in a few short hours, it would be Aiden's.

He'd arranged for one of the Raine Industries jets to fly us to Chicago. I was becoming quite fond of skipping the typical air travel headaches—a girl could definitely get used to being driven directly to the tarmac and escorted to a jet. That was one of the nice parts of the trip, but of course, there was the not-so-nice part—time with Aiden's parents.

Given the unpleasantness of my first visit, I wasn't sure how I felt about staying overnight at Aiden's family home. Between his parents and the Nadia ordeal, I was very wary. Due to the closeness of Aiden and Nadia's families, I was fairly certain she would be attending the party, so I'd prepared myself for whatever may come. Two things were evident—Nadia still had her sights on Aiden and both sets of parents were in full support of that pairing.

∾ ∾ ∾ ∾

My sisters and I landed at O'Hare a little after three o'clock and were driven to the Raine Estate. I was chatting with them about their last full month of high school when my phone pinged, alerting me of a text from Aiden.

I can't wait to see you, princess.

I feel the same about you, babe.

Come to my room as soon as you arrive.

Why?

Because I want my cock in your mouth, and I didn't think you'd want to suck it with everyone watching.

Since our picnic fuck, I'm up for anything. Besides, I've heard exhibitionism is healthy for a relationship.

So, you wouldn't mind if others watched as you swallowed loads of my come?

Aiden's dirty mouth was wetness waiting to happen—if he kept that up, I'd need to change panties as soon as I walked through the door. Over the last few months, we'd both transcended to a whole new level of dirty talk. It made for some pretty hot phone sex...all right, more than hot. It was fucking amazing!

Loads, huh? Is that a promise?
I certainly hoped so, because swallowing his come was like savoring a rare dessert.

It's a guarantee. And if you know what's good for you, you'll swallow every bit.

I looked up from my phone to see two pair of eyes on me. Although, I knew they had no idea of the contents of my text, I was suddenly embarrassed. I sent another message to Aiden, hoping to halt the vulgarity of his communication.

Bianca and Lia are staring at me like crazy. Stop texting me!!

The next message from Aiden was a picture of his fingers curved around his cock, along with the caption, "Kingston says hi."

I gasped.

"Is everything okay?" Bianca asked.

"Yes, just exchanging silly texts with Aiden," I replied.

What are you doing? I said STOP, but you only get worse. BTW, Virginia nearly exploded!

What I'm doing, princess, is providing you the incentive to excuse yourself as soon as you enter the house. You need to bring that sweet ass of yours to me.

Mmm. Is that what you want? My ass?

Among other parts of you, yes. So, don't keep me waiting.

Bossy much?

I'm the birthday boy. I get whatever I want today, remember?

How is that different than any other day, Mr. Raine?

After a few minutes, I realized he wasn't going to reply, so I tossed my phone into my purse. "Sorry for being so caught up in him. It's been a while since we've been together, and I'm excited."

"I can only imagine. I don't know how you keep your hands off of him," Lia said.

"Who says I do?"

We giggled like high school girls talking about the hot new guy in class.

"Are we almost there?" Bianca asked, glancing out the window.

I followed her gaze, but nothing looked familiar. "I think so. It's only about a thirty-minute drive from the airport." I didn't know where the hell we were — I just knew we couldn't get there fast enough. My mind was on one thing and one thing only — getting to a very worked up and hopefully very naked Aiden.

When we finally turned down the long drive, my heartbeat quickened. This was the part that was familiar — the bout of nerves I experienced upon approaching the Raine mansion. The tall, formal gates slowly opened, and the car proceeded through, eventually pulling to a stop in the circular drive. The chauffeur assisted us from the limo while Clark exited the house to collect our luggage. I looked toward the double-front doors and thought back to my last visit. Drawing in a deep breath, I started up the walkway, and hoped like hell this visit went off without a hitch.

"Wow, this place is humongous," Lia exclaimed.

"I couldn't imagine living here. It's amazing," Bianca said.

Looks can be deceiving, girls. No way would I want to live here with these pretentious, manipulative people. I hadn't said anything to my sisters about Aiden's parents. I'd decided to let them form their own opinions.

As we entered the house, we were greeted by one of the maids and then Sienna appeared, beautiful and elegant as always.

"Aria, how lovely to see you. And these must be your sisters. They're absolutely beautiful," she said, looking at the girls.

"It's good to see you, Sienna," I said, thrown off by her welcoming reception. "Yes, these are my sisters Lia and Bianca."

"It's nice to meet you, Mrs. Raine," Lia said.

Bianca smiled at Sienna and said, "Thank you for inviting us."

"Yes. Thank you, Mrs. Raine," Lia echoed.

"We're delighted you could make it. And do call me Sienna," she said. "It's so nice to finally meet the two of you. Allison has gone on and on about you."

"Is she here?" Lia asked.

"She's in the parlor with Sloan," Sienna replied.

"Your home is beautiful," said Bianca.

"Thank you. I'll have to give you a tour later."

"Wow. That would be great," Bianca replied.

I was shocked to see Sienna's pleasant side. I didn't think she actually *had* one. Maybe she was only vile to the women she didn't want to date her son.

"Come join us," Sienna said, motioning for us to follow her. "We're all in the study…well, except Aiden. He's upstairs doing God knows what. Sometimes I wonder why he bothers to come home, because we barely see him when he does."

Clark appeared next to me as if from nowhere. "Miss Aria. Mr. Aiden has requested you upstairs. A matter of some papers that need reviewing." He passed me an envelope, and I looked at it, wondering if Aiden really had some business to discuss. So, was he just teasing me with the texts?

"I'll join you all after I attend to Aiden's latest emergency," I explained, excusing myself. "Will you be okay?" I asked my sisters.

"They'll be fine, Aria," Sienna said. "Do hurry with the business matter and remind Aiden today's his birthday, not a day to work behind closed doors."

"I'll drag him down as soon as I can," I replied, turning away to open the envelope. There was one sentence written on the paper inside.

I want to hear you gag.
-A.

Fuck! Virginia must have punched my insides because my entire pelvic area involuntarily responded. Placing my hand on the banister to steady myself, I glanced around the room, relieved no one had seen my reaction, and then I trotted up the stairs—eager to see what Aiden had in store.

I didn't bother knocking. When I opened the door, he was standing on the opposite side of the bedroom, his back to me as he looked out of the window. He was wearing a navy suit, and as usual, it fit him to perfection.

"The envelope was a nice touch, Mr. Raine," I said, strolling toward him.

"I do what I can, Ms. Cason," he replied, still facing the window.

"I was wondering…" I began.

"Yes?" he asked.

"The picture you sent. It was very…distracting. I've thought of little else. So, I'm curious. Is this the part where I get up close and personal with Kingston? You know…before the festivities begin?"

"You read my mind," he replied smoothly, turning to face me, his hand already on his zipper.

My gaze washed over his gorgeous frame—he was so fucking hot. How did I ever resist him for all of those months? Moving a few steps closer, I pushed his hand aside. "Since you're the birthday boy, I'll do the honors, baby," I said, as I unzipped his pants.

He grasped my chin and pressed his lips hard against mine,

capturing my mouth with a wildness that took my breath away.

"You want it. There it is," he said, guiding me to my knees.

I shoved my hands into his boxers and released Kingston from his confined space. As Aiden's dick grew thicker and longer, I took him in, starting with the wide crown—licking, teasing and sucking as if he was supplying me with the one thing I needed to survive.

"Suck all of it," he said, grabbing my head and taking over, his dick moving in and out of my mouth, hitting the back of my throat and nearly choking me.

I hollowed my cheeks, drawing rhythmically in time with his rapid pace, my head bobbing as he watched his cock fuck my greedy mouth. He was so big. I didn't want to stop, but my jaws had already started to ache. I curved my fingers around his length, stroking him, as I bestowed attention to his balls, sliding my tongue along each one before taking them whole into my mouth.

"Ah, Aria," he said, his voice a deep rasp.

As I jacked his cock, I lavished the engorged tool with my saliva, my gaze fixed on the luscious head as his sweet treat spilled over. I rushed to taste of him, placing the tip of his dick between my lips, moving it back and forth, lightly sucking as I looked up at him. Reveling in the passion of his dark irises, I moved his cock further into my mouth, urging him to fuck it to his heart's content.

"God, Aria. That's it. Just like that," he said, fisting a handful of my hair, holding me in place as he stroked his big dick in and out of my mouth. As he went deeper, the sounds of my gagging resonated throughout the room, my struggle to take him in doing nothing to slow his pace.

"You're going to make me come," he said, slowing his thrusts.

That's what I was aiming for. The loads of come he'd promised.

He stared down at me, an all-consuming lust penetrating the heat of his gaze. "Relax your throat. I want you to swallow my cock, princess."

I prepared myself as he gradually moved his large penis deeper, then pulling out, and tracing the crown along my lips.

"What are you waiting for? Make me swallow it," I said.

Aiden guided himself into my mouth again, slowly pushing forward until his cock was down my throat. "Ah, shit," he groaned. "That's my dirty girl."

His cock jerked and a short spurt of come pumped into my mouth. I was hoping for more, but he pulled away, lifting me and placing me on the bed.

"I need to be inside you," he said, as he pulled at my pants.

"I've got it," I said, pushing his hands away. "Take off your clothes. I want to feel your skin on mine."

As I watched him undress, I reached inside my panties and rubbed my fingers over my clit. "You wanted to see me taste myself." I shoved three fingers inside the tightening walls of my sex, sliding them in and out as he watched. "Is this what you had in mind?" I asked, easing my fingers from my pussy. I smeared the lust across my lips before sliding it over my tongue. "Mmm. Do you want to taste, baby?"

Aiden grasped my fingers and slid them into his mouth, his eyes adhered to mine as he sucked my juices.

"I'm so hard for you," he said. He pulled my panties off, flipped me over and spread my legs. His hand moved between my thighs, cupping my sex. Virginia was a sensitive, throbbing mess. Grabbing my ass, Aiden spread me open and moaned when he spread me wider.

"Please don't make me wait. Fuck me," I said.

The head of his cock traced my sex, moving up and down the soaked slit, teasing me.

"Give it to me," I purred. "Please."

Aiden pushed into me, driving so deep that I nearly came undone from just the one stroke. "Oh fuck. You feel so good. I've missed this pussy," he groaned, as his hand came down across my ass. He eased back and then slammed into me again, my entire body bucking forward.

"Show me how much you've missed it. Fuck it like you've missed it," I said.

Growling like a feral beast, Aiden gripped my hips and started the deep, repetitive drives into me.

"Ahh. Right there. Holy shit," I cried out, as he continued the rhythmic blows, his strong hands holding me in place as he fucked me into oblivion. I was lost — somewhere above the clouds as this gorgeous man violently fucked my weeping pussy.

Fuck, he made it hurt so good. Too good. I couldn't take anymore. I came hard, my body quivering as he masterfully and repeatedly drove his length to the end of me. "Shit, shit, shit," I breathed, as the rapid thrusts pounded my core.

"Are you ready? Do you want my come, Aria?"

"Mmm. Yes, baby. I want it all," I said, as he pulled out of me.

I turned to face him and he pushed his dick into my eager mouth.

"Ah fuck. I'm coming," he grunted, as his cock pulsed, a continuous flow of his thick hot semen spraying into my mouth. With a hunger I couldn't explain, I swallowed mouthful after mouthful. His come was a liquid paradise. I focused on the large crown, sucking hard — milking him. I looked up, meeting his smoldering gaze as I siphoned his cock, hoping for more. A smile snaked over his lips.

Reluctantly, I pulled his delicious penis from my mouth.

"Why are you smiling at me like that?"

"You can stop sucking now. I think you've pretty much sucked me dry," he said, grinning.

"But I want more," I said, sliding my tongue over my lips, capturing any of the essence that had escaped.

He rubbed his thumb over my bottom lip. "You missed a little," he said, sliding it into my mouth.

I moaned around the pad of his thumb and he smiled again.

"Why are you smiling now?" I asked.

"Because I think I've created a monster," he said.

"Whatever. You love it."

"Damn right I do," he replied, leaning down to kiss me.

"I have your birthday gift. I'd like to give it to you now — in private," I said.

"You realize you didn't need to buy me anything. Having you here, celebrating this day with me, is gift enough."

"I'm excited to share today with you, too, but I wanted to get you something, even though you have everything."

"I didn't have everything until I found you. You know that, right?"

"I feel the same way. You've completed me in a way that continues to astound me. You've brought so much to my life," I said. I was quiet for a few moments. How did I ever think my life was fulfilling before him? He'd brought a sense of contentment and exhilaration to my world that changed my entire outlook. "Now look what you've done. You're making me all sappy. Back to your gift," I said, walking over to my purse.

After removing the box from my bag, I sat beside Aiden on the edge of the bed. He looked at me—his shiny green eyes alight with curiosity, as if this was the first gift he'd ever received.

"I hope you like it," I said, placing the box in his hand.

Removing the ribbon and wrapping, he opened the lid. "Aria," he exclaimed.

"Do you not like it?" I asked, worried I'd made the wrong choice. I had no idea what to give as a birthday present to a billionaire boyfriend.

"Quite the opposite—I love it." He lifted the Omega watch from the box. It was the Speedmaster Moonwatch Chronograph Black Dial.

"Look at the back," I said.

There was an inscription.

Let's make time stand still. Love, Aria.

It was inspired by the words he'd spoken—the same words I'd been thinking—after he'd first made love to me.

He removed the watch he was currently wearing and replaced it with my gift.

"I'll treasure this always," he said, standing and reaching for me. He cupped my face and pressed his lips to mine.

"Happy birthday, baby," I said.

"Thank you, princess. And you say I'm full of surprises. I didn't expect this."

"What did you expect exactly?"

"I'm not sure, but this is perfect," he said. "Just like you."

"I'm not perfect by any means." We both knew that, all too well.

"Yeah, I know, but I had to say that...it kinda fit the moment," he said, grinning.

"You ass," I replied, laughing. "Your mother expected me to bring you downstairs a long time ago. Let's wash up and we can join them."

Stepping into the bathroom, we grabbed a couple of towels and wiped away the signs of sex, both of us looking at the other as we did so, neither of us saying a word. I didn't know why, but watching him clean up after having fucked me was so freaking hot.

Once we were presentable, we headed downstairs. More guests had obviously arrived, given the increase in the noise level. I glanced around the room at the dozens of strange faces. The more the merrier, right? Somehow that saying didn't seem to fit this group—so there was no way the evening could end as wonderfully as it had started.

❧Chapter Twenty-Seven❧

The party was in full swing, even with the absence of the guest of honor, which confirmed my suspicions of this shindig leaning more toward a Raine Event than a celebration of Aiden's birth. No less than expected, the atmosphere was very distinguished and elegant, with epicurean cuisine, expensive beverage, and a full string orchestra. I'd also spotted a few members of the press, who added yet another layer to the exclusive and over-the-top gathering.

Aiden didn't seem to mind at all that it had started without him. As a matter of fact, he appeared bored of it already. He looked down at me, smiling as he pulled me into a dance. And for quite a while, that's where we stayed—in each other's arms and lost in the revelry of the music.

Glancing the room, I easily determined it was occupied by the most elite society members, none of whom were familiar. Aiden introduced me to several Raine Industries executives, a few of his friends from college and some close family acquaintances—which was code for prudes. It was quite the assembly. Aiden had applied his mask and fit right in. I didn't know how he volleyed so quickly from CEO to Raine elite to my Aiden. I supposed what he'd previously said was true—we all adapted to blend in—but I was amazed he did it so well.

When Aiden fell into conversation about his golf game with a college buddy, I excused myself to go in search of my sisters. Finding them proved to be difficult. There were just too many people. Stepping onto the terrace, I pulled out my phone and sent a text. They were teenagers who practically lived on their phones, so I was sure one of them would reply. After sliding my cell into my pocket, I turned around—bumping right into the one person I was hoping to avoid—Nadia Lane.

"Oh geez," I said, irked simply by her appearance.

"Hello to you, too, Aria," she said, a fake smile on her plastic face.

"Nadia," I said. "If you'll excuse me..." I moved to step past her.

"Aria, don't rush off. I was hoping to have a moment alone with you—to truly apologize for the rather unfortunate mishap last year."

Mishap? Was she insane? "You were lying on Aiden's bed naked. How can anyone construe that as a mishap?"

She waved my question away as if it were some silly joke. "I don't get caught up in terminology. But I really wanted to apologize, and I hope you'll forgive me," she said, oozing insincerity.

"I'll accept your apology in the same spirit in which it was delivered," I said, returning her cutting smile.

She caught me off guard, pulling me into a hug as she gushed, "I'm so relieved. Thank you, Aria. I was so worried you'd say no."

What the hell? She really *was* insane. I stepped back and watched as she continued her ramblings. Looking at the glass in her hand, I made a mental note to avoid whatever she was drinking.

"I know how important it is to Aiden that we get along. I don't quite understand it, but one never does understand things like this with Aiden. He's such a complex person. I suppose that's why my relationship with him has always been so complicated."

"Nadia, give it a rest. If one more person describes your relationship with Aiden as complicated, I think I'll scream."

She stiffened and gasped. Her expression faltered, but she hurriedly reapplied the facade that accompanied the evil glint in her eyes. "Well, Aria, when you carry a man's child, it does complicate things, don't you think?" she asked.

I stared at her, not knowing how to reply, and she looked at me as though she'd just thrown the knockout punch.

"I've spotted someone I simply must say hello to. It was delightful seeing you again, Aria." She smirked and walked past me, leaving me in a tailspin as I tried to interpret what the hell she meant.

What the fuck was she saying? That she was pregnant with Aiden's child? I thought back to the last time I was in Chicago. Aiden reluctantly revealed he'd had sex with Nadia the night of the gala. That had been a one-time thing though—and she obviously wasn't pregnant, so why would she say something like that?

I left the terrace, intent on finding Aiden. Unlike my fruitless hunt for Lia and Bianca, I easily found him—laughing with his brother near the bar.

Upon my approach, Nicholas spotted me, his expression transitioning from merriment to apprehension, and thereby cueing Aiden to look over his shoulder.

Aiden's smile fell into a frown as he searched my face. "What's wrong?"

"I'm not sure. Can we speak in private?" I asked.

"Sure. Nick, can you have the waiter bring over Cles des Ducs for me and a vodka cranberry for Aria?" he asked, turning to his brother.

"No problem," Nicholas replied, as Aiden and I stepped away.

"What's going on?" he asked.

"I'm hoping you can tell me. I just had a rather strange exchange with your ex."

"Who are you talking about?" he asked, his brows furrowed.

"Damn. How many of your exes are here tonight?"

"Aria, please don't start with this."

"I'm referring to Nadia. Who else?"

"Sir, your drinks," came the voice of the waiter behind us.

Aiden grabbed both glasses and passed one to me. He took a sip, his eyes not leaving mine.

It was easy to see he was already frustrated by the topic of conversation. Taking a larger sip of the drink than I should have, it burned going down.

"Okay, so let's hear it. What's going on now?" he asked.

I started to feel silly for even considering it, but I needed to ask. "Is there something I should know about you, Nadia and a pregnancy?"

He almost heaved at the question. "What? Hell no. Why would you ask something like that?"

"In the midst of another inane conversation with her, she mentioned things were complex between the two of you, because carrying your child complicated things."

Understanding crossed his face, and he let out a sigh as he shoved a hand through his hair.

"What is it? Am I missing something here?" I asked.

"Fuck. This situation with Nadia is really starting to piss me off."

"Wait. So, what are you saying? Is there something to what

she said?"

"Aria, I'm leaving town soon, and we barely have any time to spend together, so let's forget the Nadia bullshit and make the most of the time we have."

If he thought I was going to let this go, he was as insane as Nadia. "What was she talking about, Aiden?"

"This isn't the place for that type of discussion. I'll tell you everything later."

So, there was something. Something he obviously didn't want to tell me. "Aiden, whatever it is, I'd like to know now."

"I can't have one night?" he asked, his temples already pulsing. "One fucking night without trying to convince you that you have nothing and no one to worry about? That it's *you* that I want!"

"First off, don't use that tone when you speak to me. I'm not one of your sycophants who buckle every time you so much as frown at them. And secondly, I don't question if you want me, because I know you do. What I do question, is if you want someone else, also. There's a difference, asshole."

"So, this is about jealousy?" he asked.

"Don't you dare spin this around. This has far less to do with me and more to do with all of your fucking secrets that continue seeping out!"

"Are you telling me you don't have any secrets?" he asked.

"Again, Aiden…this is not about me. We're talking about you and another fact about yourself you've chosen to conceal."

"And there's absolutely nothing you've concealed from me? Nothing you've done in your past that you're ashamed of? I think we both know that isn't true," he spat out.

"Have any of my supposed secrets come back to bite you in the butt? No, they haven't so I would have to say no."

"Oh really? And the shit storm with Dane Patrick? What exactly was that if not a secret? And who the hell do you think put out that fire? Me!" he exclaimed, taking a swig of the dark liquor. "Your little secret could have destroyed your career, not to mention the PR nightmare it would have caused for Raine Industries. So, don't judge me for a past indiscretion when you have several of your own!"

I gasped, recoiling from his accusation. He was being cruel, and his temper— which he'd somehow managed to rein in until now—was flaring.

"Indiscretion? How can you reduce this to something as simple as that? We're talking about a life Aiden, not some innocent slip of your dick into the wrong woman."

"I do not wish to fight with you, Aria," he said, his voice low.

"This does not have to be a fight. I just want to understand."

"You won't necessarily understand everything about me, nor will I about you. I have a past, just as you. But do I hound you about your sexual history? No. Your ex-lovers aren't with you, and I am, so they are of no consequence. The same applies to Nadia. She is of no consequence. Just let this go."

"But, Aiden—"

"Enough, Aria! I'm not wasting any more time with this nonsense."

I could see he wasn't about to go any further, and it pissed me off. He'd turned a legitimate question about the possibility of his having a child out there somewhere, into something about my petty jealousy. And if he did in fact have a child, how could he consider the mother to be of no consequence?

He took another sip of his drink. "And one last thing, I certainly hope you don't plan on using this as yet another obstacle for us, because that shit is getting old."

With that, he turned and walked away, obviously not caring if I rejoined the party with him. Quite frankly I didn't care very much myself at that moment. After downing my drink, I decided it was time for Lia, Bianca, and I to leave.

Stepping from the terrace, I resumed my earlier search for the girls, but it was practically impossible to find them in this mob. As I perused the room full of guests, a thought brought me up short. Maybe I couldn't find my sisters because I wasn't supposed to. Maybe I needed to stay here—to stop running. After all, my running was the sole reason I'd lost so many years with my mother. Did I really want to lose out on the possibility of Aiden, too?

I grabbed another drink from the approaching waiter, thinking it would drown the anger enough to pull me back into party mode. Why had Aiden blown a gasket over a question that warranted an answer? A question he avoided by way of deflecting and giving the appearance of my being insecure? Did he really see me that way? I was secure in who I was, and in my ability to get just about any man I wanted. But did I have what it took for a man to stay? Especially with monumental obstacles consistently popping up?

I later spotted Aiden with Nicholas and some guy I didn't recognize. They each had a drink in one hand and a cigar in the other. I didn't know Aiden smoked cigars.

Walking over toward them, I asked, "Nicholas, have you seen Lia and Bianca?"

He glanced at Aiden before answering. The tension between his brother and me didn't go unnoticed. Aiden was aloof, as if I wasn't even there. "I think they were over near the auction table with Allison," Nicholas said, looking from me to his brother.

"Nick, where are your manners? Introduce me to this beautiful lady," said the guy standing between Nicholas and Aiden.

Looking at Aiden before introducing me, Nicholas said,

"Grayson Miller, this is Aria Cason."

"It's nice to meet you, Aria. What a beautiful name. Would you care to dance?"

"No, thank you. I'm actually looking for my sisters. We're about to head out," I replied.

Aiden eyed me over the rim of his glass as he took a drink. He didn't say anything. He simply turned and walked away.

❧Chapter Twenty-Eight❧

It was nearly two o'clock in the morning. After my fourth drink, I'd given up on locating my sisters and traipsed upstairs to the bedroom. I wanted to go home. I didn't want to be in this house, and I certainly didn't want to be in Aiden's room.

I'd planned to call the airline for the first flight out of Chicago. In the meantime, I needed sleep, but not in Aiden's bed. I'd get some rest in one of the bedrooms my sisters were using.

Since I hadn't unpacked, it didn't take much time at all to gather my things. After grabbing my purse and toiletry bag, I glanced around for anything I could have overlooked. My gaze fell upon the box that previously held Aiden's gift, and I let out a sigh. Just a few short hours ago, I was singing Aiden's praises. And here I was now wanting to get as far away from him as I could. A noise sounded, interrupting my musings, and reminding me I needed to get the hell out of his room.

The bedroom door opened, and in stepped Aiden. He didn't say anything, but he didn't need to. I could see he was still upset. As he closed the door behind him, he caught sight of my luggage.

"You want to go—I'm not going to stop you," he said.

Good, asshole—I don't want to be stopped. As I started to leave, Aiden was suddenly behind me, reaching over my head, and slamming the door closed.

"Why do you do this shit, Aria?" he yelled, grabbing my bag and tossing it onto the bed.

I stared at him—saying nothing. If he thought I would respond to this type of crap, he was in for a rude awakening.

He stepped closer, stopping directly in front of me. "Are you going to answer my question?" he demanded, the stench of alcohol brushing over my cheek.

"That depends. Are you going to stop yelling?" I asked, my voice calm.

He took a moment to rein in his anger and replied, "I'm damned near wasted, and quite frankly, I'm still pissed. But you don't need to leave. Let's get some sleep, and I'll answer all of your questions in the morning."

To be honest, I wasn't sure if I wanted to stay and listen to anything he had to say.

"Aria. Please. You have my word," he said. "I don't want this to be a problem for us."

"Fine," I said, dropping the purse beside the door. "But don't touch me. We sleep, and in the morning, we talk."

A drunkened grin spread over his lips.

"I'm serious, Aiden. If you touch me, I'm gone."

He stopped dead in his tracks, holding up his hands in surrender.

"And the bag you casually tossed – you can bring to the bathroom so I can change for bed," I said, as I moved away from him.

Aiden retrieved the luggage and followed me to the bathroom.

Grabbing the bag, I pulled it inside, then pushed him away and closed the door.

"I love you, Aria," he said, from the other side of our would-be barrier.

Although part of me didn't want to say it, I finally replied, "I love you, too, Aiden."

Aiden and I were back up at the crack of dawn. He was nursing a hangover, and I was still wondering if I should leave. I sat at the breakfast bar as he moved around the kitchen, whipping up some type of concoction to soothe his pains. I had a bit of a hangover myself, but it was nothing compared to the one he'd tied on.

After he'd taken a few gulps of his tonic, he busied himself with preparing an omelet for me. I looked around the kitchen – it was the same one he'd snuck into as a child. My kitchen was a fair size, but it could easily fit into this one at least three times. There were countless places Aiden could have hidden from Sienna –

behind the counter, under a cabinet, beside a column or in the pantry. I couldn't help but smile as I envisioned each scenario.

Aiden assumed the seat across from mine, his large glass of hangover tonic in tow. He took a few more gulps and then he looked at me.

"Aren't you hungry?" he asked, noticing my untouched food.

"Not very."

"You should eat."

Not wanting to debate yet another thing, I took a bite of the omelet. It was actually pretty good, so good in fact, that I continued eating without any additional prompting from him.

We maintained our silence until my last bite and his last sip, and then as if he knew his time was up, he finally started talking.

"Nadia and I were a couple—for lack of a better description— during the time I was in law school. We were involved for approximately two years. Of course, our relationship was of an intimate nature, and we always used protection—except once. As luck would have it, that one slip-up resulted in a pregnancy. Neither of us had a desire to be parents, especially me. Although Nadia wasn't ready to be a mother, she still wanted the child. I didn't."

So, it was true. He'd gotten her pregnant. She'd carried his child. I never wanted children, because I couldn't bear the thought of hurting a child the way I'd been hurt. But knowing Aiden had created a life with Nadia caused a sinking feeling in the pit of my stomach.

"Okay. So, did she have the baby and give it up for adoption?"

"No," he replied.

"Did someone else in the family raise the child?"

"Aria, we didn't have the baby."

"She miscarried?" I asked.

"Nadia was extremely eager to please me, so she set aside her wants and did what I asked of her. I convinced her to have an abortion."

I stared at him, a blank expression on my face as I realized I didn't know anything of his views on children, marriage, or religious beliefs. I'd never concerned myself with such personal issues with anyone I'd slept with. Well, except April, but that didn't really count. Certain topics violated my Fuck Rules, so I steered clear of those. With Aiden, though, everything mattered. The fact that another woman had carried a part of him inside her mattered. The fact that he would abort a child mattered.

"I know that sounds horrible, and you may consider me a selfish bastard, but that's what I did," he said. "After the procedure, my guilt forced me to at least attempt to maintain the relationship, and the fact that our parents were pushing us together at every opportunity didn't help matters."

"How did the relationship end?" I asked.

"I couldn't do it anymore. I didn't want it. I didn't want her," he said, his gaze falling to the empty glass on the table. He let out a sigh and looked back up at me. "I never wanted her."

"Yet you were in a relationship with her for two years?"

"You don't understand. You'll never understand the eccentricities of my life."

"Then tell me. Help me to understand. I need you to do that."

"Why, Aria?" he asked, staring into my eyes and revealing the shame and guilt in his own.

"I just do," I said, although I didn't think he'd say any more than he already had.

He shook his head, as if fighting with himself and then finally deciding to explain further. "It's my life and the responsibility that comes with being a Raine." His mouth twisted ruefully. "There was no room for a child, nor was there any time to be a father."

"Are you saying you convinced her to have the abortion because you didn't want the child or because you're a Raine? Aiden, I hope you aren't saying that."

"Damn it, Aria! I'm not saying that, but the two aren't necessarily mutually exclusive. I didn't just abandon her, if that's what you're thinking. She was angry initially, and then she became extremely depressed. When she started writing letters to the baby, I insisted she seek professional help. And with the help of her therapist, she gradually came back to herself."

"Did your families know?"

"They did not. They still don't, unless Nadia said something…which is unlikely."

"How do you feel about it now?" I asked.

He exhaled a deep breath and placed his hands on the table. "If you're asking if I regret my decision, no, I don't."

My gaze fell to his interlocked fingers. "Is this why Nadia has this imagined hold on you?"

"Partially, I suppose."

"And the other part?" I asked, looking up at him.

"Our families. They want me to be with her."

"It's obvious Nadia wants you, and not just because your families are steering her in your direction."

"I agree. Now can we stop talking about someone who doesn't matter?"

I certainly didn't think she mattered as much as *she* thought she did to Aiden, but why did he put up with her? Why not tell her to fuck off? It's not like it wasn't in him to be cruel. I'd witnessed that first hand. Before we ended the conversation about Nadia, I needed to know this, especially if it could explain her hold on him. I could sense his guilt, and I didn't want to re-open old wounds, but he'd promised to answer all of my questions.

"Why do you patronize her?"

He sighed. "Aria, despite what I've just told you, I'm not a monster. I care about Nadia and I'll always feel like shit for what I put her through. Do I want her to back off? Hell yes. Will I be an asshole and push her aside in the way you probably want me to? No."

I peered into his sad green eyes, holding his gaze, and as much as I didn't want to, I understood.

 single line break

❧ ❧ ❧ ❧

Aiden and I exited the kitchen and headed to his bedroom. In the absence of conversation, we were both in our heads, wondering what was next for us. It was somewhat awkward, but for some reason, I found comfort in our silence.

"I want to show you something," he said, once we were behind closed doors.

"Okay. What?" I asked.

"I said show you—not tell you. Let's get dressed."

A half hour later, we rushed downstairs and slipped out of the house. Aiden grasped my hand as we strolled across the grounds. I gave his hand a reassuring squeeze, hoping he'd take it as a sign that I was okay. He looked down at me and smiled, squeezing my hand in return.

We came upon a large building to the left rear of the main house. Aiden opened the door, and we stepped into a garage that was basically the size of another mansion. Grabbing a set of keys from the wall panel, Aiden pressed a button on the fob and the lights of one of the cars flickered.

A smile spread over his lips as he approached it. It was a magnificent car—completely black with gold-colored accents. It was both alluring and intimidating at the same time…a perfect complement for Aiden. He walked me to the passenger side and opened the door. I hopped in, and was instantly enveloped by the rich scent of leather.

"Nice car," I said, as he got in and grabbed his seat belt.

"It's alright," he replied, grinning.

"You love cars, don't you?" I asked.

"Certain cars—yes."

"Another gift from your father?"

"No, this was a gift to myself when I made my first five million."

"Oh wow. Nice gift. But I thought you weren't into excessive opulence."

"I also said I do partake of *some* of what my lifestyle affords," he countered.

"What kind of car is this?"

"It's a Bugatti."

"I don't think I've ever heard of it."

"That's not surprising—most women would say the same,"

he replied, reaching for his aviators.

"Women aren't exactly clueless when it comes to cars, you know."

"That's not what I meant," he said, with a brief glance at me. "It's not very common that women are up to speed on cars like this, that's all. I wasn't attempting to be sexist, if that's what you're getting at."

"So, you really don't need your family's money?"

"No, I don't. I'm no billionaire like Dad, but I'm a millionaire in my own right. I think I told you I've done very well with investments, and I have a few other companies."

"A few?" I asked. "How do you manage all of that?"

"I delegate. I have some very capable people at the helm."

As we drove out of the garage and down the long drive, I looked out the window, curious as to our destination. If his enthusiasm was any indicator, we were going someplace that meant a great deal to him.

We'd spent the better part of the morning visiting one of Aiden's companies. It was a large non-profit that provided children and adolescents with a complete youth music and sports program.

"You were amazing with that young boy at the piano," I said, as Aiden accelerated and merged into the highway traffic.

"You sound surprised," he said.

"I guess because you said you didn't want children...it just seems kind of odd to see you're so good with them."

"Just because I don't want children doesn't mean I'm not fond of them. There are simply reasons I don't choose to have kids."

After that, he fell quiet. I wondered if he would go into more detail than he had before, but I didn't want to push.

"I was afraid I'd become my father," he finally volunteered.

"It's hard to imagine you being afraid of anything."

"I have fears like everyone else, Aria. I just don't wear them on my sleeve."

Was that a jab at me? Did he think I wore my fears on my sleeve?

Except for the music, the drive back to the mansion was a quiet one. Aiden and I were content—holding hands as I looked out the window. When the lyrics to Labrinth's *Beneath Your Beautiful* caught my attention, I listened a bit closer, finding I easily identified with the words of the song.

It was almost as if the melody was written with me in mind. Just as the lyrics stated—I told all the boys no, and I built my walls so high that no one could climb them. But Aiden was here, asking to see beneath it all. He was certainly sharing parts of himself this weekend I didn't know existed. Maybe it was time I did the same.

After leaving the garage, we walked toward the opposite side of the property, passing the stables, and eventually coming to a stop near a large pond. Aiden released my hand and grabbed a handful of rocks. He skipped a few along the water and I watched as one took flight and bounced before plopping to the bottom.

"I wanted to teach music," he said.

"What?" I asked, caught off guard by the sudden start of his conversation.

"When I was younger, I wanted to become a music teacher," he explained. "Over the years, music became increasingly important to me, so I grasped every bit of knowledge I could about it—theory, history, instruments, composers, cultural contexts. You name it, I've studied it. I'd even gone as far as considering the medical aspects of it."

"How so?"

"Research indicates toddlers react to music first—before anything else. Studies also suggest music might have the ability to cure Parkinson's Disease and speech disorders, so as you can imagine, my medical background would have figured in. Music also plays a significant role in shaping our personalities and identities."

I could see how important this was to him. He was obviously more passionate about music than I realized. "Wow. I never really went any further than listening, wanting to play an instrument, and creating playlists. But you…you sound truly inspired. It's a shame you aren't following that passion."

"I suppose," he said. The sun reflected on the pond as another one of the rocks hopped through the water.

"So how did you first become interested in music?"

"Grade school. I began playing the piano when I was five. The teacher noticed my abilities early on and mentioned it to my mother. The following week, she bought a piano and I had private lessons twice a week."

He tossed another rock. "That went on for a few years, and I was really good. I even played publicly at events. I once participated in a recital for one of Mother's charities. They were raising money for a music program."

He looked wistful as he tossed another rock across the pond. "I had the opportunity to speak with some of the kids after the performance. That's when I first realized how the other half lived, and how something I loved and took for granted was something they longed for. When I graduated high school, I decided I wanted to help underprivileged youth with their musical aspirations. I remember being extremely excited about it when I came home. I was thirteen, and I knew what I wanted to do with my life. Imagine that," he said, smiling. "I told my father and he nearly had a coronary."

"But it's your life. You should do what makes you happy."

"When you're born into a family like mine, you're as happy as they allow you to be. Your life is not what you really want. Your life is what is expected of you — which is one reason I dated a certain type of woman — one that would meet their approval."

"Oh," I said, knowing perfectly well I hadn't received the Raine endorsement.

"They haven't been very vocal about it, but I know they don't approve of my relationship with you. I thought maybe, just maybe, if they saw how happy I was with you, they'd let it be. That they'd accept you...accept us."

I thought back to Allison's ballet. Aiden had said, if he'd known his parents were attending, he wouldn't have invited me. I'd been offended by that, but now I understood — he wasn't ashamed of me — he was ashamed of them.

"Mom and Dad's arguments about my music plans were practically incessant. I didn't get it. I mean, what's the big deal, right? He told her it would be the demise of the family and the business. Mother was extremely proud of me and wanted me to be happy. She tried to make my father see that, but he wouldn't budge, and he made her feel guilty for supporting me. She cried a lot — fighting my battles for me. It lasted until the end of my sophomore year at Harvard. Then I'd had enough, so I changed my major and went along with what Dad wanted. Every summer I was with him, learning the business. Hell, I probably know more about it than he does at this point. When I finally accepted my fate, that's when Aiden Wyatt was born. It was my escape."

"So, basically you're doing all this for your mother?"

"I suppose it appears that way, but that's only part of it. Dad is adamant that Raine Industries remain a privately-owned business, and he refuses to seat anyone at the throne that's not family."

"You have siblings, and I'm sure there are other family members," I said.

"I've played that card several times over. He feels I'm the best choice. I've never said it to him, but given his options, I agree — I'm the ideal candidate. Nicholas was the charismatic playboy until a few years ago, when Dad cut him off. Now he wants in, but Dad's thrown up his hands. Sloan does have a bit of a business edge, but not to the degree needed to run R.I. And then there's Allison — she only sees dance. She's always been that way, so he never really bothered to change it."

The water rippled as Aiden tossed one rock after another into the pond. "And what about your relatives?" I asked.

"Most of them have some position in one company or another, but nothing comparable to this. My cousin Stewart would be next in line, I imagine, but of course Dad prefers his offspring run the company he built."

A soft breeze touched my cheeks as I looked toward the horses roaming over the nearby grounds. Aiden had summed up his life as a Raine with such finality, as if there would never be a way out. "Your mother seems to be fine with this, so it's surprising she fought for anything else," I said, turning back to him.

"You wouldn't know it to look at her, or to even speak with her, but she has a lot of insecurities and worries that I've taken on, and to reduce those I do what I have to do. She lost both of her parents at an early age, and she was sent to live with her grandmother, who was also raising great-grandchildren. It was very hard for them. She didn't want that for us."

"That's ridiculous. You're one of the richest families in the world."

"I guess, but sometimes no matter what your present is, you can't shake off the remnants of the past."

That much I could agree with. I didn't think I would ever shake off my past. "Yet she still encourages your music?"

"To a certain degree, but not to the extreme she once did. It will always remain a source of tension between my parents."

"That would explain your father's response to the sheet music Sienna had given to you that morning at the penthouse."

"My father feels as though she feeds into the music thing, and he's absolutely against it, even as a hobby. Mother knows my passion for music, and she knows the sacrifice I've made, so she tries to walk the thin line between the two of us."

"I understand now…why you were so upset and didn't want to talk about it that morning after breakfast. I'm sorry I pushed."

He looked down at me. "You couldn't have known, Aria. I've never explained this to anyone before."

Grabbing some pebbles, I attempted to mimic his rock skipping. He laughed at my first attempt. I tossed another one and it bounced almost as far as his.

He looked down at me again and smiled. "Was that luck or am I missing something?"

"What?" I shrugged. "Only guys are allowed to skip rocks?"

"Yes, something like that."

"My dad taught me," I said. As difficult as it was, I wanted to go on…to tell him more about my father. Aiden was quiet. I supposed he sensed I wanted to say more and he was allowing me to do that without interruption.

"I think Dad wanted a boy, but there he was with three half-Italian girls," I said, finally breaking my silence. "We were feisty, to say the least. Since I was the oldest, I was lucky enough to do some of the things a father would typically do with a boy."

"Does that mean you can do everything I can do?" he asked

jokingly.

"Yes, but better," I said, smiling at him. "I loved my mother dearly, but with my dad, it was just different. We had this special father-daughter thing. Maybe it was partially because he did the boyish things with me. I don't know. I remember the day he taught me to catch a baseball. It was my tenth birthday. The gift he was most excited about giving to me was a glove and a bag of balls."

I threw another rock—it wasn't as successful as my previous toss, only skipping once. "Every weekend, Mom would pack a huge picnic lunch and we'd all go to the park. She and my sisters would play on the swings while Dad and I tossed the ball around. I think I grew to love it as much as he did. I still have that glove. It's the one reminder of him, other than my memories, that I brought from Dayton."

I was quiet for several minutes as I pictured those days in the park. I guess in a way I took that all for granted in much the same way Aiden had taken his lifestyle for granted. But we were both kids. What kid thought outside of that?

"I didn't really mind the tomboy stuff. Well, not that much, anyway, because I loved doing everything with him. What I wouldn't give for just one more day in the park with my family...with him. Dad was my idol. He was the one I'd go to when I needed help with homework, or some stupid grade-school drama. He always told me to ignore the people who didn't matter and they were just envious because they couldn't be me. He was great with us, so attentive and patient. I remember watching how tender and loving he was with Mom—the way he looked at her, the way he made her smile. He seemed to totally adore her, and I wanted someone to treat me that way one day. When he left, I wondered if it had all been just a show. I cried every night for weeks. I think I knew then that I didn't want to be a person that could ever be left in the ashes. I started building those walls and they became taller with each passing year. Then along came this cocky intern who flipped my world inside out."

"Fucking intern," he said, grinning.

"That's what I said," I replied, grateful he was trying to make this easy for me.

Aiden continued skipping rocks as I spoke. I reached down for a few more and attempted to rival his tosses.

"So, you know how to throw a baseball?" he asked.

"Yes. Don't you?"

"I do," he replied. "But not because my dad taught me."

"Who did?"

"The servants. I was on a little league team. They took me to all of the practices."

"Did your dad come to any of your games?"

"Maybe one or two. He would have the servants record my

games on the pretense of watching them later, but I'm not sure if he ever did."

I watched Aiden throw another rock over the pond — it skipped five times before sinking into the water.

"It was the same for all of us — it's all we knew," he said. "It wasn't until I was older that I realized it wasn't quite so normal. But we did have someone to stand in to a certain degree. The kids I work with...some of them don't have anyone at all, which is why my companies and charities are so important to me. It's also why I make it a point to support Allison and attend as many of her dance performances as possible. I support pretty much all of her crazes — not that ballet is a craze — it's just that she's...well, you've seen Allison. She's very animated and tends to experiment."

"You're a great brother," I said. "I'm sure your support means the world to her."

"I know how it is to exist in absence of that support, and I don't want her to ever feel that. Actually, we were both blown over when our parents attended her ballet last year."

Aiden and I tossed a few more rocks, laughing when mine failed to skip at all, and then falling into comfortable silence. I faced him, grabbing his hand and staring into his beautiful green eyes. "You know, you've done something I didn't think possible. Slowly, you've pulled the pieces of my heart together."

"I want to be everyone and everything to you. I want your heart, your body, and your soul, Aria."

"You have it," I said. "You have it all."

"I love you," he said.

"And I love you. It's almost as if I don't have a choice."

"Are we really doing this?" he asked.

I shrugged. "I think so."

"Don't sound so uncertain. And don't be afraid, Aria. I'm going to take better care of you than you take of yourself."

❧Chapter Twenty-Nine❧

I sat on the precipice of a life altering decision. Nothing would be the same after this. It was as though I was watching someone else's life play out before me, and it had reached a pivotal twist in the plot—the one that changed the whole story in the flicker of an instant.

A few weeks ago, I was happily immersed in a relationship I could have never envisioned. Fast forward to today and I was preparing for my departure from the city I'd called home since college. I was leaving Boston...for good.

I couldn't tell Aiden the truth. Not only would he thwart my efforts to leave, he would extend the same level of spying as he had before, involving whomever he needed in order to keep tabs on me—only this time it would be a thousand times worse. I couldn't chance that happening. I'd given him hell for what he'd done to me, but here I was about to do the same thing to him.

Aiden and I had been at his place last night, and this morning we'd come in to the office together. He knew something was off, despite my constant reassurances that I was merely worried about my sisters. That was partially true, because my decision to relocate meant for another abrupt change they had to endure.

"What the hell is this, Aria?" Aiden asked after reading my resignation letter.

"I'm resigning. Effective immediately," I replied, unable to meet his eyes.

"Did something happen?" he asked, confused by my news.

"No. Nothing happened—I merely decided I didn't want this anymore."

"I didn't get a sense you were unhappy as CEO. But if that's the case, we can come up with something that's more to your liking."

"No, Aiden, it isn't that."

"Is it your salary? We can adjust it," he offered. "Give me a number."

"Aiden, I'm moving. I'm leaving Boston," I blurted out.

He dropped the letter, leaned back in his chair, and considered what I'd divulged. "What the fuck, Aria? Don't you think this is something you should've made me aware of before now? Is it for another position? Whatever they're offering, I'll beat it."

"This is not about money or another job. I'm just leaving. Please don't try to convince me otherwise because it will be a waste of your time," I said, my voice resolute.

He looked at me, his eyes intent on mine. Understandably so, he was at a total loss. I could see the wheels turning in his head as he attempted to grasp the scope of my revelation.

"You aren't just leaving RPH…you're leaving me, aren't you?"

"Yes."

"Aria, what's going on? Is it that Dane fucker? Has he contacted you?"

"No, I haven't heard from or seen him since the day you met with him. This isn't about anyone other than me. I just want a fresh start without any entanglements or obligations."

"Is that how you see us?" he asked, stunned by my choice of words.

"It's just not easy to be with you. And I can't keep fighting everyone and every instinct that's guided me for years. It shouldn't be this hard."

"Things between us have been great, Aria. There were some stumbling blocks along the way, but we removed them all. Together. There's nothing standing in our way. This doesn't make sense. Surely there's more to this. I don't want to lose you," he said, his tone fierce. "I can't lose you." His words were tinged with a desperation that shook my resolve but didn't break it.

"It's too late. You already have. We just don't fit, Aiden. We never have and we never will. You need someone like Nadia — someone who's already firmly implanted and accepted, not someone broken like me." Her name, paired with his, was like acid on my tongue, but maybe that's what it took for him to accept what I was saying.

"Aria, I don't see you that way, and you fucking know it," he said, leaning in, his forearms resting on his desk. "There's more to this. So stop with this Nadia bullshit, and tell me what's going on."

"It's too late. Just let me go…please. You've told me that you love me. Well, today I'm asking you to prove it. Give me this. Let me go."

"Are you fucking serious? You can't drop this on me in one minute and then expect me to agree to let you go in the next. Aria, we need to talk about this."

"I'm not dragging this out. My decision is made and I'm not going to change my mind. I'm leaving Boston today, and I'm not coming back. All I ask is that you don't follow me or try to find me. I want this to be over — once and for all. Can you give me that, please?"

I saw the confusion and pain in his eyes — the most intoxicatingly beautiful eyes I'd ever seen. Eyes that had taken in every inch of my body. Eyes that once looked at me with absolute love and adoration. It was heart wrenching, but I couldn't look away — I watched as his expression slowly transitioned into revulsion and rage.

"Fine, Aria. You want out, you've got it. I'm not doing this shit with you anymore. I've had to continuously assure you of my feelings, of my intentions, and despite it all, you still leave. I accept your resignation. You needn't worry about my following you or looking for you, princess. I'm not in the business of keeping someone who doesn't want to be kept."

That's what I wanted. But, fuck, it hurt to see the look on his face and to hear the disdain in his voice. I maintained my resolve, but it was fucking torture.

"I think we're done here." All trace of emotion had evaporated from his tone. "Please see yourself out," he said, turning to his computer. He moved the mouse and clicked on something and began typing. He didn't look at me again. I took in my last glimpse of him before turning away and walking out.

Raina and Bailey were standing near the reception desk. I couldn't face either of them, especially Raina. I avoided their questioning eyes and proceeded to the elevators, relieved when the doors finally opened. Stepping in, I pushed the button to the first floor, and then looked up and saw that Aiden had joined Bailey and Raina. My eyes locked with Aiden's until the elevator doors closed, and then I finally exhaled—hoping I wouldn't cry.

The short walk from the elevator to the cab waiting outside seemed like an eternity. As I reached for the car door, I looked back at the RPH building and then settled inside the cab.

"Your destination, ma'am?" asked the driver.

"Boston International Airport," I replied.

"Yes, ma'am," he said, and we were off. I looked over my shoulder at the building until it was out of sight and then the tears I'd been struggling to dam up finally spilled over.

"Are you okay, ma'am?" asked the driver, glancing at me in his rear-view mirror.

"Yes, I'm fine. I just now said good-bye to someone, and it was more difficult than I'd anticipated."

"Maybe that means you shouldn't say good-bye," he casually tossed out, and returned his focus to the busy street.

If only it had been that simple. I thought back to the discussion I'd had with Aiden's mother.

"You're a very accomplished and beautiful woman, Aria…but you're not suited for Aiden."

I recoiled at her statement. We'd been getting along so much better—I was actually starting to think I could tolerate her. Where had this come from? Had Nadia been whispering things in her ear?

"Excuse me?" I asked.

"I don't wish to offend you. This is not a personal attack on you, but more of what you represent. Quite frankly, this is not the time for Aiden to be involved with anyone to the degree he is with you."

"What exactly do you think I represent?" I asked.

"A disruption to his priorities," she replied, and took a sip of her tea.

"Are you serious? Do you actually think Aiden is incapable of working and having a relationship?"

"It depends on the nature of that relationship, and what he has with you is more intense than he needs at this point in his life."

I placed my cup on the table and stepped away from the sitting area. "Aiden should be the judge of that—not you. Aiden feels I'm exactly what he needs, and for you to think any different is rather presumptuous, and it's demeaning to both Aiden and me."

"It's not that at all, Aria, I assure you. To be honest, I envy you. Your strength and resilience are quite remarkable, and you're a brilliant business woman. I never had the aptitude for business or any type of career. This is what I knew I would be—the person who stood quietly by her strong man, being present but not interfering with what he needed to accomplish. But you—you're very different. You will not be that quiet woman who sits back and allows her man to take on the world. That's not a bad thing though, Aria. As I said, you're an exceptional woman."

"And you'd prefer Aiden have someone unexceptional?" I asked, incredulous by her assertion. What mother wanted that for her son?

"It's not that, dear—I'm sorry—Aria. Aiden has a huge responsibility to this family, to Raine Industries, and ultimately to millions of employees and consumers, not to mention the economy," she said, as she placed her cup beside mine.

"I'm not sure what that has to do with me," I said. Sloan's conversation about the type of person that Aiden's parents wanted at his side knocked around in the back of my mind. She was right. They hadn't approved of me, and they never would.

Sienna sat back in her chair and crossed her legs. "You're too much of a distraction for him. Since meeting you, he's changed...he's lost his focus, and I'm concerned about what this could mean for the future of the family and, of course, Raine Industries."

I couldn't believe a person—a mother—could be this fucking selfish and unconcerned about her son's happiness. This was unbelievable.

"And Aiden's father, does he agree?" I had to ask, although I was sure he was the ring leader.

"He adores you, Aria. That's obvious. But why would he not?" she asked, looking me up and down. "Look at you. As I've said, you're a remarkable young lady. However, he needs Aiden's focus primarily on Raine Industries, and that will never be the case if the two of you continue this relationship. You may be what

Aiden thinks he wants, but you're simply not what he needs. You're not the type that fits with someone at the helm of a company such as ours...with a family such as ours."

"And Nadia," I asked coldly, "where does she fit in all of this?"

"Nadia and Aiden have a lengthy and rather complex relationship."

That was the umpteenth fucking time I'd heard that relationship described as complex or complicated. What the hell did that mean? Was there more than what Aiden had told me?

"Forget I asked. I will take that up with Aiden."

"Aria, this is not only what's best for Aiden. It's best for you, also. I'm sure you have dreams of marriage and family. Aiden is not to that point in his life, and it's quite possible he won't be for several years to come, if at all."

"Marriage and family never entered my mind," I said, crossing my arms over my chest. "But it's pretty unsettling to know Aiden's parents are willing to sacrifice his happiness."

"We aren't sacrificing his happiness — we're ensuring it," Sienna replied.

It was obvious that she really did believe what she was saying. "It's sad you see it that way, Sienna, and I'm sorry you feel this way. I'd hoped we would all get along. We obviously won't, but ultimately the decision of a relationship lies with Aiden and me."

"I understand that, Aria, which is why I'd hoped to appeal to your sense of duty and allow Aiden to follow the plan that's been laid out for him for years."

"What about your understanding that this is none of your business? Aiden and I have made a commitment to each other, and we're the only ones who have the right to amend that."

At that point Aiden had walked in, and the conversation ceased. I never mentioned that talk with Sienna to him because I didn't want to cause a rift and give her another reason to dislike me.

Well, Sienna, you got what you wanted. I'm out of his life. Not that my leaving was a direct result of that conversation, but it had played a large part in my decision to say good-bye to Aiden.

By the time I reached the airport, I was a blubbering mess. Kellan was to meet me at the ticket counter, and I didn't want him to see me like this. I reached in my bag for a tissue and wiped my eyes and nose.

I was headed to my new home in Belize. Lia and Bianca had relocated to Ohio. I didn't feel good about leaving them, but they wanted the chance to experience college life on their own. I was glad Ohio State was one of their final choices because it meant they could be with Mrs. Warner, someone who would love them like family. They had an apartment off-campus and had gotten settled in time for the start of the semester. We promised to video chat every day, and I warned them that I would visit often, especially since I would no longer be working, at least not anytime in the foreseeable future.

I spotted Kellan waiting for me near the ticket counter, and he walked over to meet me. I wasn't handling this as I would have wanted. He reached out to me and I fell into his arms, holding on for dear life.

"Everything's going to be okay, Aria. I promise," he said, as he grasped my hand. We checked our bags and made our way to the terminal. With my hand held firmly in his, he led me toward my new life, leaving Boston and Aiden Raine far behind.

The announcement to board was being repeated as we reached the gate. Funny how I'd finally decided to stop running, yet here I was again. At least this time I was running toward something instead of away from it.

When we were seated on the plane awaiting the quick ascent into the friendly skies, I slipped the picture out of my purse, looking at it as I placed a hand over my stomach. I looked over at Kellan, who quickly donned a reassuring smile. Despite the enormity of my sadness, I was grateful to share this journey with him.

Kellan reached for my hand, soothing my nerves with a gentle squeeze, and then he leaned in to kiss me softly on the cheek. A single tear escaped as I gazed into his eyes. He wiped it away as I leaned back and took in a deep breath, ready to embrace this new chapter of my life.

My only concerns were three loose ends: April, Bianca, and Lia. If Aiden spoke to any of them, he'd be able to get all of the information he wanted. I'd asked him to let me go and to not look for me, and although he'd agreed, it was not without very persuasive tactics on my part. I knew I'd hurt him, and it killed me to look into his eyes and lie to him, but I could no longer afford to be in his complicated world.

I'd settled quite comfortably in Belize. I'd met a few of the locals, and Kellan came to visit as much as he could. He was making arrangements to move here permanently, and I couldn't wait to have him with us every day. He'd arrived last night and was at a meeting with one of the local firms. I had come to rely on him, and although our relationship wasn't ideal, he was fine with that. I wondered how long he would be, though.

April would be coming over with Blaine next week. I was so happy they'd worked things out. She and I had also worked out the kinks in our friendship. It would never be like it once was—I never wanted that dysfunction again. We no longer shared a friendship based on need. It was a friendship based on the desire to remain best friends…to remain family.

I missed Boston. I missed RPH, and most of all, I missed Aiden. I'd considered the possibility of moving back to Boston after a few years, but I actually didn't know where I would end up, because I hadn't planned that far ahead.

I opened my laptop and accessed my email account to start a new message. Once I finished, I read it, desperately wanting to hit *send*, but something inside me just wouldn't allow me to. Instead, I read it over and over.

My Dearest Aiden,

I don't regret you. I thought that I would — I knew that I would…but I don't. Loving you made me realize I can have a life outside of my fears — that I don't have to omit part of life. For that, I thank you. And even now, after having said good-bye, my heart is overflowing with love for you. I'm pretty sure I'll always love you, but I felt I had to let you go. I couldn't stand in the way of you and your family. I couldn't force you to choose, and I didn't want to be the person who destroyed your family.

Family once meant so much to me, and I'd forgotten that. I pushed it aside because of the hurt of my childhood, which I now know was not torn apart because of a lack of love, but because there was so much of it. You have a responsibility to your family and thousands of others. Yes, I know you have just as much of a responsibility to yourself, and when you come to terms with that, I know you'll find me.

All my love…
Now and forever,
Aria

I read it again. And again. I couldn't send it, but I couldn't delete it either, so I printed the email and saved it in my drafts. After reading the printed copy once more, I folded it and went to my closet, pulling out the forbidden box and placing the letter on the top of the other memories. My gaze fell upon the crumpled note that Aiden had given me. That seemed like a life time ago. I'd never read it. I placed the box on the floor and grabbed the familiar stationary.

Aria,
Please accept these flowers as an apology for my behavior. You make me crazy, and I don't seem to know the right thing to do when it comes to you — I simply react. Let's talk. I miss you.
-A.

Placing the letter over my heart, I held it there. I closed my eyes, recalling the day in my office when Aiden had sealed his mouth over mine.

I didn't want to cry. *Don't cry. Don't cry. Don't cry.* I repeated it over and over until I'd gotten a hold on my emotions, then placed the note in the box and moved it out of sight.

Having become restless, I decided we should go for a walk along the beach. I tapped a short text asking Kellan to meet us there after his business meeting.

It was a beautiful day, perfect for a relaxing barefoot walk in the sand. The bright sun was warmer than it had been as of late — it was like an invisible blanket. The feel of the warm sand between my toes was comforting. Pulling the beach towel from my bag, I spread it out near the edge of the water. I took a seat and removed the baby carrier from my shoulders, freeing Lyric from its constraints. He'd gotten so big. I gave him a kiss on his adorably chubby cheeks. He looked so much like his father, with the exception of the chubby part.

I bounced him on my knees, speaking to him as if he could actually understand me. He was smiling and staring at just the right parts. A shadow gradually blocked the beaming sun, and I looked up from the baby, prepared to ask Kellan how things went with his meeting, but I gasped when I saw the shadow didn't belong to Kellan. I was staring into the eyes of a man I didn't recognize, a man whose eyes had once intoxicated me, a man whose eyes were now touched with an iciness that pierced my heart.

THE END

Epilogue

My heart rate rocketed as I rushed toward him. "Aiden…
why?" I asked, grabbing his arm.

He looked at me with a distasteful glare and shrugged away
from me. "I could ask the same of you," he retorted.

I'd seen contempt in his eyes before, but this was different
than anything I'd ever witnessed. He was every bit the ruthless
man I'd observed when he dealt with people who crossed him,
only this time the menacing glare was far worse, and it was
directed solely at me. I knew this would end badly. Just as I
opened my mouth to attempt another protest, he turned away and
one of the officers stepped behind me and urged me to follow
Aiden. I anxiously peered at Lyric. I didn't want this to touch
him—but it was too late.

I had yet to move. I couldn't go with them. I couldn't! I fought
the urge to run, knowing full well it wouldn't get me anywhere,
but I had to do something. *Think, Aria. Think.*

"Ma'am, if you'll come with us," the officer urged again.

There was nothing I could do—I didn't have any options.
Reluctantly, I took a step in Aiden's direction, and the police
ushered us back to my house. A short while later we were
walking up the drive to my home and there were two women

dressed in scrubs standing near my front door.

Why did Aiden have all of these people involved? I felt like a wanted criminal—a dangerous one, at that. "Aiden, who are these people?" He didn't answer me. "Aiden!"

Discussion Questions

1. Do you understand more about Aria and her struggle with relationships?

2. How did it affect you or alter the story when Aria's mom died?

3. Do you think Kellan is a better fit for Aria? Why or why not?

4. If there really were a contest called *The Writer*, would you enter?

5. Do you think Aiden will ever step away from Raine Industries?

6. Would you take a back seat to someone in the capacity that Connor and Sienna would have wanted in order to be with a man like Aiden?

7. Were you surprised when Aria resigned from RPH and broke things off with Aiden?

8. Do you agree with or understand the responsibility that was placed on Aiden in regard to his family and Raine Industries?

9. Why do you think Melena failed to inform Aria that she had met and approved of Aiden?

10. Do you think Aria would have agreed to a relationship with Aiden if she hadn't received the letter from her mother?
11. Did Aria finally forgive her mother? Or did she have residual resentment?
12. Did Melena's death play a part in Aria's allowing Aiden back into her life?
13. Which character, other than Aria or Aiden, would you most like to learn more about?
14. Do you think Aiden or Aria have any more secrets that might come back to haunt them?
15. Aria was finally able to forgive Aiden for his deceit regarding his identity. Do you think you would have done the same?
16. Did the manner in which Aiden handle Dane and Tiffany surprise you?
17. Would you email Aiden? If so, would he respond?
18. What is your favorite Aidenism?
19. Would you have rekindled a relationship with Blaine like April did?

20. Do you think Nadia will finally back off? Do you understand why Aiden refuses to forcefully tell her to back off?

Connect with Lilly Wilde

Facebook at Lilly Wilde

Twitter at @authorlilly

Good Reads

Google Plus

Linked In

YouTube

Pinterest

Instagram

Thank you for reading Touched. If you enjoyed it, please take a moment to leave a review at your favorite retailer.

Thanks,

Lilly Wilde

Touched is also available in E-book format at most online retailers.

If you would like to join the street team, please contact the author on Facebook or by commenting on the website:

www.lillywilde.com

Books by Lilly Wilde

Untouched — Book One of The Untouched Series

Touched — Book Two of The Untouched Series

Touched by Him — Book Three of The Untouched Series

Only His Touch (Part One) — Book Four of The Untouched Series

Only His Touch (Part Two) — Book Five of The Untouched Series

Forever Touched — Book Six of The Untouched Series

What readers are saying about Untouched:

"Simply Exquisite!! This book is amazing! The description of the characters is so vivid and extremely catching. I felt like I was actually living the story. I was so drawn to Aria, Aiden, and April. The communication between Aiden and Aria is so touching… I laughed throughout the book and cried at the end. Cannot wait to read more… I love the sensuality of it all. One of the best breathtaking books I have read so far. Can't wait for the next one. Great writer! Awesome Job Lilly!"

~ Review from Amazon

"Lilly Wilde gives you the same excitement we got from Fifty Shades and The Crossfire Series. Except Lilly delivered it to us in a whole new way. It was so much more realistic than the others that you not only finished it yearning for your own Aiden, but you actually think it's possible to find him. You are captured from the beginning to the end.

You fall in love with this couple. This couple is so sexy, and your mind takes you away to forbidden places and feelings. It's a great story and a sexy read. You don't want to miss out on this!!!!!"

~ **Review from Amazon**

"I loved your book! Aiden was a perfect cross between Christian Grey and Jesse Ward...The perfect man."

~ **Review from Amazon**

"I've read a lot of books, many from this genre – Fifty Shades, Crossfire Series, This Man, etc. – and in a word this book is AMAZING. You immediately become invested in the characters and take this emotional roller coaster ride with them. I found this book to have more real life undertones than some of the others I've read, making the characters more relatable. It has been said that every story has been told. Well, that may be, but definitely not in this fashion. It's a must read!"

~ **Review from Amazon**

"What else can be said about a phenomenal writer who brought to life two amazing people in a story that is not only emotionally charged, but is realistic? Aria and Aiden will capture you from the beginning and won't let you go. I can't get enough of them. Reading this, I had every emotion possible. I was happy, pissed, sad, and curious, but mostly I was captivated by their story..."

~ **Review from Amazon**

What readers are saying about Touched:

"Once again author Lilly Wilde has delivered an amazing story of love, lust, romance, intrigue, heartache, and suspense. From the first sentence of Touched *to the last, the author's way with words pulls you right into the story and leaves you wanting and wondering…craving more. Great job Lilly Wilde. Looking forward to the next step in Aria's and Aiden's journey."*

~ Review from Amazon

"Lilly Wilde, you are truly AMAZING. I couldn't and wouldn't put this book down. I fell in love with Aiden and Aria in the first book of the trilogy (Untouched) *and I fell in love with them even more in* Touched. *I had probably every emotion a person could have. It had twist and turns in every chapter. I could see Aiden and Aria in my mind and hear them talking in my head. I want* Touched by Him *out NOW. I can't wait to see how all the twist and turns play out. I can't believe you just started writing not long ago. I am a HUGE fan of yours now and for life. Your books have me shocked and amazed. Thank you for writing these books and taking me away. I will be searching for my Aiden while I wait for* Touched by Him*"*

~ Review from Amazon

"After reading Untouched *(Book 1)…I was hooked and (Book 2)* Touched *certainly didn't disappoint me… Wow, the story line is*

amazing and so real. Lilly Wilde has smashed it again. Personally I now think 50 Shades is rubbish! (Sorry to you 50 Shades lovers; yes, I used to be one myself.) Touched is way more realistic, and has so much more to offer. The main characters are brilliant, the story line is so gripping. Loads of drama, and as for the hot sex, this will not disappoint you. I couldn't put my Kindle down! Seriously this is a must read!"

~ *Review from Amazon*

"ABSOLUTELY LOVE THE UNTOUCHED SERIES. I love every detail about Aiden and Aria, who are both strong, confident, career — driven people with a love and passion so strong it's unbreakable. I was so entranced from beginning to end that I didn't want to stop reading. I enjoyed Untouched so much, and I knew would fall in love with Touched as well. The story unravels detail by juicy detail, and I love it…A LOT! This book will have you crying, screaming, and begging for more, all in one chapter. I haven't cried after reading a book since I read FSOG and this book did it…. The waterworks flooded my sheets. If you're looking for a book that has a great story line and some steamy scenes…then look no further. This is the book for you."

~ *Review from Amazon*

"Wow, I knew this series was good but I'm floored by just how good. I could hardly put Touched down; each chapter is like candy. Aria and Aiden are hot as lava together, and you'll be on the edge till "The End." I can't wait for the third book. I will read anything written by

Lilly Wilde. Anything!"

"Lilly Wilde has ruined me for other authors. Her style draws you in from the first sentence. The story of Aria and Aiden is one that I just cannot get enough of. Touched *and* Untouched *(the first book in this trilogy) made me experience every emotion possible. I feel like I am part of this story. Part of these characters' lives. And that is what a great book is supposed to do. The heat and passion in this book is intense. Once I started it, I found it difficult to put down. I simply cannot wait to read more of their story. I need more of Aria and Aiden in my life."*

"Wow, Lilly, I just want to say how amazing this was. I was hooked after book one, but now I can't wait until book three. You grab the reader and don't let go. Please hurry with #3!!!"

"I cannot believe it!!!! I never thought a book could leave me in such a state! I'm an emotional wreck, but Miss Lilly, you have done this to me with Aria and Aiden's story. I'm forever changed. I fell in love with Aiden and Aria within the first few pages of Untouched. *In the beginning, I thought this typically would be a hot, kinky, sex – craved story, but boy was I wrong!!!! It's soooooo much more than that. I was instantly hooked. Lilly pulled me deeper down the rabbit hole, curious to*

know more. I couldn't stop myself!!!! I had no control to put this book down. I felt like I was living in this story and feeling every emotion with it. I laughed, I really cried, my jaw dropped as to how much I was turned on, and I do mean a lot!!!!! I've been exposed to all things that are Aiden and like a starved, crazed woman I want more. I need more Lilly. I'll be pulling my hair out waiting for the next installment to be released. This is one trilogy you'll want in your collection, ladies! This is one trilogy I will never forget, and I know a group of ladies that never will, either. I applaud you, Lilly, on a fantastically awesome job. I'm sooooo happy that I got to experience this. You truly are an amazing writer. I'll be waiting for what's to come next!"

   ~*Review from Barnes & Noble*

"Lilly Wilde did it again! The second installment of Aiden and Aria's story was even more emotional than the first. I cannot wait for the third. This book will have you laughing and crying all on the same chapter. Lilly is an amazing writer with a talent for telling a story that is a steamy and fun to read. She makes you feel like you are a part of the story and the characters are long – time friends."

   ~*Review from Smashwords*

"This book series really makes you feel like you are a part of the action. I cried, I laughed, I got mad. You will fall deep into this series and will not want to come back to reality. Lilly Wilde takes you on a rollercoaster of emotions, and you will forever love it. To be so entwined with them is great. You will not want to put the book down, and when it's over you will literally be begging for more. I can't wait for the release of the last book."

~*Review from Smashwords*

What readers are saying about Touched by Him:

"*Lilly Wilde, there aren't enough words to describe how I felt while reading Touched By Him. I am completely Blown Away! The emotions that I felt are and WERE indescribable - I cried, I yelled, I laughed and almost threw my IPad a time or two. What an emotional roller coaster Touched By Him was.*

5++++++ STARS!!!!

Aiden Raine is by far my ONE AND ONLY BOOK BOYFRIEND. He is domineering, arrogant, sexy and sweet all rolled into one - A TOTAL ALPHA MALE!!! Touched by Him brought me to my knees! I read a lot of books…I love all types of genre but I don't think I have ever been as emotionally invested in characters as I am with those in The Untouched Series. Lilly Wilde has created a world I wish I lived in. Aiden Raine is one sexy Alpha Male - even with all his idiosyncrasies I have fallen in love with him. Touched by Him is a must read!!! Lilly Wilde, you did an amazing job and I cannot wait for Aiden, Aria and Lyric's journey to continue in Only His Touch!!!"

~ *Review from Goodreads*

"OMG!!! What a page turner!!! An intoxicating breathtaking, ground shaking continuance of the most amazing love story ever told!!! The story's turns and twists and the emotions run raw from page to page! Aiden and Aria on their amazing journey! Lilly captured me from Untouched - threw me to the wall with Touched - and brought me to my knees with Touched by him! A page turner, crying-your-eyes-out continuance of our amazing story!"

~ **Review from Goodreads**

"When you are anxious to read the next book in a series, you sometimes don't like it or it does not live up to your expectations. But OMG author Lilly Wilde did it again! I absolutely loved reading this book. It gripped me from beginning until the end. Sometimes I really wanted to smack Aiden upside the head. It was a beautiful, heart-wrenching story. Emotional, loving and HOT! Up until now Touched was my favorite, but Touched by Him just topped it. It really was worth the read and well written. I cannot wait to read the next one in this series! This one was worth more than 5 stars!"

~ **Review from Amazon**

"Touched by Him is by far the best of Lilly Wilde's Untouched Series to date! Be prepared for twists and turns in the plot that you would never see coming and pure emotion that connects you with the characters more than ever while you laugh and cry along with them.

With the introduction of a new character, Lyric, this installment of the Untouched Series will leave you blindsided in this book's underlying resonance of pure love as Aiden Raine and Aria Cason learn to explore new aspects and vulnerabilities of their relationship they never saw coming. As a reader, I took my time reading the first two installments of the Untouched Series, though Touched by Him had me always yearning for more and unable to stay away from the story for longer than a day at a time. If you think you have read all the variety available in modern erotica/romance, then be sure to put The Untouched Series to the test as Lilly Wilde will take your mind and heart to new and unexpected situations that will have you impressed that this story came together from the mind of one single author. The Untouched Series is a story you will not be sorry you picked up."

~ *Review from Barnes & Noble*

"Once again Lilly-Wilde has proven why she is untouchable as an author. I was completely enthralled in Touched By Him from the first sentence. Never would I ever think I could read not one, not two but THREE books that absolutely captured me and held me through to the words THE END!!! I cried, I laughed, I was so upset I almost through my kindle across the room and I wanted to fight!! Never have I ever read the work of an author who could reach me on so many levels and pull me thru so many emotions. When I started my journey in Untouched (Book1) and then Touched (Book2) I was captured from the start and Touched by Him did not let me down. Lilly-Wilde has a phenomenal way with words and the gift of storytelling that no one could hold a candle to.

I cannot wait for the next release. Thank you the beautiful gift that is the story of Aiden and Aria. Chomping at the bit to see where their journey leads to next!!! 5 stars from one of your biggest fans."

   ~ **Review from Amazon**

What readers are saying about Only His Touch, Part One:

"5 Sweet and Passionate Stars! From the start, this series has been great and in true Lilly fashion, she nailed this one as well. The writing flowed and story line kept you wanting more. I love Aiden! I could not get enough of this man. I loved the special moments this couple shared in the story. It was sweet and passionate. I loved that they struggled with their trust. They were like a real couple. I can't wait for the last book!"

   ~*A Book Lover's Emporium [Book Blog]*

"Another impossible to put down book by Lilly Wilde! I loved this next installment of the Untouched Series! I loved how we got to understand both Aria and Aiden's feelings of their time apart. I am hooked on this series!"

   ~*Sharing My Book Boyfriends [Book Blog]*

"This series just captures you and you cannot stop reading! Ms. Wilde sure knows how to capture her audience. Can't wait to read more!"

   ~*Hot Books and Sassy Girls [Book Blog]*

"Lilly Wilde has created a book that will reach and test every emotion you have. I was blown away with the emotional connection I had with this book. I have read all four books in the series and I am shocked and amazed at how this story continues to stay fresh and new!"

~ Review from Goodreads

"Be prepared to be speechless while falling in love again and again. This is an amazing story that will leave you wanting more. A story you will talk about after you finish the book!"

~ Review from Goodreads

"Have you ever read a book where you aren't sure if you want to love or hate a character and you feel torn? Well, that is what happened in Only His Touch. I was so torn between loving and hating Aiden from one chapter to the next. Lilly Wilde does an amazing job of showcasing the emotions of each character and you feel emotionally attached to them throughout the book.

~ Review from Amazon

About the Author

Lilly Wilde is the Author of The Untouched Series (Untouched, Touched, Touched By Him, Only His Touch and Forever Touched). She is a wife and mom who loves to fill each day with happiness and laughter. Lilly loves to dream, get lost in fantasy and create alternate worlds in which we can escape ever so often. She's down-to-earth, engaging and compassionate with a great sense of humor. Her laughter is one of the first qualities that you'll notice; you'll become instantly drawn to her witty and fun-loving spirit.

Lilly spent a lot of time daydreaming as a child which led to numerous hours of reading and eventually the writing of poetry. The first story Lilly began writing was entitled *He Lied To Me*, a novel she plans to complete in the near future. After years of starting and stopping several novels, she eventually set a goal to complete her debut novel, *Untouched*.

Her stories are of strength, growth, facing demons and stepping outside your comfort zone. They often surround topics of family and love and the beauty of both.

CPSIA information can be obtained
at www.ICGtesting.com
Printed in the USA
LVHW111521220119
604790LV00003B/239/P